CW01467488

Lamorna takes her re
waters of Fal River in anc

'What a fantastic read! Loveable characters in a picturesque setting. Lamorna captures the beauty of Cornwall and of falling in love.' – JC Berry

'I absolutely adored the Cornish comforts in this book. Lamorna's stories have a way of wrapping you up in a big cosy hug and popping the kettle on.'- Leah

## Also By Lamorna Ireland

Lamorna would love to hear from you. Find her on:

@lamornaireland

@lamornairelandauthor

@AuthorIreland

@lamornaireland

www.LamornaIreland.co.uk

Lamorna Ireland

# *Along a Cornish Creek*

# LAMORNA IRELAND
CORNISH NOVELIST & WRITER

ISBN-13: 9798853283046

To my wonderful mum, Beverley. Whose love and support knows no bounds, and whose expensive gardening obsession she passed down to me.

Lamorna Ireland

# Prologue

## 1952

The estuary water glittered and glistened, carefully splitting on a forked embankment - one leading to the open sea, the other to a labyrinth of twists and turns along the river. The patch in which a blue rowing boat floated idly in place, was enveloped in dense greens. The bank adjacent was littered with colour: the willows, dragging their yellow-green branches through the water.

From his spot on the jetty, he watched her beauty, her elegance, in wonder. A curtain of loose brown curls tumbled over a slender white neck, against the vibrant red of her bathing suit. Not like the other girls - she was a free spirit as she cut through the gentle waters with both oars. Charles Penhaligon took in their surroundings - their secret spot, where pirates once smuggled treasures. Chords of soft light speared down from above, bathing the water's surface in gold. Now, two lovers relished in each other's company, away from the prying eyes of those who must not know about their companionship. A remote corner of the River Fal, disguised as a tropical paradise with its sapphire blue waters and luscious green backdrop. Only accessed by foot from the very far corner of the Penhaligon Estate's vast gardens, a trail of fern trees guiding Charles from the restraints of his privileged life each day to their Utopia, as she joined him by means of her little rowing boat. This was their haven.

'Won't you join me on the water, Charles?'

'And get my newest addition wet?' Charles chuckled, positioning his Kodak Brownie '127' camera towards the river, focusing in on her delicate features. She wasn't accustomed to having herself captured on film and blushed fiercely at the notion, tucking a strand of hair nervously behind one ear. He looked up over the top of his camera and smiled gently. 'You are so beautiful, Gi-Gi.'

'Stop with the flattery, my dear man - and get yourself onto the water. It really is sublime. I could be out here for days!' She flung two long, slender arms into the air, her face tilted skyward and her hair dancing in the breeze. She was quick to gather up the oars before they slipped into the water, to which a tinkering laughter erupted from her chest.

His chest tightened with desire and a devastating sadness. He'd been putting it off for so long. But how could he possibly begin to articulate the truth of their future? A future where their worlds no longer connected?

It had been three weeks since he had been given the ultimatum. He had selfishly been ignoring it, relishing in the secrecy and forbidden love. But time was running out and soon he would have no choice but to step into the role he was born to inherit.

# Chapter One

Ellie Curnow drew in a long, deep breath, hanging precariously from the tree with a less than reliable harness, the rope creaking and groaning under her weight. She didn't mind this one bit. In fact, this was her favourite part of the job, with a sky-high view of the River Fal to feed her soul. In the near distance, she could see where the estuary opened into the wide sea, Pendennis Point sitting proudly at the gate.

It was a simple crown lifting for this old oak tree today, but Ellie found herself distracted. Not unheard of, but not ideal either when elevated fifteen feet up in the air, with only an old rope and harness keeping her from a fatal fall. She gave herself a mental shake, her long copper hair swinging in its ponytail, and yanked on the starter cord of her chainsaw, the throaty noise of the machine cutting through the quiet. The cutting chain was about to make contact with the branch when Ellie detected the slight travelling sound of someone shouting down below. She killed the engine and peered down on her left side.

'For a minute there, I thought I'd have to resort to waving my arms about like a mad woman!' Gloria Curnow shouted up, swapping her stick over to her right side to balance herself as she descended the little granite steps, coming directly under Ellie. For the ripe old age of eighty-nine, Gloria was marvellous and supple in her movement, but the last thing Ellie imagined her doing was waving her arms, stick high in the air, like she was

8

guiding a plane down to land. 'When are you going to stop swinging around up in this tree and come inside for some lunch?'

Ellie chuckled, her booted feet firmly positioned on the trunk and her hands steadying the silent chainsaw. Her dear old nan hadn't always approved of Ellie's choice of vocation, but she silently enjoyed the advantageous perks of having the garden well-cared for.

'Well, thanks to my swinging about, that Camellia down there should start seeing sunlight again now. And there's less of a chance of an old branch snapping off and landing on your head, Nanny!'

'I'll take that as a small victory then,' Gloria affirmed, tapping the base of the tree with her stick for no apparent reason. 'I still say you should remain a bit of femininity in your work. Your boots - and those trousers! Why do you need so many pockets?'

'Mostly for snacks,' Ellie shrugged, enjoying the tease. Gloria chortled and tutted fondly, before ordering her to finish the last branch and be inside before the soup had heated.

'You won't make an old woman walk to the end of her garden twice like that, will you?'

'Perish the thought,' Ellie retorted, yanking on the starter cord, and setting to work to finish that last branch.

'It's not like you to take so long.' Gloria said later. The soup was warmed, the bread was buttered, and Ellie came stomping through the patio doors and into the kitchen, untangling herself from the safety contraption that she was belted in to. 'You a bit distracted this morning, my love?'

Ellie sighed as she dropped the harness to the floor and stepped out of it. 'I just can't stop thinking about poor Mrs Pascoe. And seeing her house all dark and empty.'

'I know, my love. Well, I shouldn't worry,' Gloria said, her expression darkening. 'It won't be empty for long! The estate will reclaim it and it will be a holiday home quicker than a blink.'

Ellie took the soup ladle from Gloria's unsteady hands and nudged her gently towards the little table nook, pouring the steaming, thick liquid into two bowls.

The table nook - or the breakfast nook as it had most recently been named - was by far Ellie's favourite spot in their small cottage. Just a few years ago, Ellie had transformed the simple bay window into a built-in breakfast table booth. Timber framed, glossed white, scattered with Gloria's handcrafted cushions, and perfectly positioned to face the river - both of them loved squeezing into the cosy nook for every meal each day. Even now, years later, Ellie was astounded by how much one view could change throughout the year - or even daily for that matter. Today the view comprised of: a scattering of moor hens, a swan, a squirrel up in the tree that Ellie had just been attending to, and the water as still as a millpond. Just perfect.

Despite her distracting thoughts, Ellie sank into her seat, tore off a piece of her chunky bread and drank in her view as she ate with contentment. A small groan threatened to escape as she saw the mess she had yet to clear up at the base of the oak tree, but she also smiled with satisfaction as the sun peaked out from behind a cloud and beamed down on the shrubs below. That would have them thriving. A little bit of sunshine did that.

'I'm thinking I might offer to make pasties for Mrs Pascoe's wake?' Gloria announced across the table, sipping her soup delicately.

Ellie assessed her Nanny's face to determine how serious she was. 'I expect it'll be a big turnout. That's a lot of pasties.'

'Scones then. But I won't be eating no shop rubbish if they buy them in. The last funeral I went to, the pasties had carrots in them!' Gloria shuddered. Ellie laughed, shaking her head knowingly at her Nanny's fierce loyalty to an old traditional recipe. 'Margaret down the way, she was telling me how she had a chicken tikka pasty the other day. Well - I tell 'e! She always was an odd one.'

Nearly choking on her bread, Ellie composed herself and swallowed the bite she had been tackling. 'I had a turkey and stuffing one a few weeks ago.' Her eyes twinkled and her mouth twitched into a daring smile as she waited for her Nanny's reaction. There was a pause.

'Just when I thought we could be friends,' Gloria muttered into her spoon, her dry humour never dropping a beat. Ellie's laughter could be heard all the way down to the water.

\*

It was a small community that dwelled on this side of the estuary. Houses and cottages peppered the banks, and in this particular area where Ellie and Gloria lived, it comprised of mostly the elderly. So, Ellie found she was never without jobs, the old cottages and ancient trees surrounding them meant constant maintenance - something her geriatric customers couldn't manage without help. That being said, Ellie was a sucker for being a good Samaritan, and found herself shrugging off hefty quotes for customers she knew couldn't afford it and offering to do the job anyway at a heavily reduced rate. Not that she could afford to lose out on the money herself. Some of these residents were clinging to their properties for as long as they could, knowing that as soon as they showed signs of being too old to manage them, they'd be reclaimed in a heartbeat, the Cornish community fast diminishing and replaced by expensive holiday homes that sit empty for a vast majority of the year. At least, that was what was happening around other estates around the county. But it was heavily rumoured that it wouldn't be long before Penhaligon Estate followed suit.

Ellie's mind wandered again, not for the first time, to Mrs Pascoe's cottage as she packed her tools into her little boat. What if the estate did turn it into a holiday home? What then? Would this be the start of things to come? There were many estates and big stately homes around the southwest with owners who had been forced to diversify. Ellie wasn't naive enough to believe the big house was up there doing anything other than haemorrhaging money without some sort of investment to bring in the income.

She checked her wristwatch. She was going to be working until past sundown at this rate. She heaved her trusty chainsaw into the boat, and a jerry can of petrol, and gingerly stepped into the poor little vessel, finding a gap to slot her feet between all the tools and machinery she'd put on board. That was one problem with having customers scattered around the estuary. The quickest commute was on water.

The river today offered a perfect reflection of the trees and blue sky above, barely a disturbance in the mirrored surface. She cut through with her oar gently and glided along with the same elegance as the local swans, who watched her with fascination from their nests in the reeds.

'Oi - nutter! Get a bleddy motor!' a familiar voice boomed across the creek, making Ellie smile from ear to ear. She turned in the direction of her dear friend's house, to find him standing in his garden and waving at her madly.

She laughed and hollered back in his direction. 'But then I'd have to go to the gym!' She chuckled some more as he shook his head in amusement.

'Stop by on your way home!'

'Only if there's coffee!'

They grinned and waved wildly like a couple of school children, Ellie only stopping once she'd disappeared around the bend.

Jack Crawford had been a solid presence in Ellie and Gloria's life for about ten years now. Naturally, the entire hamlet gossiped over the possibilities of Jack and Ellie, Ellie and Jack. The only two youngsters on this side of the river - shacking it up. But really, they were more like brother and sister than husband

and wife material - much to the disappointment of most of the residents along the creek. Even almost a decade on, she knew the same wishful thinking was shared amongst the older residents over their cups of tea.

'Ooh, wouldn't it be lovely? Ellie and Jack.'

'They'd make such a sweet couple.'

'If only I was fifty years younger.' This was something often repeated amongst the female counterparts of these conversations, and it often had Jack blushing brighter than Gloria's lavish blouses.

Ellie's little boat pushed up against the bank moments later, and she turned it skilfully to its side, hoisting herself out to secure it to an old mooring post. As she gathered her tools, she glanced up at the house of her next customer and gasped.

'For goodness' sake, Harold! I told you I was coming up this afternoon to do that!' Ellie raced up the garden from the water's edge towards the house where Harold, a ripe old age of eighty-eight, was seen climbing a rickety old ladder, scooping congealed old leaves out of the gutters. 'Does Irene know you're out here!'

'I am perfectly capable of clearing me own gutters, young lady,' Harold grunted, throwing a big slop of leaves down to Ellie's feet. 'Be a good girl and pop the kettle on, will you?'

Ellie plonked her tools down on the grass and began scooping the sludge Harold had deposited haphazardly all over the lawn into a nearby bucket. 'How about you go and pop the kettle on, Harold. You've made a lovely start to the gutters, now let me crack on.'

It mostly didn't bother her when these sorts of comments were made, particularly given the generation of most of her customers. She knew that the likes of Harold found it odd to have a maintenance *woman*, despite it being twenty-three years into the 21st Century. Still, on the odd occasion, the flippant comments that implied her place was better suited in the kitchen fixing no more than a hot beverage irked her to no end.

'Is Harold up that bloody ladder?' Irene was heard shrieking from inside the cottage.

'Now you're in for it,' Ellie teased, her good humour clicking back into place as Harold clambered back down to the safety of the ground in school-boy panic.

'I only told him to put the ladder out ready for you,' Irene huffed and puffed, wiping soapy hands on her tabard apron as she scolded her husband with nothing more than a stern look. 'Honestly, it would take just one wrong step and you've fallen off and broken your neck. Ellie, dear. Would you like a cup of tea? Bit of saffron cake?'

'Yes to both. Sounds delicious.' Irene shuffled back into the depths of the cottage and Harold hovered, looking a little downtrodden. Ellie's good nature got the better of her. 'Harold, would you mind holding the bucket up to catch the sludge. Save messing up your lawn.'

It was nearing to half past six by the time Ellie's boat finally reached the bank bordering the bottom of Jack's garden, and her limbs were heavy and lagged from a long day. She found Jack in his newly fitted kitchen smearing adhesive to the back of a tile, the bare concrete floor littered with little white spacers.

'Going well, then?' Ellie teased, beelining to Jack's fridge and grabbing a can of something fizzy.

'I bloody hate tiling,' Jack muttered, pushing the tile in place, and slotting the spacers in. 'Should have gone for splash backs.'

Ellie pushed herself up onto one of the barstools - she was just shy of 5 ft 4 and often found any stool or chair adjusted to Jack's height a struggle - and swigged on her can of pop. 'Looks good though. What colour is the grout going to be? Please say grey.'

'Of course,' Jack scoffed, as if it was the most obvious choice. Ellie pinched her fingertips and thumb together and kissed them in true French chef style, then resumed to drinking her long-awaited cold drink. Her can placed on the counter once again, she must have drifted into deep thought for a little longer than usual because Jack regarded her with a mix of amusement and concern. 'Long day?'

'Not particularly,' Ellie said, shrugging off Jack's question and altering her vague expression to a more focused one.

'You just look like you're a million miles away.'

'Pondering,' Ellie said, her index finger circling the rim of the tin. 'I'm fine. I just go a bit thoughtful when there's a death in the community. Reminds me that Nanny is no spring chicken.'

'Don't let *her* hear you say that,' Jack chuckled, though his smile showed understanding. 'I did like Mrs Pascoe. It's sad seeing her cottage so still and empty.'

Jack fitted the last tile and retired his mucky tools to a bucket of warm water to soak. 'Thank Christ that's done! Tiling is so boring. You want to stay for dinner tonight? I'm having risotto and it's near impossible to make it for one.'

Ellie chuckled, passing Jack a beer. 'Sure. Hey, maybe you can make extra and use the leftovers as grout! The last one you made was the perfect consistency!'

Jack's bottle paused before it reached his now wide mouth. Ellie's laugh ruptured and echoed against the newly plastered walls, and she cried in protest as Jack lobbed a dollop of adhesive at her.

'Well, now you're getting bugger all!'

# Chapter Two

It was a big day for Lavinia Penhaligon, and she didn't know where to begin. After all, it wasn't as if she was at full capacity with her housekeeping team, nor her gardening staff. In fact, it had been many years since Penhaligon Estate had the required amount of people to simply make a dent on the upkeep of the place. The house and the surrounding gardens were far from perfect, but it would have to do... for now.

She ran a hand down the polished mahogany stair banister, checking for dust as she descended the grand staircase to the main hall. If she was to convince her only son that Penhaligon Estate was worth the trouble of uprooting himself from the perfect life he had built back in Milan - nothing short of glamorous - then she needed to at least ensure the place was free of dust and cobwebs. She was well aware of George's opinion on period properties and their oldish ways. Coming across one of the cleaners - Jill, was it? Or was that Peggy? - she asked them to check all of the banisters around the house. She only had them for another hour. She needed to get her money's worth.

'Goodness. Someone must be getting married,' Tressa's voice was a drawl as she rounded the corner from the direction of the drawing room, a book in one slender hand and a glass of wine in the other. Tressa, Lavinia's first-born, wore mustard-yellow trousers, high-waisted over a white turtleneck top. An unusually professional attire for someone who essentially wandered around the house idle most days.

'Why do you say that?' Lavinia asked, choosing not to comment on her eldest daughter's choice of midday beverage. That was one argument she could do without today.

'The place hasn't been this full of staff since Cousin Olivia's wedding.'

'This must be for our dear brother's home warming.' Wenna, Lavinia's youngest, sprang into view larger than life, her beautiful golden locks matted in a mess of little plaits she had clearly done herself - out of idleness, Lavinia expected. She really must find these girls something to do around the estate. It was clearly beneath them to pick up a duster every now and again. 'When does he arrive, Mother?'

'Yes. When should we roll out the red carpet for His Lordship?' Tressa rolled her eyes, scowling at her sister's enthusiasm.

'Oh, stop it you two. You sound horribly bitter and jealous,' Lavinia scolded, her eyes set a little harder on her eldest.

'On the contrary. I couldn't think of anything worse than being in charge of this dump.'

Without another word, Tressa crossed the hall, sliding a pair of sunglasses on to her face, and headed out to the gardens. A loaded silence was left behind in the hallway as Lavinia and Wenna exchanged knowing looks.

'It will be lovely to have him home,' Wenna said, squeezing her mother's forearm - ever the peacekeeper.

'Bless you, darling. It will be.'

Wenna was right. It would be wonderful to have George home, if not to shake up this infuriating pattern the Penhaligon women had fallen in to. And the eldest of the four Penhaligon women was not much better.

'Lavinia! Lavinia!' Her mother's shrill cries echoed into every corner of the large house, and it took all that Lavinia was not to cuss to the high heavens.

'Lavinia!' Beryan bellowed, as she marched through the hall as fast as her cane and dodgy hip would allow. 'I must insist that somebody speak to that incompetent wally out in the garden. Where's Ernie? Doesn't he know that one of his apprentices is destroying my wisteria?'

'For goodness' sake,' Lavinia muttered under breath, before composing herself and giving her best attempt at looking sympathetic to her mother's current dramas. 'What do you mean, Mother? Show me.'

'Look! Look!' Beryan cried, as she led the way to the breakfast room, pointing her cane menacingly in the direction of the pergola. Joseph, a young apprentice Lavinia had recently convinced her head gardener to take on, purely to save money, was indeed hacking away blindly at their poor ancient wisteria. Lavinia cringed outwardly as he cut into fresh shoots and created great gaps in the foliage. It was clear he didn't have a clue what he was doing.

'Joseph! Joseph, darling - please stop!

The boy looked bewildered and lowered his shears, his bright red hair standing on end from a mixture of morning breeze and perspiration.

'Morning, Mrs Penhaligon. Ernie has just asked me to prune the wisteria.' His eyes were suddenly as wide as dinner plates. 'Oh god, this is the wisteria, right?'

Lavinia couldn't help but chuckle, though her eyes closed in exasperation. 'Yes, Joseph. This is the wisteria. But you're far from pruning it.'

'You're hacking it into permanent submission!' Beryan added unhelpfully from the safety of the patio. Her cane and kitty heels were not fit for the lawn and its morning sogginess. 'In other words, you're ruining it! Killing it!'

'You're not killing it,' Lavinia reasoned quickly, seeing the blood drain from the poor boy's spotty face. 'But you do need to be more precise and careful. We don't want our prize wisteria to become misshapen or patchy.'

'Yes, Mrs Penhaligon.' There was a long pause as Joseph held the shears in midair. Then lowered them again. 'Should I use something a bit smaller then?'

'Yes, Joseph. Perhaps some secateurs would be more suitable.'

As the young lad skulked off to seek better tools, Lavinia's hands reached up to her face as she attempted to shake away her frustration. Things would be easier once George was here. It just had to be.

She turned to her mother, a sheer force for a lady in her early nineties and coaxed her gently back into the house and into the breakfast room.

'I could do with a beverage, Mother. Won't you join me? A nice cup of Earl Grey perhaps.'

'I don't see why we must hire such incompetence, Lavinia. I mean really, how much are we actually saving?'

Lavinia pinched some fresh tea leaves into a strainer and dunked it into a teapot of hot water, as Beryan lowered herself unsteadily into a wing-back chair nearest to the unlit fire. 'It's a significant difference financially between hiring an apprentice or hiring somebody qualified. Believe me, I've looked.'

'Then Ernie needs to whip them into shape.'

'Ernie is seventy this year. I do think we need to-'

'Don't be so ageist, Lavinia. The man has a few more years in him yet.'

This was a sore topic for her mother - Lavinia knew this. Ernie had been a gardener at Penhaligon Estate for almost five decades and Head Gardener for four of them. For as long as Lavinia could remember, Ernie had always been spotted on the grounds and in the gardens, working like a Trojan. But there was no denying his age and his depleting ability in such a physically taxing job. And it showed in the gardens - wild and overgrown -

the lines of the lawn no longer pristine. Fallen trees and debris littered the parkland from last winter's storm and a blanket of moss and weeds were slowly taking over the long driveway and front yard at the front of the house. Penhaligon Estate had gone wild and was lost to the public eye.

'I'm telling you now, Lavinia - that man is no more ready for retirement than I was to see that ghastly online stuff installed around the house. For goodness' sake, who needs to look things up online every second of the day? It's just laziness.'

'The Wi-Fi is very much needed, Mother - if we are to consider the notion of opening the doors of Penhaligon House to guests.'

Beryan grumbled, her wrinkled neck wobbling in disapproval. 'Do not even get me started on *that.* I've lost the battle with these silly little modern ideas, but I stand firm on Ernie.' A distant shouting could be heard out in the gardens as Beryan powered through with her rant. Lavinia's eyes trained distractedly to Joseph who was now running down the garden path. 'Us oldies must stick together before we are cast out of the equation for good. He's strong as an ox. Just you see him mark another ten years with us.'

'Mrs Penhaligon! Mrs Penhaligon!' Joseph cried, gasping for air as he stumbled into the breakfast room, Beryan harrumphing disapprovingly at Joseph's dirty boots on the antique Persian rug beneath him. 'I'm sorry to barge in, it's just...it's Ernie. He's fallen over. He's hurt, really bad. I think he needs an ambulance.'

'Oh, my goodness,' Lavinia cried, springing into action as Beryan thudded her stick against the ground in annoyance at Joseph's poor timing.

'He's beginning to be a thorn in my side, that boy,' Beryan grumbled, sitting tight as Joseph and Lavinia dashed away through the gardens to find Ernie.

Lavinia heard Ernie before she could see him, his pained

grunting and swearing echoing against the canopy of the rhododendrons.

'It was him! That bloody boy... getting in my way all the time!' Ernie shouted, pointing a muddy finger at poor Joseph.

'I wasn't doing anything, Mrs Penhaligon,' Joseph cried, his eyes wide with panic. 'I swear!'

'That's the problem - he d'unt do nothing 'round here!' Ernie growled, a fresh wave of pain washing over him and rendering him semi-unconscious.

Lavinia retrieved her phone from her pocket and began dialling for an ambulance. 'Joseph, I need you to go to Trixie in the kitchen and request for some blankets to keep Ernie warm.' The faint sound of the operator could be heard as Ernie regained conscience long enough to shout in agony. 'Hello...yes...ambulance please. Joseph - now please!'

As Joseph skidded across the gravel back towards the house, Lavinia rearranged her legs from under her to prevent further pins and needles, straightening her floral skirt to keep her dignity. She wasn't exactly feeling like a spring chicken herself these days. She looked down at poor Ernie in despair, realising now more than ever that she could not allow this arrangement to continue. Starting tomorrow, she would have to start the search for a new gardener, whether her mother liked it or not.

# Chapter Three

It had only been a week. And yet there was a noticeable emptiness to Mrs Pascoe's cottage. A sadness and a sense of sudden abandonment. Sorrow trickled in as Ellie gingerly stepped over the stinging nettles and brambles threatening to invade the crumbling path which led to the front door, Jack following close behind.

'Doesn't feel right doing this, does it?' Jack mumbled in Ellie's ear as she turned the old front door key, the mechanism clacking open loudly.

'I know. I don't think Mrs Pascoe would have minded one bit, though. You know what she was like. She'd be telling us to pop the kettle on. Help ourselves to the biscuit tin.'

Jack and Ellie laughed softly, feeling the need to keep their voices low as they stepped straight into the sitting room, the air cold and stale. It was as if Mrs Pascoe's life in this cottage had simply just been put on pause. Like she'd be back at any moment. A basket of wool and knitting needles sat by the foot of the old armchair closest to the fireplace, no doubt containing some unfinished projects that she was working on for the knickknacks stall in the community hall. Jack veered off towards the little sunroom at the back whilst Ellie headed to the kitchen to check for perishables in the fridge. It looked as if a lovely neighbour had already been in - no doubt Vivian next door - as the fridge was empty and freshly cleaned, the dishes cleared and left to drain, and a basket of clean and folded laundry had been left on the breakfast table.

The community here really was wonderful, Ellie thought fondly.

'Hey, Ellie?' Jack's voice echoed through the small space. He appeared from the sunroom, his head slightly dipped from the low beamed ceiling and a cat sprawled happily in his arms. 'Did Mrs Pascoe have a cat?'

Ellie gasped and cooed, leaping forward to run her hands through the friendly feline's grey fur. 'Awww, hello gorgeous!'

'Hello!' Jack responded, a grin on his face and his eyebrows wagging at Ellie playfully.

'You plonker,' Ellie laughed. The both of them fussed over the cat for a while longer. 'What do you think then?'

Mrs Pascoe and her late husband Robert had never had children and so there would be no extended family available to sort through her things other than Robert's sister, who lived all the way up in the Lake District. Not to mention she was nearing three digits in her age and so would perhaps struggle with the shifting of furniture. Only a week had passed but Robert's sister had already been in contact with the neighbours about packing away the life the Pascoes had built in five decades. Of course, the youngest and most able residents of the hamlet had been summoned.

'Shouldn't take very long to clear,' Jack said, putting the cat down on a nearby armchair and pulling his vibrating phone out from his back pocket. 'But I still say it's too early to start shifting things.' Excusing himself from the room, Jack slipped back out into the little sunroom with his phone to his ear just as there was a timid knock on the front door. Ellie turned to see Mr Williams, a small and nervous-looking man of his late-sixties, peeping his head around the door in way of greeting.

'Hello, Ellie me 'andsome. I wondered if it was you and Jack I could hear,' Mr Williams said with a hint of relief. He lived in the next terrace house along, attached to Mrs Pascoe's right-side whilst Vivian was to her left. Mr Williams lived alone now after losing his wife to dementia only a few years back - his three children all grown up and living their own lives. Ellie had always found him to be a kind and familiar person to wave to each day, often spotting him in the pub on Friday nights or taking his little terrier for his daily morning walks.

'Sorry if we worried you at all, Mr Williams,' Ellie said. 'Vivian gave us the key.'

'Not to worry, my love,' Mr Williams said kindly, now stepping fully into the cottage and digging his hands into his trouser pockets. 'Thought I'd check all the same. Ah, there you are Mr Fluffles!' Mr Williams rushed forward to retrieve the cat from the sofa, scooping him lovingly into his arms before taking his prior position by the door. 'Mrs Pascoe liked to leave this one little bowls of mackerel, bless her heart. I suppose I will have to start doing the same now. Shouldn't have thought the dried kibble I've been putting down for him will cut it anymore.'

Ellie smiled fondly, reaching out and petting the cat's small little head. 'Mr Fluffles, eh?'

'My granddaughter's choice of name,' Mr Williams grumbled, though a loving smile pulled in the corner of his thin, aged lips. 'Oh dear, I think Mr Fluffles here will be quite confused to find this place empty for the time being.'

'She was quite something, our Mrs Pascoe.' She then looked up in alarm to find poor Mr Williams sniffling loudly, using poor Mr Fluffles as a handkerchief to catch the escaping tears. Ellie was relieved when Jack returned from his private phone call, a look of bewilderment on his face as he found Ellie making feeble attempts to comfort Mr Williams. She exchanged wide eyes with him, silently pleading him for support.

'You alright there, Mr Williams?' Jack asked, managing to sound both sympathetic and encouraging with his loud voice shaking up the saddening tone about to take hold. 'Ah, is this

24

your cat?'

'Hello, Jack. Yes, this silly thing is mine.'

Jack and Ellie waited patiently for Mr Williams to compose himself, Ellie offering a couple more feeble pats on the shoulder in way of comfort.

'Anyway,' Mr Williams finally announced, setting Mr Fluffles down and reaching for a handkerchief in his back pocket. 'You'll forgive me for having a moment. I was very fond of Mrs Pascoe, and she did a lot for me when I lost my dear Jennifer.'

Jack and Ellie nodded in sympathy and Mr Williams continued. 'Silly bugger, I am. I was actually hoping to catch you, Ellie. The house -' Mr Williams pointed in the vague direction of Penhaligon House. 'They're advertising a new gardener's job!'

'Penhaligon?' Ellie asked. Mr Williams nodded and Ellie politely feigned interest. 'Oh, right.'

'I just thought you'd like to know, because it's a generous salary - or at least I thought it was.'

Ellie's eyes widened then, her thoughts flying to her diminishing bank balance and the hefty number of unpaid bills waiting for her on the kitchen counter at home. But it was the big house after all, so the anticipation was dampened somewhat. 'A salary? That surprises me.'

'Why's that, my dear?'

'You just don't see well-paid gardening jobs very much anymore, despite the labour and skills that go into it.'

Jack nodded in full agreement and Mr Williams did also, muttering 'quite right, quite right' and explaining in great depth how he had heard about it through the fast-working grapevine of the community. In the meantime, Jack had found the job advertisement on his phone and was now showing Ellie.

'It's for Head Gardener, Mr Williams,' Ellie clarified, pulling a face. 'I doubt I'll be qualified for that but thank you anyway.'

'That's a shame. But perhaps you should apply either way. You never know what opportunities might arise. Though, don't tell people around here you heard it from me. They'll be after me for compromising their gardener's availability.'

'I'll think about it. Thank you, Mr Williams.'

Mr Williams smiled warmly, seemingly pleased with himself. 'I always thought you were made for bigger things, my dear.'

'Here, here!' Jack bellowed, triumphantly.


The birds chirped cheerfully outside, hopping, and fluttering from bird feeder to bird feeder on the Mountain Ash in front of the kitchen window. Ellie occupied the little breakfast table, her paperwork spread across the entire tabletop, her index finger stabbing into the clunky keys of her trusty old calculator. She'd done these calculations three times now, in the hopes that one more time would perhaps prove that she had simply added up the numbers wrong. She punched at the equals button, her heart sinking as she gave in to the idea that the results had been correct all along.

A headed letter lay amongst various other house bills and invoices, addressed to her and Nanny as tenants of the cottage, informing them that rent would be rising by at least twenty percent. They knew it would happen eventually. The estate hadn't increased their rent for many years now and it was only to be expected with the rising cost of just about everything. But that was just it. Everything was going up. Everything except Ellie's income. She would need to raise her fees at some point, but she couldn't just throw her prices up in one go without consulting her regulars. Times were hard for everyone around here, so putting her customers out of pocket would do no good. If anything, it would put her out of a job entirely in cases where her customers could no longer afford the luxury of having Ellie to maintain their gardens, spruce up their houses and clear out their gutters.

One thing was absolutely certain here. Their outgoings were now officially more than what was coming in. With Nanny's measly pension and Ellie's inconsistent payments coming in from customers, it was looking pretty grim for them both. Ellie gripped the breakfast table with both hands and took a steadying breath, her mind racing for solutions. Ellie was practical through and through, rarely a moper. But there was only so much she could do here.

Her mind settled on the conversation with Mr Williams earlier that morning. At the time, she'd dismissed the news of Penhaligon Estate's job vacancy for Head Gardener. It was of no interest to her. She was unqualified and the reputation which proceeded the people who lived up in that big house gave her little motivation to be employees to them.

But at this current moment in time, she was sat between a rock and a hard place. Perhaps she couldn't afford to be too choosy.

With Ellie weighing up her depleting options, Gloria shuffled into the kitchen from the hallway, falling into a spurt of hacking coughs, perching a gnarled hand on the kitchen worktop to steady herself. Ellie looked up in concern.

'That's not sounding good,' Ellie declared, watching her eighty-nine-year-old grandmother ease herself into the chair next to her with unusual frailness. 'Are you alright?'

'I am *quite* alright,' Gloria confirmed, waving Ellie's concern away with an impatient hand. 'Don't you dare start fussing over a couple of splutters. I'm just feeling a bit chesty, that's all.'

'I'll make you a lemon and honey drink,' Ellie said, shooting up from her seat and putting the kettle on.

'Fine,' Gloria accepted, picking up some of the bills sitting in front of her on the table. 'These look ominous.'

Ellie squidged some honey into her Nanny's favourite teacup and began slicing a lemon. 'Ominous is a good word for them.' She poured the boiling hot water into the cup and brought the concoction over before continuing. 'We've got a bit of tightening up to do with the old finances, I'm afraid. Rent is

27

going up.'

'Robbing bastards,' Nanny muttered, viciously.

'To be fair, it was expected. With cost of living at the moment...,' Ellie said, trying to be reasonable but not fully believing in her own words. 'I think I need to start looking into other forms of income, Nan. As great as it is working along the creek and being close to home, it isn't steady and I'm certainly far from raking it in.'

Gloria sipped her honey and lemon drink, pondering for a moment. 'What were you thinking? Same line of work?'

'Maybe. It's where I enjoy my work - something outdoors.' Ellie hesitated for a moment, aware that what she was going to say next wouldn't go down as well as that hot beverage her Nanny was currently sipping. 'Actually, Mr Williams mentioned earlier that the estate was looking for a new gardener. Well, Head Gardener actually.'

'Penhaligon Estate?' Gloria's sharp blue eyes narrowed over her cup.

'I know it's a bit ambitious. I don't really have any qualifications, but Mr Williams seemed to think I wouldn't need any. His brother went to school with the old Head Gardener - Ernie. He reckons he doesn't have a single qualification to his name, so I thought -'

'No, you can't work there,' Gloria said, firmly, shaking her head. 'No. No, absolutely not.'

'You don't think I could -'

'Oh, I think you can do just about anything you set your mind to, my girl. But no, I will not see you working in that horrible place, amongst those... those people.'

Ellie would usually have thrown back a rebuke of some kind, but she had never seen her grandmother distressed over something like this. Vexed, worked up over something perhaps, but never truly upset as she was right now. It took Ellie by surprise, and she simply gaped at her grandmother, confused and disappointed.

'Nanny, we're about to be in a lot of trouble here if I don't find myself a better paying job.'

'Raise your prices!'

'You know my customers can barely afford what I charge them now. If I throw my prices up, then I'm no better than the estate raising the price of their rent. Am I?'

Gloria appeared to back down for just a second, accepting that Ellie was right at least about that, but seemed to find a second wind, smacking the tabletop vigorously. 'I will not see you working for them. I won't.'

Ellie's entire body sunk and arched in defeat as she nodded to show a reluctant acceptance of her Nan's wishes. She offered to make them both a late lunch and quietly sauntered to the kitchen to prepare some sandwiches. She would just have to scour the jobs in this week's paper later and hope she could find something. Time would soon run out.

Feeling somewhat downtrodden, her concern for the bills growing as the afternoon dwindled by, Ellie decided to take action and head to Jack's to use his Wi-Fi.

Despite it being Jack's house which was under renovation, with mostly exposed mortar and stripped ceilings, it was his which had the reliable Wi-Fi. A running joke between them, Ellie was exasperated by the unreliability of working internet in their little cottage on a daily basis. Luckily, she wasn't one to spend hours browsing the web and, according to Jack, she was the only person in her thirties left on this planet who didn't have social media. He was exaggerating of course, but that was the common reaction from people when she told them she didn't have any of these social media platforms society seemed to function around. For most part, she wouldn't have time spare to sit and 'scroll' as people do, and she didn't much care for socialising in person. Why would she want to do it online?

It was times like these though, where she really longed for a reliable Wi-Fi, so she could simply sit at her own breakfast table and browse the local job vacancies with no issues. Then again, sitting in Jack's newly completed kitchen, perched on the end of his huge breakfast island, and overlooking the glistening waters of the estuary, was certainly a bonus which made rowing down the river to simply Google something worthwhile. Jack placed a coaster down next to his laptop, which Ellie was tapping away on, and sat a steaming cup of coffee on top, protecting his brand-new grey-marble worktops with pride.

'Why you don't just get somebody out to check your internet...' Jack tutted, placing his own cup of coffee on a coaster, and picking up his paint brush to continue priming the kitchen walls. 'It's probably something simple. You're paying all that money per month.'

'Yeah, yeah - I'll look into it,' Ellie said, waving the notion off, her eyes fixed to the screen as she scrolled through some vacancies.

'Heard that before,' Jack said, rolling his eyes. Ellie tore her gaze from the screen to watch as Jack's steady hand glided the brush effortlessly down the wall, perfectly cutting in along the edge of the door frame. His work was slow and precise, but it was always finished to the highest standard.

'I could watch you paint all day,' Ellie sighed, entranced as he dipped the brush into the paint and scraped off any excess on the edge of the tin. He glanced up, his face splitting into a grin.

'Like a bit of painting porn, do we El?' Jack said, waggling his eyebrows and making a point of sticking his bottom out as he stroked the brush down the wall once more.

'You've got paint on the framework,' Ellie pointed out.

'Ah, shit,' Jack muttered, dropping his silly act, and jumping into action to correct his mistake.

Ellie chuckled from her spot at the breakfast island, taking a sip of her coffee. 'Serves you right, you goof.'

'I wonder why Gloria has such a thing against you applying for that job,' Jack pondered, his focus back on his wall. 'Sounds right up your street.'

'I'm not sure,' Ellie replied, frowning. 'She was really distressed about it. She does not like the people who live up there, that's for sure.'

'She's a mysterious lady, our Gloria,' Jack said, feigning drama. 'Maybe she has a history with the family. A connection we didn't know about. A secret lover.' Jack waggled his eyebrows for the second time, and Ellie chuckled. But a slight frown remained on Ellie's face. Jack was just making a joke, but Ellie couldn't help thinking that Gloria's reaction suggested this wasn't far from the truth. Her reaction seemed too personal - too raw.

'Anything?' Jack asked, nodding at the laptop as a prompt.

'Nothing,' Ellie sighed, leaning back on her stool, and putting her full focus on her cup of coffee. 'Nothing in the outdoors or gardening sector anyway.' She suddenly looked miserable as a wave of realisation washed over her. 'If it comes down to it, I'll just have to grab any job. But I don't think I can bring myself to be locked away inside a shop nine hours a day, and I'd be useless as a waitress. I *need* to be outside.'

'I agree. You'd go *doo-lally* stuck inside all day.'

She felt Jack's eyes on her as she buried her face into her hands in despair.

'El, that job is perfect for you. Maybe you need to have a proper conversation with Gloria tonight and get an explanation from her. I love her to bits - you know I do. But she needs to be reasonable here.'

Ellie nodded slowly, staring out to the water, and thinking how much she would miss it if she had to get a job away from the creek. At least if she got the job at the estate, she could see the creek from the gardens. Or she assumed she could. If she could see the estate and gardens from the creek, she'd be able to see the view in reverse, surely? And if she was honest with herself, the idea of getting her green fingered hands on those Italian gardens, the kitchen gardens and even that walled flower garden, excited her beyond belief. She'd seen old professional photos of it in a book from the library once and often wished the place was open to the public. The older members of the creek community often recalled the days where the entire estate opened its doors and welcomed the surrounding communities for family days, fayres, and charity garden events. But for decades now the estate had been closed off, a mystery behind its old stone walls and high hedges, poised on top of its hill out of reach. Getting a sneaky look-in at the secret gardens and stately house was surely enough of a reason to go along to an interview - simply to be nosy.

Her mind set, Ellie closed the laptop. 'I'll speak to her tonight. Maybe catch her with her dentures out. She can't argue back without her teeth.'

Jack snorted loudly, almost swiping paint all over his door frame again. 'You've got such a dark sense of humour sometimes. I bleddy love it.'

A barn owl hooted in the distance, marking the start of a clear spring evening. The nights were still drawn in, it only being mid-March, but Ellie could feel the anticipation of lighter evenings ahead. She wasn't partial to either, but there was something pretty magical about listening to the nocturnal side of nature awaken in the darkness. There were times when she would simply take a mug of something hot and sweet out onto the patio and listen to the gentle lapping of the water at the bottom of the garden, their little cottage behind her flooding the lawn in light and casting the surrounding trees and shrubs into shadow and silhouettes. The clear sky, framed by the treetops, would glisten with the stars above, and the sound of Gloria's programmes would ring out from the living room, followed by her loud cackle.

It was a similar sort of evening, though the stars were not visible through a blanket of grey clouds. Ellie finished watering the plants on the patio before closing the door and locking up for the night, switching the outside light off. It was only ten o'clock, but she had heard Nanny turn off her TV and head to the bathroom to brush her teeth, so it wouldn't be long until she was sound asleep. But she also wouldn't be distracted by Strictly Come Dancing or Doc Martin. Ellie had been putting off the conversation all evening. It was now or never.

'Nan?' Ellie poked her head into Gloria's bedroom to find her applying some face cream.

'I was just about to say goodnight. I'm having an early one if you don't mind.'

'Course not. Just quickly,' Ellie began, pausing to receive a goodnight kiss on the cheek. 'About that job up in the big house...'

Gloria sighed and sat gingerly on the edge of her bed, her bedside light glowing behind her. 'My reaction was a bit much earlier, that I will admit. But I really am quite uncomfortable with the idea, my love.'

'Can I ask why?' Ellie asked, as gently as possible, taking a seat on the little wicker chair beside her nanny's vanity table and gathering her long legs beneath her. 'It's clearly something personal.'

'It is,' Nanny answered, vaguely. 'Let's just say one of the women who occupy the house now were not particularly kind to me once upon a time. Some might say I deserved it, but I don't believe so. Not fully. I haven't seen Beryan Penhaligon for quite some years now - decades even - but I shouldn't think any amount of time will ease the tension between us. I would like to explain this to you properly one day, Ellie. But not tonight. I'm tired and you look like you could quite happily fall asleep standing up yourself.'

Ellie couldn't hide the disappointment on her face, but it was a fair request. She'd left it too late tonight. She nodded her agreement and helped her Nan into bed, tucking the duvet around her frail body. 'Night, Nan.'

'You work so hard for us, my love,' Nanny said, reaching up to stroke Ellie's cheek. 'I know you've made many sacrifices over the years when it comes to your own... your own ambitions and goals. Like I said, it's late tonight. I'm not saying no about the job just yet, but I'm not necessarily saying yes either.'

Ellie's spirits lifted a little as she smiled and kissed Nanny on her powdery cheek.

'We'll discuss it in the morning. Let me sleep on it.'

It wasn't a yes, but it was much more than Ellie could have expected without so much as a chance to discuss the matter properly. Perhaps, if Gloria was willing to share some of her secret quarrels with the estate, Ellie could reason with her and make her see that this could be the answer to their problems, and maybe even a chance for Gloria to gain some form of closure. Ellie would just have to discover more tomorrow morning after a good night's sleep.

# Chapter Four

Bright lights flashed in contrast to the dark night as George Penhaligon made a reluctant journey to Milan Malpensa airport by taxi. A tanned hand gripped the taxi's grab handle as he thought about what awaited him on his return home to Cornwall. He'd probably arrive at the estate just in time for dinner tomorrow. Perhaps if it was late enough, he wouldn't need to see the inevitable state of the place for another day. He could lay weary eyes on it after a good night's sleep, perhaps a little more optimistically than he was currently feeling.

The last time he had been at Penhaligon Estate was Christmas, a mere five months ago. He wasn't about to give himself false hope that things had improved in such a short space of time. His memory flicked back in mild horror to the peeling paint, the crumbling walls, the loose roof tiles, the unruly garden slowly enclosing the house in a cage of brambles and vines. Not to mention the ancient electrics and dodgy plumbing. His head began to pound in that familiar way it did when his mind was filled with... well, just about anything. Here in Milan, his mind usually buzzed with to-do lists, and meetings, and publicity events. But it was satisfying work which made the moments of stress worthwhile, often signed off with a night out in the city.

But Penhaligon Estate was a different level of stress. It was a burden on George's shoulders. It was a job never completed.

'Grazie. Buonanotte,' George said, paying his fee and stepping out of the taxi onto the pavement before the airport entrance. The airport was its usual hustle and bustle as George stepped through the automatic doors, and he felt the lingering glances from a group of young ladies on what he assumed was a hen party arriving for a weekend of celebrations. He was used to the attention he received. With his rich, chestnut hair and golden tanned skin, people wouldn't be blamed for mistaking him as a local *Italian stallion*. And he'd be lying if he said he didn't enjoy it. Why shouldn't he? He worked hard on his physique.

George groaned at the harsh reminder that Penhaligon Estate did not have a gym. He could go for a run around the estate perhaps, but at the peril of his poor ankles as soon as he hit the first rabbit hole. Maybe that would be the first thing he installed. Bring the estate firmly into the twenty-first century, starting with a fully equipped fitness centre. Tressa would surely be pleased. How his sisters managed with the archaic ways and lack of modern comfort in that big house, he struggled to understand. Perhaps that was why Tressa was the way she was.

George ordered a large brandy at the only bar open for business and settled onto a stall, soaking up the last of the Italian ways and waiting for the announcement to his gate.

The Cornish weather welcomed George back in his home county with appropriately predictable grey skies and scattered showers. He shook his head in disappointment, trying not to think about the luscious blue skies and scorching hot temperatures he'd left behind back in the Mediterranean. He gripped the steering wheel of his hire car, the 'Coming Home Trees' appearing in their usual spot. Usually, the sight of these trees gave George permission to wind down, even look forward to a week or two back in Cornwall - usually for the holidays or a birthday. This time, they didn't have the same desired effect and he wondered when he'd be passing them again.

His phone rang through the blue-tooth system and George braced himself before pressing down on the green phone symbol on the dash screen.

'Hello, darling. How was the flight?' Lavinia's voice filled the car.

'Fine, Mother. Like any other flight.'

'And the hotel?'

'Also fine,' George said, smiling at his mother's way of fussing.

'Oh well, don't overwhelm me with too much detail, will you?' Lavinia's voice huffed through the speaker.

George rolled his eyes toward the car roof and added, 'it had a bed; it had a bathroom; it included breakfast. It was fine. I'm going to be there earlier than planned. I should be there by lunchtime.'

'Wonderful. I'll let Trixie know to include you in the numbers.'

George bit down on the concerns he almost shared out loud. Surely, they didn't still pay Trixie to prepare three meals a day for just the four of them. That was a conversation for another time. 'Okay, Mother. Thanks. I'll see you soon.'

The house appeared in view almost two hours later, and a sight beheld George that had him cussing out loud. He blew out bated breath and tapped the steering wheel in agitation. It was so much worse than he remembered. The Italian gardens which surrounded the house were wild and out of control; most of the downstairs windows and half of the second-floor windows had been totally claimed by the wisteria and the varied clematis. His car pulled up to a moss and weed infested driveway, and the boxed hedging which sat beneath the windows on the house front was riddled with blight. What on earth was Ernie playing at?

The front door, tired and peeling, opened to reveal his

youngest sister, who flew down the stone steps to greet him.

'George!' Wenna sang, wrapping her small arms around his middle. 'Thank God you're here. The house is stifling without you around. Are you really staying? Please say you are!'

George chuckled, returning the embrace, and kissing the top of her head. 'For now. How are you? How's the course going?'

'Which course?' Wenna asked bashfully, her eyes wide.

'The... um, was it the hair and nails course?'

'Oh, that one. No, that one didn't work out. Think I might try a business diploma.'

George's smile was tight as he tried his best not to show a glimmer of disappointment. Not disappointment in his youngest sister, but disappointment *for* her. That she had not found that interest, that passion. The way she flitted from job to job and project to project, never seeing any of it through. She was, in his view, lost and he didn't know how to guide her without coddling her. Perhaps studying business would be a good all-rounder while she decided, he thought reasonably.

'Great idea,' George said, committing fully to his smile as he closed his car door. 'I can help you find the right course after dinner, if you like.'

Wenna reached into the boot and dragged George's bags out onto the mossy gravel. 'Nah, another time. Let's get drunk tonight!'

George scoffed, declaring firmly that it wasn't going to happen before prising his heavy bags from his sister's bony hands.

'Come on,' George said, jerking his chin in the direction of the front door. 'Let the torture commence.'

Inside the house, the interior was untouched. Tidy, clean, and typically old-fashioned. It could probably do with a lick of paint and the old carpets would benefit from a shampoo, but it was mercifully preserved. At a quick glance, he wouldn't need to throw money at the interior just yet. The dinginess of the rooms, the sun attempting feebly to peek through the gaps of the overgrown climbers outside, was a harsh reminder of the issues externally. If his face wasn't already a hard grimace, it was practically contorted as his other sister rounded the corner, her own expression thunderous.

'Hello, Tressa,' George said, warily.

Tressa forced a smile and headed for the stairs. 'Hello.'

'Crikey, it's barely midday. What's got your knickers in a twist so early?'

'Why don't you ask our dear mother? Her precious son will cheer her right up, I'm sure.' Tressa disappeared without so much as feigned politeness towards her brother who she hadn't seen for over three months.

George pinched his lips together and nodded, as if confirming exactly what he had been expecting. 'Brilliant.'

'Just ignore Tressa,' Wenna called from the back of the hall, gesturing for him to follow her towards the drawing room. He did as he was told, setting his bags at the base of the stairs. 'She's just pissed off because Mother won't let her get involved with the interviews.'

'What interviews?'

'Oh, didn't you hear? Ernie fell in the garden last week and broke his hip.'

'Christ! Is he alright?'

'Well, not precisely. He's, like, a hundred years old. Pretty sure breaking a hip finishes you off for good at that age.'

'Cheerful. He's seventy. That's hardly ancient.'

George's main concern was with poor Ernie, a familiar part of his childhood here at Penhaligon Estate - but a dominating part of him was instantly relieved. There were extenuated circumstances for the state of the gardens, a valid reason. He didn't need to panic just yet.

'Yeah, so Mother has started doing interviews for somebody

to cover Ernie until he's back on his feet.'

Worry set back in again. 'She can't be serious. Poor old Ernie isn't just going to bounce back from a hip break. Not at his age.'

'That's what I said. And to be fair, that's what Tressa said too. Honestly, Mother has been insufferable. But it's a start. Maybe this temp person will do a good job, and Mother and Granny will realise Ernie is just too old to run an estate like this.'

'See?' George winked. 'Sounding like a true businesswoman already.'

Wenna rolled her eyes but there was an extra spring in her step as she led the way into the drawing room, a space mostly comprising of mahogany furniture and loud floral wallpaper. The midday sun beamed through the gaps in the window and bathed the cluttered space in golds and yellows, the small frame of Beryan sitting in her armchair in the far corner.

'Hello, Granny,' George smiled, closing the gap, and placing a gentle kiss on his grandmother's powdery cheek. 'You're looking well.'

'That's usually a polite way of saying you look passable for an old woman,' Beryan said wryly, her eyes twinkling at the anticipated arrival of her only grandson.

'Still sharp as ever, I see,' George chuckled.

'Yes, well... one must remain hard and sharp as flint to not appear redundant around here,' Beryan mumbled in her usual irritated way.

'A Christmas Carol?'

Beryan's face broke into a broad smile. 'I missed you darling boy. Your sisters barely know the difference between their Austens to their Kardashians.'

George suppressed a laugh as he glanced at his youngest sister, her arms thrown into the air in exasperation.

# Chapter Five

It occurred to Ellie, as she stumbled her way through the thicket of brambles onto an unused path leading to the main house, that she had never once in her adult life set foot on the grounds of Penhaligon Estate. She had faded memories of once traipsing through the parkland as a primary school pupil, for a day out Ellie had never known the Penhaligons to be an open-gates sort of family, their house, and gardens open for all to enjoy. Whenever she was forced to drive, walk, or paddle by, it looked as locked up from prying eyes as it always had.

It was a rough bit of track she ventured on now and Ellie was glad she had her trusty work boots on, though her bare legs were taking a battering from the intruding hedgerows. If she got the job - and this was a very big 'if' - she'd have to figure out the best route. Walking this path in the harsh elements of the winter months didn't sound too appealing, and her little red Leyland Sherpa wasn't too trustworthy these days - even on short trips up the road. Perhaps she could go by water, but she would need to suss out an easy path from the little pebbled beach up to the gardens.

She gave herself a mental shake. Less than forty-eight hours ago, she'd thrown away the notion of going for this job at all. She'd woken the next morning, fully prepared with persuasive arguments to present to Nanny in way of convincing her of the benefits, only for Nanny to yield over breakfast, giving reluctant permission for her to apply. The cynical side of Ellie couldn't help but believe that this was Nanny's way of avoiding telling the truth behind her initial reaction. But she'd bounced into action all the same, motivated by the inevitable trouble they would be in soon without better income. She'd been shocked when the voice of a stern woman had invited her in over the phone for an interview the very next day.

Now, here she was working out the logistics. Who was to say they'd even hire her? It was all hypothetical nonsense at this point.

But, either way, she needed a more consistent wage. She needed to know that the money coming in at the end of the month was more than just enough to keep their heads above water, and with Nanny's state pension barely making a dent now, Ellie needed to make sure she covered enough for the both of them. She owed that much to Nanny.

It didn't take long for the house to come into view, its limestone grandeur gleaming in the morning sunshine. It was pretty, as far as stately homes go. She couldn't deny that. The surrounding park land shimmered lazily in silvery morning dew, a herd of Belted Galloways creating hazy silhouettes in the near distance.

This was what you call a commute, Ellie thought, her chest swelling as she drank in that gloriously sweet air.

Now she just had to hope that qualifications weren't mandatory.


'We are ideally looking for someone with qualifications in horticulture. Going by your - rather brief - CV, it appears that you have...well, none.'

The woman now holding Ellie's CV whilst pacing the carpeted floor in front of her had introduced herself as Lavinia Penhaligon at the start of the interview. The Lady of the estate. She was taller than Ellie had imagined. Slender and well-poised, but sturdy. Ellie couldn't quite pin point what she meant by that, but sturdy seemed an appropriate adjective for a woman like Lavinia. And now, she was ripping her to shreds.

'So - do tell me - why should I hire someone with absolutely no qualifications other than a near-expiring chainsaw license?'

It was a fair question. And Ellie stumbled silently on possible answers, each less impressive than the other. Eventually, she shrugged a little and took the plunge.

'I know qualifications are important to most employers. But honestly, I've seen people in my line of work qualified up to the eyeballs, and at the end of the day if they can't do a decent dove joint or tell the difference between a rudbeckia and a cosmos, then really, it's just a fancy bit of paper isn't it?'

Lavinia's expression didn't so much as budge, but Ellie ploughed on. 'True skill comes from practise and experience, not from a silly bit of paper that costs an arm and a leg to get.'

The woman's eyes bored into Ellie's with growing interest as she considered her for a while.

'If I may pry a little,' the older lady next to Lavinia continued, glancing at the blasted CV over her daughter's shoulder. Ellie had almost forgotten she was there, perched in her armchair behind Lavinia with an impressive air of both frailness and legacy. 'You didn't finish college. Why not? That was almost fifteen years ago now. Have you ever thought about finishing?'

This was why Ellie hated interviews. They stripped you bare, giving people permission to ask impertinent questions like this. How dare she ask that, Ellie thought. Yes. Of course she'd considered it. But when money is always concerned, suddenly the idea of finishing college was a bit pointless and risky. The silly old woman had no idea of the sacrifices Ellie had had to make over the years.

'Extenuated circumstances,' Ellie finally responded. 'Family related.'

'I can see that you live down on the creek, in one of our

cottages,' Lavinia said, straying from Ellie's lack of qualifications to her relief.

Ellie was just about to respond when the old woman suddenly leapt forward with surprising agility and snatched the CV from Lavinia's long fingers.

'Ellie Curnow?' The woman's voice was curt and laced in sudden malice. 'You are related to Gloria Curnow?'

It was both a question and a statement, and Ellie wasn't entirely sure whether to answer.

'She's my Nanny.'

Her CV, as useless as a chocolate teapot at this point, was suddenly cast to one side as if it had burned the lady and the woman immediately started rising from her chair, unsteady on her cane in her distress.

'Thank you for your time, dear. But I don't think you're suitable for the role at this moment in time,' the woman said, gesturing towards the door in dismissal.

'Mother, what are you -' Lavinia said in surprise, trying to navigate herself out of her chair as her mother began edging past her. She turned to Ellie, her hands gesticulating in agitation. 'I apologise, Miss Curnow. I'm not sure what has come over my mother so suddenly.'

Ellie didn't know what to do, but suddenly felt the urge to escape from this stifling room, the dark burgundy curtains and bottle green vintage wallpaper suddenly pressing in on her. She was utterly perplexed, and her face showed it as she watched the two women have a strange, silent dispute right in front of her.

'Shall I just...go...?' Ellie muttered, rising from her chair, her eyes still trained on the strange scene unravelling.

'Sorry...yes...' Lavinia stumbled through her words, a look of frustration and exasperation which seemed to run deep. 'Good luck with it all, Miss Curnow. Perhaps we will see you in the future, with some qualifications under your belt.'

It was a blow to the stomach and Ellie barely muttered out a coherent response before flying out of the drawing room, her face burning and her heart pounding down into her stomach. Her legs didn't feel attached to her as they carried her down the long corridor, through the pretentiously large hallway and out into the blinding sunshine.

It had been a mistake coming here. She felt utterly stupid for even thinking this would be a good idea, that she'd allowed people to convince her something quite as absurd as this horrible family actually needing someone like her. Of course she was unqualified. Of course she was absolutely useless to any employer on paper. Just because she'd got by all these years doing her own business on the creek, did not in any way whatsoever make her suitable for something as big as this.

But how dare they.

Perhaps Nanny had been right about them.

Her eyes smarted and the ground beneath her swam and blurred as the tears arrived. Why, whenever Ellie was angry, did the tears always come? She crossed the vast driveway, the small gravel stones making her footfall unsteady, just as a shiny black Audi flew around the corner and skidded to a halt. Ellie cried out and slammed her hands onto the bonnet to stabilize herself, throwing glares and curses into the dark window where the large silhouette of the driver could just about be seen in the glaring light.

'Slow down, you idiot!'

And there it was. Her Nanny's rage surfacing over Ellie's usual coolness and manifesting at that very moment into something that was probably about to get her arrested any moment now. The driver's door flung open, and a large bulk of a man unfolded out of the car, his tall stature casting Ellie into shadow, his handsome features distorted in vexation.

'Did you just punch my car?' The man's voice was deep and velvety like chocolate, even in irritation. 'And did you just call me an idiot?'

'Yes to both,' Ellie declared, standing strong though her legs were about to give out from under her any moment now from all the adrenaline. 'You nearly ran me over! It's a driveway, not the bloody A30!'

In an odd sort of U-turn, the handsome man's frown loosened into amusement, his hands finding their way into his trouser pockets as he leaned casually against his vehicle. 'Well, I apologise. I hope you're not hurt.'

'Only my pride,' Ellie muttered, straightening her top and averting her eyes. 'I've just made a total tit of myself in there for a job I'm not even qualified for, so... I don't know why I'm telling you that. I chat shit when I'm pissed off. The women in there were too snooty to even consider my actual skills...anyway...'

Ellie turned to go but a sudden realisation nudged her from within the pit of her stomach and she slowly turned on her heel. 'You don't... live here...do you?'

'I own the estate,' the man said, the amusement beaming from his face and dancing in those dark chocolate eyes as he held a hand out. 'Lord Penhaligon. And the snooty women in there... I expect that is my mother and grandmother. And you are?'

'An idiot,' Ellie said, defeated as her hand disappeared into the man's large hands. They were warm and sturdy, and Ellie could have stayed there in their warmth all day if she wasn't currently dying with mortification. She muttered her feeble apology, took back her cold hand and disappeared down the road back to the creek where she belonged.

The sunny, blue skies of the morning soon dispersed into dark, ominous clouds as a cold evening drew in. The Old Creek Inn gleamed like a beacon across the darkening waters of the estuary, spilling out with merry patrons of all ages, a rumbling sound of laughter and cheer echoing out through the old windows and thatched roof. It was clearly the end of a working week - a typically busy Friday night with tradesmen, fishermen and familiar faces of the creek community lining the wooden benches along the front of the old building. Across the narrow road was the adjacent beer garden which faced the moorings down below, people attending to their precious boats even in the dimming light. Ellie's tiny rowing boat could be seen bobbing happily next to its larger counterparts. Jack and Ellie ascended the concrete steps, passing a long row of old men sat just outside the main door, smoke billowing from their pipes and cigarettes.

'Ellie, m'love? You comin' to finish the patio next week?' Larry said through spluttering coughs.

'You're booked in for first thing Tuesday, Larry,' Ellie said, slowing in front of the old patrons, her hands on her hips. 'Got the sand being delivered Monday afternoon. Spoke to Carrie earlier about it.'

'Right you are, Bird.'

'And Jack, m'boy!' The next man spoke up, next to Larry. 'Hope you're coming to fit the new shower this week. The missus is going spare over it.'

'Saved Wednesday onwards for you, Paul!' Jack said, pausing behind Ellie. 'She chosen the tiles yet? Can't finish it off without the tiles.'

'I'll give her a nudge. See you on Wednesday.'

Making a little more progress over the threshold of the pub, Jack and Ellie were once again accosted by Mr Williams, who was elbowing the air between them.

'Heard you went for your interview today! Good girl! When do we start addressing you with your new title then?' Mr Williams must have read the expression on Ellie's face and feebly attempted to back down his enthusiasm. 'Never mind. Never mind. Plenty of jobs out there for you, me 'andsome. I'll leave you two to your evening then.' Mr Williams dipped his bald head, and playful smiles played on the old features of him and his drinking companions. A ripple of knowing chuckles cascaded down the line of Cornishmen sat along the front outside, Paul and Larry included.

'Oh, behave you lot,' Ellie scoffed, rolling her eyes to the drizzly dark sky and storming into the depths of the busy pub. She knew it was all in jest, but it didn't half get on her nerves when she couldn't be seen walking around with her best friend in public without the *wink-wink-nudge-nudge* from their nosy neighbours of the community. Finding a vacant table in the corner nearest to the roaring fire, Ellie shuffled into the seat and caught a glimpse of Jack's amused face. 'Why do you find it so bloody hilarious when they make those jokes? I find it infuriating!'

'I find it hilarious how infuriated you get!' Jack chortled, hovering by their table. 'It's clearly a horrifying concept to you.'

'What is?'

'Us. You and me. Boyfriend and girlfriend. Clearly a terrible, terrible notion.' Jack nudged her and winked. He scoffed loudly as Ellie's face turned more sour. 'Come on, Ellie. I know you've had a stinker of a day, but you know they mean well. Besides, you can't blame them. A beautiful specimen like myself...your slightly above average looks - oof!'

Jack's laughter rumbled amongst the low beams and through the steady chatter of neighbouring tables as Ellie's arm made contact with his stomach.

'With your quick humour and dashing good looks, how have I resisted over the years?' Ellie said wryly, resuming her defeated position.

'Beats me,' Jack said, the amusement slipping momentarily from his face. 'Anyway, drink?'

As Jack headed towards the bar to get them both a drink, Ellie sighed in shame at her behaviour. Both she and Jack had had a long week, and their Friday night tipple at the pub was a weekly tradition they had done for a long time. Usually, a couple of hours full of their usual goofiness, laughter, and banter - it was the best cure to see them into a much calmer weekend. It wasn't fair on Jack for Ellie to bring the mood down like this. So, what if she hadn't got the job? So, what if they had been rude to her and belittled her - what had she expected? But she still had those increasing bills to pay. The panic had settled in to stay this afternoon when she'd realised how unemployable she really was.

Ellie loved the steady trickle of jobs from her loyal customers along the creek. She loved the predictability - hopping into her little boat and doing the same jobs for each customer across the seasons. But it didn't pay enough. It was steady, yes - but it wasn't consistent, and it wasn't guaranteed every single month. She would need to pull herself out of this self-pitying mood and try again tomorrow. There had to be plenty of jobs out there in the gardening or outdoor sector. Just standard gardening jobs. She'd been too ambitious going for Head Gardener.

Before she had a chance to fall back into her funk, annoyed with herself for even putting herself into such a ridiculous position, Jack returned with two drinks - a pint for himself and a half pint of lemonade for her.

'Ah, thank you,' Ellie said, smacking her lips together in thirsty anticipation as she reached for her drink.

'I almost pushed the boat out and got you a full pint, but don't want you off your face on sugar,' Jack said, wryly. He held out his pint. 'Want a sip of a proper drink?'

Ellie pulled a face. 'No, thank you. Horrible, bitter stuff.'

'Just like my soul,' Jack cried, holding a hand to his heart for dramatic effect. A tightness in Ellie's chest loosened as she felt things ease between them, the banter returning once again. She was going to ask Jack about his renovation and the progress with his kitchen when her attention was drawn to the entrance of the

Inn, a familiar man crossing the threshold and scanning the inn.

'Shit!' Ellie gasped, throwing herself under the table, much to Jack's confusion and amusement.

'What are you doing?' Jack asked, chuckling away as he poked his head under the table to find Ellie squishing herself in between the table legs. Ellie hushed and waved him off frantically, which only made Jack laugh more.

'Shut up!' Ellie whispered, fiercely. 'That's him! From earlier!'

'The Lord?' Jack asked, seeking him out gleefully. 'Oh shit, he's coming over. Act cool, Ellie - wait, you're under a table. You've failed already. Oh...alright, mate?'

Ellie closed her eyes, wanting the floor below to swallow her whole, as two polished tan shoes came into view in front of their table.

'I'm sorry to disturb you,' the familiar deep voice from earlier rumbled above her. Despite herself, Ellie thought about the handsome face which went with this voice, momentarily entranced. 'My name is George Penhaligon. I was looking for a Miss Ellie Curnow.'

Ellie couldn't see Jack's face, but she only needed to hear the utter delight and amusement in his giddy voice to know that he was loving every moment. 'I'll just get her for you!' Jack trilled, rapping his knuckles on the sticky tabletop.

Slowly, Ellie emerged. It was, of course, completely unhelpful just how ridiculously good-looking George was. His chocolate brown eyes, against his golden tanned face, twinkled the same way they did on the driveway of Penhaligon Estate just a few hours ago. He was in a dark navy cotton shirt, held taut against muscles which could only be achieved by regular visits to the gym. Ellie checked herself before she could be caught gawking at his arms. She didn't need anything else added to the list of embarrassing things she had achieved this afternoon.

'Hey! Sorry, I... umm...dropped something on the floor. I've found it now. Can I help?' Ellie babbled, alternating between crossing her arms and awkwardly stuffing her hands inside the front pouch of her hoodie.

'I was wondering whether you would be able to come up to the house tomorrow morning, for a meeting?' George asked, formally.

'You must be joking,' Ellie said, forgetting herself for a moment, her hands flying up to her mouth. Jack was clearly ready for another blow to the stomach as his body trembled with the urge to burst into laughter. 'Sorry, that was really rude. I just mean, I'm surprised you want me back for a meeting at all.'

A reassuring smile formed on George's face and Ellie near as well fell into those dark eyes of his. She would put it down to the exhaustion of the day catching up with her. 'Not that I was there in person for your interview, but I would hazard a guess that you weren't given a fair try earlier. My mother and grandmother can be...forces of nature. I'd like a chance to interview you myself. They don't know this yet, but they will soon.'

Ellie's stomach clenched in discomfort. 'I don't know. Your grandmother made it very clear I wasn't suitable for the job.'

'Well,' George started, putting his hands into his pockets, his legs apart in a strong stance. 'I'm the Lord, so really it's down to me who is hired and who is not.'

Some of the neighbouring tables became notably still, and Ellie caught the eye of Mr Williams, who was peering indiscreetly over his pint.

'Are you still interested in discussing the position?'

Ellie wanted to say *no she wasn't.* She wasn't interested in setting foot in that damned house ever again. And she certainly never wanted to be in the same room as those awful women ever again. But there was something encouraging about George and for a reason she couldn't explain, Ellie didn't want to let him down.

'Alright,' Ellie finally said. 'Thank you. What time?'

'How does half past nine sound? We'll discuss the position over breakfast.'

Ellie felt Jack fidget beside her but tried to ignore it. 'Sounds great.'

George's warm smile broadened, and with that he said his goodbyes, gave Jack a polite nod and headed back out of the door. For a moment, Jack and Ellie sat in silence, the loud ambiance of the pub continuing around them as if the Lord of the estate didn't just casually stroll in and back out again. It was Jack who finally spoke first.

'So, are you going to take it?'

'He hasn't offered me the job. Just a second chance at applying.'

'He's going to offer you the job,' Jack confirmed, confidently. Ellie noticed that his features were suddenly taut, his jaw tensed as he stared at the door where George had only just exited from. 'He clearly has intentions of hiring you. Why else would he make the effort to come and find you... in person? How did he know you'd be in here anyway. Makings of a stalker there.'

Ellie was distracted and pondering over tomorrow's dreaded breakfast meeting but was tuned in just enough to note a hint of annoyance in Jack's voice. She turned to him and studied his face for a moment. 'My address was on my CV. Maybe he stopped by at the cottage first. Oh god, I hope not - I'm going to get an earful from Nanny if he did.'

'Why's that?'

'She wasn't keen on me taking a job at the house in the first place. No reason given - just doesn't like the family apparently. I haven't told her what happened this afternoon yet. Not sure I will. But she won't have appreciated George Penhaligon turning up at our doorstep.'

Jack cleared his throat and took a large swig of his beer. 'Your Nanny was always an excellent judge of character.'

# Chapter Six

'You did what?' Lavinia cried, gripping the back of the dining chair as she stood over her nonchalant son. George, knowing how easily galled his mother could get when challenged, took a small sip of his coffee, readying himself for the fight.

'I have invited Miss Curnow back,' George repeated, calmly.

'Does your grandmother know about this?' Lavinia asked, her voice rising an octave.

'Not yet. I'll speak to her.'

'Why on earth did you do that? The girl was completely unqualified.' Lavinia threw her arms up in the air and paced the drawing room floor.

'Mother, how many responses did you get for the job advertisement?'

Lavinia paused to look at her son. 'Don't be contrary, George. You know full well she was our only applicant. It appears nobody wants to work these days!'

'Well, then. We can't exactly say we are overwhelmed with choices here. And unqualified she may be, but it sounds like she has a lot of experience. She's also local to the creek, so this would look good on us too.'

'I wasn't aware we'd have to be seen to be charitable to the creek community whilst hiring somebody to manage our entire two-hundred-acre estate,' Lavinia responded tartly. 'It must be somebody competent and... and...'

'Qualified?' George offered, one eyebrow raised. 'Did Ernie have qualifications?'

'I really can't talk to you when you're like this. It's exactly what your father used to do to get his point across. It really is quite frustrating,' Lavinia ranted. She finally gave in with an audible huff and took a seat opposite her son, buttering a piece of toast in a ferocious manner. 'Just do what you like. You're the Lord now, I suppose. Interview the silly girl but do let me know when you plan to tell your grandmother so I can run for the hills.'

'I shall warn the entire county,' George joked, smiling at his mother to make quick amends. 'I don't mean to undermine you, Mother. You know I don't. But time is of the essence and the garden is in need of someone's leadership sooner rather than later. I met her briefly and she seems like a hard worker.'

'Is she pretty?' Lavinia asked, almost accusingly.

Now it was George's turn to frown, his cool composure slipping. 'Is that how shallow you think I am, Mother? Thank you for that.' When his mother didn't answer, he pressed on. 'I wasn't paying attention to her appearance. I was more thinking how passionate and knowledgeable about her work she was.'

That part was true, but George had perhaps not been entirely truthful when he said he didn't notice Ellie Curnow's appearance. Because she had been pretty - that he would not be able to deny. But he was also very aware of the reputation that proceeded him, particularly with his family. People called him a womaniser, a ladies' man, a Casanova. Yes, he'd had his fair share of dates and fleeting relationships. And yes, he liked the way women looked at him and the effect he had on them. That was why he took care of himself and his own appearance. But recently, he'd become bored of the dating scene and the same line of women with the same appearances, the same styles. All the same. There had been something new and disarming about Ellie. Unapologetically real and unfiltered. She had been refreshing, and for the first time in a while George's interest had been peaked. Even now, he tried not to smile in front of his mother at the thought of her fiery temper, reflected by her equally fiery auburn hair thrown into a long ponytail, her small oval face dappled in freckles. He'd almost found himself disappointed when he'd finally tracked her down at the pub, only to see her close and personal with the man she'd been having a drink with. Potentially her boyfriend, partner, or even husband. He really didn't know anything about her.

George shook himself out of his thought trail, thinking how pointless and ridiculous this little infatuation was. He needed a Head Gardener, and she was potentially the person for the job. He could just leave it at that.

She arrived, a little cautiously George noted, at 9:25am. She was early - that counted as a good sign in George's books. That should mean that she would be prompt and reliable. He didn't blame her for her guarded entrance into their large hallway, taking in her surroundings as if she were walking into a trap.

'My mother and grandmother won't be joining us, you'll be pleased to know,' George joked, a little unsure why he said that. But he hoped it at least put her at ease. He gestured towards the breakfast room where two placements had been laid by Trixie with their finest dinnerware. 'I thought we'd have a spot of breakfast and talk about you and the role. Then we'll head outside after, and I can show you the gardens if you like.'

'Great,' Ellie said, taking the seat which George held out for her. 'I noticed your magnolias are coming out in full now. You can see them from the walk between here and the river.'

'Yes, the garden does seem to become a splash of colour this time of year,' George recalled, not much enjoying the stiffness of their conversation so far.

'Like most Cornish gardens, it's a Spring Garden,' Ellie explained. 'And a well-developed one at that. I'd be interested in seeing your champion trees on the walk in a moment. They must be such an asset to the garden.'

George paused, only for a second, as he flicked his napkin out to the side and placed it on his lap. Champion trees? Spring garden? On one hand, a wave of relief washed over him to hear her speaking with such knowledge. On the other hand, it dawned on him that he knew very little about the technical sides of gardening himself. His competitive nature meant that he didn't want to appear a novice.

'Yes, of course,' George smiled. 'I hope you're hungry. Trixie - that's our cook - has prepared her wonderful Eggs Benedict for us this morning.'

'Starving,' Ellie replied, holding her stomach. 'I've been up since 6am. I usually have breakfast early.'

'Well, at least I know you'll be OK with early starts,' George said, mentally checking off another worthy attribute.

'Not sure I know any gardeners or tradesmen who don't start early. Doesn't bother me in the slightest. In fact, I quite like the early mornings on the river.' George noticed a small smile play on Ellie's features, a fondness as her mind drifted to the place where she called home.

'Have you lived down on the river for long?' George asked, now pouring them each a coffee from the cafetiere.

'All my life,' Ellie said. She took the coffee George offered with thanks and took a large sip. 'I live in the little thatched cottage with the blue door, right at the end of the track. Stone's Throw, it's called. It's usually the first one to know when the tide is too high.'

'And do you live alone? With a partner?' George pried, knowing this was an unnecessary question but finding himself wanting the answer all the same.

'With my Nanny,' Ellie said, though she looked a little sheepish at this. 'I know. A bit unusual. A thirty-something year old living with her eighty-something year old Nanny. But that's a long story. We're very close.'

'That's nice,' George said, smiling fondly. He wished he could say that he would feel the same if he lived with his grandmother in such a small cottage, but he knew that even living with her in small doses in their large stately home was pushing it. 'So, you work mostly in the community?'

'Yes. Most of my customers are the folk along the river. Garden maintenance. Tree felling, crowning - whatever is needed.'

'Oh, so you're a tree surgeon?' George said, peaking at his copy of Ellie's CV.

'Well, I have my chainsaw license - if that's what you mean,' Ellie said, shyly. 'Not sure I would call myself a tree surgeon necessarily.'

'You're far too humble, you know,' George said, kindly. He was glad to see Ellie return his smile warmly and relax a little in her chair. 'A chainsaw license will be very handy. As you know, we have the small bit of parkland as you come in from the main entrance. Then of course there's the trees in the gardens. The woodlands. There's a lot of difficult maintenance dotted around, and going by the recent invoices Ernie has had to bring external people in for this.'

Ellie nodded along, listening intently. Trixie arrived with their breakfast, and they ate in silence for a bit. The sun was beginning to beam in through the large windows across the table, almost willing them to finish quickly and get outside for the tour. But George was quite enjoying getting to know her.

'Have you managed people before?' George asked, wiping his plate clean of the Hollandaise sauce with his last bit of toasted muffin.

'No. No, I haven't,' Ellie mumbled. 'But I'd be willing to go on any training courses to learn. I think if I know what I am doing and I have a vision, the leading of the team will go from there.'

George considered that answer. 'Not always quite as simple as that, but yes - I know what you mean. Having a vision is a really good start. I'm sure there would be some leadership training I could look to enrol you on. It's not a big team, but there would obviously be a lot of delegating involved. My mother informs me that our youngest recruit Joseph may need some heavy guidance too. I believe he's doing an apprenticeship with us through the Duchy.'

Ellie nodded some more, and George wondered whether she was beginning to feel a little overwhelmed already. They finished their breakfast; George replenished their coffee mugs and suggested they took them out into the garden for the all-important garden tour. George had almost reprimanded his mother for doing the interview with Ellie yesterday without at least a tour of the garden. George had been involved in recruiting a lot in Italy, and he had learned recently that applicants showed their potential much more when you put them into their natural environment. Ellie was clearly much more comfortable surrounded by the camellias and the magnolias, than she was boxed inside the high walls of Penhaligon House.

'I'll confess, I have always wanted to walk through these gardens,' Ellie beamed, walking beside George, and taking in her surroundings like a child in a sweet shop. 'It's a shame the gardens aren't open to the public anymore. The community down on the creek reminisce all the time about it.'

'Do they?' George asked, curiously. It had been something that had crossed his mind a couple of times, wracking his brain for ways to make the estate money. But he hadn't realised the community had such an attachment to it.

'Of course. Our hamlet of cottages is attached to your estate, after all,' Ellie said. George thought he noted a bit of a tone to her voice for a moment, but she was soon gasping in delight as they entered the kitchen garden. High, red-bricked walls surrounded a perfectly symmetrical formation of vegetable beds. Despite the bareness and lack of productive crop, it was still quite a sight to behold. A long tunnel ran through the middle, made entirely of trained apple trees snaked around wire framing, creating a perfect canopy walkway. 'Oh, my goodness. This is incredible. These apple trees must have taken years of training.'

'Yes, I believe this is Ernie's pride and joy. I remember him starting these when I was a young teenager.' George wondered what Ernie would think of all this and felt a small pang of guilt. He knew full well that Ernie was a proud, slightly territorial man when it came to his garden. But at the end of the day, a broken hip at his ripe old age wasn't something that would fix itself any time soon, and the gardens needed endless care and attention - something he was clearly struggling with. 'I'm sure that at some point, when Ernie is feeling well enough, he would probably like for the three of us to meet and discuss the gardens. He has his methods.'

There was that nod again. Like Ellie was simply agreeing but had other thoughts running through her mind. 'And I have my methods.' That took George by surprise, and he near as much stopped in his tracks. 'But that seems fair enough. He has cared for these gardens for a long time. So, does that mean the position is only temporary?'

Had his mother made this temporary or permanent? He realised he didn't know and floundered for a moment. Until he remembered with a pang that it was his decision. 'It will be permanent. Ernie, as much as he won't like to admit it, is extremely elderly. I'd be concerned about him returning to full duty, but I'd like to think he would return as a volunteer perhaps.'

Ellie snorted, her eyes wide. 'From what I've heard about him, I'm not sure he's going to like being demoted from Head Gardener to volunteer in one move. Sorry, I don't mean to be rude or condescending. But does he know you're replacing him? Is this even legal?'

George's brow furrowed and he scowled. He didn't like

being contradicted at the best of times, especially with a big oversight such as this. Had his mother even had a conversation with Ernie? He was suddenly annoyed with both Lavinia, and himself, for not checking before taking over.

'We've...we've offered him a retirement package,' George fabricated, feeling his neck going red. 'He's very much aware of the situation and supports our decision.' He made a mental note to research retirement packages tonight which he would now have to present to poor old Ernie at his home next week. His to-do list was already growing, and he'd only been home for a couple of days.

'That's okay then,' Ellie said, looking relieved. 'I'd hate to be stepping on old toes.'

'Not at all. Let me show you our prestigious Italian gardens. Being somebody who has lived in Italy for over ten years now, it's quite easily my favourite part of the estate.'

Their feet crunched against the pea gravel pathway which hugged the side of Penhaligon House. Ellie stopped occasionally to admire a plant or check out the box hedging lining the beds. Her attention eventually turned to the several entwining climbers now engulfing the house.

'As you can see, the garden has started to take over a bit in Ernie's absence,' George said, conversationally, studying Ellie's reaction. She seemed completely unperturbed.

'Shouldn't be a problem, though you have a wisteria and a climbing rose getting very close to one another here. It's a shame because they'll be depriving each other of sunlight and space to bloom properly.'

George crossed his arms and looked up to where Ellie was referring. 'What would you do then?'

'It would take a bit of doing, but I would properly heavily prune them back for this year and look to train them in opposite directions. I expect they started being trained but lost control eventually - now both are headed in the same direction. That clematis in the middle as had it, I would say. Do you mind?'

Ellie gestured to the wall, indicating that she wanted to check in closer. George nodded. 'Go ahead.' He watched in slight admiration as she took her cardigan off, rolled her sleeves up and carefully hoisted herself onto the small retaining wall holding the flower bed. It was clear that the smart clothes she wore today were not her first choice of attire and she felt much more comfortable being less constrained. George watched with fascination as she lifted the new leaves up with one arm and stuck her head in amongst the branches and twines, near enough disappearing into the dense growth to figure out which belonged to which climber. She started pulling at dead pieces, hopping back down to the ground to retrieve a metre-long piece of thin vine. 'Yeah, that clematis has been completely suffocated. I would probably trim it right down, clear this strip of wall, then begin pruning here, here, and here. The wisteria can go that way and the rose that way.' Her arms gesticulated in the directions as she spoke. 'Maybe - though I wouldn't hold your breath - maybe, the clematis will come back with more space to thrive. They're usually quite hardy things once matured, so it's a huge shame.

George smiled, realising his instincts had been right. 'You know your stuff.'

'Don't need a piece of paper to tell you that,' Ellie said, smiling coyly. 'I know I don't have the qualifications your grandmother and mother were hoping for, but I have been working in gardens all my working life. Been learning all about plants and their names, and best ways to care for them since I was little. Despite not being given a chance to study, I read horticultural magazines and books all the time. I've been to talks and mini courses in my spare time. I'm completely up to date with the latest methods, sustainable gardening, organic gardening...'

'Finally,' George muttered, smiling, and folding his arms

across his broad chest.

'What?' Ellie asked, looking bewildered.

'For the first time since you arrived, you've started to actually sell yourself as a worthy applicant. I was beginning to think you didn't want the job at all.'

Ellie had the right mind to look a little bashful. 'I was just a bit wary today. Sorry, I didn't mean to come across as apathetic.'

'No need to apologise,' George said, waving her off. 'You weren't being apathetic. Coy, maybe. I'm sure your interaction with the eldest women of the house would have had most people wary and perhaps even running for the hills.'

'Perhaps not the hills,' Ellie said, teasingly. 'Maybe to the nearest pub.'

George laughed, heartily, and something eased between them.

'Well, I would hire you in a heartbeat,' George said, clapping his hands together. 'But I suppose I had better run it by the powers that be - that's my grandmother and mother, in case you hadn't cottoned on to that. They're already pretty upset with me for bulldozing their recruitment strategies.'

For the second time that morning, Ellie snorted, turning away to hide her expression. George chose to ignore it.

'Shall we head back inside and discuss salary, etcetera? Then you can at least go away with some information to digest and consider in the meantime.'

Ellie agreed, looking pleased. 'Sounds great. And thank you. For giving me a second chance at this.'

Something warm and unfamiliar swelled in George's stomach as he looked down at her with smiling eyes. 'You're welcome.'

# Chapter Seven

The next week flew by. George offered Ellie the job the very next day and she agreed to start the following Monday after she had had a chance to wrap up jobs with her regulars. She was relieved when George confirmed he was perfectly fine with her still picking up the odd job here and there with her customers, just so long as she wasn't killing herself trying to squeeze it all in. She'd already had her most faithful customers passing their congratulations on to her, but showing clear disappointment and despair at the thought of not having their lawn regularly cut or their hedges shaped when they were needed, or their gutters cleared out twice a year. These were all jobs she could tackle in the weekends, if really needed.

When the following Monday finally arrived, Ellie's stomach was practically doing somersaults, making her queasy and jittery all at once. Nanny had been uncharacteristically quiet about her opinions on the job, practically force-feeding her a bacon sandwich before she left and reminding her that she needed to keep her strength up for the mental overload of a typical first day. Several times, on her walk to the estate, she nearly turned around to head back to the safety of her little cottage and the predictability of her day-to-day. She was a creature of habit, and this was about to rock her boat entirely. Somewhere deep down however, there was a glimmer of excitement. She just needed to grab hold of that feeling and let it surface.

At least George would be able to put her at ease this morning. He'd done so already on their two other encounters. She wondered, with blushing cheeks, whether he had a small part to play in that excitement she could feel swelling in her stomach.

'Good morning, Miss Curnow,' Lavinia Penhaligon said, shortly. Ellie's heart and stomach raced towards the floor as the woman gave her an appraising look, no doubt taking in Ellie's attire - practical, but not in the least bit feminine nor fashionable. Her old rucksack slung over her shoulder was probably the finishing piece. 'George has been pulled away to deal with something at the council. I'll take you down to meet your team and get you settled.'

'Oh. Oh, right,' Ellie stuttered, prickles of regret seeping in. This job was suddenly starting to feel like a really bad idea.

Lavinia was tall for a lady, particularly one in her sixties. Ellie had always been on the shy side of 5ft 4 and slight in stature, often giving people false pretences to her ability as a gardener. Her size had never once bothered her or hindered her in any way, but suddenly walking alongside Lavinia's 5ft 11 rectangular frame made her feel inferior - almost child-like. Ellie was seconds away from breaking into a small jog to keep up with the lady's strides, before they finally arrived at an old stone-faced outbuilding, the front lined with empty terracotta pots, wheelbarrows, and old pallets. It was a dreary, little grey building with a galvanised roof, dirty old windows which surely let little to no light inside, and a tatty old door with its paint blistered and peeling. There was a bit of chatter coming from inside, which came to an abrupt halt when Lavinia rapped on the door. A boy with a striking head of red hair popped his head out of the door and looked utterly bewildered when he clapped eyes on Lavinia.

'Hello, Mrs Penhaligon,' the boy said, his voice cracking slightly. His eyes darted to Ellie before returning to Lavinia nervously.

'Joseph, this is Ellie. The new gardener.'

Ellie frowned, wondering whether Lavinia purposely left out the other part of that job title to show her dislike towards George's decision. All the same, Ellie wanted to make a good impression. George had already warned Ellie that this Joseph was the nervous one who would probably benefit from some kindness and guidance. Ellie gave a little smile and a wave. 'Hi, Joseph. How are you?'

Joseph's features relaxed slightly, and he stepped out fully from the stone threshold to greet her. 'Good, thank you. We're just popping the kettle on for some coffee. Do you want some?'

Ellie let her bag slip from her shoulder and started digging around for her flask. 'Coffee would be fantastic, thank you. Can I have it in this please?'

Joseph smiled in response and took her flask inside the little building. Lavinia shrugged and huffed a little. 'Well, I think I'll leave you to just get settled for a moment then.' She gave the outbuilding a slightly scornful glance and Ellie realised that Lavinia had absolutely no intentions of stepping inside. A bit too rough around the edges for Her Ladyship, Ellie suspected. 'If you wouldn't mind leading everyone to the Kitchen Gardens in half an hour, I'll do the morning briefings with you this week - if you won't mind. You should get an idea on how we do things around here quite soon enough.'

'No problem,' Ellie replied, stiffly. 'Shall I bring a notepad and pen?'

'Yes, that might be best. I'll leave you be, then.'

Lavinia headed back towards the warmth and luxury of her stately home, leaving Ellie with the draughty, leaky little stone hut behind her. That said, it had plenty of character and seemed to hold a warmer welcome inside than she would probably receive in the main house. She took a deep, easing breath through her nose, drinking in the calmness of the dewy, early morning, and tried to remind herself why she was here.

'Here we go,' Ellie whispered to herself, before ducking her head and stepping down into the little stone shed.

'Would you like sugar with your coffee, Ellie? Oh! Sorry, Miss... umm....' Joseph stuttered, his spoon hovering over three flasks, which were currently sat on top of a portable workbench, the holes being re-purposed as teaspoon holders.

'Please call me Ellie,' she insisted. 'I hate formalities. No sugar for me, thank you. Interesting coffee station you've got there.'

'Yeah,' Joseph chuckled, nervously. 'We haven't got much counter space in here, as you can see.

He wasn't exaggerating, Ellie thought. This was clearly more of a storage shed than anything else, with a variety of different seats - from a camping chair, to a turned over vegetable pallet, to a stack of compost. On the compost, his back against the cobweb-covered wall, a man in his mid to late fifties sat eating a packet of cheese and onion crisps, his swollen belly sticking out through his fleece jacket and a scraggly, gingery-grey beard trailing down his barrelled chest. The scowl on his face matched his body language perfectly; he was a bear not to be poked. Ellie averted her eyes for a moment and when they returned, his scowl remained focused on her. She smiled nervously.

'This is Dave,' Joseph said, simply.

Ellie nodded her head. 'Alright?'

Dave chewed his crisps slowly before nodding back. 'Alright?'

This was going to be long day, Ellie thought.


Her notepad and pen clutched in one hand and a full flask of coffee in the other, Ellie took deep breaths as they crunched their way along the pathway, through camellias and under the overbearing rhododendrons towards the Kitchen Garden. At the same time, Lavinia strode in with a basket draped over her arm.

'Joseph, dear? Could you please fill this basket with some

kale and any carrots that may be ready for picking?' Lavinia held out the basket expectantly and Joseph ran forward to oblige. 'Miss Curnow, my son informs me that you have a plethora of ideas in modern gardening.'

Ellie squirmed, not liking where this over-exaggeration of her ability was going. 'Well, I - I didn't...'

'You may notice that our Kitchen Garden has been somewhat neglected recently,' Lavinia pressed on. Joseph returned with the basket, a measly bit of floppy kale and two tiny carrots.

'Sorry, that's all we have,' Joseph muttered. Lavinia looked almost triumphant at the way this proved her point; Ellie suppressed the desire to roll her eyes. The woman was like a cartoon villain.

'With your new modern ways, it would be wonderful to see the Kitchen Garden brought back to its former glory. We used to be able to source all our fruit and vegetables from this very garden, but we now have to have it all delivered, which seems rather counter-productive. Shall we expect to see great things happening here over the coming weeks and months?'

Ellie considered being truthful and admitting that she'd actually never grown a vegetable in her life. She was more about the trees and the shrubs, and flower gardening. But there was something about the lady's expression which set a challenge between them, a quiet competitiveness which Ellie was suddenly unwilling to back down from. 'Absolutely. Leave it with us. I'm sure between us and the rest of the team, we can have these beds bursting with potential harvest.'

Rather than looking somewhat impressed, which was the reaction Ellie naively hoped for, Lavinia blinked at her with mild amusement. 'The rest of the team? Miss Curnow, this is the entirety of your team.'

'Oh.'

'I'll leave you to it.'

When Lavinia had returned to the house, Ellie remained rooted amongst the weed-infested vegetable beds, Joseph and Dave waiting expectantly. Three people. Three people to not only work some form of a miracle in this over-sized vegetable patch, but to also maintain the other two-hundred acres of the estate. It was impossible.

'I don't think Ernie liked vegetable gardening that much,' Joseph said, watching Ellie's expression.

'Dunne-av-time-izwha-tiz!' Dave grunted, causing Ellie to jump out of her boots. It was the first time he'd spoken a full sentence since she'd arrived.

'What was that?'

'Dave said we don't have time. That's the problem.'

Ellie nodded her agreement. 'I can't believe you've been running as a team of three. For how long?'

'Long-e-nuff,' Dave said, seemingly disinterested as he tapped a heavy boot against the edge of the first bordered bed. 'Nearly a year now.'

'Right... that's a conversation I need to have with the Penhaligons at some point,' Ellie said, feeling a surge to jump into action. She wasn't going to be defeated by a vegetable patch and a passive aggressive old woman in a trench coat. 'Do we have a stash of newspapers or cardboard or something...?'

'I think there's a stash of cardboard somewhere. Trixie might have newspapers for lighting the fires in the house,' Joseph said.

'Great, can you grab a wheelbarrow and source as much as you can?'

Joseph, excited by his task, ran off to find a wheelbarrow.

'I'm thinking we should try a no-dig approach,' Ellie explained to Dave. 'There's definitely a big weed and pest problem here, so if we start with a no-dig, lasagna technique this may give us a healthier base to work with.'

Ellie assessed Dave's expression and waited for the scowling to return but was pleasantly surprised when Dave nodded in agreement. A simple nod was all she needed.

'OK. Where are the tools?'

They worked solidly for the next four hours, before a symphony of rumbling stomachs reminded them that it was lunchtime, a mizzle of rain setting in to cool them down. They started picking all the scattered garden tools up to store in the wheelbarrow, tidying the area to avoid any potential hazards. Once it was all clear and safe to leave unattended, Ellie and her tiny little crew of two were about to head back to their little stone hut when a tall man cladded in waterproofs came stomping down the garden path, his dark curls protruding through the hood. It was George and he was beaming, despite his shoulders hunched from the rain.

'This is looking promising,' George shouted from across the vegetable patch. 'I see you've got everyone working hard already, Ellie.'

A low growl erupted from Dave, and Ellie was pretty certain it wasn't his stomach. 'I would say it's the other way round,' Ellie said, diplomatically. 'They've worked solidly all morning. We're about to stop for lunch actually.'

'I won't get in the way of that. Could I just have a quick word with you, Ellie.'

Ellie glanced apologetically at Dave and Joseph. Dave, who had warmed up to Ellie significantly over the last few hours, took Ellie's flask from her hand.

'We'll pop the kettle on,' he said gruffly, giving George a once over before following Joseph through the archway leading back out of the walled garden.

'Christ, wouldn't want to meet him down a dark alley,' George said, quietly.

'He's alright, actually,' Ellie said, though smiling at the similar first impressions she had had only hours ago. 'He's warmed up a bit as the morning has progressed. But best not upset him.'

The mizzle eased and Ellie released her ponytail from her cap, giving her head a shake to release all the water droplets. She noticed George watching her and felt a bit of unease set in, feeding her ponytail back through and returning the cap on her head. She knew she looked ridiculous to him right now, in her baggy work trousers and fleece, her steel-capped boots adding to the masculinity of her full attire. But at the end of the day, she was a gardener. She was certain that someone like George Penhaligon was used to women in dainty outfits, perfect hair and nails and full make-up. She looked down at her bitten down nails, now black from the soil - the grooves and calluses on her hands also prominent and lined dark from the tonne of earth they had been moving about all morning. Her coppery hair, though usually straight and tied in a long ponytail, frizzed in strange little baby hair curls around her face from the dampness in the air. It was safe to say that Ellie's day-to-day appearance would never catch the eye of someone like George.

'Mother's doing, I suppose,' George said, wryly - looking around at the much tidier - albeit bare - Kitchen Garden. 'Trust her to get you straight on this. She's been banging on about not being able to grow her own vegetables for ages.'

'Can she not get hands on with this part?' Ellie asked. It was a genuine question which she tried to ask without sounding pedantic. She failed miserably and George's face split into an amused grin, his eyes gleaming. 'I mean...if it's important to her. Does she enjoy gardening?'

'She enjoys the idea of gardening. And she enjoys the garden. But if it means Mother has to get down and dirty - or break a sweat at all - you can forget it. She'd much rather get you lot to do it.'

'Oh, right,' Ellie mumbled, looking around at the results of their labours and feeling a little silly. 'Was this not a priority then?'

'It wasn't pressing, but it's something that needed doing

eventually. It's important to Mother, so this will keep her happy.' George must have noticed the disappointment on Ellie's face because he added, 'you're doing a great job already. Just don't let Mother bully you into doing her own biddings.'

'Might help if I know who I'm meant to actually be taking orders from,' Ellie rebuked, releasing a sigh, and clapping her gardening gloves together to beat off the dirt.

'Technically, you're the boss when it comes to the garden,' George pointed out. 'You'll start to see what takes priority as you settle in.'

Ellie smiled and nodded, appreciating the vote of confidence. 'How did this morning go? Lavinia said you had something to deal with at the council.'

'Oh - yeah, all sorted,' George said, waving it off. 'Got a cottage down on the river which needs to be sorted out. Its previous resident has just passed away. Oh -' He closed his eyes, the realisation clearly washing over him.

'Mrs Pascoe's cottage, you mean?' Ellie said, a pang of nerves running through her as she studied George's strange expression.

'You know her?' George said, attempting to be nonchalant.

'Everybody knows everybody down on the creek,' Ellie said, rolling her eyes. 'What's happening with her cottage?'

'Well,' George began, looking wary. 'First it will need gutting. Typical old fisherman's cottage. Damp everywhere. Old carpets and decor. So, I need to find someone to-'

'I know somebody!' Ellie cut in, seizing the opportunity. 'Jack! My friend Jack. He's a brilliant carpenter. And I could do the garden. I used to cut Mrs Pascoe's little lawn out back once a fortnight during the summer anyway.'

George considered this for a moment, his deep brown eyes looking down at her and making her stomach flip oddly. He frowned. 'This is the bloke you were with at the pub last week?'

'Yeah, he's my best friend. Look, Mrs Pascoe was a very

beloved character in the hamlet and neighbours are rightfully upset about her passing. Her funeral is on Friday. I just think people might find it easier if it's Jack and I going in there and renovating it, rather than a van-full of strangers gutting the place.'

George nodded, still considering but clearly seeing Ellie's point. 'You won't find it too much alongside your role here?'

'Not at all. But let me speak to Jack and confirm his availability. I bet we can have the place ready in time for the new tenant.'

George's brow furrowed and his expression was almost unreadable, but he nodded again in acceptance. 'New tenant... right... - well, if you're sure. Speak to your friend - Jack - and we'll go from there.'

'Great,' Ellie said. 'Thank you. Can I ask one more favour while we're here?'

George chuckled. 'You don't ask for much, do you? What is it?'

'It's about that little stony hut we're meant to call a staff room.'

# Chapter Eight

George went to bed feeling uneasy that evening. When he'd gone to the council to request a change of use for the cottage, not once did he consider how the community along that river would react. It didn't matter to him. All he knew was that the estate needed to start making more money, and holiday lets made fast money - much more than long-term rentals. What he hadn't bargained for was Ellie's crude reminder of the community spirit to actually jolt a little bit of what felt like guilt. So much so that he couldn't bring himself to correct her when she'd assumed the cottage was being renovated for a new tenant. The truth was, he wanted the cottage modernised and ready for holiday bookings by the start of the summer season. Somehow, he got the impression Ellie would not be happy about this.

'Oh dear,' Wenna's voice was heard from the doorway. 'That's a troubled look.'

George's little sister bounced into his room, studying his expression with concern.

'What's up?'

'Nothing,' George lied, clearing his throat, and slapping a smile on his face. 'Where've you been the last few days? I've hardly seen you.'

'Friend's hen do,' Wenna said, rolling her eyes.

'Going by that tone, sounds like you had... fun?'

73

'It was alright,' Wenna said, vaguely. Lost as ever, George thought, now turning a percentage of his worry over to his little sister. Suddenly, she bounced on his bed and crossed her legs in a burst of excitement. 'Anyway, I hear we have a new Head Gardener. And she's a bit of a fitty!'

George, realising he wouldn't be going to sleep any time soon, got comfortable in his red tartan armchair in the corner. His room had remained exactly the same as it had been before he had moved to Italy all those years ago. It was simple and traditional, but comfortable and familiar. But he quietly admitted to himself that it wasn't a scrape on his sleek, modern apartment waiting for him back in Milan. He sat back, hooked his ankle over his knee and gave his sister an appraising look.

'Who have you been speaking to?'

'Joseph.'

'Oh,' George said, not realising he had rolled his eyes until Wenna tutted, loudly.

'Oh, don't be like that. He's a sweetie really. He just doesn't work well under pressure. We all love Ernie dearly, but he shouted at Joseph every day when he was here, and it makes poor Joseph a bag of nerves.'

George couldn't deny that. Ernie was a proud man but irked at the slightest inconvenience, and from what George could remember from his childhood, Ernie wasn't great with children or youngsters. He smiled at the sudden bursts of tiny memories filling his head like a bowl of marbles. Of times when he and his sisters had caused havoc in the gardens, all at Ernie's expense and often being shouted at and told to 'play with the traffic'.

'Wait,' George said, suddenly realising. 'Joseph called Ellie a fitty?' He didn't know Joseph all that well, having only met him a few days ago. But from the handful of small interactions he had had with the young apprentice, somehow that type of language didn't seem to match up.

'Well, I may have embellished that a little. He said she was pretty. And really, really nice. Said she was encouraging and didn't yell at him when he accidentally spilled loads of compost everywhere.'

'So, you talk to Joseph a lot then?' George grinned, his eyebrows dancing mischievously. He laughed as she threw a pillow at him.

'Not like that,' Wenna cried out, but laughing in good humour. 'He's just sweet and I don't exactly have many other people around here to chat to.'

George's smile faltered with that comment. He did often worry about Wenna being lonely. She never made the early escape to university, like George did. She wandered around the estate like a little lost fairy most of the time and didn't seem to have many hobbies in the outside world. His other sister, Tressa, was even worse. They were like two women from a period novel, rattling around their home with no real purpose, waiting to be swept away by handsome suitors in possession of a good fortune. The small Austen reference was not without purpose as George thought about his sisters wasting the hours away every day with futile existence. He understood Tressa's frustrations at not being involved in the interviews when he first arrived.

'How did the taster session go for that business course?' George asked in way of lighter conversation.

'Oh, it was awful, and the lecturer was a miserable old bag - so I left after the first break. Not for me.'

And with that, George buried his face in his hands - any hope for Wenna getting out, and doing something meaningful with her life, quashed once more.

George was awake and downstairs for breakfast early the next day. He was a morning person anyway, but his night's sleep had been broken from racing thoughts of to-dos, mixed with a howling wind rattling his old single-glazed sash windows in his bedroom. He'd promised to walk the estate with Ellie this morning so they could come up with a priority list of things for her and her team to tackle first.

George used the word 'team' sparingly. After putting in a request for a warmer, more practical staffroom for the gardeners, Ellie had rightfully pointed out the size of her team. All two of them. But the estate's finances were a huge concern already. How would they be able to afford to hire any more people?

Despite his growing list of concerns, he was looking forward to taking that walk around the estate with Ellie and having some time to get to know her a little more. He couldn't quite work out why, though.

He walked into the kitchen to find Trixie, their beloved house cook, at the island counter with her arms dusted up to her elbow in flour, her hands cutting butter into small cubes at expert speed.

'Good morning, Sunshine!' Trixie sang, spotting George and giving him a beaming smile. She'd greeted him this way for as long as he could remember and it warmed him through to hear her call him that, even now. 'You're bright and early.'

'Always early, Trix. Not so much on the bright though.' George, now at least a foot taller than the old cook, ducked down and pecked her on the cheek in greeting. 'What are you making? Scones?'

Trixie nodded. 'Your grandmother wants them for this afternoon. Cream teas with some old friends.'

'Good for her,' George said, popping a piece of bread in an old toaster which looked ready to explode any moment now. He eyed it warily. 'At least someone in this house has some form of a social life.'

Trixie remarked George with a look and chuckled loudly. 'The Penhaligon women, I've come to learn recently, are a little bit like bears. They hibernate in the winter, then come out to play a little more in the warmer months. See them in the summer before you concern yourself over them. They liven up a bit then.'

'That makes me feel a little better knowing that.' George's toast popped up, with everything around it unscathed. 'Don't suppose you're making extra of those scones, are you Trix?'

'I can do.'

'Yes please. Got some gardeners to sweeten up.'

'Ah, yes,' Trixie smiled, knowingly. 'I've heard all about the new Head Gardener.'

'Let me guess,' George said, sliding up onto the breakfast stool and biting into his buttered toast. 'Wenna? Talking about how pretty she is... or *fitty* was the word she used last night.' George rolled his eyes and shoved the first half of his toast into his mouth in one go, brushing his hands together to rid the crumbs.

'No. Your mother actually,' Trixie replied. 'Says you only hired her because she's pretty...or - fit. As you youngsters call it.'

George's voice was deadpan. 'I'm nearing forty. I'm hardly a youngster. And I don't use the word fit, just to be clear.' George paused and threw his frustration over to the other thing Trixie had said. 'Mother said...? God, she's unbelievable.'

Trixie held up flour-covered hands in surrender. 'Don't shoot the messenger. You know what she's like, my love.'

'Mother? Yes, we know exactly what she's like,' Tressa's voice was heard as she entered the kitchen, immediately appraising her brother in the way that always made him feel like he was in trouble. 'What has she done now?'

'Nothing!' Trixie tutted, knowing full well that Tressa would hold on to any opportunity to be absolutely furious with her. 'What is this by the way? Why are you all waking up so early? I haven't even prepared the breakfast room yet, and you lot are wandering around like hungry hyenas and making me feel tardy!'

'I can go back to my room and ring the servant's bell if you would rather,' Tressa drooled, a twitch of a smile playing in the corner of her mouth.

'Don't be contrary,' Trixie scolded. George chuckled from the safety of his spot behind the kitchen island, adverting Tressa's imminent glares.

Trixie was another permanent fixture to Penhaligon House and Estate, and George had never known the place without her. She was a second mother, a friend, and a confidante when things went wrong - this became particularly true in his teen years, where he found himself constantly in trouble. He watched as the poor old woman scrutinised Tressa's slow meander around the kitchen, opening and closing cupboards absently.

'What are you after, child?' Trixie huffed, clapping her hands together to rid of the excess flour. She bustled Tressa to one side, encouraging her to sit on the far side with George - out of the way of her working kitchen. 'Are you self-serving? Am I making you something?'

'I'll self-service,' Tressa mumbled, shuffling to the cereals, and pouring herself some *Cheerios* with about as much enthusiasm as a sloth. Usually, George would roll his eyes or make a dig at her to wind her up, but his brow furrowed in concern as he studied her complete a basic cereal breakfast and take a seat.

'You alright?' George asked.

Her head snapped in his direction, as if he'd electrocuted her. 'Yes, I'm fine!'

George's hands shot up, palms faced outward, as he pulled a bewildered face. 'Sorry I asked.' He drained the last of his coffee. 'On that note, I'm off.'

'What are you doing?' Tressa asked, almost accusingly.

George crossed the kitchen, placing his plate and mug in the sink. 'I'm taking Ellie - that's our new recruit - around the estate for a couple of hours, then I have a difficult conversation to have with Ernie.' His heart sank at the reminder of that.

'Elaborate,' Tressa demanded, twirling her hand in circles over her bowl.

George sighed, considering for a moment whether he *should* elaborate. 'Mother never actually clarified whether the Head Gardener job was permanent or whether it was just temporary.'

'Well, of course it needs to be permanent. Ernie is far too old to continue - without the broken hip!'

'Exactly. But we can't say that, because else we'll be done for discrimination. So, I've offered Ellie permanent, but I'm going to have to hope Ernie accepts my retirement package offer.'

'Oh, well,' Tressa began, straightening in her stool. 'Perhaps I should be grateful to our dear mother for not letting me get involved in these dastardly deeds.'

It was bitter cold as George and Ellie walked around the estate. They had just reached the far end of the parkland and were now stood on the brow of the hill looking back upon Penhaligon House. It had always been George's favourite view in the entire estate, with many times in his childhood spent racing up to this very spot to enjoy some time of peaceful isolation. There was once a time when the house was a constant bustle of people: WI groups, family and friends, historians - sometimes it bordered along hectic for little George, so this was where he escaped the madness and kept out of trouble. Now, at thirty-eight years old, he still got the same thrill at taking in the entirety of the estate from his little spot on the hill.

He zipped his inner fleece up to his chin and stuck his frozen hands inside his coat pockets. Beside him, dressed in similar upper layers but donning shorts of all things, Ellie appeared unaffected by the blistering morning chill.

'You can tell you're used to the cold,' George said, trying his best not to let his teeth chatter.

Ellie turned to look at him and burst out in laughter. It was a wonderful sound which took George completely by surprise. 'It's not that cold!'

'It is if you've lived in the Mediterranean for almost ten years!' George rebutted, pretending to be offended. In fact, he was glad to see Ellie loosen up a bit today. She'd ripped into him on more than one occasion this morning - something he was much more used to.

'I bet it's been a culture shock, coming back to the drizzly Cornish weather after sunshine and siestas,' Ellie observed, kicking a rotten tree trunk. 'Do you miss it?'

'Like you wouldn't believe,' George said, rolling on his heels in earnest. 'But duty called here. Mother has been pestering me to come home and run the estate in the flesh for months now.'

'So, you didn't choose this?' Ellie asked. Her full attention was on him, and he felt a bit analysed all of a sudden.

'I accepted that I would have to stand in as the new Lord years ago. With my grandfather gone. My mother being female,' George rolled his eyes at the archaic misogyny. 'Perish the thought.'

'But you didn't choose it,' Ellie confirmed.

George considered his answer but decided on the truth. He felt he could be truthful with her. 'No. No, I didn't choose it. It was more a case of I was chosen.' He laughed then. 'That sounded completely naff.'

'Yeah, I'm not going to lie to you. That sounded totally naff.'

They both laughed loudly, and this time George felt himself absorbing her laughter, storing the sound of it deep in his memory.

'You have such a fantastic laugh,' George admitted before he could even think it through. Ellie's laugh dissipated and was quickly replaced by a flushed face and an awkward smile. George immediately regretted saying it, feeling the air between them shift. He coughed nervously. 'Anyway, shall we move on to the Flower Garden?'

'Yes!' Ellie said, seemingly glad for a change in subject. George led the way, and they stomped down the hill back towards the main gardens surrounding the house.

'I know I've been a bit demanding already,' Ellie began a few moments later, as they crossed under the red-bricked archway into the Flower Garden. George's heart sank a little as he saw how overgrown and leggy the sections of beds looked, old perennials strangled by weeds and brambles. He was no gardener, but even he could see that yet another row of box hedging was suffering from a bad case of blight.

'You haven't been demanding,' George argued. 'You asked for a decent break room for your team. Which I'll be sorting in the next couple of days, by the way.'

'Thank you. The boys will be pleased. Actually, this is quite a big one, but I need to say something about it. Is there any budget at all for hiring more gardeners? A team of three isn't much when you have over two-hundred acres to look after.'

George's jaw tightened and his stomach clenched. He was afraid this would be her request. If he was being completely honest, there was currently no budget for anything. He knew his mother had done her best over the last few years, but finances really were not in order at all. He got a headache just thinking about it and realised he really couldn't avoid it any longer. He needed to sit down this weekend and crunch the numbers. Maybe even hire an accountant if Lavinia didn't already have one.

He had clearly hesitated for too long because Ellie sighed audibly. 'I didn't think so. I just really don't think it's going to be sustainable long term. Look, I know I have only been here five minutes, but there's a reason why these gardens are in such a state. I don't know how this Ernie bloke has managed all these years.'

'You're right.' George nodded, rubbing his face before hooking his hands onto his hips in agitation. She was right, and

George realised, feeling a little foolish, that these gardens hadn't got like this overnight. They weren't overgrown and wasting away because of Ernie's absence. These gardens had been slowly suffocating for years now because Ernie and his tiny little team were quietly drowning.

'You've got Joseph on apprenticeship wage,' Ellie offered. 'I mean, I feel bad for him working to the bone for pittance. But maybe we could put out for more apprenticeship positions. Or start up a volunteer program.'

'No one is going to want to work for free,' George scoffed.

'I disagree. I know lots of people who do things for free. Like Wendy three doors down from me. She dedicates hours to the Parish Council. And Barry - he's teaching Cornish to people in the Reading Room twice a week, for the pure love of it. Maybe there's people out there who don't have a garden of their own. People who are lonely and would just like a couple of hours speaking to people and being a part of something. I'll bet I can get WI involved in some way too.'

George watched her as she suddenly came to life, animated about the people of her own community. There he was again, studying that freckled face of hers, scattered across a Duchess nose.

'Surely you could find a budget to feed people a meal,' Ellie continued. 'Free breakfast or lunch as payment for their hard work.'

George's face split into a wide smile. 'And this is why I hired you.'

# Chapter Nine

Ellie felt elated that evening and practically skipped home in the semi-darkness, along the little pathway linking their hamlet and the estate. Although no decisions had been made or set in stone just yet, she had felt like George had listened and taken in her feedback and concerns. She was beyond relieved, having gone home the previous day with a heaviness in her heart that she had perhaps made the wrong decision accepting the job. Now, she had hopes for the months ahead. She navigated the little blue gate at the top of their front garden path and stabbed at the keyhole of their door with her keys, blindly unlocking and stepping inside the dark hall. The smell of beef stew hit her nostrils and had her tummy rumbling in earnest. She could hear Nanny's voice, chatting away with the accompanying deeper chords of dear Jack. Perfect - she couldn't wait to tell him everything and hadn't had a chance yesterday.

'Hello, you!' Ellie sang, patting Jack's back affectionately as she peeled off her coat and hung it on the back of a chair. 'Hey, Nan. Smells gorgeous!'

'Oh, Lord. You're chirpy,' Gloria grumbled, though she smiled in amusement as Ellie planted a cold kiss on her powdery cheek. 'What's got into you?'

Ellie held her hands out in feigned defence. 'Can I not be chirpy without raising suspicion?'

'Usually means you're up to something - so, no,' Jack

retorted, grinning back teasingly. 'Go on, then. What have you done? What do I have to do?'

Ellie gasped with laughter, then surrendered to defeat. 'Okay, well played. How would you like to be hired to renovate Mrs Pascoe's cottage?'

A strange sort of rigor mortise came over Jack as his drink paused at his lips. It wasn't the reaction she'd been hoping for and suddenly the kitchen fell silent and vacant. An awkward pause lingered as Ellie studied the multitude of expressions cross Jack's face. Even Nanny had stopped bustling in her little cooking area to listen in.

'Hired by who?' Jack asked, Ellie aware that he knew exactly who.

'G-George... You know, the -'

'The Lord... yes, I know who you mean.'

Further silence followed and suddenly Ellie wanted to retract the whole conversation. 'It's good money, and I'm going to be doing the garden. And...' She released a sigh of frustration, suddenly feeling annoyed. 'You don't have to do it. I just thought... you said... we *literally* talked about it last week - how much nicer it would be if we could be the ones to go in and do the work. Better than some company with total strangers going in and gutting the place.'

'She has a point, my love,' Nanny piped up, surprising Ellie.

'I meant as a renovation project for us,' Jack explained. 'Not to line the pockets for them up in the big house. Let me guess - holiday home?'

'No, he didn't mention holiday letting at all. Just wants it nice and modern for a new family to move in.'

'Yeah - alright, alright!' Jack relented. 'I'm just not sure about him, is all.'

'*Him?* What, like - *He Who Must Not Be Named!*' Ellie bit, sarcastically. 'He's not bloody Voldemort, Jack. I was the one who pushed for it. George mentioned that he would be getting the place ready for the new residents...'

'Way to give it five minutes,' Jack cut in, leaning back on his chair with his arms crossed. 'Mrs Pascoe's not even in the ground yet, for Christ's sake.'

'Oh my god!' Ellie cried, throwing her arms up in the air in exasperation. 'Forget I said anything! When are we eating, Nan? Have I got time for a shower?'

'No, I'm dishing out now and you're not buggering off upstairs in a huff while Jack is here as a guest for dinner.'

'He's hardly a guest. He's part of the furniture half of the time. Though, that might change if he keeps shitting on my excitement.' She sent daggers his way and he returned it with a sarcastic smile.

Ellie washed her hands and started buttering chunky slices of home-made bread ready for dipping in Nanny's rich beef stew. She was absolutely starving, and her spirits lifted a little at the thought of sinking her teeth into one of the dumplings currently marinating in the thick gravy.

'I'll think about it. The cottage work.'

'No pressure,' Ellie said, a little more sulkily than she intended.

'Oh, Lord help me,' Nanny mumbled. 'The youth these days.'

Weeks flew by after that night. Mrs Pascoe was finally laid to rest - a beautiful, full service reflecting how popular she really had been amongst the community and beyond. Though she couldn't be sure, Ellie had sworn she'd caught a glimpse of Beryan Penhaligon at the back of the church during the service, but she'd been nowhere to be seen at the wake. Nanny had nearly killed herself over making scones and saffron buns and, despite the nature of the day, it had been a day of laughter, good food and sunshine down on the river.

Jack, after a painful amount of deliberating, accepted the job to renovate Mrs Pascoe's cottage, confirming through Ellie that he could start work at the start of May. Just three weeks away.

Ellie and her small team were well settled now in their much bigger, much warmer break room. It was the old laundry room, just adjacent to the kitchens in the main house, with just the servant's yard between the two sections. It hadn't taken much to transform it into a comfortable space, with only the old drying rack suspended from the ceiling hinting at its previous purpose. George had since provided a simple wooden table and some seats which he had sourced from various rooms around the house. Dave had brought in his old microwave, mumbling that it was a good excuse to get a new one for home. Although, since being so much closer to the kitchens, Ellie had recently befriended the lovely Trixie who now made it her mission to keep them well-fed.

'Thank you so much, Trixie. Delicious as always!' Ellie said, bustling into the kitchen to return their plates.

'Just pop them by the sink. Thanks, my love,' Trixie said, gesturing in the direction of the sink. She was busy rolling out some pastry ready to make pasties. 'Well, as I said - it's no trouble feeding you lot. I'm only making extra of what I do for the family. Broke my heart knowing Dave and Ernie were down in that wretched little shed, eating cold sandwiches from home. But they were on the other side of the estate, near enough. I offered many times, but Ernie wouldn't have it.'

'Well, we really appreciate it,' Ellie said, placing a hand on Trixie's shoulder in gratitude as she passed back through. 'Got to fuel the body when it comes to gardening. Dave is much less feral after one of your meals.'

Trixie barked with laughter, knowing Dave's temperament all too well. 'Where in the garden are you today then?'

'Italian gardens,' Ellie confirmed. 'We've drained the pond.' She pulled a face, baring her teeth nervously at the momentous task they had started. Trixie echoed her expression.

'Golly gosh, you're brave. I'm surprised Beryan hasn't hunted you down.'

Ellie paused in the doorway, her face drained from colour. 'I ran it by George first. It was inundated with algae and blanket weed. Half the plants were dead.'

'I'm only pulling your leg, girl. But that pond is Beryan's prized spot, along with the pergola at the back of the sundial garden. I'd head for the hills if she finds out.'

'I haven't seen her since she and Lavinia interviewed me,' Ellie said, trying not to externally shudder at the memory.

'She's been cooped up with a bit of a cold for a week or so. Hasn't been out and about much.'

Ellie nodded, pausing in the threshold of the back door, her mind wandering aimlessly. Something was bothering her, but she couldn't pinpoint what.

'You alright, my love?' Trixie said, penetrating Ellie's vague thoughts.

'Yeah. Sorry - just tired. Right, best crack on.'

Back in the Italian Gardens, Dave was standing in the now empty pond, scrubbing the lead lining with a bristled garden broom. He huffed and puffed, sweat pouring from his brow.

'Take it easy, Dave. Get Joseph to take over for a minute.' Ellie gestured at Joseph to swap jobs, to which Joseph leapt into action. He handed Dave the scraping tool, which he was using to dig out the weeds and moss in between the cobbled stones surrounding the pond. Ellie assessed the old pump, which was now lying on the nearby grass in pieces.

'We're gonna need a new pump,' Ellie declared, hooking her hands onto her hips. She sighed. She knew George was worried about the finances but had needed to get several orders authorised just this week. None of this was ever going to be cheap when it came to bringing the garden back up to standard.

'Do you reckon George would let us put some fish in here when it's done?' Joseph asked, already getting out of breath.

'Heron will get 'em,' Dave muttered, now easing himself onto a nearby bench.

'Are you alright, Dave?' Ellie asked, taking the scraping tool out of his hands, and encouraging him to stay seated. 'You look a bit peaky.'

Dave waved her off, struggling to catch his breath whilst growling at them both not to fuss. Suddenly, he clutched his chest, and his face became strained with pain.

'Joseph - get George, now!' Ellie shouted.

The ambulance had pulled into the entrance yard within twenty minutes, the peaceful surroundings of Penhaligon House morphing into a scene of flashing blue lights and people springing into action. When the paramedics had arrived on scene, Ellie had guided poor Dave down to the soft grass and into the recovery position. George and Joseph had come running just moments later.

Now, an hour and a half later, they were taking cover back in their new break room. Joseph was making them all a strong coffee and Ellie was filling in the accident book with George's guidance.

'You did really well,' George encouraged, taking back the accident book, and sitting down next to Ellie. Despite her mind being far away with poor Dave at this point, she didn't fail to notice the way George stood out like a shiny red Ferrari amongst a line-up of muddy Defenders in his tailor-cut suit and polished shoes. 'Your quick thinking probably saved his life. I take it you're first aid trained, then?'

'It was on my CV, if you remember,' Ellie said, smiling coyly. 'Yeah, I try to keep my first aid up to date for my Nanny.'

Joseph set a hot coffee in front of George and Ellie, before settling down in his own chair with a drink. Ellie smiled warmly, feeling sorry for the poor boy who seemed to be doing his best to not look shaken.

'Thanks, Joseph.'

'Yes, thank you Joseph,' George said, stretching out a large, tanned hand to grab his coffee before leaning back in his chair. Poor Joseph stumbled out a shy reply, his wide eyes fixed on George, like a child looking up to a cool big brother. 'Thank you for your quick action today as well.'

Trixie came bustling in, looking rather wretched from the whole incident, carrying a tray of sweet things. 'Are you all alright, my loves? What an ordeal! I've got some millionaire shortbread here. Eat it up please and get some sugar in you.'

Ellie thanked Trixie and was the first to dive in and grab a slice. They were chunky, generous pieces, oozing with sticky caramel. She turned her attention to Joseph, who had become very quiet. 'Are you OK, Joseph?'

Joseph looked up at them all with a slight vacant expression, then smiled weakly. 'I'm OK. Will Dave?'

'The paramedics reckon he had a small angina attack,' George said. 'They've taken him to Treliske for some assessments. I'm sure he'll be OK.'

Joseph nodded but didn't look completely convinced.

'I'm sure he will be well looked after,' Trixie said, placing a mothering hand on Joseph's shoulders. 'I must crack on but eat up please.'

'First Ernie with his hip. Now Dave,' Joseph continued after Trixie's rushed exit, looking miserable. 'Ellie's right - we need more gardeners.'

Ellie smiled tightly at George, knowing the concern behind this. 'Have you thought more on my volunteer idea? Apprenticeships?'

George nodded, a grave expression on his face at the mention of money. He let out a heavy sigh and snatched a piece of millionaire shortbread from the plate in hopes of a sugar-fix sorting out all his troubles. 'Let's give it a go.'

To Ellie's horror, George recommended they discuss the matter of a large recruitment campaign over dinner that evening, with the rest of the Penhaligon family. She was keen to see the team grow, so she reluctantly accepted and rushed home to clean herself up at the end of the working day. Dinner would be at 7pm, prompt - so, she had a good hour to rid herself of the stagnant water smell from draining the old pond. Nanny had immediately been against the idea, which played havoc with Ellie's nerves over the evening.

'Don't do it,' Nanny had said, as soon as Ellie had told her where she would be for the evening. 'Don't do it. You'll only have those wretched women ganging up on you again - like they did in your interview. Horrible so-and-sos!'

Ellie was still none the wiser as to what Gloria's real issue was with the Penhaligon women, besides the obvious. But every time she asked, her hot-tempered Nanny would tell her it was nothing of anyone's concern now, let her be. One thing Gloria Curnow was spot on with, those Penhaligon women were a piece of work and Ellie felt she was about to be thrown to the vultures.

'So, how are you finding it, Miss Curnow - your new role?' Lavinia asked, quite pleasantly, over the dinner table. They had just taken their seats, not too soon after Ellie's arrival, and Trixie was bringing out glass goblets filled with prawn cocktail salads. Ellie had smiled warmly at her, before beaming down at an old favourite. This was Nanny's usual go-to starter whenever they hosted a special dinner with friends. She summoned the will to relax a little, maybe even try to enjoy her evening, with Trixie's delicious food as an added bonus.

'It's good. Thank you,' Ellie replied, lamely. Apparently, her ability to articulate herself had gone. She quickly swallowed the prawn she had been caught halfway through eating, to elaborate. 'I hope you're pleased with the progress we are making in the garden.'

'Mmm, yes,' Lavinia said, taking a bite from her own salad. Ellie waited for a little more in her reaction, but that appeared to be it. She looked up at George pleadingly, who smiled with a mixture of sympathy and apology. Despite her nerves, a lot of Ellie's attention kept beelining to George's appearance. He wore a simple baby-blue linen shirt, which pulled taught around his biceps and across his broad shoulders. As usual, his sleeves were unbuttoned and gathered up to his elbow, freeing his tanned forearms of which Ellie constantly had to rip her gaze from. She blinked, dazed as she caught herself doing it for the hundredth time.

'How's Dave doing?' The young woman to her right asked. She had been quiet and reserved from the start and had immediately made Ellie feel like she was under great scrutiny. She was quite clearly Lavinia Penhaligon's daughter. She had the same strong jawline as her mother, and steely blue eyes designed to cut the coldest of glares. Ellie had managed to recall her introducing herself formally as Tressa Penhaligon.

'I had a text message from him earlier,' Ellie confirmed. 'Simple and to the point, as Dave does. I have tomorrow morning off, so thought I would pay him a visit at the hospital.'

'Marvellous idea. Send him our regards,' Lavinia said, smiling with encouragement. Ellie returned the smile, thinking that perhaps the Lady of the house was at least trying so she should too.

'It was Ellie's quick thinking here which saved Dave,' George pointed out, finally speaking up. Small talk. This was all small talk. Ellie gathered all her willpower to prevent her leg from bouncing under the table, as it did when she was agitated.

'Is it, indeed?' Lavinia retorted, wiping her mouth with her napkin, and sipping her wine. 'Well, good for you. Did you hear that, Mother?'

The attention was drawn to the old lady sat to the right of her daughter - the one who had so readily dismissed Ellie at the interview.

'Yes - very good, very good,' Beryan grumbled, picking at her prawn cocktail salad, and pulling out a rocket leaf with distaste. 'Must Trixie use these silly salad leaves? Whatever happened to just having iceberg lettuce?'

'Don't mind Granny,' Tressa said, smiling in amusement. 'She's just in a terrible mood after seeing that her beloved pond has been emptied.'

'Tressa,' Lavinia said, in a warning voice.

Ellie's stomach jolted slightly as she confirmed this fact with the cold hard stares she was receiving from the old woman across the large mahogany table. 'Oh, well - I can assure you, it will be returned to its former glory very soon. But it was quite desperate for a good clean. Cyanobacteria. It's quite toxic, actually.'

'Well, I wasn't planning on bathing in it, my girl,'

'Granny,' George warned, his tone not dissimilar to that of his mother's - his face darkening in sternness. Ellie decided she had best not retort, knowing that the side of her personality inherited from Gloria would rear its ugly head without invitation. She was certain that the two women would watch carefully for any slip ups and excuses to see her gone.

They finished the remainder of their starter in painful silence, and Ellie thought she wouldn't be able to take it any longer when a girl burst into the room in a wonderful flurry of chaos and joyfulness, which Ellie quite possibly could hold gratitude for the remainder of time.

'Sorry I'm late everyone! I would like to say I have the most brilliant excuse - but I don't,' the girl said to the room breathlessly. Going by her features, she was quite clearly another Penhaligon - George's second sister. But her smiley demeanour; her floaty skirts and jangling bangles on her wrists; her unkempt, mousy brown hair, feebly controlled by little braids she had possibly added herself in idleness, gave her such a contrast to the rest of her family that, to Ellie, she was a breath of fresh air.

'You *must* be Ellie!' the young girl cried, reaching across her older sister, and shaking Ellie's hand. It was small but held a firm shake. 'George has told me all about you. You are doing such a marvellous job of the gardens.'

Despite the exasperation radiating from the other Penhaligon women, Ellie couldn't help but smile broadly, joining in on the young woman's enthusiasm. Ellie decided right away that she liked her with all her heart.

'Thank you so much!' Ellie said, gratefully. 'I'm glad my small team's efforts are being noticed.'

'Oh, I know - crikey. You guys must be exhausted. I was saying to George only yesterday: I don't know how you're doing it all with just the three of you.'

'Well, poor Dave is in hospital as of this afternoon - so...,' George commented. The girl gasped in horror, asking if he was alright. George added: 'Angina attack. He's in for monitoring.'

'Wenna, will you sit down already,' Beryan cut in, harrumphing loudly. 'You're making the place look untidy.'

Wenna hurried around the table and chose a seat on the other side of Ellie. Suddenly, Ellie felt she had a sort of ally beside her and immediately appeared more confident.

'Oh, poor Dave. I find him so funny. Don't you find him funny, Ellie? People think he's just a grumpy old man, but if you get to know him, he's actually got a brilliantly dry sense of humour!'

'Yes!' Ellie agreed, wholeheartedly. That was exactly what she had explained to Jack just the other day. She liked Wenna even more now, to know that she took her time to get to know the staff around the estate. 'I was actually saying just a minute ago that I will be visiting him tomorrow morning. If you're free at all, I'm sure he'd love to see you.' Ellie wasn't sure why she had jumped straight into inviting one of the Penhaligons along with her, into her banged-up little van, for a trip to Truro, but she was relieved when Wenna accepted gladly.

'Do you think we could stop into the town centre on the way home?' Wenna pleaded. 'There's a darling little indie clothes shop at the top of Pydar Street, and I could do with some more-'

'If you are quite finished monopolising the conversation for the entire table,' Lavinia scolded her youngest. 'I do believe Trixie is about to bring out the main course. Please discuss your personal plans in private.'

Feeling equally scolded, Ellie joined Wenna in looking rather bashful before exchanging a slightly amused smirk with her as the older women became distracted with the arrival of Trixie's main. It wasn't until Ellie returned her gaze to the centre of the table that she noticed George staring right at her. He too wore an expression of great amusement, his eyes dancing and his lips turned upwards in a handsome smirk, making Ellie's tummy somersault in spectacular ways.

# Chapter Ten

George watched in both shock and awe as Ellie slowly earned her place of acceptance from even the most disagreeable of the Penhaligon women. It was starting to get late, and the remnants of Trixie's delicious Eton Mess dessert lay defeated in the middle of the dinner table. Beryan had taken herself off to bed straight after her last spoonful of dessert, claiming that she was exhausted for the day. This had left him with his mother - who was uncharacteristically optimistic after their table debate over George and Ellie's new recruitment idea - his youngest sister, who was her usual animated self and currently barking with laughter over something Ellie had said, and Ellie leaning back in her chair and clapping her hands in paralysing mirth. But the most shocking of all was Tressa. She wasn't perhaps as bent over with amusement as the other two were, but George had observed a noticeable difference in the way she sat back in her chair, her shoulders relaxed, and a wine glass perched loosely in her hand. She watched Ellie and Wenna in muted amusement, her teeth even occasionally showing in a genuine smile. It warmed George's heart to see his otherwise forbidding sister removed from her stern shell, her features softening and showing her true elegance.

'So, it is decided,' Lavinia announced, clapping her hands in triumph. 'I will put out an advertisement in the local papers on Monday for weekday volunteers, with the promise of a hot breakfast or lunch. George and Eleanor will make contact with the colleges across Cornwall about a couple of apprenticeship placements.'

'Do you think perhaps now you might reconsider my idea on setting up a social media platform for the estate?' Tressa said, much more politely than George was used to. He was disappointed to see his mother frown at this and was ready to jump to Tressa's aid.

'That's a great idea,' Ellie chimed in, beating George to it, and clearly not noticing Lavinia's initial reaction. 'So many Cornish estates are on social media now. I'm not on it myself, but I know many who simply follow the pages just for the photos and a glimpse into these stately homes. People are proper nosy on these pages.' George didn't miss the gratified expression Tressa sent towards Ellie for her support.

'At least then we can pop a post on our page about the recruitment for free,' George added.

'Oh, alright,' Lavinia lamented. 'Seems a bit unnecessary to me, but fine.'

'Tressa, why don't you take charge of the social media front,' George suggested. The sudden beaming expression which settled on his sister's face took him by surprise and he felt a pang of guilt in exchange. She simply wanted involvement in the estate, and this would be a positive start.

'Can I make use of that photography course I did last year and take the photos for the page?' Wenna asked, her usual enthusiasm unwavering.

'Yes, that's fine,' Tressa said, importantly. 'If you'll excuse me, I'm going to retire to my room and make a start on setting up the pages.'

They all bid their goodnights to her and with that Lavinia followed suit, thanking Ellie for her efforts with such geniality that George could quite easily have believed he'd entered an alternative universe.

'Well,' George said, a few moments later in Trixie's kitchen. He, Ellie and Wenna had cleared the dining table of the remaining dishes and were now washing up and clearing away anything Trixie had not had a chance to do before heading home for the night. 'I don't know whether to be scared, suspicious or just in absolute awe of you Ellie Curnow.'

'I agree,' Wenna laughed, abandoning her cleaning duties, and instead helping herself to the Eton mess leftovers. 'Not many people can say they've dined with the entire Penhaligon family and survived it. Mother and Granny can be a piece of work. And you got Tressa to crack a smile.'

Ellie laughed and shrugged amiably. 'We're all people at the end of the day. Though, I'm not going to lie: your grandmother terrifies me.'

Both George and Wenna chuckled in unison, nodding in understanding.

'Yeah, that's Granny,' Wenna said. 'Don't take anything she says too personally.'

Ellie smiled in understanding and the three of them finished clearing the kitchen. It was almost midnight when George and Wenna finally saw Ellie off, her rusty old van chugging noisily down the drive and out of sight.

'Well, she...is delightful!' Wenna announced to no one in particular, taking immediately to the stairs with the intention of finally going to bed. George gave in to a stifling yawn which had been threatening to erupt for the last thirty minutes, before following closely behind.

'You two certainly gelled.'

'If you marry her, I think I shall be her Maid of Honour. We're definitely best friends now. In fact, scrap that - even if you two don't marry, I will still be Maid of Honour at her wedding.'

George scoffed loudly, feigning ignorance to that comment and trying to ignore the slightly irritating sensation of warmth he felt at the idea. 'You are such a hopeless romantic, Wenna.'

'Ha! You didn't deny anything though. I was right the other day, wasn't I?' Wenna teased, arriving at her bedroom door, and leaning against the frame. George stopped in the corridor which would eventually lead to his, his hands in his pockets patiently. 'She is pretty fit. You couldn't stop looking at her.'

George scoffed again, throwing his hands out of his pockets to mark the end of his patience. 'That's enough from you. Go to bed.' He stormed off in the direction of his bedroom, his sister's laughs chasing after him.

The next morning, he caught a glimpse of Ellie as she picked Wenna up for their trip to visit Dave in hospital. Wenna had asked if he would be joining them, but George was accepting enough to know that Dave was not his biggest fan and would probably not appreciate his visit as much as the girls'. He politely declined and decided to use his day to explore some of the outer parts of his estate, including the hamlet and properties along the river. He'd known their boundaries stretched far and wide into pockets of land around and beyond the estuary, but it was this week upon examining the estate land registry that floored him with the sheer acreage he was now in charge of.

His morning trickled by slowly, giving him plenty of opportunity to drink in the vast and changing views along the river. Every section and every bend were different. Occasionally, he'd come across a property - a single cottage or a row of terraces - marked with the matching burgundy red wooden gates and windows, showing their attachment to the estate. George tried to recall the names of the residents for each property. His father would have known them all, by first and last name, as would his grandfather.

It occurred to him that it had been a very long time since he'd allowed himself to think about his late father and grandfather. Only five years sat between their final days on earth. George hadn't long turned eighteen when his grandfather

Charles went first. Heart attack. So quick and so unexpected. George was suddenly bombarded with expectations of being the next Lord of Penhaligon Estate, with immediate effect. Then his father passed away from his long fight with Leukaemia five years later. In his youthful naivety and grief, he'd declined and fled - seeking a life entirely different from what was already laid in place for him. His adventures around the UK, starting and finishing University, stumbling into the world of viticulture, and finally settling into life in and around parts of Italy in his late twenties - Lavinia never stopped chipping away and encouraging him back to his inheritance. He never understood why Lavinia didn't just give up tradition and hand it to Tressa, but he had recently come to realise that there was a lot of things that Lavinia didn't give Tressa credit for.

It wasn't the rolling hills of Tuscany or the glittering waters of Lake Como, but George couldn't deny that the Cornish hills rolled, and the estuary glistened like a thousand diamonds - just in their own rustic way. He reached the highest point and looked back on his efforts, taking in the glory of the estuary in its entirety, or at least the estate's section of it. On a sunny day like today, the water was aqua blue and sparkling in the late spring sunshine. Boats and yachts peppered the mouth of the estuary where it opened up towards the wide sea - fishing villages and private beaches lining the side of the coast before finally leading to Falmouth itself, Pendennis Castle sitting as an historical landmark.

George had almost done full circle of his estate, and finally arrived in Ellie's little hamlet from the opposite side around lunch time.

The sheer quaintness of the place captured George's interest as he descended a sloping path onto the pebbled beach. The muddy embankment curved around beneath a track road which led to the other cottages further along on the opposite side and an upturned rowing boat was surrounded by piles of lobster pots and crab pots. His feet were starting to hurt now, blistered by the wellington boots he had never taken the time in his past visits to break in. A huddle of people gathered by a row of three parked cars, one of which was a small white van overflowing with nets and other such fishing equipment, waders flung over the open back door. Their conversation ceased as they noticed George approaching, and all five heads turned his way, a friendly but curious smile on their faces. They muttered their cheerful greetings and he returned with an equally jovial 'Good afternoon'. He followed the line of embankment down the bumpy track to explore the houses further down, catching the tail end of what one of the people in the huddle was saying.

'Is that him? Younger than I thought he was.'

It hadn't occurred to him that news would have spread fast across the estate of his return, and his usual confidence suddenly felt uncharacteristically depleted. What if he failed? Failed the estate? Failed the people of the estate? The sudden realisation of responsibility floored him for a section, and he took refuge on an old bench which faced the water. He took a deep breath through his nose and exhaled out of his mouth. Somehow, stepping out of the garden walls of Penhaligon House made the people, who would be relying on him, so much more real - reminded him of who and what was really at stake. He allowed himself a few more minutes at the run-down bench, his hands steadied on his tired thighs from all the walking, and his line of sight following a trio of moor hens as they glided down and around the corner of the river bend.

'Right. Onwards.' He slapped his thighs with determination and heaved himself back up onto his sore and blistered feet. A little way up the track led him past private gardens, houses, boat sheds, more houses, the backs of small run-down garages and even a tiny orchard of around eight to ten apple trees, all in full spring blossom. Finally, he reached a small stream just off from the main estuary, the track ending at the old garage with blue double doors. A concrete slab acted as a little step over the trickling water, leading to a simple blue gate, a thatched cottage just beyond that. He realised instantly that this was Ellie's cottage. Stone's Throw Cottage.

Blue gate, George noticed. Not the estate's burgundy red. He was just contemplating why, being sure that Ellie's cottage was under the estate, when the front door opened, and an elderly lady stepped outside onto the cobbled step. She was bent over with age and reliant on a cane. From a distant glance she seemed a similar age to Beryan. Her cane tapped warily against the stone as she shuffled into a stable position to pull the door shut, and as she looked up, she spotted George standing at the end of the path. She became frozen to the spot and George frowned at the strange reaction. He decided to go and introduce himself - check if she was okay.

'Sorry to interrupt the start of your afternoon, Ma'am,' George began, formally. 'I thought it best to introduce myself.'

'I know who you are,' the elderly lady croaked. George realised with a pang that tears sat in her eyes and her thin lips trembled. She looked up at him with such pain in her eyes that George didn't know whether to comfort her or retreat. She heaved a big, trembling breath. 'I know exactly who you are. Oh...'

Despite himself, George took a step forward and assisted the poor old lady into the little wooden bench to the left of the front door. He was a giant beside her tiny frame and did his best to appear less so as he took a seat beside her. Her blue-grey eyes were striking and still held the spark of a strong woman with a story to tell. He recognised those eyes immediately. They were Ellie's eyes.

'You look exactly like him,' Ellie's Nanny gasped. She looked away then and gazed out to the garden, her hands poised on the top of her cane for support. It seemed like she was going to say something else, and then the silence fell and lingered between them. George studied her aging face and allowed the silence to stretch a little further before he said, 'I assume you mean my grandfather, Charles. I've been told on numerous occasions how much I look like him. Did you know him well?'

She nodded, her lips quivering from tiny sobs. 'I did... once. But a very long time ago. You must ignore me. Silly old woman, I am.' She suddenly tapped her cane on the path and composed herself in a frustrated manner. 'I haven't set eyes on your dear grandfather for many a decade now, and I'm afraid your appearance was so familiar you took me by surprise. Anyway, good day to you. I was on my way to post a letter if you'll excuse me.'

George, utterly bewildered by this queer exchange, stood up and supported her onto her feet, grasping desperately for something to say.

'Ellie is doing a fantastic job with the gardens - Mrs Curnow,' George said, throwing out the best he could to extend their exchange.

'Call me Gloria, please,' Gloria requested, no trace of a smile on her sad face. 'I'm glad. Ellie seems to be enjoying it.'

His efforts weren't enough and before he could conjure up another attempt at small talk, the lady had pivoted carefully on her little feet and shuffled her way past the gate and around the corner. George remained at his standing spot, both unnerved and intrigued by Gloria's reaction. It had been immediately obvious that Gloria and his grandfather held some history. But what exactly? As far as he had been made aware, Charles and Beryan had been sweethearts from the very beginning. As far as he would like to believe, his doting grandfather had always been faithful and loyal to both Beryan and the rest of the family. So, what on earth had happened in the past between Gloria and Charles to elicit such a reaction. If he didn't know any better, he would say that Gloria's expression mirrored that of someone who had once had their heart broken. But by the actions of his grandfather, that he did not want to believe.

After that, George had lost his motivation to explore the rest of the hamlet and, suddenly feeling invasive, decided to return to the house. His arrival had been timed well with the return of Ellie and Wenna, who had both jumped out of Ellie's van in a state of mirth. Both munching heartily into a pasty each, they stomped across the yard to greet George.

'Good Lord, brother. Perhaps we should have brought something back for you. You're looking rather peaky,' Wenna observed, concern being outweighed by mostly amusement. She held out the pasty in her hand, half-eaten and wrapped in paper. 'Pasty?'

'No, thank you,' George muttered. He glanced at Ellie, who was digging in unapologetically and with gumption. 'I...um...met your grandmother earlier.'

Ellie paused mid-chewing and suddenly concern edged along her features. 'How? I mean, how did that go?'

'Why do you ask?' George asked, suspiciously. 'Like that, I mean.'

Ellie shrugged and avoided the question. 'How did you end up meeting her? Where were you?'

'At your cottage?' George's eyes narrowed more.

'Why were you at my cottage?' The amusement which had danced around Ellie and Wenna had quickly dissipated, and now only this odd wariness sat between Ellie and George, Wenna observing bewilderedly from the side. Ellie's voice was sterner the second time. 'Why were you at my cottage?'

'Because it's part of the estate. I was exploring the estate and came across it. Your grandmother -'

'Nanny,' Ellie corrected.

'Sorry?'

'It's Nanny. Not Grandmother. She doesn't like it. She prefers Nanny. Grandmother makes her feel old and stuffy,'

Ellie's words were fast and clip, and she seemed agitated all of a sudden. Her pasty forgotten and poised in her hand.

George rolled his eyes to the sky. 'Nanny, then. Your Nanny just happened to step outside when I appeared.'

'What did you say to her?'

'Nothing!' George was uncertain why he sounded defensive now. 'Why...why is your gate blue?'

'What?' both Ellie and Wenna asked in unison.

'Why is your gate blue? It's part of the estate. It should be burgundy red.'

Ellie's pasty nearly flew from her hand as she threw her arms into the air. 'I don't know! Nanny didn't like the burgundy red so asked me to paint it duck egg blue. It's been like that for years now - no one has said anything about it.'

'Well, it has to be red.'

'Fine, I'll paint it back.'

Another pregnant pause swelled between them and Wenna slowly stepped in, as if she was treading on ice. 'So, Dave is doing well. He'll be discharged this afternoon.'

'I hope you didn't bring up the gate with Nanny,' Ellie cut in. Wenna muttered her apologies as she backed away, setting her attention back on her lunch.

George sighed, his temper rising. 'I didn't say anything out of sorts with your Nanny. I simply went to introduce myself and she...' George sighed a second time, resigning in the fact this conversation wasn't going anywhere good. 'Look, she seemed to get quite upset seeing me. I had barely said hello and she began to say that I looked exactly like my grandfather. And this seemed to upset her. I'm sorry, Ellie. I didn't mean to cause an upset. I actually wanted to say hello and tell her how brilliantly you are doing.'

Ellie's face, still contorted with concern, eased slightly into surprise at this compliment.

'I promise you,' George pleaded, his temper disappearing. 'I wasn't trying to cause any distress. I just wanted to say hello.'

'No, I believe you,' Ellie muttered. 'I don't know what, but I think something must have happened years and years ago which has left Nanny a bit sour. Was she rude?'

George waved the notion off. 'Not at all. Just...sad.'

Ellie's eyes glazed as she went into deep thought. She looked like she was about to say something else, her mouth opening and shutting like a fish, but she suddenly decided against it and closed off again.

'I think I'll head home to check she's okay,' Ellie said, an apology in her tone. 'She can get herself in a bit of a pickle when she's upset about something.'

'I'm sorry if I've done something wrong,' George said, feeling a sudden urge to close the gap between them, not wanting her to go when he felt responsible for her change in mood. She had been so beautifully happy just five minutes before.

'It's not your fault. Nanny is a mystery at the best of times. I'll go and check on her,' she offered him a small smile and backed away towards the direction of her van. 'Bye, Wenna. Thanks for the laughs this morning.'

'I'll text you later!' Wenna's chirpy voice cut through the tension, as she waved Ellie off. 'Turn your phone on, old woman!'

George felt Wenna's attention seep over to him, which he tried to ignore, his trailing eyes watching Ellie's van disappear around the bend. Two things bothered him. He felt beyond wretched for what had happened with Ellie's Nanny, though he still couldn't figure out what had actually gone so wrong. But he suddenly realised at that moment that he did not like watching that rusty old van of hers disappear down the drive like that. He didn't like saying even a quick goodbye to Ellie Curnow - even though he knew he would see her the very next day. It jangled him beyond measure. He felt pathetic. What on earth was the matter with him? He needed to be more careful and keep these unexpected feelings tucked away where they belonged.

# Chapter Eleven

The month of May arrived soon enough and with it the summer colours of the garden bursting into bloom. The volunteer programme was a roaring success, and within a couple of weeks Ellie went from being in charge of a team of two to being in charge of a growing team of twenty-two and counting. Just as Ellie had thought, and hoped for, people from all over the area and different backgrounds had been drawn to the programme for simply the desire to socialise with like-minded people, to enjoy a complimentary meal, and to gain experience working in a large stately garden. With the extra hands, the garden soon began to take shape and Ellie finally felt like she, and her team, were having a real impact on the grandeur of the gardens at Penhaligon House.

One particular morning, Ellie found herself waking to the early summer sun beaming in through the gaps of her curtains, the birds chirping away merrily in the trees outside her bedroom. She realised, with a sudden burst of joy, that this was the first time she was waking up with instant eagerness to get back to the estate. Her vision for the gardens had become clear now that she had the manpower (for want of a better word seeing as three quarters of her team were now female) to not only maintain what grew and flourished in the garden now, but to be able to make changes and create new spaces with realistic ambition. She often shared her visions with the Penhaligon sisters - Wenna would bounce off Ellie with their ideas, often adding quirkiness to Ellie's designs, and Tressa began to work wonders with the way she presented and blogged the progression of the gardens on their new social media platform. The Resurrection of Penhaligon Gardens, she kept calling it - though Ellie diplomatically suggested they seek out a less ominous name. Even now, Ellie found herself surprised by the friendship which had kindled between her and the sisters, particularly with Tressa, who was clearly a difficult person to befriend. But Ellie had found an amiable side to Tressa, disguised by a cold front which she didn't understand but respected on Tressa's terms. She had, naturally, had a few run-ins with the eldest sister over decisions with the gardens, but this was only to be expected when two women as feisty and strong-minded as Ellie and Tressa put together.

Ellie practically jogged down her little lane to the estate and arrived before the curtains of the Penhaligon's sleeping quarters had even begun to twitch.

'My goodness, I thought it was only me mad enough to be arriving at work at this ungodly hour,' Trixie declared, as Ellie strode into the kitchen to fill her little kettle. 'I know you're an early bird, but any reason why you're a whole hour early, my love?'

'No reason,' Ellie shrugged, throwing her widest smile at her favourite cook. 'But it's set to be a beautiful day and I have about fifteen of the volunteers all in together today, so wanted to do a quick reccy and get a to-do list going before their arrival.'

'I did see that on your little white-board thingy,' Trixie said, pointing a wooden spoon in the direction of the new white-board that Wenna had installed a couple of days before. This was so Ellie could easily note down how many volunteers would be in each day, and therefore how many breakfasts or lunches Trixie would be preparing. 'Good job I had a delivery yesterday from the butchers. Six packs of bacon, two large trays of eggs, and a shit load of sausages.'

Ellie laughed and smiled bashfully. 'Sorry, Trixie. I've created so much more work for you, haven't I?'

'You're doing the estate the world of good, my love. The gardens haven't looked this wonderful in a very long time. I'm sure even Ernie will agree when he eventually feels well enough to come along and see for himself.'

Ellie nodded, though she was unconvinced that would be the case, when the time came.

'Although, if your team gets any bigger, I may need to do a bit of recruiting myself. Do you know how many cooks and kitchenhand this place would have had once upon a time?' Trixie complained, though her voice remained light and in good nature.

'We couldn't function without your good food, so you're very much appreciated,' Ellie said, sending her a kiss through the air and taking her kettle back to the little breakout room. This space had since evolved, of course, with more chairs and tables squeezed into each corner to accommodate the growing team. Ellie threw herself down into one of the old armchairs and started writing down things on her to-do list which she had thought of on her walk over. She would have three people edging the front lawn this morning, to redefine those edges. There was a big trailer of manure in the back yard ready for another small group to mulch the beds in the Italian gardens. Then there was the huge task of getting the seeds sown for the extensive amount of vegetables Lavinia was requesting for harvest time this year. From the amount Ellie had ordered, she had visions of the Kitchen Garden bursting with harvest: carrots, cabbage, cauliflower, squashes and pumpkins, courgettes, leeks. Wenna had kept herself busy over the last week putting her textiles skills to good use in making a scarecrow, saying that a newly replenished Kitchen Garden needed its own scarecrow to watch over the new crop. From the glimpses of its progress Ellie had caught in passing, she couldn't wait to see it installed, nor could she wait to see Lavinia's reaction. Something told Ellie it wasn't going to be quite to Lavinia's taste.

The volunteers began arriving in spurts, along with Joseph and Dave. Dave had made a gradual return this week, with strict orders to take it easy. He was on light duties, and Ellie had decided to assign him to driving the little ride-on with the trailer of manure to and from the back yard. It was going to be a busy, fruitful day, so Ellie got the hot teas and coffees out to the smiling faces of people donned in their gardening gear and had them all huddle in the yard for a quick briefing. She'd done a few of these over the past couple of weeks, with her trusty clipboard which she now used to keep track of the jobs each day, but it still made her nervous when all eyes were on her, waiting for her direction. It wasn't something she was used to, having worked alone for so many years. But she couldn't deny that she actually quite enjoyed it.

'Morning, everyone. Once again, thank you for your time and your enthusiasm,' Ellie began, her voice bouncing against the walls of the house blocking in the servant's yard. 'I've got three areas of the garden I'd like covered today, and I've split us into small teams for each of those. I'll get you into your teams and then go through the jobs with each of you.'

She started splitting them off into their groups, ensuring that there was a fair mix of age and ability in each one. She had started briefing the lawn edging group as George came into view inside the kitchen, speaking with Trixie before ducking his head and stepping outside into the yard. Surprisingly, he was in much more casual attire, his suit trousers and shirt left upstairs for another day. Ellie paused her instruction and looked at him expectantly. He looked furious; his features darkened in a deep scowl.

'What's up?'

He shook his head. 'Later.'

Unspoken words hung between them, and Ellie took the hint. She gave her team an encouraging smile to distract away from the fuming Lord next to her. 'Okay, everyone. Grab your tools from the shed and head to your areas. I'll come and see you all in five minutes. Breakfast is at 9am!'

Ellie studied George, whose murderous eyes burnt into the walls of the main house, his large chest swelling up and down as his temper rose. His hands were clenched tightly by his side and, though Ellie's main focus was on his mood, a side of her was slightly distracted by his exposed tanned forearms, flexing in agitation with the sleeves rolled back. She stood by his side patiently for another minute, allowing him a moment to calm his breathing.

'Okay?' Ellie asked, gently. For someone always so calm, it was quite alarming to see him so worked up. Without too much thought, she placed a steadying hand on his upper arm, immediately regretting it as she felt his muscles ripple under her touch. She drew her hand away as fast as she had placed them, her face flushed from her reaction. She hadn't even realised that his fierce eyes had now fixated on hers. He blinked ferociously and snapped out of whatever trance he was in. 'What's going on?'

'Tressa,' George muttered, in way of an answer. 'I could bloody well kill her.'

'Why? What has she done?' Ellie asked, in alarm. In the short time she'd known the Penhaligons, she knew the sibling relationship between George and Tressa was strained and that she could be a little bit lacking in any form of affection towards her family, but this was a different level entirely.

'See, this is why...' George began, pointing his finger at nothing in particular and pacing the space in front of Ellie. 'This is exactly why we don't let Tressa loose on anything with the estate. She's irresponsible. She's lavish. She's... argh!'

Ellie, still none the wiser, waited patiently as George

111

widened his pacing spot and ran his hands through his dark brown hair. She wasn't good in moments like these. She wasn't the type of person to jump straight in with words of comfort, knowing exactly what to do to save the day. She was more of an observer, feeling intrusive if she was to try any form of comfort while he was having his moment. She didn't know George well enough and so she waited patiently.

Finally, he drew in and then breathed out a big sigh, before walking back and facing Ellie with his face tired and strained.

'Sorry,' George muttered.

'It's okay. You've got nothing to be sorry about. What has she done?'

'She's blown three thousand pounds on marketing and events,' George said. He spoke quickly, as if saying it quicker would make it hurt less. Ellie gasped, her hand flying up to her mouth.

'Three....thousand...pounds? Events? What events?'

'Well, that's just it. According to Tressa, Penhaligon Estate has a programme of events coming up, starting with a summer fayre! Then a vintage rally! A festival!' George spat, his temper rising once again. 'None of this has been run by me. Mother knew nothing about this either. Wenna said she didn't, but I beg to differ. Three - thousand - pounds. We don't have that sort of money.'

In utter defeat, George flumped down on an upturned crate and put his head into his hands.

'I spoke to the accountant last week. He hasn't gone through the estate's finances for ages, because Mother hadn't been keeping up to scratch with it all. He said Penhaligon Estate is in a lot of trouble and we're going to find ourselves up to our eyeballs in debt.'

Ellie allowed that information to sink in, chewing her lip grimly and selfishly thinking straight away about her own employment. Trixie's. Joseph's and Dave's. With the estate having no money, where would they fit in all of this?

And then there was the community down on the creek. Her community. Nanny's cottage. Almost everything along that river was tied into the estate. What would become of them? Naively, up until now she'd never contemplated or considered how important the estate was to the infrastructure of everything she had ever known. Growing up, Penhaligon House had always been a mysterious mansion up on the hill and, in Ellie's young eyes, had been where rich people lived surrounded by wealth, jewels and treasure. Even later on, with a more realistic mind, she'd still always assumed the people who dwelled in this big house were well-off in life. She'd never considered that, although they were asset rich, it did not mean they were cash rich - and an estate as large as Penhaligon could not go on like this without bringing in some money for the upkeep.

'We need to start finding ways to bring in money,' Ellie said, sitting down next to George on an upside-down bucket. 'The older generation down on the river talk about the days when Penhaligon opened their gates to the public all the time, hosting big community events and charity fundraisers. Maybe it's time you opened the gates once again. Before I had gotten the job here, this had been the first time I'd set foot on the main grounds. You're all so shut off from the rest of the world.'

George nodded. 'I've said this to Mother and Granny before. I completely agree with you. But they've become so private over the years. I'm not sure what they would make of the place becoming open to the public again.'

'It's either that, or not have the money to live here any longer,' Ellie shrugged, annoyance outweighing her sympathy for a second. 'They already have us gardeners traipsing around the place. It's hardly much different throwing the occasional event. Or... ' The ideas started flooding in and her eyes went wide with growing excitement. 'Or garden tours! I went to one once down Penzance way, and it included a guided tour by the head gardener and an evening supper afterwards. It was really lovely.'

George looked up and smiled. 'You're really good at this. Coming up with fresh ideas. You make everything seem so simple.'

Ellie blushed a little at the compliment and nudged her knee against his. 'It can be simple. These things don't have to be all-singing and all-dancing.'

She paused and looked up at the house, gazing into each of the ten windows in view from the side of the big house, half expecting at least one of the Penhaligon women to be spying on them. 'Actually... she may have buggered up with the marketing costs, but Tressa is actually full of great ideas. Between you and me, I think she's frustrated that she doesn't get more say in things.'

George frowned and did the same as Ellie, peering up at the house as if checking he wasn't being overheard. 'Hmm, yes...well. After today's nasty surprise, I'm starting to see why. Mother did always say she wasn't level-headed enough to make important decisions in the line of business.'

Ellie went to argue, and George held his hand up, apology in his expression. 'I appreciate what you're saying Ellie. But you don't know my sister like I do. Tressa grew up with a silver spoon in her mouth, and where Wenna and I set our silver spoons down to explore the real world - me more so - Tressa never did. She thinks money grows on trees. And this exact stunt, spending three thousand pounds without so much as a thought... that's why she can't be trusted.'

George's harsh words took Ellie by surprise and echoed in her mind hours later.

With the volunteers happily busy with their jobs, Dave taking lead safely on his little ride-on, Ellie had decided to use a couple of hours to walk the parkland and woods with Joseph, marking the trees with special forestry paint for tariffing. Ellie distracted herself from her and George's conversation, by talking through the tariffing process with Joseph.

'So, this small area of trees here was selected last week,' Ellie explained, stomping over the moss and twigs around the base of the pines. 'George confirmed them. They're all getting a bit scraggly, and we need to fell some trees for weathering, or the house won't have any firewood next winter.'

Joseph, a good student as always, listened to Ellie carefully, following her around the site like a little puppy.

'Basically, we need to count, classify and convert this area of trees using this tariff table,' Ellie explained, tapping her clipboard. 'This will estimate to us the volume of timber we'll get and how many of these trees we need to fell. Here's a tape measure. You need to measure the trunk's diameter. I would do it for these three at least.'

They spent ten minutes carefully measuring the trees, Ellie helping Joseph with some of the bigger ones. Then they sat down on an old log to make the conversions.

'Where did you learn all of this?' Joseph asked, his voice full of awe as always. Ellie could always count on Joseph to make her feel way better about herself and her abilities than she usually did.

'I took a few horticulture courses here and there over the years. Got my chainsaw license five years ago and became quite fascinated in forestry. I've only ever done a bit of felling and crowning on trees along the river. I'm not a qualified tree-surgeon or anything.' She looked up at the sky-high pines and the rest of the woodlands in front of them. 'I think we'll probably have to hire some professionals to do this lot. I'll be able to cut them up afterwards, but I've never felled anything this high before.'

'I just think you're so fantastic,' Joseph gasped, shaking his head in disbelief. 'You would never guess you don't have "qualifications".' He aired quotation marks around the word qualifications and Ellie burst into laughter.

'I have some "qualifications",' Ellie admitted, echoing Joseph's actions around the word. 'Just not the "qualifications" that Mrs Penhaligon would like, with a fancy certificate.'

'I think she is actually quite a nice person, deep down,' Joseph said, randomly. 'She's just a bit scary.'

'Definitely scary,' Ellie agreed, her attention on her tariff chart as she did some calculations on her phone.

'She's been quite kind to me over the last six months,' Joseph continued, looking out to the parkland in a pondering way. 'I was a bit useless when I first started, and I got on Ernie's nerves. Lavinia gave me a chance.'

Ellie nodded, unsure how to comment. It wasn't that she disagreed with Joseph about Lavinia - she was just yet to see it herself. 'That's good to hear. And you're far from useless.'

'My mum would say otherwise,' Joseph said, chuckling away. But as Ellie looked up at him, she saw years of hurt cross his young, pimply features. She suddenly felt a wave of protection over him - like a big sister. She placed a hand on Joseph's shoulder, giving him her full attention. 'You are not useless. You are a fantastic gardener.'

Joseph nodded. 'Thank you, Ellie. Since you started, I've begun to believe that might be true.'

Ellie's heart swelled and suddenly how she viewed her position here as Head Gardener changed indefinitely.

# Chapter Twelve

Jack heaved his bulging toolkit and electric drill case through the front door of Mrs Pascoe's cottage and plonked them into the open space of what was once her living room. Now stripped of her furniture, the heating having been switched off for weeks now, it was cold and empty. He stood still, his hands wedged onto his hips, a deep sigh erupting in his chest unexpectedly.

He was regretting agreeing to this already.

Since Ellie had started at the Penhaligon Estate, he had hardly seen her. He was happy for her, he really was. He couldn't be prouder of her actually. But a selfish side to him missed their daily exchanges, even if it was just a goofy wave across the water as she passed his house on her little boat. At least he would have an excuse to see her more again now that they were working on this cottage together. It was just that niggling feeling he couldn't seem to get rid of - like something wasn't right. Why did he feel like he was betraying Mrs Pascoe's memory being here? It's not like he knew her all that well before her passing. But she had always been kind and friendly in their passing, offered interesting conversations at community events, and had been something of comfort and familiarity in the hamlet.

'Jack, Jack, Jack, Jack!' Ellie's voice sounded up the garden path. Jack chuckled to himself as the chaos that was Ellie burst through the front door. 'I have arrived!'

'And the whole hamlet knows it,' Jack retorted, laughing. 'Do you need a hand with your lot?'

'Nah, it's okay. I'm only strimming and chain sawing today, so I carried them up. The garden is an absolute jungle. I haven't done so much as cut her grass for months. What are you going to start with?'

'The bathroom, I think. Start upstairs and work my way down.' Jack looked up at the ceiling, as if observing the monstrous work ahead of him through the plasterboard. 'Might need your hand getting the bathtub outside. It's an iron one.'

'Surprised the old floorboards can hold the weight,' Ellie gasped. 'Right, I'll bring the strimmer through. And Nanny has sent some rock buns.' She placed a round Tupperware tub on the old kitchen counter and headed back outside to retrieve her machinery.

Jack took one last heaving sigh, blowing out hot air noisily through his mouth and clapping his hands loudly. 'Right! Get on with it, Jack!' He grabbed his toolbox and marched upstairs, the old cottage staircase creaking under his weight. The landing was not much more than a square patch of carpet, one step leading to the single bedroom on the left and another step of old vinyl leading to the bathroom. A mint green bathroom suite sat under brash turquoise walls and patterned brown tiles. It made Jack's eyes hurt and he couldn't wait to rip it all out, despite his morals with Mrs Pascoe's memory. The sound of Ellie's strimmer broke through the quiet and Jack peered out of the window to see her traipsing through the long grass in her overalls, her orange safety helmet and face shield sat upon her head, out of proportion with her petite frame. He couldn't help but think how adorable she was.

It had always amazed Jack the way Ellie threw herself into these jobs - the way she could easily put most of the male traders that Jack knew to shame simply by the fact that no job was too big for her. She never hung around, usually head-first straight into even the most laborious of jobs, waiting until the job was done right before collapsing into an exhausted heap. She had always been a worker. They'd often indulged in the idea of setting up a business together, taking on renovation projects and putting their skills together to transform houses into homes. This, Jack supposed, was close enough to that dream. This was it. So, what was it that prevented Jack from leaping with joy over the prospect? Was this not what he wanted? To spend more time with her? To be with her?

*Yeah - but, not as a colleague!* He thought grimly.

The strimmer's engine cut out all of a sudden and Jack peered out once again to find Ellie on her phone, the strimmer hanging from her harness. She was smiling, he noticed. Not that it was rare to see Ellie smile - in fact, she often had a big smile on her face which was what Jack loved about her. But this seemed different. Was she blushing? Jack took a step forward to get a better view, but soon threw himself to the side of the window as Ellie turned and met his gaze. Great - now it was obvious he had been spying on her.

He gave himself a shake and started ripping up the hideous old vinyl, revealing old wooden floorboards underneath. When he got downstairs with the vinyl rolled up ready for dumping, Ellie was stood in the threshold of the back door from the little sunroom.

'Who was that?' Jack asked, trying to sound nonchalant and attempting to cover his tracks from his spying.

'It was Wenna,' Ellie replied, now stabbing her fingers into the screen at an attempt to put a text together.

A strange trickle of relief set in for Jack. 'That's the youngest one, right?' By one, he meant Penhaligon, and Ellie understood that code. She nodded. 'So, that wasn't the Lord.'

Ellie's hands dropped in front of her as she fixed him a deadpan expression. 'Really?'

'What?' Jack cried, in defence. He peeled open Gloria's Tupperware tub and extracted a rock bun, biting into it a bit more animalistically that he had intended to.

'You know he's called George. Why do you keep saying 'The Lord'?' Ellie said the final bit in a forced posh voice, crossing her eyes in a mocking way. 'You make him sound like a right ponce!'

'He is, isn't he?' Jack bit, without thinking. He felt Ellie go still in his peripheral vision and put all his focus on his rock bun, which was unsurprisingly delicious. 'I mean, he just wears suits all the time and goes around in his shiny sports car.'

'Actually, he sold the sports car this week,' Ellie informed him, her voice suddenly sounding a little edgy. 'Don't think they're as well off up there as people think. You're right about the suits, but he's not a ponce.'

Before he could retort with something light-hearted and sarcastic, Ellie had already headed back into the garden, the sound of the strimmer kicking back into life telling him that the conversation was well and truly over.

Great. Now he felt like a prejudiced asshole.


By lunchtime, Ellie had strimmed the entire garden, the air filled with the smell of freshly cut grass. The grass had been so high - almost up to their knees - that Ellie had had to strim back the worst before tackling the rest with the mower. She was raking up the worst of the off cuttings when Gloria had stepped through the open front door, her cane in one hand and a wicker basket in the other.

'Ellie! Nanny's here!' Jack yelled toward the direction of the garden. He rushed forward and relieved the poor old woman of the basket, the delicious smell of hot pasties wafting up through the weaves. 'Oooh - ansome! Thanks, Gloria.'

Gloria was silent as she looked around the empty room, leaning on her cane and her lip trembling. 'It's as if the poor woman never existed.'

Jack paused his search in Gloria's basket for his pasty and rubbed his face nervously, feeling uncomfortable. 'This was partly why I didn't want to do this. But Ellie's right. It's better her having people she knew coming in and doing this, than the Penhaligon's bringing a big company in to tear the place apart.'

Gloria nodded, not seeming convinced. 'I feel a tension in the air.'

'I'm sure we'll all feel a little better when the cottage starts taking shape.'

'Not the cottage,' Gloria grumbled, pointing her stick at Jack and then at Ellie as she came back into the house, the bottom of her dungarees coated in grass cuttings. 'You two! Don't you two start falling out over all of this again.'

Jack and Ellie looked at the wise woman, bewildered.

'How did you -?" Jack began. 'I mean, what do you mean? Everything is-'

'Jack seems to think I've joined the Dark Side or something since getting this job at the big house,' Ellie stated, matter-of-factly. She took a big bite into her pasty and challenged Jack with a look, who was silently protesting next to her. 'I'm right, aren't I?

After a few more excruciating seconds of him gaping like a fish, Jack threw his arms up in the air in defeat, grabbed his pasty and took an impressively large bite. 'Fine, I may have been a little off-hand with my comment towards...'

'George...' Ellie offered, through her own mouthful of food, her eyebrows raised expectantly. The expressions that played on her face sometimes - it didn't half disarm Jack in a way he couldn't explain.

'George,' Jack repeated, swallowing his mouthful. 'I'm sure he does a lot more than just wear suits and drive flashy sports cars.'

Ellie appeared mildly satisfied and they both glanced at Nanny, who simply stared perplexed at the both of them. 'Well. What a relief to get that cleared up. Such fickle nonsense between you two at the moment. I ought to bang your heads together. Bring the basket back with you when you're finished.'

And with that, Nanny left with a scuffle and a huff back towards their cottage, leaving Jack and Ellie in silence as they finished their pasties.

'What?' Jack asked, when he caught Ellie staring at him for the fifth time.

'Is this what it's going to be like from now?' Ellie asked, sadly.

'What do you mean?'

'Us. Falling out all the time. You've been giving me a hard time ever since I took the job.'

'No, I haven't!' Ellie shot him a loaded look and he yielded reluctantly, releasing a heaving sigh. 'Are you happy? Are you enjoying it?'

Ellie's face softened. 'Very much.'

'Then that's the main thing, isn't it?'

Ellie frowned, dissatisfied with that response. 'No, it's not. I miss you - and the banter.'

Jack held her gaze for a moment, and he suddenly felt completely disarmed, lost in her pale blue eyes, and feeling like a total wretch. He wanted to tell her how he really felt. The unexpected and maddening jealousy he felt over the time she now spent with George and his family up in the big house. 'Ellie, I-'

Heavy footsteps halted his attempts at a confession and a wide set of shoulders maneuvered through the narrow front door.

'George!' Ellie gasped, and Jack didn't miss the subtle way she composed herself and tamed her hair. He felt an immediate knot tighten in the pit of his stomach as he straightened up to full height. Despite his previous comments, it seemed that George was going to show Jack up on this occasion by wearing a casual pair of khaki green chinos and a simple black shirt, his sleeves rolled up to his elbows - not a tailor-cut suit in sight.

'You must be Jack,' George said, offering an outstretched

hand.

'We've met actually,' Jack said, accepting his handshake all the same and giving it a firm squeeze. 'At the pub. With Ellie.'

'Of course,' George said, smiling politely. 'Yes, I remember now. Thank you for agreeing to take this project on with such short notice. I understand how busy you must be.'

George buried his hands into his pockets with casual confidence as Jack's arms folded themselves across his large chest. The pause was short but palpable as everyone hurried to find something to say.

'Jack is the proud owner of Willow Bank, the big pink house just a few properties down the river from our cottage,' Ellie explained.

'Soon to not be pink,' Jack added, smiling at Ellie.

'Renovation?' George asked, with genuine interest. Jack nodded in response. 'Quick turn over or forever home?'

'Somewhere to settle, I hope,' Jack replied, his eyes darting to Ellie poignantly. George nodded in feigned understanding and turned his own attention to her.

'Hope you don't mind me popping by unannounced. Thought I'd just see how you're getting on. Check you don't need anything.'

'You can pick up a tool or a paintbrush if you like,' Ellie offered, then burst out laughing at George's horrified expression. 'I'm joking, I'm joking! Do you want to come through and see the garden first? I've just cleared all the overgrowth, so you'll be able to see the potential, not to mention the actual size of the garden.'

And with that, Ellie led George through the cottage and out into the back garden, leaving Jack alone in the carcass of Mrs Pascoe's kitchen.

# Chapter Thirteen

'I don't even know if the old thing still works, but Mother said it should be in here,' George's muffled voice could be heard from the outer side of an old stone shed. The sunlight beamed through the gaps of the wooden door and dust particles bounced on something large covered under dust sheets. The iron bolt on the old wooden door - swollen from damp and age - was wrenched open with a loud clunk as George and Ellie peered into the darkness.

'It's just the same as I remember it,' George chuckled, pulling the sheets off the 1961 Massey Ferguson 35 and instantly feeling eight-years-old again. The 'super red' paint was as vibrant as it had been the day George's grandfather had given the old thing a new spruce of life, after buying it from a local auction.

George had felt a rush of excitement from seeing the old bit of machinery again, but nothing in comparison to the animated celebratory dance Ellie was currently pulling off next to him.

'Oh my god, oh my god! How long have I been working for you? Why is this the first I'm hearing of this beauty?' Ellie practically squealed. She went to rush forward, but seemed to remember herself, glancing at George with pleading eyes.

George laughed and gestured an invitation. 'Be my guest.'

Ellie scuffled forwards like an animated child in a sweet shop and swung a leg around to sit at the wheel. She dipped her head and located the key still in the ignition. 'Top notch security here, I see.'

George flinched. 'Christ. My grandfather was never the most careful of people.'

'Rural crime is a thing, you know,' Ellie said, giving the key a jiggle until it finally clunked clockwise and engaged the engine. It choked and died out several times, Ellie persevering rigorously. George waited in anticipation, watching her in awe as she finally succeeded, the old engine firing up and settling into a chugging rhythm. Like some strange epiphany, amongst the dust and the dirt, his gaze was glued to her as she feathered the throttle and tested all the gears with the confidence of a person who knew her way around machinery, her hair glimmering auburn in the natural light and those freckles accentuated. She bore old dungarees over a tatty white t-shirt and clunky, old work boots - and yet, right now, she was radiant.

'What?' Ellie asked, pulling him back from his dream-like state and looking self-conscious all of a sudden, hooking a curl of hair behind her ear.

'Nothing. I've just never seen a girl so easily excited over an old tractor before,' George said, smiling fondly.

'Ssh!' Ellie hushed, leaning forward, and placing a hand on either side of the bonnet. 'She'll hear you!'

George attempted to shake some sense into himself as his heart swelled in a ridiculous manner. Clearing his throat, he sprang into action and gave the double doors of the old outbuilding a shove out into the open yard, giving way for the tractor. 'Go and give her a spin then.'

'You not coming?' Ellie said, sounding disappointed. He hesitated at this, suddenly forgetting all other plans and appointments he had this afternoon and simply wanting to just hop on and take the tractor out with her. What on earth was the matter with him today?

'I really shouldn't...'

'Oh, come on. Have a bit of fun, for once,' Ellie said, grinning mischievously. George felt the irony in this and wanted to laugh. Not that long ago, back in Italy, people might have said he did nothing but have fun. It was only since taking his place as Lord of the estate that the fun had stopped, and responsibility had kicked in like a punch to the gut. It had only been a few months and yet his life had changed drastically. He was still trying to figure out whether it was for worse or for better. This was Ellie's way of basically saying 'lighten up'! He realised at that moment that Ellie only knew him as this newly serious version of George. She was right. He needed to 'lighten up' - just for a bit.

He leapt onto the trailer attached behind and Ellie gave a little whoop of victory.

'You're a bad influence, you are,' George teased, trying to ignore the dusting his expensive Italian jeans were getting.

'Thank goodness for that,' Ellie replied, wrenching the gear stick forward into first. 'I'd hate to be a good influence.' And with that, she expertly raised the clutch, the tractor springing forward and crawling out of the shed for the first time in years.

The old relic had a surprising amount of spirit to it, effortlessly transporting both George, Ellie, and the trailer to the far side of the parkland, where piles and piles of logs lay waiting to be collected and stored for weathering. A metal log-cutter stand had been left amongst the sawdust and chippings, and a bonfire pile had been started out of branches and foliage from the felled trees.

'You've been busy,' George remarked, hopping off the trailer just as Ellie secured the tractor and cut the engine. Peace was reinstated around them, and the sound of birds twittering could be heard again.

'You'll be surprised how much I can get through with my old chainsaw,' Ellie said, smiling proudly at the fruits of her labour. 'Joseph is to thank for a lot of this as well. He's been out here all week, lugging logs around. He asked to have a day in the Kitchen

Garden today for a rest.' Ellie chuckled at this, and George noticed a sort of fondness cross her pretty features. Like a teacher speaking about her students.

'You're amazing.' It was said before George had a chance to stop himself. Ellie's face flushed instantly but he didn't care, she needed to hear it. 'You are! The difference you've made to not only the gardens but to the growing team as well. You did all that. And I think you really enjoy it too. The pride in your face talking about Joseph, your little apprentice. It says it all, really.' He crossed his arms across his chest and gave Ellie a challenging look, one eyebrow raised, and the corner of his mouth lifted into a smirk. 'Aren't you glad that I encouraged you to take the job on now?'

'Emotionally blackmailed, you mean?' Ellie teased, before giving in and nodding. 'I do love it. I really do.' She gazed out across the parkland, her chest rising as she took in a lungful of fresh open air.

'Thank you,' George said.

'For what?'

'For everything you've done - everything you're doing. Couldn't do it without you.'

This seemed to take Ellie aback, her eyes widening as she continued to look out across the estate, her cheeks now ablaze. 'That's nice to hear.' Her eyes met his and she smiled warmly. 'It would be a shame for all this effort to go to waste though. You need to open the gardens up to the public again.'

George nodded, knowing she was right and feeling guilty that his sister Tressa had been telling him so for so much longer.

'And your sister Tressa has all the ideas for it,' Ellie added, as if she had been reading his mind. 'I know she cocked up a bit with the overspending.'

'Three thousand pounds worth of overspending,' George reminded her, nodding for her to continue.

'Okay, big time cocked up. But she does have some amazing

ideas.'

'I'll speak to her. I think starting with the open day would be a good test run. We can talk about the possibility of being open more regularly after that.'

Ellie nodded and started the arduous task of lifting the logs onto the trailer. 'That's fair. Now roll up your sleeves and help me with these logs.'

'Thought you coaxed me out here to 'lighten up'. Not to do manual labour!'

'Nothing better to loosen the tension than a bit of fresh air and physical work. That's what my Paps used to say.'

Realising that he would need to keep up with this girl as she heaved several logs onto the trailer at a time, George shook off his jacket, unfastened his shirt cuffs and rolled his sleeves up as Ellie had requested. His tanned forearms now exposed to the sun, his back and torso now benefiting from the breeze felt through the thin material of his linen shirt, he couldn't help but smile as he caught Ellie looking. Perhaps she wasn't as immune to his looks as she made out. That was a minor relief to George. He'd been beginning to think his age had caught up on him and he no longer had the charms he once had with the ladies in his life back in Milan. Or that perhaps Cornish girls were harder to impress.

He hoisted some of the damp logs into his arms, his shirt immediately soaked from the excess moisture. That was going to be an expensive dry-cleaning bill. He was surprised at how heavy the logs were and equally at how strong Ellie was to be throwing the logs onto the trailer like they weighed nothing.

'What do your parents do for a living then? Was it them who got you into gardening?'

Ellie began laughing bitterly and George knew he'd asked the wrong thing. 'Ah, jeez. I hate it when this dreaded question comes up.'

'I'm so sorry, I shouldn't have asked,' George spluttered. 'I'm sorry for your loss.'

'No, nothing like that. I don't know my dad. Never have and never will because even my mum doesn't know who he is.' George struggled to hide his expression. 'Don't ask. And my mum... where do I start with Mum? I mean, besides having a one-night stand with some bloke when she was just eighteen, getting pregnant with me and then spending the next two or three decades chasing her youth... you get the picture. Nanny was furious but supportive and was very hands on from the moment I came along. But my mum soon got fidgety and wanted to travel.'

George was speechless as he listened intently, his arms fixed around the log he was still holding.

'It's why I live with Nanny,' Ellie continued, looking suddenly embarrassed. 'It's why I *still* live with my eighty-nine-year-old grandmother at the lame age of thirty-two. Not that I don't enjoy living with Nanny - couldn't imagine not living with her actually. But my mum has... some problems with her health... mentally. Have had to bail her out of some sticky financial issues in the past.' Ellie stumbled her way through the explanation, dodging details which George did not pry on further. 'That's why I never completed college or went on to do any more big qualifications really. And with Nanny's age behind her, and a next-to-nothing pension... the money had to come from somewhere. So, I've been working as much as I can to pay the bills and keep money back whenever my mum decides to make another stupid decision on her travels. Think she's in India at the moment, staying at an Indian Ashram. Probably pretending to be Julia Roberts in *Eat, Pray, Love.*' Ellie rolled her eyes and huffed out a large breath of frustration. Silence fell between them for a moment as a buzzard mewed loudly in the sky above them.

'Bet you wish you never asked now, don't you?' Ellie chuckled, side-glancing at him self-consciously. George gave her a smile which he hoped would be received as something of comfort and admiration - and not pity. Because he felt nothing but admiration for her right now.

'Your Nanny is eighty-nine years old?'

With that, Ellie burst into laughter. 'That's what you got from that sad little tale of my childhood. She is remarkably well-preserved for her age.'

'Remarkably well-preserved,' George agreed, grinning from ear-to-ear. 'Right, I'll avoid questions about your family from here on out. Can we get these soggy logs shifted now please? I've ruined an expensive shirt and I'm freezing my gonads off now.'

'That's what you get for dressing like an expensive ponce all the time,' Ellie retaliated, not missing a beat. 'You need to get yourself some decent outdoor wear.' Their laughter could be heard from all corners of the estate as they finally cracked on with the task in hand.

\*\*\*

Later that evening, warmth from the day was still present in the southern parts of the house and an orange glow streamed in through the windows from the setting sun. George found Tressa in the library, lounging across a velvet chaise longue like some regal character from a period novel. Resisting the urge to roll his eyes towards the ceiling, George took a deep breath and stepped into the room.

'You want to organise a public day? Go for it,' George blurted out, one hand on his hip and the other making strange attempts at authoritative gestures which mostly consisted of pointing at the floor. 'You have a budget of one thousand pounds, and not a penny more. And it's just the gardens in this instance. Granny would have a fit at the ideal of the general public traipsing in through the house. Not to mention the entire place needs redecorating and we don't have the money for it. So... a thousand pounds. Try to triple that in takings. Then maybe we can start buying paint, or something.'

There was a pause between them as George waited for a response, out of breath from his nervous outburst, whilst Tressa remained annoyingly still... poised even.

'Right,' George said, awkwardly. 'That's all I have to say. You'll need to liaise with Ellie in regard to the gardens.'

George turned on his heel and was ready to exit when Tressa finally replied. 'What changed your tune?'

'Sorry?' George said, prickly.

'Just yesterday you were chewing my ear off about the money I had spent for future events. All investments by the way, but we won't go into that again. And now this!' Tressa's tinkering laugh made George's eye twitch as he gritted his teeth. 'She's got right under your skin!'

'What are you talking about?' George huffed, suddenly feeling fourteen-years-old again when he and Tressa would relentlessly wind each other up.

'Ellie, of course. I'm glad of it. She's a nice girl.' His face must have betrayed him as Tressa laughed some more. 'Relax, brother. It will do you good to dote upon a girl like her. And thank you. I'll start the preparations tomorrow.'

Utterly perplexed and - for once - speechless, George simply nodded and took himself off to freshen up before dinner, with visions of Ellie's auburn curls and sapphire blue eyes at the forefront of his mind.

# Chapter Fourteen

Ellie practically skipped home that evening, along her little lane and back down to the hamlet along the river. After an afternoon of humping logs with George, exchanging stories and getting to know him on a whole new level, Ellie's heart was bursting, and her cheeks ached from the dopey smiles that had spread across her face the entire time. As much as she'd scorned Jack for his comments on George's clothes, she had to admit even she was glad to see George let loose from his tailor-cut suits, rolling up his sleeves and getting hands-on with the tasks around the estate. She had politely pointed out to George that people much preferred a leader who led from the front. Someone who wasn't afraid to get involved in the physical labour - and he'd agreed with her.

'Evening, Ellie!' Larry Franklin chirped from his little front patio, watering his plants. 'Another late one, I see?'

'You know me, Larry,' Ellie said, beaming up at one of her old neighbours. 'Your geraniums are looking lovely!'

'Thank you, me 'ansome. How's the job going?'

'Love it,' Ellie replied.

'I bet those gardens are looking spectacular this time of year. I haven't set foot on that estate for some twenty year now. Used to love their annual open days, we did.'

'Well, keep your ears to the ground. Not set in stone yet, but you never know.'

Larry chuckled gleefully and waved Ellie off as she bid him goodnight.

Negotiating the little garden gate, Ellie's jovial nature dimmed at the sound of Nanny coughing and hacking inside the cottage. She really needed to convince her to see a doctor. Nanny's cough had been getting increasingly worse over the weeks. Inside the kitchen, the windows were fogged with condensation and the pots bubbling away menacingly on the old stove. Steadying herself with a hand on the counter, Nanny erupted into another fit of hacks. Ellie rushed over to the bay window and wrenched it open to clear the air, then gently but firmly guided Nanny away from the kitchen area towards the little breakfast table to take over the cooking. Despite her resistance, Nanny did as she was told and took a seat, though she grumbled inaudibly under her breath as Ellie turned down the hobs and checked the pork chops inside the oven.

'You trying to set fire to the place, or something?' Ellie exclaimed.

'That's enough of that cheek, thank you very much,' Nanny grumbled, placing her handkerchief over her mouth to cough again. Deciding the pans were under control, Ellie reached up for a glass, filled it with water and plonked it in front of Nanny. She frowned as she watched her frail hand bring it shakily to her thin lips, sipping it and placing it back down in relief. 'Thanks, my love. Those chops will need turning.'

Ellie did what was needed, dished the food up ten minutes later and sat at the table with Nanny, glancing at her occasionally in deep concern.

'You can stop looking at me like some sort of invalid, an' all,' Nanny grumbled again. 'I'm eighty-nine years old. I'm allowed to cough without raising concerns, aren't I?'

'It's because you're eighty-nine years old and coughing like you just smoked a twenty-pack which concerns me, Nan.'

'Well, happens to the best of us,' Nanny said matter-of-factly, as she cut into a boiled potato. 'Take me now, I say.'

Ellie kept quiet, chewing on her pork chop to stop herself from biting back. She really hated it when Nanny made comments like that, like she was welcoming the Grim Reaper at the door with open arms. Like she was giving up. Nanny had always been as strong as an ox, so talk like this just didn't sit right with Ellie.

'How was work?' Nanny asked, like she did every evening.

Ellie's smile must have given her away as she nodded and said, 'it was good.'

'Oh, dear Lord. I know that dopey expression.'

'What?' Ellie protested, through a mouthful of potato. 'I said it was good. Got the rest of the logs shifted up to the yard for weathering. Dave's repaired the cold frames in the Melon Yard so I can crack on and gloss them tomorrow. George seems quite happy with the progress. Today, he actually got hands-on and helped out in the parkland with me.'

Nanny listened politely as Ellie listed all the achievements from this week. She was semi-aware of mentioning George's name more times than was necessary and Nanny's eyes narrowed in response.

'You've taken a bit of a liking to him, haven't you?' It was more of an accusation than a question. Ellie merely shrugged, not denying it, then jumped in her seat as Nanny dropped her cutlery onto her plate with a loud clatter. 'If you'll excuse me, I'm not feeling very well. I'm going to bed.'

As Nanny heaved herself out of the chair, a bewildered Ellie also stood up and gave her some assistance with her stick. 'Why are you so cross, Nanny?'

'What about Jack, you silly child?' Nanny suddenly blurted.

'What about him?'

'You know exactly what I mean. That poor boy has been head over heels for you since he moved here.'

Ellie shook her head, keeping her temper at bay. 'We're

good friends, Nanny. Nothing more.'

'Utter rubbish!' Nanny spat, waving off Ellie's help and shuffling her way towards the kitchen door leading to the hallway. 'You two have had something good going here for the past year at least. Then some fancy Lord comes along and distracts you from him. Poor boy d'unt stand a chance.'

'Do you know what, I think it *is* time for your bed, Nan,' Ellie fired up, her temper getting the better of her. 'And your bleddy meds. And you're going to the doctors tomorrow, whether you like it or not. I'm calling them first thing and driving you there myself.'

Nanny grumbled and griped her way out of the kitchen and shut the door of her downstairs bedroom with surprising force for her age. Ellie stood in the kitchen and closed her eyes, shaking her head sadly. What on earth had happened once for Nanny to feel such hatred towards the estate, and George for that matter? She was frozen to the spot for a moment before she gave herself a little shake and proceeded to tidy up.

Gloria Curnow had a temper, there was no denying that. It's where Ellie had got hers. But this was a step too far, even for her hot-headed demeanour.

When the kitchen was all cleared, Ellie brought Nanny a cup of tea and a rice pudding for her supper. She was so small and frail, now in her nightgown and tucked up under her sheets reading a magazine.

'Got you some supper,' Ellie muttered, pushing her back against the door and squeezing herself in.

'Thanks, my love,' Nanny mumbled, as Ellie placed the tea and rice pudding on her bedside table. Ellie gasped as she heard sniffles and realised her dear Nanny was crying. She grabbed Nanny's frail hand and gave it a squeeze. 'I've been a right rotten so-and-so. What must you think of me!'

'Stop it! Don't be so bloody daft. We're both as stubborn as the other,' Ellie said, sitting on the edge of Nanny's bed, her hand still encased around hers. 'Nan. If it's causing you too much pain, should... should I call it a day at the estate?'

'Don't you bloody dare!' Nanny said, fiercely. 'Don't you bloody dare, my dear girl. You're clearly very happy working there and I'm just being a miserable old woman.'

Ellie tried to choose her next words very carefully. She didn't want to start another argument, but at the same time she was desperate to know. 'Nan, when you saw George for the first time, he said that you seemed upset. Something about his grandfather.'

Nanny nodded. 'Charles Penhaligon.'

'What happened?' Ellie pleaded. 'Something must have happened for you to get so upset.'

'It was a very long time ago, and it doesn't matter anymore. I married your dear Paps and lived a wonderful, fulfilling life.'

'Nan, did you and-'

'It doesn't matter now,' Nanny said, firmly. 'Like I said, it was a long time ago. Thank you for my supper, my love. I'll be going to sleep in a minute if you don't mind.'

Accepting her loss, Ellie nodded and kissed her Nanny goodnight. As she reached the threshold of the door, Nanny called to her. 'Ellie, my love. Please don't call the doctors tomorrow.'

'But your cough!' Ellie protested.

'I'm almost in my nineties. I'm bound to have some ailments. It's probably all the pollen in the air. Please, my love. Let me see how I am in a week's time.'

Again, Ellie knew when she wasn't going to win, and repeated her good nights before closing the bedroom door gently.

It was only 9pm with a bit of the daylight and warmth lingering into a quiet summer's evening. Ellie decided she needed to clear her head and so grabbed her hoodie and trainers before rushing down to her little boat at the bottom of the garden. It sat there, bobbing gently against the embankment, sulking pitifully from its weeks of not being used. It had been used every day for many years, but since Ellie had gotten the job at the estate, she had not needed so many ventures out on the water to reach her river-side neighbours.

She had been light as a feather earlier and now her heart felt heavy with niggling concern. Getting out onto the water never usually failed to calm her and so she gave her little boat a guilty pat, gave it a gentle push and leapt on board, allowing herself to drift out into the centre of the estuary. Her thoughts were filled with speculations about Nanny's past and growing worry for the woman's refusal to see a doctor, as she gathered the oars and dipped them inside the still water. Ellie immediately released a deep, long sigh as she drew through the first stroke, propelling herself along and in the direction of Jack's. It was often the default direction she took, and this evening was no exception - even if Jack had been one of the hot topics for her and Nanny's disagreement.

She channelled her focus on the boat, on her arm muscles protesting as they pulled the little vessel along. Perhaps going out rowing after a day of lumping logs around wasn't the best decision. Every now and again, she would pass a property, their garden sloping up to the house where residents were out watering their thirsty plants after a hot day. The odd neighbour would catch sight of Ellie and give her a little wave, to which she returned merrily, despite the heavy pit in her stomach. And when she rounded another bend, Jack's property coming into view, she realised with a disappointing jolt that all his windows were dark with no sign of life inside. Unusual for him, as most evenings it beamed with light in at least two of the rooms where he was doing renovation work. No, tonight it was clearly all shut up and Jack had gone out. Perhaps he had gone to the pub.

With new-found determination, Ellie continued to row, this time towards the mooring area just down from their local. It was a steep climb up four flights of concrete steps to The Old Creek Inn, when she'd finally tied up her boat. The mezzanine patio was peppered with loud and merry people drinking ciders and beers, some disguised behind clouds of cigarette smoke. Inside, the Inn was packed with bodies and Ellie squeezed herself through the crowd to get to the bar.

'Alright, my love?' Gary, one of the bartenders, called out to her as he pulled down on a tap. 'Jack's around. Not sure where though.'

'Thanks, Gary. Busy tonight!'

'Silly season is upon us!'

She didn't recognise a vast majority of the crowd, which often happened in the peak seasons when holiday makers were about. She continued to push her way gently through, but Jack was nowhere in sight. She was about ready to call it a day when she found herself sandwiched in by a small group of men, who clearly had had too much to drink.

'Excuse me,' Ellie mumbled at someone's chest, trying to find a gap to slip through.

'No problem, love,' the man slurred, humour in his voice. 'Can I buy you a drink?'

A scattering of chuckles rippled through the men and Ellie gritted her teeth. 'No, thanks. Just trying to find my friend.'

'I can be your friend,' one said.

'I can be more than a friend,' another added.

'Piss off,' Ellie spat, now shoving herself through and scatting two of them flying. A proceeding of leers and cackles erupted behind her as she finally clocked eyes on Jack, who had just come back into the bar area from the toilets. He saw her and gave a little wave.

'Alright? You look hacked off,' Jack observed as Ellie approached him and took a place at the side of the bar with him.

'That's because of those assholes over there.'

Jack looked over Ellie's head to see who she was referring

to. 'Ah yes - the stag group. Gary's already given them a warning and refused to sell any more drinks to two of them. I think one of them has puked in the loo, too.'

'Classy,' Ellie murmured, sending them some shooting looks before ordering a lemonade from one of the younger barmaids. 'How was your day?'

'Was alright,' Jack said, non-committing. He leaned his forearms onto the bar and accepted a cider which had been placed next to Ellie's lemonade. Upon closer inspection, Ellie realised this must be his third or fourth cider, going by the gentle swaying he was now adopting.

'Jack?' Ellie cooed, placing a hand on Jack's forearm. 'Are you alright?' She was relieved at least when he placed a large, warm hand over hers, picked it up and encased it with the other.

'I'm a bit tipsy,' He admitted.

'I can see that,' Ellie said, smiling. She then leaned her head on his shoulder, some of the tightness from earlier loosening as she realised things were redeemable between her and Jack. 'Nanny isn't very well, and she won't let me take her to the doctors.'

'Well, we know where you get your stubbornness from. Ow!' Jack let out a high-pitched squeal which didn't match his size, in protest of Ellie's elbow driving into his ribs. They both watched as the stag group cleared out through the entrance, leaving the Inn noticeably less rowdy.

'Thank God for that,' Ellie muttered.

'They really annoyed you, didn't they?'

'They'd have annoyed you too, if you'd seen the way they'd herded around me just a minute ago. I'm no delicate flower, but even I found them a bit intimidating.'

Jack looked down at her, his expression darkening. 'I didn't realise they'd tried it on with you. Bloody wankers. I'll go and have a word with them...'

'Don't you dare!' Ellie cried, grabbing Jack's arm, and pulling him back onto the bar stool. 'They're gone now. Let's just have a nice drink and a catch up. I feel like we haven't had this for a long time.'

Jack smiled and agreed, swigging his cider, and reaching for a pack of playing cards on the side of the bar. 'Go Fish or Rummy?'

It was a short but enjoyable thirty minutes of catching up, playing a couple of games, and finishing their drinks before Ellie decided she'd best head back, realising she would now be rowing back in the dark. She offered to row Jack home to the bottom of his garden too, not trusting him to walk home safely whilst intoxicated. Stepping outside onto the mezzanine patio, Jack got distracted chatting to some regulars whilst Ellie checked that she had enough battery on her phone to use it as a torch.

'Ellie!' It was Jessica, one of the girls who worked in the kitchen. 'Did you bring your rowing boat tonight?'

'Yeah, why?'

'You need to get down to the mooring. Some guys have hijacked it onto the water.'

Ellie cussed loudly and took off towards the concrete steps, only semi-aware of Jack calling after her and following closely behind. When she got down to the bottom, she found three of the same men who had herded her earlier out on her little boat metres away from where she'd left it. The night was filled with their hyena-like laughter as they rocked the boat side-to-side, both oars floating in the water far out of reach. On dry land, two police officers were now attempting to coax them back in whilst the remainder of the group howled in mirth at their friends' antics.

'Fellas, you need to get back over here now - for your safety,' one of the officers barked, firmly. 'And you lot pipe down.'

'What the hell?' Ellie gasped, standing in between the officers and the remaining stags. 'That's my bloody boat!' Jack finally caught up and stood behind her.

'Don't worry, we'll get it back. These lot have had too much to drink,' the female officer said. 'One of the other boat owners must have called them in and we got sent over. What's your name?'

'Ellie Curnow.'

'Okay, Ellie. Bear with us and we'll get your boat back.'

'Alright, Ellie?' one of the men heckled, splashing his beer all over the ground. 'How's about that drink, now? I can do more than rock your boat, tonight!'

The jeers and laughter were cut short from the group as Jack launched himself at them in a fury Ellie had never seen before, his fist making contact with the bloke's jaw. There was a brief commotion as both Ellie and the officers threw themselves into the mix, each trying to separate the aggressors before it turned into a full fight. Ellie positioned herself in front of Jack and pushed him away, encouraging him to calm down.

'Jack, don't!'

'Yeah, Jack. Down, boy. Listen to your missus.'

There was a horrifying crunch followed by a crack as one of the stags on board her poor boat put their foot right through the floor, crashing into a drunken heap. A fresh wave of giggles and cackling erupted from the group which sent Ellie's rage flying through the sky, and before she could calculate right from wrong, she was shoulder barging the closest drunk straight into the water.

'We need backup at the Old Creek,' the officer shouted into his radio. 'Backup and a van at the Old Creek, now.'

A peaceful evening on the river turned into a night of chaos as Ellie's arms were restrained by the female officer, closely followed by Jack being restrained as he attempted another drunken launch at the men. A cacophony of shouts and commands surrounded them, footsteps descending the concrete steps from the pub as half of the customers, and even Gary, came down to witness the scene unravel. And yet just one figure stood out from the crowd as Ellie realised who it was.

It was George. He looked down over the slate wall from the top of the steps in muted horror, a far cry from the expression he had worn only this afternoon - the kind of expression which had caused butterflies in her stomach. Now, she wanted the ground to swallow her up as she, Jack and the drunken stags were gathered under control like criminals. A police van arrived, blue lights flashing silently against the white front of the Inn and filling the darkness with blinding lights. After that, it was hard to pick out any faces and George's disappointed face disappeared into the night.

# Chapter Fifteen

On what felt like the hottest day of the year so far, the scorching sun sweltered down on the Italian gardens, and the limestone from Penhaligon House beamed cheerfully. Dave and Joseph could be seen giving the plants under shade a good watering before they too would be under the summer rays. Inside the house, in the drawing room, Ellie shrank into one of the mahogany desk chairs whilst George sat casually on an adjacent wing-backed armchair, a coffee poised in his tanned hands. He observed Ellie for a long time whilst her eyes darted notably towards the door and the open window, flooding with sunlight.

'So, you pushed a man into the river,' George stated, as if this was perfectly normal behaviour. He had noticed the darkness under Ellie's eyes and a look of worry on those features the moment she'd come into work this morning, and knew he'd have to go easy on her. She'd had a rough night.

'More importantly, said *man* and his chums stole my boat.'

'I heard,' George said. When Ellie looked at him questioningly, he replied. 'I'd heard there was a commotion down at the Inn and that the police had been called. I went down to offer my assistance and find my Head Gardener is one of the people getting arrested.'

'Didn't get arrested,' Ellie pointed out. 'Just a slap on the wrist.'

'It's not great for business, though - is it?' George pointed out, sternly. 'Having the Head Gardener of the estate *almost* arrested.'

'Do you know what else isn't great for business? Having your work boat trashed by a bunch of drunken bell-ends.'

George frowned and appraised Ellie some more, watching her body become more shut off the more defensive she became. 'Would you like some coffee?'

'No, thank you.'

'Some water maybe? I'm sure you've probably got the hangover of the century after last night.'

Ellie's arms became uncrossed as she sat up, looking enraged. 'I wasn't drinking! Look, Nan went to bed early because she wasn't feeling very well. We'd had a bit of a barney, so I took the boat out to clear my head. Ended up at the pub and had a catch up with Jack - who, admittedly was a bit tipsy. I had a lemonade and was there for less than an hour. In that time, those... assholes harassed me, hijacked my boat, and kicked a hole in the bottom with their big fat foot.'

'They harassed you?' George asked, trying to keep a growl out of his voice as something undetectable rose from within him.

'Yes! Circled me like a bunch of horny teenagers. Don't look so concerned, I can handle myself.'

'Clearly,' George agreed, a hint of humour in his voice despite himself. 'And you're sure you weren't drunk.'

'George, I don't drink. At all. So yeah, pretty sure.'

'Oh.' He was surprised for some reason, like an adult going to the pub and not drinking was unheard of. A flash of annoyance crossed his face then at the thought of those idiots giving Ellie unwanted behaviour and suddenly he was pleased with her actions. He was about to tell her so when there was a loud honk of a vehicle outside on the drive. Ellie and George exchanged confused looks and rushed to the front door, George wrenching the old Georgian door open to reveal a 1981 Citroen H van chugging to a throaty stop in front of them. Wenna jumped out from the driver's door and skipped on over to give them both a hug in the way of a greeting.

'Good morning, love birds!' She sang, then stopped suddenly at the sight of George's expression. 'What?'

'Nothing!' George snarled, pointedly. He tried to send a non-verbal message her way signifying that what they had discussed yesterday had been called off and things had changed, drastically. He quickly changed the topic over to the strange piece of scrap metal sat before him, hoping Ellie hadn't fully acknowledged what Wenna had blurted out. 'What the hell is that?'

'Feast your eyes on Penhaligon Estate's new venture!'

'An old banger,' George said, deadpan.

'For God's sake, brother. You have no imagination. It's going to be a coffee van - obviously! My coffee van.'

'That's a brilliant idea!' Ellie exclaimed, stepping forward to take a closer look at the old relic. 'Can I pop the hood?'

'Beg your pardon?' Wenna asked.

'The bonnet. Can I look at the engine?'

'Oh!' Wenna cried, laughing. 'Absolutely! Be my guest!'

Whilst Ellie opened the bonnet to reveal the old engine, Wenna rushed over to her brother with a questioning look.

'What happened?' Wenna whispered fiercely. George hushed her back, batting her away.

'Not now!' George whispered. A few silent gestures were passed between them before George shooed his sister back towards the van, where Ellie was now headfirst inside the bonnet, admiring the engine.

'How's it looking in there, Ellie?' Wenna asked, laughing. 'Is this where you tell me the engine is held together with Sellotape or something?'

'Not at all!' Ellie said, pulling herself out and wiping her hands on her work trousers, adding oil stains to the existing grass and paint stains. 'Looks in pretty good shape for its age to be honest. The engine looks newer than the van, and well maintained - so should be okay.'

'Phew, that's a relief!' Wenna breathed, giving her brother a nervous side-eye.

George's eyes narrowed as he looked over to the family cars. 'Wenna, how did you pay for this? Where's your little Ibiza?'

'Sold it,' Wenna replied, scrunching her nose up nervously. 'Bid for this on eBay and collected from Bideford last night. Slept in Tesco carpark in Wadebridge actually, because I got tired. So, if you'll excuse me, I'm going to pop off and have a shower. Don't give me that look, brother! You'll see that it will be a fantastic asset to our new events venture here in the estate. Our own pop-up coffee van!'

'You haven't made a single coffee in your life,' George pointed out, as Wenna passed him to head through the front door.

'I'll sign up to a course or something later. Bye, Ellie! Catch you later.'

'Another course,' George sighed, when Wenna had disappeared into the depths of the house. 'She won't have the first clue about running a coffee van.'

'I don't know!' Ellie rebutted, optimistically. 'Could be the perfect job for her. She's brilliant with people and her business is mobile, so at least she can change up her scenery whenever she gets bored.'

George snorted and nodded, agreeing with her. 'You know her well then. She really does have the attention span of a flea, so this won't last. May be useful for the open day though. Do you reckon something can be done with this thing in time for that?'

'Oh, easily! I don't mind helping her out.'

'By helping her out, you do know it'll mean 'doing it all', George pointed out, wryly. 'My sister isn't one for getting her hands dirty.'

'We'll see,' Ellie smirked. 'Now, are you done lecturing me? Just, I've got a lot to do.'

'I wasn't lecturing you!' George argued. Ellie snorted, crossing her arms in disbelief. 'Okay, I *was*. I didn't know the full story. Wish I could have chucked them all in the river myself now.'

The annoyance on Ellie's face slipped and she uncrossed her arms. 'Oh.'

George cleared his throat, suddenly feeling uncharacteristically self-conscious. 'What did... I mean... Jack couldn't have been too happy about the whole ordeal.'

'Not massively.'

A loaded pause fell between them. George searched for something to say, fighting the urge to ask Ellie about her and Jack. Because from what he had seen last night, there was clearly an Ellie and Jack, and all the signals George had thought Ellie had been sending him yesterday afternoon he had misread completely. He opened his mouth to speak just as Joseph rounded the corner, calling for Ellie.

'Ellie, there's been a delivery down in the coach yard. I think you need to sign for it.'

'Be right there!' Ellie replied. She turned to George. 'All good?'

'Yeah! Yeah, all good,' George said, waving her off. He glanced at Wenna's van and released a sigh of exasperation before heading back into the house himself.


In the afternoon, George had nestled himself into the old study. It was one of the smaller rooms of the ground floor, with mahogany panelled walls and a large desk to match, which dominated most of the room, alongside floor to ceiling bookshelves, giving the room a stuffy feel. Despite all of that, George had always liked this room, it being where his grandfather Charles had worked the estate from, and many Penhaligon men before him. When George had been a little boy, he remembered sneaking in to see his grandfather, despite being told sternly by both his mother and grandmother not to disturb him when he was working. Charles always kept a large glass jar behind his desk, filled with humbug sweets. He would give George a cheeky little wink before filling his grandson's pockets with the minty favourites and sending him back on his way. George had found the jar under the desk as soon as he'd started rummaging through all the paperwork which needed sorting. Sadly, it was empty.

In fact, the whole room seemed neglected and forgotten. He'd thrown open the window, which faced out to the small sundial garden just to the right of the main Italian gardens, and he'd slowly revealed dusted surfaces underneath mountains of unorganised paperwork for the estate. Their accountant must have a nightmare dealing with the finances for this place, George thought. Coming across an old file box, he opened it to discover some of the contracts and paperwork for the resident properties being rented down on the river. He discovered old carbon copies of receipts and invoices for rent paid from days before Direct Debits, as well as letters and Christmas cards to Charles and Beryan from grateful residents of their time. George felt a pang of guilt as he realised that he didn't know the people of his estate at all, let alone have the type of relationship where he would exchange Christmas cards or letters. He read a handful, noting the genuine love and gratitude people showed to Charles as their Lord. How times had changed.

Perhaps he could write a letter or something to his tenants, introducing himself as the new standing Lord and announcing all the plans he and his team had set out for the estate. It was a bit late coming, he admitted. But it would be a start. Yes - make some connections. Perhaps a monthly newsletter delivered free to their doors. Joseph - or maybe one of the volunteers - could do that on a quiet morning or something.

He was feeling surprisingly closed in all of a sudden, finding the confinements of the space filled with a chaos of paperwork overbearing, so he grabbed a couple of the box files and left his grandfather's study in pursuit of his laptop and somewhere more open and airier to work.

A couple of cups of coffee later and a much more comfortable spot in the library, which was now flooding with late afternoon sunlight, George had churned his way through half of his first newsletter. It had been harder than he thought, and he had found himself embellishing in parts to make the first few months of his place as Lord sound less of a snore-fest.

'You'll be glad to hear I have over twenty stallholders already for the open day,' Tressa announced as she floated into the room with her usual air of superiority. 'Fifteen pound a stall and twenty-five pounds for food vans.'

George looked up from his laptop and gave Tressa an approving look. 'That's a promising start. Oh, can you reserve a food van spot for Wenna. She's gone and got herself a van to convert into a coffee van.' He rolled his eyes, thinking Tressa would participate, but instead she lowered her notebook to glare at him.

'And you're rolling your eyes because...?' Tressa challenged.

'Well...it's Wenna!' George stuttered under Tressa's stare. 'You know how long these little ideas of hers last. She's twenty-five this year and still doesn't have a clue what she wants to do with her life.'

'Yes well, having an idea on what you want to do with your life often doesn't make the blindest bit of difference,' Tressa muttered, bitterly.

'What do you mean?' George asked, his voice not unkind as he appraised his older sister.

'Nothing,' Tressa said, now turning her attention to his laptop. 'Is that a newsletter?'

'Yes - though, a pretty dull one so far.' George leaned back in his chair, glaring at his newsletter as if it personally had annoyed him by not writing itself. 'I found a load of letters and Christmas cards to Granny and Grandfather from years ago. The people of the estate seemed to genuinely love him and everything he did. I'm pretty sure people here don't even know my name or what I look like.' He recalled the other day when he had stumbled his way through Ellie's little hamlet, and the questioning looks he had received from some of the villagers.

'It's not just you, believe me. You've been away living the Italian dream, whilst I've been stuck here the entire time. I shouldn't have thought anyone would know me either.'

'But why is that?' George asked, leaning forward in his chair. 'How have we dropped our public relations with the estate so much! We're still claiming rent from these poor people, but we do nothing for community spirit.'

'You're asking the wrong person,' Tressa sighed, perching herself on the arm of George's chair and reading his first draft over his shoulder. 'This is...'

'Boring,' George affirmed.

'Why don't you do a Vlog?' Tressa suggested.

'You're joking, right?' George said, arching an eyebrow. 'Can you see me doing a Vlog?'

'Well, yes actually. Not to expand your head any more than it is, but you're charismatic and - apparently - attractive.' This time it was Tressa's turn to roll her eyes. 'I could never bring friends home after school because they would all turn to inarticulate mush whenever they saw you. And don't act like you didn't know! You appeared everywhere we went, flexing like a total ponce.'

George pulled a face which showed he couldn't deny it, then burst out laughing. 'I was such a tool!'

'Such a tool,' Tressa agreed, smiling. 'Come on, then. Let's go.'

'What?'

'Film the Vlog. If we start in the entrance hall, then you can take the viewers around the garden and give them a taster of what is to see for the open day. It will double up as advertising for the event. Maybe we can get Ellie in on it and you can do a cute little interview or something.'

'Jesus Christ,' George muttered under his breath, hoisting himself out of his chair and following Tressa obediently towards the entrance hall.

# Chapter Sixteen

Penhaligon Estate's first public open day in over thirty years was fast approaching. With the date finally set for the last weekend of July, preparations were fast under way. Ellie had never been so busy, ensuring every part of the gardens was fit for the public eye, not to mention safe to walk through. Her and Tressa had been working tirelessly over the last couple of weeks, figuring out risk assessments, public liability insurance and licensing to name a few. The entire event had gone beyond Ellie's duties as Head Gardener, but she had to admit that she was enjoying it, albeit a little stressed over the whole ordeal. And yet it wasn't this which had kept her awake for the last few nights.

'Ernie is coming back?' Ellie had gasped when George had first broken the news on the Friday night. 'I thought you'd offered him early retirement?'

'Well, I had,' George had replied, bashful. 'But I'd given him time to think about it. He hadn't actually confirmed his decision. I thought, with some time at home with his wife, he might have come to the conclusion himself that retirement was the best option.'

'So - what - I'm out of a job?' Ellie had scoffed, her eyes filled with hurt and panic.

'No! Absolutely not! He will just want to do the odd shift here and there. Keep his toe in, so-to-speak. Your position does not change. We need you.'

George had done his best that afternoon to ease Ellie's concerns, but she couldn't help feeling like things were about to go pear shaped for her. It wasn't like her, and George were on the best terms since the boat issue. He'd seemed distant ever since and so Ellie, annoyed with his reservations, hadn't made much of an effort herself.

It was now the day of Ernie's return and there was a ripple of unease coming from Ellie, George, Dave, and Joseph - even Lavinia, who was finally starting to show small appreciations for the work Ellie and her team had put into the gardens and parkland.

'Eleanor, my dear,' Lavinia began, as they stepped out onto the gravelled driveway. 'Ernie is a long-standing member of this estate.'

She wasn't finished, but Ellie used her pause to direct a loaded look at George as they positioned themselves in a line in front of the house, ready to welcome Ernie.

'It will be very hard for him today, to return to the estate and find someone new in his position. And though he has done some marvellous work in his time here as Head Gardener, I'm sure he'll be able to see that you too have... done some good work here too.'

It was an improvement from what Ellie had been expecting her to say so she simply smiled and nodded, unsure what to say in response anyway and taking up her position. She felt George's eyes on her just as there was a bustle through the front door.

'I don't see why we have to stand on ceremony,' Tressa complained, throwing her long, skinny arms across her chest, and sticking some large sunglasses on her face. 'We look like a line-up of servants in a Downton Abbey episode.'

'I do have a fondness towards Ernie, you know I do Lavinia,' Beryan added, stepping out on the gravel cautiously with her cane. 'But I shan't be staying out for long. It is far too hot for me today - I cannot stand it!'

Ellie chanced a look up at George and, despite herself, shared a small smile with him as he rolled his eyes in exasperation. That smile quickly vanished however at the sound of tyres crunching on the driveway.

Ernie was far more fragile than Ellie had pictured him, and she immediately felt like the worst person in the world when a small sense of relief trickled through her at his fragility. There was no way this poor man was fit for work. So why was he here?

'Ernie, how wonderful to see you back on your feet again?' Lavinia said, the first to step forward and greet the old man with a polite kiss to the cheek. 'Hello, Mrs Jenkins. How lovely for you to join us too. George, Tressa and my mother, Beryan, you know. Wenna couldn't join us this afternoon, I'm afraid. She's off doing a barista course today. Making coffees for a new venture of hers.' Despite her best efforts, Ellie noted the snobbery in Lavinia's voice and disapproval of her daughter's new career path. As Ernie and his wife nodded politely, Ellie caught Tressa's eyes rolling to the sky. Whether it was for her mother's attitude towards Wenna's plans or Tressa's own opinion of her sister's plans, Ellie wasn't sure.

George stepped forward to greet the couple, towering above their frail frames. There was a moment of pleasantries between those who already knew each other, Dave, and Ernie clasping hands along with a gentle embrace, Dave supporting Ernie has he found his footing again. Even Joseph exchanged a timid hello with his previous boss. Ellie found herself shrinking back.

'Please come inside and we shall have a spot of tea before a tour of the gardens,' Lavinia said, waving an elegant arm towards the house in a welcoming gesture. Ellie pressed her lips together and raised her brow with a loaded expression at Joseph and Dave. Dave gave her a knowing wink, seemingly trying to sooth her rising temper.

'This is Ellie, Ernie,' George cut in, stopping his mother in her tracks as he distracted the Jenkins from their journey to the dining room. Ernie's grey eyes bored into Ellie's as he appeared to size her up. His mouth pursed in agitation whilst his wife smiled pleasantly.

'Hello, Ellie,' Mrs Jenkins said, though her smile seemed strained as she gave her husband a gentle nudge. 'Say hello to Ellie, dear.'

'Hello.' Ernie's voice was hoarse and clipped as he turned and shuffled his way towards the house, very much reliant on the crutch he now bore his weight on.

Lavinia led the way to the dining room, with Lavinia and Beryan close behind the Jenkins.

'Right, guys - let's go and make a start on that fruit cage,' Ellie said to Joseph and Dave, a heavy sigh in her voice.

'Ellie,' George began. 'Aren't you going to join us?'

Ellie's face distorted into a surprised grimace, and she shook her head. 'You don't need any of us trampling inside on those lovely carpets in our big, muddy shoes.' It was a strange comment, even Ellie had to admit. But she was cross and embarrassed. And the last thing she wanted to do right now was sit in a stuffy room, around a shiny mahogany table, feigning politeness whilst Lavinia and Beryan made endless digs in her direction. Irritation crossed George's tanned features, but he nodded all the same, accepting Ellie's decision.

'Will you at least join us for the tour, so you can talk Ernie through everything you've done?' George asked, a small plea in his voice.

Ellie nodded and held up her walkie-talkie in answer. 'We'll be in the kitchen garden. Installing your mother's fruit cage.'

'I don't understand,' Joseph declared a few minutes later, as they walked into the kitchen garden and made a start on rolling out the netting. 'Does this mean Ernie is coming back as...the Head Gardener again? Are you still staying, Ellie?'

Joseph's face was etched with concern as he looked at Ellie for an answer.

''Course Ellie is still staying, you daft boy,' Dave said, gruffly. 'Does Ernie look in much state to be running the gardens again? Now, I got a lot of time for Ernie - I've worked with him for many, many years. But I'll admit he's coming on a bit and the gardens are too big for him.'

Dave paused his monologue of the decade as the three of them simultaneously lifted the heavy roll of netting, Joseph and Dave carefully unravelling it against the metal frame whilst Ellie began securing it in place with black cable-ties.

'The garden has finally got some direction for the first time in years,' Dave continued, more out of breath this time from the heavy lifting. 'George knows that. We need you, love.' The last bit was directed at Ellie, and she suddenly stopped cable-tying to look up at Dave, her eyes swimming all of a sudden. 'Oh, bleddy hell. Forget I said anything if it's going to make you blubber. I don't manage emotional women well.'

Ellie chuckled and wiped her nose with her free hand. 'You don't know how nice it is to hear you say that, Dave.'

'Yep. Well. I don't give compliments often,' Dave said, clearing his throat and taking sudden interest at the large oak tree standing proudly over the kitchen garden wall.

'Like Dave said, Joseph,' Ellie continued, feeling some of her confidence trickling back. 'I'm not going anywhere. I'm sure Ernie will appreciate all the hard work that has been taking place over the last three months and maybe he can give us some pointers before the big day.'

Ellie glanced at Dave for some approval, and he simply smiled and nodded, affirming that she had adopted the right attitude to the bizarre situation they had found themselves in.

'Thank god for that,' Joseph said, breaking the moment. 'Ernie really scares me.'

With some new-found confidence and determination from Dave's little boost, Ellie joined the Pehaligons and the Jenkins on the garden tour as promised. But it was soon made clear to Ellie, despite her best efforts, that Ernie was far from pleased with their circumstance. She led them steadily through the flat paths of the Italian gardens first, aware of Ernie's unsteadiness on his feet. Proceeding to grunt and grumble at every attempt of Ellie's to make pleasantries and engage in conversation related to the progress of the gardens, even Ernie's wife began to lose patience.

'For goodness' sake, Ernie! I'm ever so sorry about my husband. He is being particularly difficult this morning,' Mrs Jenkins huffed.

Ellie smiled with understanding and was about to wave Mrs Jenkins apologies away when Lavinia cut in. 'Perfectly understandable. Ernie has been the heart and soul of this place for countless years. I'm sure Eleanor here would be delighted for your advice and expertise.'

That had just about done it for Ellie as her hands clenched into tight fists. Her mouth and temper were about to get the better of her when George stepped forward, placing a hot hand on her shoulder.

'Actually, Mr and Mrs Jenkins. Ellie here has been a skilled gardener since a very young age, just like you Ernie. In fact, she's been maintaining resident's gardens down along the river all this time without our knowledge. I've been speaking to the community along the estuary, and she too is the heart of that community. I think we can all agree that the gardens here on the estate are in excellent hands. Wouldn't you agree, Mother?'

There was a sternness and authority to George's voice that Ellie hadn't heard before and she watched with wonder as Lavinia shrank back without so much as a remark. Mrs Jenkins smiled widely in agreement and Ernie even had the decency to look up from the bench he had now situated himself on to give

Ellie a proper appraisal. His face was still solemn and distorted in a level of irritation, but he seemed to actually acknowledge Ellie now. She suddenly felt a wave of sympathy towards the old man, remembering now that his entire livelihood had been snatched away early from just one misjudgement of a step on a ladder.

'How lovely to have a local girl take my Ernie's place,' Mrs Jenkins said, as gracious as ever. 'We must have crossed paths at some point. We live in the next village along, you see. Do you attend the WI meetings in the old Memorial Hall?'

Ellie cleared her throat and tried to find her voice. 'No, I don't. But my Nanny does. Gloria Curnow?'

There was a strange, harrumphed sound and a smack of Beryan's cane against the gravel which Ellie chose to ignore as Mrs Jenkins burst to life. 'Yes, of course! My goodness, I know your Nanny very well. Lovely Gloria, Ernie! Ellie is her granddaughter.'

Ernie made an effort this time to find a new pitch in his monotone grumble, showing genuine interest in this news.

'We've...' Ernie gave a little cough, suddenly looking a little bashful. 'We've known Gloria for many, many years. In fact, her daughter - your mother, I assume - used to go to the Old Kea school with our two.'

'How is your mother?' Mrs Jenkins asked, pleasantly.

Ellie's pause was palpable enough to not go unnoticed, but she tried to recover herself. 'She's well, thank you.'

'I don't think we've seen your mother for many years. Does she live in Cornwall?'

'No. Actually, she's traveling through Asia at the moment, I believe.'

'Goodness, what a life! I always marvel at people who go traveling like that. How long as she been traveling for?'

It was a question she really didn't want to answer - not in front of the Penhaligons.

'A while,' she answered, vaguely.

'Well, how long exactly?' Mrs Jenkins pushed, eagerly. 'Our Goddaughter travelled for a whole year in her gap year, just before she headed to Bath Spa University. Didn't she, Ernie? Can you imagine? Travelling for a whole year!'

All attention was on Ellie all of a sudden and she realised then that she couldn't mutter her way out of this with vague answers. 'Well, she's been traveling for about...fifteen years now? On and off? Guess she's got the traveling bug!' Ellie added in the last line awkwardly, in hopes that a splash of humour would disguise the reactions of the older members amongst them. Beryan's grumbled 'good gracious me, how absurd' wasn't far off from the reaction Ellie had foreseen, and she almost chuckled at the accuracy. Ellie's eyes darted to Tressa whose usual apathetic expression was replaced with a form of interest, and then to George, who's dark brown eyes were now upon her with concern. Or was that pity? Either way, it made her uncomfortable and she now wished she could just be left alone to get on with her mountainous to-do list. Mrs Jenkins was appearing to seem as though she regretted her enquiry, and the topic was soon changed over to the upcoming open garden event.

Mr and Mrs Jenkins were soon back on their way home again an hour later, with Ernie somewhat satisfied for now that his gardens were indeed in good hands. The Penhaligon women retreated to the house and Ellie took herself to the kitchen in pursuit of something sweet for a pick-me-up. Trixie soon had her tucking into a slice of *Bakewell Tart,* a steaming hot mug of coffee in tow.

'Joseph and Dave seemed quite positive about the visit,' Trixie said, in way of comfort as Ellie stuffed big bites of tart into her mouth whilst looking miserable. 'They said Ernie admitted to liking the stumpery garden. Wasn't that the new bit you were unsure he would like?'

'He said it looked like something from Jurassic Park,' Ellie said thickly, through a mouthful of icing, sponge and almond. 'Hardly think that constitutes as liking it.'

'Oh. Well, what about the renovation of the old rill? I bet he was pleased to see the water flowing once again, with all the lovely herbaceous bedding surrounding it. That's my particular favourite, I have to say.'

Ellie merely shrugged, stabbing her fork into the dessert, and ripping off a chunk. There was a clatter of cutlery against porcelain, as Trixie dropped what she was doing to dig her hand into her hip and shoot Ellie a stern look. 'My goodness, girl - whatever is the matter? This isn't like you to be such a wet fart.'

Her mouth wide open with half-chewed cake, Ellie looked affronted.

Then, she couldn't deny that with the early starts and the late finishes; the extra work she had been putting in to help Jack finish Mrs Pascoe's cottage; the work she was doing on Wenna's van, and the usual maintenance around Nanny's cottage, she hadn't been herself recently. But that wasn't just it. Where could she begin in explaining? She just felt so out-of-sorts at the moment, and she couldn't quite figure out why.

'Well?' Trixie demanded.

'I don't know what's the matter with me!' Ellie eventually began, throwing her arms up in despair. 'I don't know what I'm doing here half of the time. It's like the blind leading the blind! Tressa keeps adding to my massive to-do list for this bloody open day. Things have drifted between me and my friend Jack ever since I took the job here and I don't know what to do about it. Nanny hasn't been very well and won't go to the doctors even though I nag her daily for it. I'm pretty sure Lavinia and Beryan hate me, and I feel *this small* when I'm around them, even for a second. And Mrs Jenkins asked a perfectly reasonable - but kind of impertinent - question about my mum. But because my relationship with my mum is somewhat unconventional and let's be frank here, completely weird, I ended up making everyone uncomfortable by admitting that my mum has been traveling the world non-stop since I was a teenager because apparently she would rather slum it in some hostel in the middle of Thailand than even attempt to have a relationship with her only child. Unless, of course, she has debt that needs paying off. Then she's right there on the phone kissing my arse!'

Trixie's delicious Bakewell Tart was suddenly impossible to swallow past the lump that had now formed in Ellie's throat. She let her fork land with a clatter on the side plate as weeks, months, perhaps years of tears rushed out of her in waves. Trixie was there in a flash, and Ellie apologised over and over into Trixie's shoulder as she stroked her hair soothingly.

'There, there. Hush. Let it all out,' Trixie cooed, gathering Ellie up into the type of hug only a well-practised mother and grandmother could conjure up. 'We all need a good cry sometimes. No good holding it all in, and I think you're a little too good at doing that. You haven't been yourself for a few weeks now. And you're doing too much! I've said it to George a couple of times now.'

Ellie pulled herself away and accepted a piece of kitchen roll from Trixie, sniffing loudly. 'That'll explain why he keeps giving me weird looks every time I see him. Giving me a bloody complex.'

'I think he's just been a bit concerned with everything you've taken on - what with the gardens, the growing team of volunteers, the open day. He's quite fond of you, you know.'

Ellie scoffed and blew her nose. 'Yeah. Alright. Because I'm such a catch!'

Trixie stiffened and smiled at someone behind Ellie.

'What's the matter?' George's voice sounded behind her, a genuine gentleness and concern in his tone.

'She just needed a little pick-me-up, didn't you love?' Trixie said, giving George's arm a motherly pat before returning to her task. 'Can I get you anything, George my love?'

'No thanks, Trix,' George replied, not taking his eyes off Ellie who was now doing her best to compose herself and wipe any traces of tears.

'I'm fine. Honestly, I'm fine,' Ellie insisted, getting up from her stool. 'Just needed a bit of sugar. I'll be leaving early today if that's alright. Things to do at home. See you tomorrow.' And with that, feeling rather mean, she left George looking helpless and darted out of the kitchen before he had the chance to respond.

# Chapter Seventeen

*'Hi, Guys! My name is George Penhaligon, and welcome to Penhaligon Estate.'*

George's voice continued in the background of the vlog currently playing on Tressa's laptop as both Tressa and George watched it with juxtaposed expressions. Tressa wore the smug look of someone who had poured hours into the editing of this video, whilst George cringed behind the palm of his hand, his elbow poised on the desk and one leg twitching nervously.

'See? It's good, isn't it?' Tressa said with triumph.

'Oh, yeah... yeah,' George forced himself to say, frowning as he watched himself on the small screen, stumbling his way through a Q&A with a nervous Joseph about apprenticeships on the estate. 'Do you think I say 'guys' too much? I never noticed that before. Do I say 'guys' a lot?'

'A bit. But it doesn't matter; no one will notice. What do you think? Shall I post it?'

Despite his tribulations, George plastered an enthusiastic smile on his face, knowing full well how long this had taken his sister to put together. 'Yes! Go for it. I'm sure it will give some people a good laugh.'

'It's perfect timing for the open day too. I've advertised the event everywhere, but a little glimpse into the estate might boost those extra ticket sales.'

'Okay, good. Good,' George said, nodding and biting his lip.

'That's good.'

'And you're keeping remarkably calm about the whole thing,' Tressa said snidely, patting George on the shoulder. 'It's going to be fine. I've got everything in hand.'

George smiled up at his sister. 'I know you have.'

'Who's that?' Tressa suddenly said, taking herself towards the window and looking out to the driveway, where Wenna's rusty, old Citroen H van was transforming into a cute little bistro van for serving coffees. George hoisted himself out of his seat to stand beside Tressa, his stomach doing a little flip as he first noticed Ellie, her coppery hair tied up with a head scarf in a cute little retro bun and her bangs framing across her face as she took a circular saw to a big piece of plywood and cut into it expertly. He then watched as she blew off the dust and hoisted it up effortlessly, sliding it through the back door of the van and disappearing inside it. Wenna came into view, carrying a small potted bay tree which she now placed carefully in front of the serving hatch and adorning it with little battery-powered twinkly lights. George couldn't help but smile as he watched his sister titivate happily with the finer detail of her new little business, sporting a set of dungarees all too similar to the ones Ellie adorned almost every day. Was his little sister idolising Ellie? Then the person in question came into view and suddenly George's smile was wiped from his face.

'That's Jack,' George said, finally answering Tressa's question. 'Apparently he's plumbing in a sink and the coffee machine in the van.'

'Is he, indeed?' Tressa drooled, taking a step closer to the window. George clucked disapprovingly and nudged her hard in the arm. Tressa then suddenly took flight towards the door and out onto the driveway. George followed reluctantly.

'Almost finished?' Tressa asked, in the way of greeting, and successfully catching the attention of Jack, who stopped what he was doing to exchange a smile. George frowned and seeked out

Ellie to check her reaction. She was still busy inside the van, the sound of a drill coming to life to confirm that.

'What do you think? Doesn't she look adorable?' Wenna sang, clapping her hands and practically dancing on the spot.

'It looks great, Wen,' George said, meaning every word. He'd been watching Ellie and Wenna slowly transform the old van for a couple of weeks now. Ellie had carefully sprayed it to a classy cream colour a few days ago, which had certainly brightened it up and made it fit for an open day at a stately home. George wasn't overly convinced the running of the van was much more reliable, but they had mostly focused on cosmetics for it as a stationary coffee van which George was perfectly content with. It would be ready in time for the open day, and for now that was all that mattered.

'It's ready for a test run in a moment, if you want to be my first customers!' Wenna said, like a gleeful child in role play.

'Give me five minutes to fit this,' Jack said, waving an elbow joint at them and climbing into the van. Two minutes later, the side hatch was pushed forward, revealing an excited Ellie who secured the supporting poles in place.

'Sorry, we're closed,' Ellie joked, laughing along with Wenna who now became animated as she too climbed into the van and started finding all the equipment to make a coffee. They both stumbled and tripped, followed by a groan of pain from Jack who was headfirst under the sink, fitting the elbow joint, and being trampled on apparently.

'Don't mind me, ladies!' Jack cried out, wryly.

While Wenna gathered her equipment together and Ellie checked her most recently fitted counter with a spirit level, George stepped closer to admire the handy work. With the side hatch open, he could now see the extent of Ellie and Wenna's labour - mostly Ellie's. He was astounded at the quality in such a short space of time and ran his hand along the varnished wooden serving shelf running along the side of the van, the perfect height for customers to personalise their coffees and complete transactions. Wenna passed through a little wicker tray filled with sachets of white and demerara sugar, which George placed on the shelf, followed by a paper cup filled with wooden stirrers and a small jar of little bite-sized cannolis.

'The rest are in the freezer in Trixie's kitchen,' Wenna explained, as George raised an eyebrow at the cannolis. 'I just wanted you all to try them. They're bought though. I didn't make them.'

'No one had thought for one second you had made them, Wenna,' Tressa said, stepping forward and peering in through the hatch with her arms crossed. 'I'll try a latte when you're ready to go.'

Despite Tressa's little remark about Wenna's baking skills - or there lack of, Wenna became doubly excited that even Tressa was on board with the whole thing and showing a remarkable amount of support. George almost wanted to embrace Tressa with gratitude for the kindness and patience she had shown Wenna these last couple of weeks. It certainly made a huge change from the way they usually treated one another. But perhaps this was what they had been missing all this time - finding their own ways of contributing to the family business and feeling like they all had their own personal purpose in it all.

Jack finally announced that the sink and the coffee machine were all safely plumbed in and ready to go. Ellie jumped out and geared up the generator as Wenna squealed and started fiddling with the coffee machine on the back counter. George and Tressa waited on the driveway in anticipation as the machine was clicked on and started gurgling.

'Oh, I forgot. It takes about fifteen to twenty minutes to heat up,' Wenna said, despondently.

Tressa sighed and shuffled back towards the house. 'Give me a shout when you're ready. I need to post this vlog.'

'You've all done a great job,' George commented, mostly to

pass the time but also meaning every word. He ran a large hand across the wooden counter, admiring every attention to detail. He looked up at Ellie. 'Did you even fix the engine problems?'

'Engine is fine. But I wouldn't chance the chassis on the A30,' Ellie said, pulling a face when she knew Wenna wasn't looking. 'It's fine for on the estate.'

It was a tight space inside, and George watched with an odd sense of feeling left out as the three of them procrastinated with their own little jobs whilst navigating around each other, Jack's bulk of a body getting far closer to both Ellie and Wenna's than George could handle. He decided to take a new position in the doorway of the little van, at the top of the steps, just as Wenna was measuring out her milk into a stainless-steel jug.

'OK, it's nearly up to temperature,' Wenna said. 'George? Latte?'

'Cappuccino, please.'

Wenna paused and gave George a pleading look which immediately had him chuckling. 'Latte sounds great.'

And with a sudden whoosh, Wenna started heating up the milk with the steam wand, the frothing sound quickly escalating to an ear-piercing shriek. She was burning the milk and George couldn't hide his expression of agony. Years of living in Italy had seen him knowing the difference between an expertly made cup of coffee and an absolute shambolic one. Both Ellie and Jack seemed to have the same concern as their polite expressions flickered occasionally at the sound of the milk hissing ferociously against the metal jug.

They watched in silent anticipation as Wenna turned the steam wand off, gave the jug a hard tap on the side, shooting molten hot milk flying in the air. Lowering the mug of freshly strained coffee, Wenna put all her focus into swirling her milk into the golden-brown liquid, only to end up with a mound of froth which instantly collapsed in on itself. Wenna lowered her jug down with a despondent thud.

'That didn't go very well,' Wenna muttered. George's heart ached for her and when she looked up at Ellie, she too was giving Wenna a small, sympathetic smile. 'This didn't happen at the course. What have I done wrong?'

'Can I butt in?' Jack asked, tentatively approaching the coffee machine.

'Yes, please,' Wenna said sadly, stepping to one side.

'Firstly, give yourself a chance. It's a brand-new machine and not the same as the one you'll have used at your course.'

Ellie frowned, looking at Jack with confusion as he emptied the group head of the old coffee and reloaded it with some freshly grounded stuff. He then poured a small amount of milk into the jug.

'I would only fill the milk to here for one coffee,' Jack explained, indicating the amount with the tip of his finger. Inserting the steam wand into the jug, he angled himself so Wenna could watch over his shoulder. Now George was frowning as his little sister got close and personal to Jack, her chin practically resting on his shoulder. What was the matter with his sisters today?

'The key is to sit the end of the wand just in the surface of the milk, like this,' Jack continued. 'If it starts hissing, just adjust the position. It should be nice and quiet, just like this.'

As Wenna edged in closer and Jack started whispering 'nice and quiet' to the milk like some sort of lullaby, George suddenly felt like he was intruding in some sort of moment, creasing his brow in annoyance and confusion. He almost burst into laughter as he caught Ellie's expression, her arms folded, and her chin dropped to her chest as she stared at the strange intimate moment Jack and Wenna seemed to be sharing. She glanced at George and her expression collapsed into shared humour, her shoulders shaking in silent mirth. She tilted her head towards the back exit of the van and shuffled her way past Jack and Wenna to escape onto the driveway with George.

'Okay, while those two are getting steamy with the steam wand - Ha! Get it?' Ellie cried, slapping her thigh and chuckling to herself. 'I need to just check you're happy with the new signage we've started putting around the gardens. You know, the ones for stupid people to remind them not to do stupid things, like fall in a pond.'

George laughed along and followed Ellie around the corner into the Italian gardens. He was utterly perplexed by her cheeriness considering the spectacle they had just witnessed.

'Sorry - I know she's your little sister - but don't you think her, and Jack were kind of cute, then?' George looked at her, incredulous - unsure how to respond. Ellie rolled her eyes at his expression, completely missing the point. 'I know, I know. She's your sister. Big brother duty and all.'

'Don't *you* care?' George blurted out, before he could stop himself.

'About what?' Ellie asked, pointing at her first sign which read 'DO NOT CLIMB ON CORNISH WALL - VERY OLD'. 'Your grandmother requested this one. I think this is aimed towards children, don't you?'

'Yeah, Granny doesn't like children very much,' George remarked.

'So, what don't I care about?' Ellie asked, now leading him through into the Kitchen Garden where there were more signs dotted all over the place.

'Well - Jack... flirting,' George clarified, now feeling completely childish for asking. But it kind of bothered him how little she cared, and he wasn't sure why.

Ellie laughed then, hooking her hands onto her hips and giving George a strange look. 'Why would I care about Jack flirting? And was that even flirting? You should see him down at the pub after a few pints! Total slut.' A look of mild realisation washed over Ellie then. 'Jack and I are not a couple, just to clarify.'

'You're not?'

'No!' Ellie scoffed, rolling her eyes to the sky. 'Honestly, the amount of people who mistake us as a couple. Are men and women not allowed to be friends without it being something more?'

'I think Jack might like it to be something more,' George remarked, his stomach clenching in anticipation at that moment from the conflict of emotions bubbling away.

'Don't. You're sounding like Nanny,' Ellie scoffed again, now facing away, and adjusting a sign which had been hung on the fruit cage to warn members of the public about sharp metal on the wire.

'We've gone a little over the top with the signage,' George declared, scanning the Kitchen Garden and spotting about ten just where he stood.

'We've definitely gone way over the top with the signage,' Ellie agreed. 'But Tressa is taking the risk assessments and public liability very, very seriously.'

'Better this than getting sued, I suppose,' George said, sighing. 'So, you and Jack really aren't a couple?'

'Nope,' Ellie said, a small smile forming on her pretty face, and like a teenager talking to his first crush, George's features broke out into a wide smile.

# Chapter Eighteen

Only two days to go before the big day and the shared nerves amongst everyone at Penhaligon Estate rippled through like tidal waves. Tressa had morphed into a crazed loon with a clipboard and the inability to leave the walkie-talkies silent for more than five minutes. Ellie cringed as her own device burst to life for the umpteenth time that morning, with the urgent sounds of Tressa demanding someone come and help her with the chairs for the front lawn where they would be serving Trixie's cream teas. She grabbed the device from her beltline and turned the volume down, restoring the peace for Ellie in her surroundings once more. She needed head space today, her head fogged from stress and over-thinking.

Ellie finished raking up the last of the dried leaves and petals on the stretch of path she was on, scooping it all up and into her wheelbarrow. She'd been at it for a good three hours so far, slowly making her way down the long, snaking path which led from the back of the formal gardens all the way down to the estuary, lined with tree ferns and towering echiums. Despite the efforts she put into the formal gardens and the parkland, Ellie had to admit she'd grown a personal fondness for this tropical haven. It felt other-worldly, like she was two-inches high exploring a prehistoric jungle - especially when she found herself working underneath the large, umbrella-like leaves of a Gunnera.

She rounded the corner to a new stretch of path, a fresh blanket of mushed up petals, leaves and moss waiting to be cleared. The scratching of the rake against the gritty path proceeded once again as Ellie absent-mindedly took in her surroundings. At some point, this jungle would need more of their attention. Perhaps, one day, they could even create some little paths under the canopy of the gunneras and ferns. Ellie started envisioning the place becoming alive with visitors and dog walkers, perhaps even trails for children. The possibilities were endless. Then she spotted a glimpse of red brick through the shades of green, her curiosity instantly peaked.

Placing the rake down against the wheelbarrow, Ellie ducked and climbed through the over-growth towards the red brick. It was a wall. An old wall standing around ten feet high and now, on closer inspection, Ellie wondered how she had missed it until now. Then again, a lot of the brickwork had been claimed behind a thick screen of ivy and moss. She parted a particularly heavy over-hang of both ivy and clematis, and her heart jumped in excitement as she revealed an old arched wooden gate. The style of the gate seemed older than Penhaligon House - perhaps 17th or 18th century. Ellie wasn't good with dates, but the old iron supports criss-crossing the gate, along with the matching cast-iron handle, made her think it had to be at least one of those.

In her excitement, Ellie grabbed her walkie-talkie and turned the volume up, only to have a barrage of voices, bringing her back to reality. Tressa seemed to be having some sort of disagreement with Dave, who was now muttering incoherently back to her about lawn care. Ellie turned the volume back down, rolling her eyes in the process, and reached for her phone instead. She stabbed out a quick text to George, describing her rough whereabouts and telling him to get down to her as soon as he could. For good measure, she did something completely out of character and shot a selfie in front of the gate, sticking her tongue out in excitement. Pinging it off to George, she suddenly felt lame and doubted herself. Would he see the funny side to that? She really hoped so. It was usually her who mocked other people for doing this. But she was practically giddy with excitement, now looking up the jungle path impatiently for signs of George.

As she waited, she retrieved her secateurs from her tool belt and snipped away at the vines dominating the front of the mystery door. She pawed at the solid wood, desperate to open it and reveal whatever existed behind. A few jiggles of the cast iron handle told her it was locked - or jammed. There was the smallest of gaps where the old wood had split from weathering, but as Ellie peered through it, all she could make out was green foliage and overgrowth. She scraped at the ground beneath her and revealed a patch of the old path. It wasn't dissimilar to the jungle path she had just been sweeping, so why was it that just this part of the garden had been lost and forgotten?

Ellie glanced at her phone, but no response from George. Returning her attention to the gate, she now scanned the wall protruding from behind the overhang of climbers and ivy. It was well-preserved, with minimal wear and damage. She could carefully tame back the climbers and expose the wall. Perhaps a bit of grouting and re-pointing here and there. She noticed one brick in particular was sitting loose in its place and she gave it a gentle wiggle. Yes, it was completely loose. She had a sudden urge to pull it out just as approaching footsteps sounded behind her.

'Did you seriously send me a selfie?' George chuckled, marching down the path and ducking under the low canopy of leaves to reach Ellie.

'Be honoured,' Ellie quipped, her attention still on that loose brick. 'That was my first ever selfie.'

George reached her side, slightly intimate in proximity from the lack of available space in all the overgrowth.

'What are you doing?' George asked, his breath tickling the back of her neck.

'Resisting the urge to pull out this loose brick,' Ellie said. 'Have you seen this gate before? You don't sound very surprised to see it.'

'I think I hid around here a couple of times, playing hide and seek with Tressa, Wenna and some cousins when we were little.'

'So, what's in there then?'

George shrugged. 'No idea. Never been past it.'

Ellie turned around and looked at him in disbelief, allowing her hand to drop. 'And you've never been interested to know?'

'Well, not when I was little - no. We had so much garden and estates to explore, it didn't cross my mind.'

'Said the rich kid,' Ellie muttered, laughing as George nudged her in response. 'Well, it's locked. And I'm dying to know what's in there. Did Ernie have any old keys? A big iron ring of them, like Filch.'

'Who?'

Ellie's face fell in mock disappointment. 'The caretaker at Hogwarts... Harry Potter. Oh, never mind you muggle. Remind me after this to educate you in some Potter culture or we can't be friends.'

'Maybe there's a key behind that loose brick,' George suggested, reaching over Ellie's shoulder to pull at the brick himself. His chest pressed gently against Ellie's back and a silent gasp escaped her mouth as she breathed in his scent. She put her focus on that pesky brick, trying to ignore the reaction of her body towards George. Bits of old mortar crumbled away as he revealed a small gap in the wall and Ellie, peering into the darkness, caught sight of paper in amongst the cobwebs and moss.

'It's a letter,' George observed, pulling it out and carefully wiping off the dust and dirt. As he turned the letter over in his hand, his face darkened in concern, his eyes flicking up to meet

Ellie's.

'What is it? Let me see.' Ellie took the letter from George's grasp. The ink was smudged but the letters legible enough. 'Who's Gi-Gi? I wonder who wrote this. The handwriting is beautiful.'

'I know that handwriting very well,' George said, seriously. 'I've seen it countless times in the last few weeks, sifting through paperwork for the estate.'

'Your grandfather?'

'Yes,' George nodded. Now it was his turn to watch Ellie with concern. 'What is it?'

Ellie's face was as grey as the crumbling stone behind her as she glared at the letter now poised in her hand like something toxic, implications making more and more sense as she began to fit the pieces of the puzzle together. Nanny's tribulations towards Ellie's job on the estate. Her initial behaviour towards George. Her vague confessions to having a history with Charles Penhaligon, the owner of the curled lettering on the envelope of that letter which potentially held all the secrets. 'I think I might know who Gi-Gi is.'

George's brow wrinkled and his eyes softened in concern at Ellie and the letter. 'Really? Who?'

'Nanny,' Ellie breathed. 'George - I think our grandparents may have had an affair.'

They had had no luck in finding the key to unlocking that mystery gateway, and given the age of it, they had been unwilling to barge it down in any way. Both Ellie and George had agreed that the wall, the archway, and the old door were a beautiful addition to the gardens and needed to be carefully and sensitively renovated. They would find another way of unlocking it to reveal the lost gardens beyond.

In the meantime, the letter bothered them both. It was now

the end of the day. The gardening team had gone home - over an hour late from their usual finish - and Tressa had finally put her walkie-talkie down for a rest. Penhaligon House was settling down for the evening and Trixie was now announcing her departure to George and Ellie, who were both sat up at the counter in her kitchen, pouring over the unopened letter.

'There's a cooked chicken in the Rayburn, George,' Trixie instructed, as she put on her jacket. 'Have what you like with it. But I think your mother and grandmother wanted a garden salad after today's hot weather, so maybe shredded with some Caesar dressing.'

'Thanks, Trix,' George said, barely looking up from the letter.

'And not that it's any of my business but hearing you two debating over there - that letter needs to go to the person it's addressed to.' Trixie held up her hands to signify she was done with her brief lecture, blew them both a kiss and gave a little wave goodbye.

'She's right,' Ellie said, seconds later. 'It was written for Nanny. She needs to be the first to read it. If you're OK with that.'

George nodded, rubbing his face with both hands, and looking as distressed as Ellie felt. 'Yeah. Absolutely. Completely agree.'

A heavy pause fell between them as they both stared at the letter, sitting temptingly on the counter.

'Do you really think they were having an affair?' Ellie asked, her voice small with worry.

George shook his head, his lips pressed together. 'I don't know. Are you hungry?' Ellie's expressions of worry were quickly exchanged with amused confusion. 'When I'm stressed like this, I just need to eat. I need something a bit heartier than a salad though, don't know about you.'

'Not really a salad girl at the best of times, to be honest,' Ellie remarked.

'Perfect,' George said, smiling. 'Pasta?'

In less than half an hour, Ellie had watched George whip up two steaming bowls of creamy pasta and four plates of chicken Caesar salads for the Penhaligon women. She laughed as he took a carton of apple juice from the fridge and poured the golden liquid into a wine glass, swirling it gently.

'I hear this was a good year,' George remarked, winking at Ellie as he placed the glass on the counter in front of her. 'Shall we take this onto the patio at the front?'

Ellie nodded, her stomach rumbling at the delicious smell of the pasta wafting up at her as she collected both her bowl and her glass of apple juice, following George out into the cooling summer evening.

'Well, this is a bit different,' Ellie said, as they tucked into their meal minutes later.

'What is?'

'Sitting here and enjoying the fruits of my labour - well, my team's labour. My God, this pasta is good!' She looked up to see George smiling, a new expression on his face she couldn't quite work out. 'I take it you learned to make dishes like this in Italy.'

'Mmm, kind of,' George said, taking a swig of his cider. 'I could already cook fairly well from my university days. But I've perfected my dishes the Italian way if you know what I mean.'

'Not in the slightest, but sure.' Ellie chuckled along with George, took a huge bite of her pasta, and sat back in her chair, looking out to the gardens which were now bathed in a golden sunset light. The estuary glistened aqua in the distance, creating a strange ache in Ellie's chest. An invisible pull towards the water. 'I do adore that view.'

Again, she felt George's eyes on her and couldn't deny the heat rising in her cheeks.

'Stop looking at me like that,' Ellie warned, glancing sideways at George with the smallest smirk.

George pretended to look affronted. 'Like what?'

She didn't have a way of answering that, not without

sounding arrogant and presumptuous. But she knew the looks he'd been giving her recently. And she had felt the shift between them. She'd enjoyed it, and she didn't want to ruin something by pointing out the obvious. Instead, she gave him a knowing smile and returned to her food just as Wenna stepped out onto the patio, slightly breathless.

'Well, well. Doesn't this look romantic,' Wenna teased, leaning her hands on the back of George's chair. Ellie smiled in amusement at George's deadpan expression.

'There's a Caesar salad for you in the fridge downstairs,' George said.

'Oh, thanks dear brother. But I've already eaten.' Wenna suddenly looked giddy, and Ellie creased her brow at her in a silent question. Wenna paused for a moment, as if she was contemplating answering her or not. 'Jack and I had an early dinner at the little pub down the road. He's gone to Truro now for a friend's stag do.'

'You and Jack?' Ellie asked, trying to ignore the slightest twisting sensation in the pit of her stomach. 'You went on a date?'

'Yes. Kind of. I hope you don't mind,' Wenna said, twisting the hem of her floaty skirt in her hands and giving Ellie a pleading look. George looked first at his sister in mild annoyance and disbelief, then at Ellie in scrutiny. She could feel him analysing her reaction.

'No, of course I don't mind,' Ellie forced herself to say, plastering a supportive smile on her face and dampening that rising ache. 'We're just friends.'

Wenna's body sagged in relief. 'Good. Thank you, beautiful lady. I'm going to take myself off for a hot bath now and leave you both alone.' She wagged her brows suggestively, earning herself an eye roll from George, and shuffled back inside. Ellie almost immediately felt George's eyes burning into the top of her head.

'Alright?' Ellie asked.

'Yes. You?'

Ellie chewed on her food, her eyes narrowing at George across the table. 'Wenna and Jack, eh? How do you feel about that?'

'Fine,' George said, shrugging casually. 'How do you feel about that?'

Ellie scoffed, loudly. 'We're just friends. We always have been just friends. Why can't anybody get that?'

'Perhaps because Jack has made it clear he wanted to be more than just friends. You're not the best at noticing signals.'

Ellie was tiring of this conversation fast, putting her cutlery down with a loud clatter. 'What is that supposed to mean?'

'It's not necessarily a bad thing. You're just very humble and laid back. You're a very beautiful woman, Ellie. You just don't flaunt it.' George's face softened and Ellie was suddenly breathless, holding on to his every word. 'You'... unique.'

Ellie rolled her eyes at that, the momentary spell broken between them. 'That's just a polite way of saying I'm weird.'

'You're definitely that, too,' George agreed, smiling. 'Nothing wrong with a beautiful little weirdo. You keep people guessing, that's for sure.'

The sun was beginning to slip down out of view and a nearby owl hooted cheerfully, distracting Ellie for a second. Such conflicting emotions ran through her as she returned her attention to George. He looked nervous, a serious look on his face as he reached out for her hand. His tanned hands were warm and large around her petite ones, her nails black from soil and years in the garden. For once, she suddenly felt self-conscious about her lack of effort in her appearance. She was certain George was used to holding perfectly manicured hands, slender and feminine.

'Ellie, I'd like to take you on a date. If that's all right with you,' George said, his voice soft and tender. 'I know it's a strange situation between us - working here together. But I really do like you, and I've respectfully kept my distance all this time, thinking you and Jack... well - now that's been cleared up. What do you say?'

'Umm,' was all Ellie could manage as she gazed at his hands, cocooned around hers. At his face, waiting patiently and expectantly for an answer. At her surroundings, so beyond her real world. Then she caught sight of a figure standing in a window of the second floor. Lavinia's face was pinched with distaste - Ellie could see that even from where she was sitting. She suddenly ripped her hand away, George's eyes widening in surprise.

'I don't think it's a good idea,' Ellie said, her eyes darting up again at the window. George noticed this time and turned around, following her line of sight. A mixture of hurt and understanding crossed George's face as Ellie shot up out of her seat. 'I really like you, and you don't know how much I want to say yes. But...'

'Ellie...'

'It's just not a good idea. Let's not open that can of worms. I think I should go, actually. It's late and I need to check Nanny has taken her meds before bed.'

'Ellie, come on,' George huffed. 'Don't just run off.'

'I'll see you tomorrow,' Ellie assured him, smiling. 'Thank you for a lovely meal.'

And before he could argue with her any further, and before that expression of hurt and disappointment could break her down enough to change her mind, she turned and marched off into the darkness, towards the path which joined both her old life and this new life here on the estate. Her heart felt heavier with every step she traipsed back to her little hamlet, as the distance between her and George stretched out. Her exposed legs endured scrapes from low-lying brambles and stinging nettles as she relied on familiarity to guide her home, forgetting all about the handy torch on her phone and instead walking blindly through the darkness. It wasn't until she reached the hamlet, the glow from neighbours' windows offering a bit of light as she tackled the narrow path along the embankment, that she realised she had left Nanny's letter in Trixie's kitchen. She thought about messaging George, asking him to keep it somewhere safe, but quickly thought against it. She had just rejected him, like the stupid idiot she felt. And as if she wasn't confused enough, she froze in the gateway of her and Nanny's cottage, Jack's large silhouette sitting on the nearby bench taking her by surprise.

'Jack? What are you doing here?'

Jack got up and the light from the porch flooded his anguished face. 'I think Nanny's gone to bed. I didn't want to disturb her. Can we talk?'

'Yeah, of course.' Ellie rushed forward, grabbing her keys from her pocket.

But before she had even had a chance to unlock the front door, Jack's nerves got the better of him. 'I went on a date. With Wenna.'

Ellie paused and smiled kindly at him. 'I know.'

'You do?'

'Wenna told me herself.'

'Right. Course she did,' Jack said, looking the most stressed Ellie had ever seen him.

'I thought you were in Truro this evening for a stag do.' Ellie's brow furrowed as she watched Jack's strange behaviour. 'Jack, are you -'

'Can I just try something a moment?'

'Sorry?'

But before she could question him further Jack stepped forward, cupping her face in his warm hands, and locking his lips on hers in a deep, passionate kiss.

# Chapter Nineteen

Utterly bewildered, Ellie could do nothing in response. They finally pulled away from one another, Ellie's eyes still wide and Jack's hands still gently cupping her face. His eyes searched hers for some kind of answer.

'Well?'

'Well, what?' Ellie cried. 'What the hell was that?' Ellie started chuckling in disbelief. 'You just snogged my face off and now you're asking 'Well?' What do you want, a review or something?'

Despite his agitations, Jack's face broke out in amusement. He dropped his hands from Ellie's face and straight to his hips, looking down at the floor.

'Did you feel anything at all?' Jack asked, shyly.

'Beside your tongue?' Ellie asked. They burst out laughing, Ellie hushing as she finished unlocking the front door. She tip-toed across the flag-stoned floor to the other side of the kitchen, quietly closing the door which led to Nanny's room. Nanny's loud snores echoed through the landing, indicating that she was still fast asleep. As Ellie tip-toed back to the island to pop the kettle on, Jack took his usual seat, rubbing his face with his hands in distress.

'Ellie! I don't know what I'm doing,' Jack groaned into his hands. 'I went on a date today with a beautiful, funny girl. It was great. But I couldn't stop thinking...'

Ellie and Jack's eyes met across the island.

Jack took a deep breath. 'I couldn't stop thinking about you. I didn't even make it to Truro for my mate's stag do. I started painting my skirting boards in the hallway instead and I just felt guilty.'

'Why?' Ellie asked. Jack responded with a shrug.

'Ellie, I've been pining after you for some time now. And you have never noticed.' Ellie squirmed uncomfortably from where she stood, thinking about what George had said earlier about her not noticing signals. 'But it's okay. That's what makes you cute. It's what makes you even more attractive. It's like you don't notice how bloody beautiful you are.'

Ellie's eyes darted sideways and a chuckle erupted involuntarily from her chest.

'You see?' Jack chortled, wryly. 'You can't hear a compliment without turning into a giggling five-year-old!' Ellie mouthed a silent 'sorry' and busied herself in making two coffees, despite desperately feeling like she needed some alone time. Suddenly, this entire evening had become too much. Ellie peeled back the lid of a nearby Tupperware container.

'Do you want a slice of Victoria Sponge?'

'Hell yes.'

Jack watched intently as Ellie cut two generous slices of sponge and transferred them onto two side plates. She added a fork to each and slid one plate towards Jack, followed by his coffee. He thanked her and they ate their late evening treat in companionable silence. After only a few minutes, Ellie felt Jack's appraising eyes back on her.

'The kiss,' Jack began. 'It felt weird, didn't it?' Ellie gave a shy, apologetic nod. 'I thought so too. I just needed to know. Whether there was a you and me. I feel so comfortable around you that I just needed to know whether there was something beyond that familiarity.'

Ellie simply nodded, allowing Jack this moment to think out

loud. She had never seen him like this before, and she was beginning to quickly realise that, despite his compliments to her a few minutes ago, this was not about her.

'Are you going to see Wenna again?' Ellie asked, feeling content enough to know that it didn't bother her now as much as it did back at Penhaligon House. On the contrary, she would be thrilled for the both of them.

'Yes, I think I am,' Jack said, decisively. He then returned his attention to Ellie. 'I don't want things to change between us.'

'They won't,' Ellie said, with a promise. 'We're sat here casually enjoying a slice of cake after you just rammed your tongue down my throat. I'd say our friendship is as tough as nails.'

Jack smiled warmly and reached over to wrap his arms around her shoulders. 'Thanks, Ellie.'

'You're welcome,' Ellie replied, pressing into him in a return embrace before pulling away and planting a kiss on his cheek. 'Now, are you going home? Because I'm bloody knackered and want to go to bed.'

When Ellie woke up the next morning, all the memories of her strange evening came flooding back as she groaned into her pillow in response. She allowed herself a moment or two of self-pity before her mind snapped to the more pressing mystery of yesterday.

Nanny's letter.

The problem there though was that the letter was in Penhaligon House - and Ellie hoped desperately that George had had the good sense to hide it away somewhere safe - and given Ellie's rejection of George last night, she was less than eager to bump into him today. Could she perhaps message Wenna and ask her to bring it down to the cottage? Or ask her to pass it to Jack. No, this would take too long. She needed to retrieve it today, before it got lost or misplaced into the wrong hands.

Beryan or Lavinia came to mind here. Though Ellie did not know what was said in this letter, given her current suspicions between Nanny and the late Charles Penhaligon, it didn't seem too difficult to piece together a fabrication of some sort. Sighing heavily and relenting to the idea that today wasn't going to be kind to her, she heaved herself out of bed to get ready, nonetheless.

'Morning, Nan,' Ellie whispered, popping her head round Nanny's bedroom door to find her sitting up in bed with a glass of water.

'Morning,' Nanny croaked.

'How are you feeling?'

'Fine. You were back late last night,' Nanny stated, not accusingly but with a loaded question.

'Just sorting out some last-minute stuff for the open day,' Ellie said, quickly throwing together a lie which would avoid her admitting that she had actually had dinner alone with George. 'Do you want me to bring you in some porridge before I head to work?'

Nanny put her glass down and started peeling back the sheets. 'No, I think I'll have my breakfast on the patio this morning.' A great eruption of coughs and splutters took over Nanny's body and Ellie rushed forward in aid, putting the glass of water back in the old lady's hand and encouraging her to take another sip. 'I'm alright. I'm alright.'

'Clearly,' Ellie muttered with a wry smile, worry framing her eyes. 'Nan, you need to go back to the doctors.'

Nanny growled out a response, shaking her head fiercely. 'I'm alright! I don't need to see a doctor. I'm old.'

'Right, so that's that is it?' Ellie snapped, putting the glass of water back down with a thud. 'Look, you asked me to leave it last time. But it's been weeks now and you're no better. I'm making you an appointment. No arguments.'

'Christ - take me now,' Nanny muttered wickedly to the

ceiling.

'That's enough of that talk, too,' Ellie said firmly, wagging an accusing finger in her Nanny's direction.

When she got to Penhaligon House, the weather had decided to take a slightly metaphorical turn and Ellie was dampened from a light mist setting in. She stomped through the back door into the kitchens, shaking off droplets of water from her hair and jacket. As she looked up George entered the kitchen, a mug of coffee in one hand and Nanny's letter in the other. Ellie pressed her lips together, her heart leaping and plummeting painfully into her stomach at the sight of him. So much for avoiding him today.

George stepped forward and placed the letter on the counter, nodding at it pointedly for Ellie to retrieve. 'Coffee?'

'Please,' Ellie replied, shyly. She picked up the letter and put it in the inside pocket of her coat. 'Thank you for keeping the letter safe.'

'Of course,' George said, not smiling. He turned his back on Ellie to make the coffee and she considered breaking the ice between them, apologising for her abrupt exit last night. But just as she opened her mouth to speak, in bustled Trixie with her arms ladled with shopping bags and a rush of chaos about her as she huffed and puffed the way she did when she had a busy day ahead of her.

'Morning, you two! Hope you're done in here because I need you out. Out, out, out, out! Lots of love to you both but bugger off!'

In spite of herself, Ellie smiled fondly at Trixie and assured her she'd be out of her way. Even George gave a little chuckle as he finished stirring Ellie's coffee and handing it to her. Their eyes met for a second and Ellie suddenly felt a little lost in those deep browns of his. As Trixie muttered madly to herself, emptying the contents of her shopping bags to every available counter surface available, George tilted his head towards the door leading to the rest of the house, signalling to Ellie that they both go that way. In understanding, Ellie led the way through the narrow doorway, feeling George close behind as they climbed the small staircase up to the Penhaligon residence. It was quiet and still, the rest of the family still soundly asleep. George led the way to the breakfast room and invited Ellie to sit down so she could drink her coffee.

'Have you had breakfast?' George asked, breaking into conversation.

'No, not yet. But I'm not very hungry.'

George nodded and sat down next to Ellie, the end corner of the long breakfast table between them.

'I'm sorry,' Ellie said. George's eyes widened in surprise, his dark brows creasing in confusion.

'Why on earth are you sorry? Ellie, I'm not the kind of bloke to sulk and have a wobble for being declined for a date.' He leaned back in his chair, crossing his ankle over his opposite thigh and nursing his coffee in a large, tanned hand. 'Actually, I wanted to check that you're okay. And that I didn't offend you by my asking last night. Check I haven't got a lawsuit heading my way for sexual harassment.' George smiled kindly to show his teasing and Ellie broke into a small chuckle, easing her tension a little.

'Can we just pretend then that none of that conversation happened and I didn't make a total tit of myself last night?' George asked.

'No,' Ellie said simply, shaking her head with a small smile on her face. 'Because I don't want to forget it. And perhaps if I was lucky enough for the conversation to be had again, I might be braver to say yes next time.' George frowned, perplexed by this but nodded all the same in small understanding. 'I was just startled last night. That's all.'

'And it didn't have anything to do with my mother looking down at us like some sort of Disney villain?' George asked, his mouth lifting in a wry smile. Ellie shrugged, not denying it. 'Didn't take you as a girl who cares much about what other people think. Particularly when it's none of their business.' There was a crossness in George's voice now, a sharp tone directed at his mother, wherever she was in the house.

'Well, you clearly don't know me as well as you think then,' Ellie retorted, lightly. 'Because I care far too much what other people think. Annoyingly so, actually. Let's get the open day out of the way and... see where things take us.'

Ellie's entire body and soul practically screamed at her in protest of this ridiculously rational bargain she had struck with George, and it was clear by his expression that the idea of taking things slow in order to get the impending stresses out of the way first was not something he was keen on. But, like the perfect gentleman, he nodded in agreement and held out a large, tanned hand. Ellie snorted in amusement and slotted her hand into his to shake it. He then gripped it firmly and brought her hand to his mouth, kissing it gently. The smile to follow was her undoing, and she felt her legs become jelly.

'You know, I'm not accustomed to being rejected like this,' George said, teasingly.

'Mmm, clearly,' Ellie retorted, feeling the playfulness settling back between them. 'Probably do you good, to be honest.'


'Where did you find this?'

That evening, after much deliberation, Ellie eventually plucked up the courage to give Nanny her letter. She wasn't sure what made her so nervous about the whole thing, but when she saw the blood drain from her Nanny's face, she began to think her nerves had been justified. Gloria had been silent for a few minutes since the grand reveal of the letter, empty plates sat before them on the dining table for dinner. It wasn't until Ellie rested a gentle hand on Nanny's wrinkled arm and placed the letter in her gnarled hand.

'George and I discovered a walled garden yesterday, at the base of the gardens where it almost meets the river,' Ellie began, her voice soft as she assessed her grandmother's expressions. Pain was etched into every wrinkle of her face and Ellie's heart ached for her. 'We haven't been able to get into it yet but there was-'

'A loose brick in the wall,' Gloria finished, her voice thick with emotion. Then a shuddering breath passed through her lungs, and she clasped the letter with both hands, her eyes burning into it as if she could read the letter through the weathered envelope. 'How much have you read?'

Ellie's lips parted in surprise, and she leaned in with earnest. 'I haven't opened it, Nan. I haven't read a single thing. I would never breach your privacy like that.'

Nanny's head bobbed with gratitude as she looked from Ellie back to the letter, turning it over and over in her hands - contemplating whether to open it or not. Ellie knew her cue and squeezed her Nanny's shoulder gently.

'I'm going to make you a cup of tea, Nan. And then I'm going to give you some privacy.'

When she'd set the mug in front of the old woman moments later, leaving her with a reassuring pat on the hand and heading out into the garden to water the plants, Ellie's stomach knotted with a cocktail of emotions. At the forefront, doubt - had she done the right thing passing Nanny the letter? It may have been addressed to her, but was stirring up the past like this fair to her when so many years had gone by?

Protection and curiosity were two other emotions that kept Ellie hovering inconspicuously around the patio area, watering the same plants more than once in her distracted passing of the patio doors. It wasn't until she heard the faint sound of sobbing that she took the decision to no longer mind her own business.

'Nanny, I'm so sorry,' Ellie gasped, stepping back inside, and leaping to Nanny's aid. 'I should never have... I didn't want...'

Nanny's voice was barely audible beneath the sobs as she said, 'I'm glad you did.' She clutched the letter to her bosom and filled her lungs, a heaving sigh releasing through trembling lips, which pulled upwards on each corner in a ghost of a smile. 'I'm so glad you did.'

# Chapter Twenty

Even seventy years later, Gloria recalled the day she had first met Charles Penhaligon - in every glorious detail.

It had been during the Indian summer of 1951 - the vibrant reds and oranges on trees showing the tell-tale sign of a changing season whilst a warm, hazy weather lingered on well into the autumn months. Gloria was eighteen - just - full of life, and ready to embrace the world. Her auburn curls cascaded down her delicate shoulders, and her sapphire blue eyes sparkled with excitement and curiosity. It was a time when dreams felt within her reach - all she had to do was grasp it with both hands.

One particularly hot October day, Gloria had been one of three who had taken over a little cove beach just along the River Fal, where the creek opens up into the wide sea. The sun beamed down on the sandy shore, painting the beach in shades of gold. Gloria wore a polka-dot two-piece swimsuit that accentuated her youthful charm, as she danced and frolicked in the foamy spray of the lapping waves - her two best friends watching her safely on dry land. She loved the thrill of adventure and was always the first in the water, no matter the time of year.

'Dearest Gloria, please don't ever change,' one of her dearest friends giggled, her dark brown curls bobbing cheerfully at her ears as she shook her head in fond amusement. Bee - as everyone called her - was the embodiment of sophistication, and her calm demeanour brought a sense of tranquillity to the lively trio. She returned to her novel, licking a fingertip and flicking the page over happily as she lay in the sand.

And then there was Lizzy, the wild spirit of the group - the life of the party. Her infectious energy drawing others towards her like magnets. She simply twirled and danced along the shoreline, making everyone around her laugh until their sides ached as she begged Gloria to return to the sand so they could start the picnic they had brought.

'I'm starving. I shall start the food without you in a moment.'

'Fine!' Gloria cried, her laughter carrying out across the cove as she reluctantly waded back out of the water. 'Oh, please tell me that your mother packed her famous egg and bacon pie.'

'It wouldn't be my birthday without it!' Lizzy stated, holding the pie up over the picnic basket as evidence. 'Who would like some eggs?'

'Oh, dear lord. It's the Old Truronians,' Bee scoffed, peering over her cat eye sunglasses. 'Those boys are insufferable.'

The three young women watched in bemusement as five young men, donned in checkered squares and lavish stripe patterns of swim boxers and matching shirts, bee-lined in their direction. One stood out amongst them for Gloria in a heartbeat, before each of their handsome features could sharpen in better proximity. Charles' size and stature was, in Gloria's keen eyes, far superior and desirable to that of his fellow men, and when they finally stood before them on the warm sand, she gave him her best dazzling smile. He was instantly captured by her beauty, and she knew it.

'I'm afraid these sands are claimed, boys,' Gloria said, boldly.

'Really?' Charles said, a mischievous smile pulling on those full lips, his tanned features glowing in the sunshine, his hands in his pockets in casual calmness. 'And it is you ladies who have claimed them, is it?'

'Of course!' Bee joined in. Gloria noted the blush in her

cheeks as she too bestowed on Charles' charm. 'I'm sure there will be another beach further along perfect for you lot. Ta-ta!'

The boys all chortled and chuckled at her boldness, and the other lads jostled Charles forward.

'Go on, Charlie-boy! Tell them!'

The arrogance which crossed Charles' face only lured Gloria further in and her legs practically went to jelly as he revealed a set of perfectly white, straight teeth.

'I do believe we have a problem here, my dear ladies. You see - these sands are privately owned. They are otherwise engaged if you will. I'm afraid you will not be able to claim them.'

His voice carried an amusement disguised in authority, and the trio stared at him, perplexed.

'What are you waffling on about?' Bee cried out, her patience worn thin and that calm demeanour of hers dropping like a cloak. 'We come here every weekend, and tonight is a particularly important evening because it's our Lizzie's birthday. You are spoiling it with your male presence. Do be gone!'

'H-h-happy birthday, Lizzie,' a shy, skinny boy suddenly said, coming forward with his ears raging red.

'Hello, Robert,' Lizzie said politely, though her eyes rolled to the sky.

Robert Pascoe!' Another boy jeered. 'He speaks! In front of a girl, no doubt! What do you think, Lizzie? Fancy becoming the next Mrs Pascoe?'

Despite the boy's unkind jeering, Lizzie's face pinked and she sent gentle eyes in Robert's direction, rewarding him with a friendly smile.

'So, I take it you are the Lord's son then?' Gloria said, continuing the topic of the beach claim. 'And this beach is part of the Penhaligon Estate.'

Charles' dark eyes settled on Gloria's skin, every part of her tingling under his gaze. 'Aren't you an intuitive little thing? I am. Charles Penhaligon, madam. And you are?'

'Gloria. Gloria Retallick.'

That moment had sealed a fate between them and before Gloria knew it, her heart was entirely with Charles Penhaligon. They courted - much to their families' distaste. They found ways to spend their days together without being under the scrutinising eyes of those who fought against their relationship. They wrote love letters to one another, hiding them in inconspicuous places around the estate. And Gloria affectionately became Gi-Gi, a name she adored and treasured, her heart swelling in her chest every time it passed his lips.

Her friendship with Lizzie stuck like glue - her and Bee being asked to be bridesmaids for Lizzie and Robert's quick wedding that following Spring - Lizzie indeed becoming Mrs Pascoe and settling happily in a little fisherman's cottage in the hamlet they grew up in. But a void fell between Gloria and Bee, and she could only put it down to jealousy.

Gloria was acutely aware of the way Bee was around Charles. The way her body reacted and the way her face glowed. It was astoundingly clear that the closer Gloria and Charles grew, the colder Bee was towards her oldest friend. It both broke Gloria's heart and enraged her in equal measure.

It was August 1st when Gloria first realised she was pregnant with Charles' baby, and from there her life began to unravel. At first, she was able to disguise the bump, cleverly hidden under loose fitting frocks whilst she desperately clawed at solutions for the future. They were worlds apart - her and Charles. How could they bring a baby into the world together, where society saw its parents segregated by an invisible class system decided upon archaism and tradition? But as her stomach swelled, so did her love for her unborn child, as did her resolve to make this work. She would simply tell Charles - they would marry, and as far as everyone would be made aware, they'd have a beautiful baby in happy wedlock and all would be well. But of course, it would never be so simple.

'I'm in an impossible position, Gi-Gi,' Charles said one day, under the canopy of the sweet honeysuckle. 'There have been many a time where I dreamed of taking your hand and asking you to be my wife.'

'But?' Gloria asked, a tremble in her voice as she halted the news of new life growing in her swelling belly.

'Look, darling,' Charles continued, pain contorting every muscle on his handsome face. 'I must take up my position with the estate. Father will be stepping down within the year and I am duty-bound to take his place.'

Gloria searched in his eyes for an answer, for an explanation as to why he told her this now. Why he fixated on his becoming a Lord, and why this made the slightest difference to their courtship. He stumbled over his words, like he was taking a wide berth around a truth that would be the inevitable undoing of their relationship. But he didn't have to say it. Suddenly, it dawned on Gloria.

'You mean to end this,' Gloria stated.

He looked beyond wretched, and it was all Gloria could do not to step forward and place a comforting hand on his cheek. But she remained rooted, bracing herself for what he was about to say - her whole world crashing at her feet.

'We're from different places, you and I. Darling, there's no easy way to say this.'

'Then don't.' Gloria's features were riddled with contempt as she backed slowly away, desperately keeping her hands from flying to her stomach in a natural protective reaction.

Charles pleaded, his chest heaving in despair. 'I don't know what to do. I don't have a choice.'

'It's alright,' Gloria whispered, hating herself in that moment of weakness where she put Charles' reassurance before her own dignity. After all, things were far from alright. 'I understand.'

'You're quite the homemaker, Lizzie,' Gloria had said one morning to her dear friend, her smile never reaching her eyes. She had been a ghost of a person since that dreadful day and hadn't seen Charles since. Her short time with him seemed like a distant memory already, and if it wasn't for the baby growing inside of her as a bitter-sweet reminder, she would have convinced herself easily that it never happened at all. Lizzie, newly married and blooming in womanhood, smiled proudly in her tiny kitchen.

'Would you like a cup of tea, Gloria? Robert will be home any moment and would love to see you, I'm sure.'

'No, I mustn't stay for long. Mother wants me to cycle to the shops later for some groceries.' She gripped the chair in front of her, suddenly barrelled over with pain somewhere in the pelvic area. Her hand immediately rushed to her stomach, pressing the material of her dress down and around the swell. She realised then, through the cramping, what she had revealed as Lizzie's eyes became wide like dinner plates.

'Oh, Gloria...' Lizzie gasped. 'You're not...?'

'Oh!' A sudden dampness pooled down below as her back and pelvis became hot in agony. She collapsed into the chair which Lizzie offered with shaking hands, and both young women cried out at the sight of the blood seeping through her dress.

'You mustn't tell anyone, Lizzie!' Gloria cried through wails of pain and instant grief. 'Please - promise me you won't tell anyone. My parents could not take the shame. They don't deserve it. Please!'

'I... I promise,' Lizzie had managed through barely a whisper. 'I'm so sorry, darling Gloria.'

Even seven decades couldn't erase the pain - the loss Gloria had endured that year. Now, in the present day, flashes of memories pooled to the surface of a brain fogged with age.

Being told by her parents - stricken with grief for their own daughter's scandal - that losing her baby had been for the best. For the *best*? How anything as agonising as losing one's child could be for the best, Gloria would never begin to understand. And though she had understood her parents' own grief in her recklessness, those words had harrowed her for years to come.

Her thoughts delicately edged around the day she first found out about Bee and Charles. Or Beryan as she chose to return to once she had declared she would be the next Lady of the estate. How Beryan had come to Gloria, only months after Gi-Gi and Charles had become no more, to inform her that their families of equally elevated status had rejoiced in the engagement of Charles and Beryan, and that she would not be welcomed to the wedding.

'I just don't think it's appropriate - considering the circumstances. I hope you'll understand.' Beryan had been cruel, motivated by a thirst for something that apparently sat high above friendship. Not that Gloria would have wanted to be at the wedding - she couldn't think of anything more torturous in fact - but it had been the deliberate rejection, the sudden shift in social class between them. The way Beryan had accentuated her social superiority over Gloria had made her feel like a second-class citizen.

But Lizzie had been true to her word - her parents also keeping the whole ordeal a secret from everyone in the hamlet. Even Charles never discovered the existence of his own unborn child. Or so she had been led to believe.

Dabbing her wrinkled face, the tissue she had been using for the past hour rendered useless now, Gloria retrieved an old shoe box, hidden in the depths of her wardrobe behind old dresses and coats. It was tatty, torn in one corner and discoloured from age - but it held some of Gloria's most treasured items.

Inside, a collection of letters not dissimilar to the one Ellie had given her last night, bound together with some tatty string. Some old photographs lined the bottom of the box, to which Gloria couldn't bring herself to look at in this moment. It was one thing having words bring her back to that time. She didn't need the visuals to accompany it. She added the newest letter with the others and closed the lid, looking up at the framed photograph of her and Joseph on their wedding day.

'Oh, Joseph,' Gloria croaked. 'I didn't deserve you.'

Joseph had come into Gloria's life five years later. He'd been a welcome distraction and a breath of fresh air, a local mechanic someone in the hamlet had hired to fix their car. She recalled with fondness how she'd told him off for the amount of oil he had spilled on the ground. The kindness and safety of his eyes had captured Gloria immediately. It was her who had asked him on a date, and he had loved her boldness. When they'd married a couple of years later, she had wanted to move away - start a new life far away from the estate. But Joseph had fallen in love with the river, the people, and had picked up quite the custom as the creek communities' local handy man. Cars, gardens, house maintenance - he did the lot. And so, Gloria shut away the memories of a dark past, the big house and the people within a dark shadow easily ignored where it could not be seen, and Gloria and Joseph built a beautiful life together. They raised Fiona, their tenacious daughter, to be strong and practical and independent. And goodness, was she all those things. What Gloria hadn't banked on was for history to repeat itself.

'How can you not know his name?' Gloria had cried out, the day her daughter had broken the news of being pregnant. Both crushed by the confession and somewhat elevated by the fact her daughter had felt she could come to her in this hour of need, Gloria had found everything in her being to offer her daughter the support she had never had. 'You bedded him, but didn't think to find out his name?'

'I told you, Ma! He was touring with his band. He'll be halfway up the country by now!'

'What is the band called? Perhaps we could trace him. He must be accountable, Fiona.'

'I can't remember,' Fiona had admitted bashfully. 'I was...I wasn't...'

'You never are these days!' Gloria had spat, referring to her eighteen-year-old daughter's fast-growing issue with alcohol.

Of course, it is true what they say. Things do happen for a reason, and through the darkness and the constant rain, there is always light - and perhaps even a rainbow. That rainbow had been their darling Ellie.

Fiona did her best, with the support of Gloria and Joseph, to raise Ellie as a single mother. But her addiction and growing mental health issues meant that they had had no choice but to step up as permanent guardians to the young Ellie. Fiona took this as an opportunity and dealt with her issues in the only way she felt would be possible - travelling.

Gloria fingered through the wad of postcards and letters from her daughter - years and years' worth of travel and 'managing' her needs. Gloria didn't necessarily resent her daughter's decisions in life - in a way she sort of admired them - but it floored her in sadness for best part at what Fiona was missing out on, what Ellie missed out on with not having her mother present in her life. She was so proud of the young woman Ellie had become despite things.

She realised in that moment that her darling granddaughter deserved the truth. The whole, messy truth. And so, she picked up the shoe box, shuffled into the kitchen where she found Ellie filling out order forms at the kitchen table, and placed the box in front of her. Ellie looked up, alarmed.

'Everything alright?'

'I think it's time I was truthful with you. I'm going to tell you everything.'

A warm, encouraging smile crossed over Ellie's gentle features. 'Thank you, Nanny. I would like that. And I'm here for you. Just as you have always been for me.'

Gloria's lips puckered nervously, fresh tears welling in her blue eyes. She squeezed Ellie's hand and took a seat beside her.

'What I will tell you, we will discuss only once. You see, I have carried these secrets for so long, but the letter you gave me last night - well, it's done me the world of good. I can't explain it. You see, the letter - from Charles - it told me that he knew.' Her eyes glistened with tears and a smile of relief spread over her face. 'He knew - all this time. And he cared. And I don't know why, exactly - but that's given me so much comfort.'

'Knew about what, Nan?'

Gloria drew in a long breath, installing some much-needed courage. 'Alright. Here goes.'

# Chapter Twenty-One

*January 27th, 1953*

*Dearest Gloria,*

*I write to you with fresh knowledge of something I have felt ashamed to learn that you experienced entirely alone. I am sorry for the way we parted, and I am sorry for everything you have been through since. Please know it had not been my intention to cause you so much grief and that, up until now, I had had no knowledge of the child. Our child. I assure you that this secret you have borne will stop with me and go no further.*

*My darling Gloria, the pain and suffering you have been through. It grieves me to learn this, and I feel my own selfish loss for a child I had never and will never meet. I understand your position and hold no resentment in your choice to keep the pregnancy from me. I blame myself entirely and do hope that one day you can forgive me for my actions. I do also hope that one day you and Beryan can be friends again, though I know this shall be difficult given the circumstances. Again, I hold nothing on you to make a decision for anyone's benefit other than yourself. I want you to be happy, Gloria. You deserve to be happy.*

*The doors to Penhaligon will always be open to you and your family. I hope this letter reaches you in time and that you figure out my trail. I couldn't risk this letter falling in the wrong hands. I want to make amends for what I have done and look ahead to the future.*

*I wish you all the best, Gloria. I really do.*

*Yours,*
*Charles*

# Chapter Twenty-Two

'Tell me my app is just broken and the weather is not about to piss all over my open day on Saturday,' Tressa cried out, storming into the study and slamming her phone down on George's desk.

'*Your* open day?' George challenged. He glanced at Tressa's phone and cussed under his breath. A line of dark thunder cloud symbols covered the forecast from tomorrow all the way into Sunday. 'Can we bring any of it inside?'

'Would you like to run that by Mother and Granny?' Tressa paused for a moment, considering the idea despite her remark. 'I suppose we could bring the trade stalls inside and create a one-way system in just a couple of the rooms.'

'Let's hope the stalls distract from the tiredness of the place,' George muttered, noting the discolouring of the walls around him and the patches of damp on the ceiling. As Tressa stormed back out, muttering incoherently under her breath with the added foot stomp here and there to punctuate her frustration, George's phone buzzed on the desktop.

'Ciao, Antonio,' George greeted his friend into the screen. An Italian blue sky mocked George from behind Antonio as his friend walked casually down the street, glasses reflecting and his brilliant white teeth gleaming. 'You couldn't have called at a crueller time, friend. The British weather is keeping up its reputation.' He looked out of one of the large windows in the study to glance at the moody, grey sky.

'See, this why I not bother to visit England,' Antonio said down the phone. 'When are you coming back, amico?'

A part of George wanted to say 'right away' - 'tomorrow' at the very best. But then Ellie walked around the corner from the kitchen gardens into the little courtyard in front of his window and he found himself saying, 'not for a little while, friend. I have business here to sort out.'

A hearty laugh erupted from Antonio. He appeared to be walking somewhere coastal, a glimpse of sparkling water spotted behind him.

'Where are you?' George asked, trying to make it out from his friend's background.

'Lake Como,' Antonio answered dismissively, before returning to his reason for mirth. 'What's her name, amico?'

'Ah, what are you talking about?' George groaned, knowing exactly where he was getting on, knowing Antonio.

'Last you told me, it would be quick visit to England, no? Sort out castle or whatever.'

'It's a house, Antonio. Well, an estate. I don't own a castle.'

'Semantics, amico.'

'No, they're very dif - do you know what, never mind. Anyway, to what do I owe this pleasure of you calling me and torturing me with your glorious Lake Como scenery?'

A sudden ejection of Italian profanity burst through the screen as Antonio argued with someone out of shot about picking up their litter. George stood patiently, smiling fondly at his hot-headed friend. He glanced up to see Ellie had come back into view again, and though he felt like a Peeping Tom watching her from his study as he did, he couldn't help himself. Antonio's words of justice continued to burst through his phone as he watched Ellie take her gardening gloves off to retrieve her own phone from her back pocket and answer it. She looked suddenly concerned, her shoulders hunched in like she carried the world on them. George watched intently as she nibbled nervously on her thumb, occasionally speaking down the receiver and running her hand down her long ponytail. She nodded and seemed to agree on something as George became acutely aware of Antonio returning to their video chat.

'People want to visit our beautiful country, but they cannot be bothered to put rubbish in bin,' Antonio ranted, gesturing down the phone in irritation. 'Now, if girl involved. I won't be seeing you for a little while now, no?'

George chortled. 'How are the clients holding up?'

'Bene. Is why I'm in Como.' Clearly bored of speaking in English, Antonio reeled off a sales report of their wine merchant business in Italian, claiming that two new restaurants were opening in tourist-heavy areas of Lake Como and that they'd been recommended as the best wine merchants from friends in Milan.

'Fantastico!' George exclaimed, before responding back in Italian and thanking his friend and business partner for holding the fort in his absence. Antonio had joined his company only a couple of years ago, but he had years of experience having grown up on an old family vineyard. When George's then-small wine merchant business began to grow into a successfully large company, George happily invested with Antonio to help them widen their field across Italy. Without Antonio, he never would have been able to come back to Cornwall to tackle his own family affairs. Antonio was now busy doing the visits and the quality checks of their wine, whilst George attempted to keep up with the admin side of things over email and conference calls. But with an entire estate to save from financial ruin, he was beginning to realise that where he gave one the attention it needed, the more he neglected the other.

'It all sounds great, Antonio. Listen, perhaps we should arrange to talk like this over video more often to keep us both in the loop. I feel like I've just left you to run things solo.'

'True. True. You have,' Antonio nodded. 'It's no problem for now. You have bigger...uh, how they say...bigger fish to fry, no? It's nothing! No problem, amico. I'll let you know later how the sign up goes with new client.'

'Grazie, Antonio. Ciao!'

As he ended the call, he hadn't noticed Ellie come inside and rap lightly on the study door.

'Hey,' George greeted her warmly. She seemed out of breath and agitated, and naturally he stepped forward wanting desperately to comfort her in some way. 'Everything alright?'

'Yeah, fine,' Ellie replied, dismissively. 'Would you mind if I took off for a couple of hours? I finally managed to get a doctor's appointment for Nanny. It's in the Health Centre in Truro though.'

'Of course! Is she okay? Anything I can do?'

Ellie paused her fidgets of agitation for a moment to smile appreciatively at George. 'Thank you. I just need a couple of hours to drive her down. She's not going to like it, but tough shit. I'm fed up with hearing her barking away and looking so uncomfortable. It worries me.'

'Understandable. Did you give her the letter?'

'I did.' Ellie said, some of her worry sliding from her features. She sighed deeply.

'And?'

'Let's just say, the letter gave her some much needed closure.'

'Oh, really?' Ellie nodded in reply, smiling. 'That's good. I take it it's all top secret.'

'As I've said before,' Ellie said, coyly. 'My Nanny is a mysterious woman. But don't worry. Your grandfather's integrity is intact. In fact, I rather admire the man - even if I never got to meet him.'

'I think he very much would have liked you,' George said, smiling down at her.

Ellie returned the gesture and a comfortable silence fell between them for a moment. 'Anyway, I won't be long, and I'll make up the lost hours.'

'No need. I'm pretty sure we owe *you* hours. Not the other way round. I am meant to be meeting Jack at Mrs Pascoe's old cottage this afternoon to do a snag check before completion. Perhaps I could check in if you're back?' It was potentially a futile attempt to be more involved in Ellie's personal life, given that her only active family member couldn't stand the sight of him without causing her great distress, but he wanted to at least try. Besides, after whatever revelation occurred in the Curnow house last night, perhaps he would be on safer grounds now with Gloria.

Ellie surprised George by saying, 'That would be lovely, actually. Make sure you're nice to Jack, please.'

'Why wouldn't I be?' George asked, acting affronted.

'Don't go doing the whole 'big brother' act,' Ellie teased. Of course - she was talking about Wenna and Jack. Not his hang-up from the previous possibility that Jack was some sort of rival. In fact, he'd been so focused on him and Ellie, he'd neglected his brotherly duties to be unnecessarily vexed by Jack pursuing his baby sister. Except, when he thought about it, he found he was oddly pleased by the idea of Wenna finding someone. Perhaps someone to ground her a little. Perhaps Jack would make her grow up a bit.

'I'm going to shoot off now, if that's okay,' Ellie said, backing out of the door and interrupting George's thought trail.

'Absolutely. Take as much time as you need. You've got a full team today. Why don't you take your Nanny out for tea and cake after her appointment? Soften her up a bit.' He winked and Ellie brightened up at the idea.

'Actually, that's a really good idea. There's a little tearoom just outside of Truro that she loves. Haven't taken her there for ages. Thanks, George.'

'You're welcome.' A moment hung between them before Ellie disappeared, leaving George to begrudgingly return to his work.

George had done many nerve-wracking things in his time. He had spoken in front of hundreds of people at wine conferences. He had invested thousands of pounds of his own money, taking huge risks and working the tricky business of the wine industry. His move from Cornwall to Italy, entirely on his own, had been one of the most terrifying things he had ever done. And yet, none of these milestones matched the nerves he felt right now as he stood at the little blue gate leading to Ellie and Gloria's little cottage. He'd finished his meeting with Jack and found himself astounded by the quality of finish - the way Jack (with the help of Ellie, of course) had transformed the place. He'd thanked Jack and discovered that, without the unspoken rivalry that had existed between them previously, they actually got on pretty well. And now, with a little posy of Sweet William grasped in his hands, he creaked open the gate and approached the door to the cottage with caution.

Ellie answered the door immediately, and George was momentarily inert by her appearance. It quickly occurred to him that he had never really seen Ellie out of her work clothes, and though he still found her unbelievably adorable in her khaki shorts and weather-proof jackets, her simple little summer dress that she wore now suddenly bore him the inability to piece together a simple greeting.

He babbled his way through a clumsy 'hello' and thrusted the posy of flowers into her hands, leaning down to place a tender kiss on her cheek. Her sweet, flowery fragrance swaddled him and pulled at something primal deep within.

'How did the appointment go?'

'She has a chest infection. I mean, I could have told her that,' Ellie said, rolling her eyes and quickly thanking George for the flowers. She led him through into the kitchen, George ducking every couple of steps to avoid the low beams, and continued to tell him about the afternoon whilst finding a small vase to place the flowers. 'Anyway, she has antibiotics now. Doctor wants to see her again in two weeks' time to make sure it has cleared up. Make sure it hasn't progressed to pneumonia or...' Ellie suddenly paused and released an unsteady but sharp breath through her nose, her hand poised on the counter and tapping away in agitation. George observed her bottom lip beginning to tremble and he shot forward, gathering her up and pressing her into him.

'Hey, hey,' George soothed. 'It'll be alright. She'll be fine. If your Nan is anything like you, she's strong as rock and will be just fine.'

Initially, Ellie stiffened in George's embrace, hesitant of his comfort. Then, within seconds, her body relaxed and melted into him, her arms snaking around his middle. They remained like that for what felt like a lifetime, in the quietness of Ellie's kitchen, until a light thump was heard from somewhere further into the cottage. Ellie peeled herself away, wiping her face and not making eye contact.

'I just hope...' Ellie pondered, then shaking her head. 'I keep thinking the stress of the letter, me working at the estate - stirring up old emotions. I feel like I've finished her off!'

George wiped away a stray tear on her cheek and shook his head gently. 'Don't think like that. It's not true.'

'No, I know. I'll just check on her a minute. She was just getting freshened up.'

'Anything I can do here?' George asked, looking at the ingredients laid out on the counter ready for dinner.

'Yeah - can you start peeling the veg? I won't be long.'

Ellie disappeared through a door and George was left to his devices. He busied himself with peeling the vegetables, as per Ellie's request, and took his moment of solitary to absorb his surroundings. Though it was cramped and busy in its decor, there was something about this cottage - this kitchen - that he instantly loved. The Moroccan yellow wall paint clashing against the pale blue kitchen cupboards reminded George of the kind of busy warmth of an old Italian kitchen, and the cold flag-stoned floor was remedied with handwoven rugs scattered around in patches. As George filled a saucepan with hot water, he looked up to gaze at the glittering water at the foot of the garden. Everything about the design of this kitchen had been purposely angled towards the river - the focal point.

He was about to make a start on prepping the chicken when Ellie returned, looking somewhat relieved.

'She's on her way. Thank you for doing those,' Ellie remarked, tilting her head over the saucepan. 'Oh, dear. You've done fancy batons.' She held up a carrot baton between her thumb and forefinger, tutting away teasingly.

Looking bewildered but amused, George shrugged. 'Yeah? So?'

'Nanny prefers them cut in discs. You wait.' She nudged her head towards the door just as the very woman shuffled into the room, her head bent over from age as it was when George last came across her. She paused briefly to cough into a handkerchief, Ellie darting forward to help her only for the old woman to bat her away impatiently.

'Don't fuss, my love. I'm fine.'

The old woman came level with the kitchen island where George was situated and raised her head shakily to acknowledge him.

'Hi, Gloria,' George greeted her cheerfully. 'How are you feeling?'

Gloria mumbled away about the joys of being old but thanked him politely for his query. A pregnant silence fell between the three of them and George fought for something charming to say.

'George brought you some Sweet William, Nan,' Ellie said,

stepping in. She pointed at the flowers, which were now sat proudly in a vase on the kitchen table.

'Oh, I love Sweet William. Thank you, George.' She made an effort to tilt her head upwards to make eye contact, though this proved to be difficult for the poor lady with her spine curved over the way it was. It didn't help that George stood well over 6ft, which would make any person of Gloria's height strain to reach eye-level.

Another silence fell.

This would take time, George thought to himself. He would of course respect this for Gloria's sake. For Ellie's too.

'Are you staying for dinner, George?' Gloria piped up, edging her way towards the hob to turn them on for the vegetables.

George glanced at Ellie for approval, with her returning a smile and nod of encouragement. 'That sounds lovely, Gloria. If you'll have me.'

'We always make plenty, so you're very welcome. Ellie, m'love - help me with the meat. George, you pour the drinks.'

Feeling somewhat grateful for a purpose and a role in their evening, George jumped straight to it, taking orders from the two ladies. When all drinks had been poured, Ellie accepted hers with a smile of encouragement directed at him. Their eyes locked on each other; they sipped their beverages as Gloria opened the lid of one of the saucepans. 'Who the bloody hell cut my carrots all fancy?'

George and Ellie snorted in unison and finally the tension was broken.

# Chapter Twenty-Three

'I can't believe I let you talk me into this,' George groaned, as he followed Ellie into the tiny entrance hall of The Reading Room, a timber-framed chapel-shaped hall which acted as the hamlet's village hall. The floorboards creaked under foot and there was a distinct damp smell within, mixed with the scent of TCP and perfume.

'Hey, you're the one who said you wanted to get more involved with the community. No better way to mingle than with a night at WI Bingo!' Ellie sang, clearly enjoying every moment of George's discomfort as he smiled politely at those glancing his way in curiosity. 'Honestly - it's the highlight of the quarter!'

The queue edged forward towards the table of ladies selling tickets, George surprised at the volume of people crammed into this tiny hall. 'So, what's at stake here? Cash? Wine?'

'Okay, I want you to take your standards from up here,' Ellie said, holding a hand flat above her head, 'and bring them to around about here. It's the WI. They're not made of money. There might be wine. But it won't be your posh stuff. Oh good - Nanny's here already and she's got the dabbers.'

'Dabbers?' George asked, feeling like a fish out of water as Ellie stoically ignored him and approached the ticket table.

'Alright?' Ellie sang cheerfully, the ladies smiling back. Their side glance to George prompted Ellie to add, 'This is George Penhaligon. He's just moved back from living in Italy and wanted to show his support - didn't you, George.'

'Absolutely,' George said, sounding much more confident than he felt. 'Good evening, ladies. Lovely to meet you.'

The ladies trilled happily between them, shaking his hand delicately before passing over their bingo books.

'Would you like some raffle tickets too, my love?' The older lady of the two asked, her arthritic hands poised over a line of tickets ready to rip out of the book. 'A pound a strip.'

'Why not?' George replied, cheerful and confident all of a sudden. Ellie had been right to recommend this - it would be a perfect way to get in with the locals. He hoped Charles would be nodding in approval right now. 'I'll take five strips please.'

Receiving some approving looks from the women in closest proximity, George handed over a £5 note and followed Ellie into the tight space of the hall, which was lined with tables from all sides. Nanny was spotted on the first chair on the last row, closest to the stage, in conversation with a woman George recognised from seeing out on a dog walk the last time he had ventured down as far as the hamlet. George observed in quiet amusement as people of all ages swarmed happily into the tiny hall and proceeded to decant whole picnics onto the tables in front of them.

'I didn't realise it was 'bring your own',' George whispered to Ellie. 'I would have -' He abandoned that sentence as Ellie emptied the contents of her rucksack, littering their table with an array of different snacks. Nanny tutted and told Ellie to clear the table, plucking a party-sized bag of crisps off her ticket book.

'You're surely not going to stuff your face with all of this at once. Put it all away!'

Giggling like a little child, Ellie did as she was told and scooped the majority of the snacks back into the bag. She then wrenched a packet of tortilla chips open and waved them under George's nose. *'Dorito?'*

'Got any drinks in that rucksack of yours?' George asked,

popping a *Dorito* in his mouth. In danger of spitting the crisp back out all over the table, George burst out laughing as Ellie extracted a pack of party tumblers from nowhere, followed by a bottle of *Shloer*.

'Wanna get *Shloer*-faced?' Ellie asked, winking. 'Actually, I'm going to grab a coffee too. It's going to be a long evening.'

'You're absolutely mad,' George remarked, chuckling away as Ellie scooted off in search of caffeine. 'How are you feeling, Gloria?'

'Fine, fine,' Gloria answered, dismissively. She then held up a pack of markers with two shaky hands. 'Which colour dabber do you want to use?'

'On its own, number eight! Five and six, fifty-six.'

'I had no idea Bingo could get so intense,' George whispered to Ellie twenty minutes later, when the hall was filled with a silence of concentration and light competition. Dozens of heads were bent over their tickets, dabber pens poised at the ready. Ellie snickered quietly, her shoulders shaking in mirth as Nanny hushed them both loudly. George leaned into Ellie and added in whisper, 'we're going to get kicked out in a minute.'

'A regular occurrence,' Ellie joked.

When the hall had eventually filled up with people, just before 'eyes down', George had been surprised with the mix of people the event brought. It wasn't just the WI members and local people of the hamlet - George recognised lads from The Old Creek Inn, coming in with their six-pack of beers; he'd noted young families with children as young as six dotting numbers with the help of their parents.

'Two and two, twenty-two,' the bingo master called out. George's head lifted in bewilderment as everyone began quacking like ducks around the hall. Ellie giggled behind her hand at his reaction as the more enthusiastic quacking from children lingered and bounced against the magnolia walls. 'Legs eleven!'

Everyone in the hall gave out a wolf-whistle, followed by George letting out a giggle of disbelief. 'What is happening?' There was a ripple of laughter across the whole hall and even Nanny looked up and smiled at George in amusement.

More numbers got called out and finally George realised that one of his tickets was fully dotted on all the numbers. 'Oh. I think I have a full house. Umm...bingo? Bingo!'

All eyes were in his direction, and the bingo master looked up sternly over her half-moon glasses.

'Sir, was this for the number I just called out or the number before?'

'The number before I think,' George said, hesitantly.

'Then you're too late, mate,' a male voice sounded curtly from somewhere in the table rows.

'I'm very sorry, Sir. But I've already called out the next number.'

George couldn't hide his disappointment but smiled politely, picking his dabber back up again. Ellie nudged his arm in support and muttered, 'you've got to get in there quickly. Fast sport this bingo.' George's smile spread more widely across his face then until the same male voice sounded again.

'Don't think his Lordship over there is used to hearing the word no, Madge,' the bloke said, jeering with his mates on the same table. George's forehead puckered into a deep frown and his top lip pulling up in one corner in a look of confusion and annoyance.

'Bit unnecessary,' George muttered.

'It's rude is what it is,' Ellie said, stretching herself up to look over the sea of heads. She must have spotted the offender because she then shouted, 'Oi, Jamie! Shut your pie-hole. No one likes a sore loser!'

Jamie was clearly about to retaliate when Nanny, to George's absolute astonishment, beat him to it. 'One more word from you, Jamie Hancock, and I'll be marching you straight back to your mother and telling her about that time I caught you smoking behind the bus stop.'

Chortles and chuckles rippled across the crowd and Jamie had the right mind to look bashful, dipping his head back down and out of view.

'Right, crack on Madge,' Nanny called out with fierce authority which only reminded George fondly of where Ellie got her own fire. 'We've all got homes to go back to and I'm eyeing up those tea-towels!'

A whopping two hours later, and the bingo master had called out the last numbers and thanked everybody for their attendance and support.

'So, how was it? Popping your bingo cherry?' Ellie said in a normal volume now that chairs scraped against the wooden floor and the mass collection of coffee mugs clinked across the echoey hall.

'Well, I feel a bit of a betrayer to be honest,' George joked, holding his winnings in his hands. 'There's you and Nanny valiantly defending my honour and I've gone and won the tea-towels Gloria here wanted.'

'Bleddy thief,' Gloria deadpanned and George and Ellie ruptured into laughter.

'Well, I would be honoured if you took these off my hands. Peach coloured tea-towels with floral embroidery isn't really my style. Come on, I'll walk you both back. Let me take the bags.'

The gentle walk back through the dimming light of the summer evening was a pleasant one, and George realised how much he had enjoyed his evening, despite some of the unwelcome attention he received from some people. Many of the villagers approached him after, shaking his hand and thanking him for coming along to support. He'd taken the opportunity to remind those who listened of the estate's open day and told them he hoped to see them there.

'Could I be cheeky and ask that the WI have a stall to sell cakes?' the lady introducing herself as the treasurer had asked, to which George had wholeheartedly agreed. He would deal with his sister's grumbles over adding another cake stall later.

Now, the ivory moon gleamed bright in the darkening sky and ominous streaks of cloud edged into view.

'Don't like the look of those clouds,' Ellie remarked at the same time as George had a similar thought.

'Looks like bad weather is coming in after all,' George sighed, thinking of the complications that would now arise with the open day.

'Excuse me? Mr Penhaligon?' A small gentleman George recognised as being one of the close neighbours of Mrs Pascoe's cottage was jogging up to them, negotiating the pebbles and stones underfoot whilst avoiding the clumps of seaweed the high tide from earlier had brought in.

'Hey, Mr Williams,' Ellie said in greeting whilst giving Nanny her arm for support.

'Hello, Ellie dear. Good evening to you, Gloria. You're looking very well.' Mr Williams was all pleasantries, a wide friendly smile upon his face, until he turned his attention to George, to which he had to tilt his chin upwards in order to meet eye-to-eye. 'Gosh, you're a very tall chap, aren't you? I hope you don't mind my approaching you after such a lovely evening, but I really feel I must take the opportunity to speak to you about something.'

George's initial friendly smile faltered, replaced with a light frown as he gestured for Mr Williams to continue.

'You see, it's about Mrs Pascoe's cottage,' Mr Williams continued. 'Jack and Ellie have done such a fantastic job of brightening the place up. Really spectacular work, Ellie.'

'Thank you, Mr Williams.'

'But I couldn't help but notice that you've had quite a few visitors recently. Visitors with clipboards. Not to mention the tell-tale sign of a key-safe newly installed on the front door. If I didn't know any better, Mr Penhaligon, I would say that you're planning on making our dear Mrs Pascoe's cottage into a holiday home.'

George felt Ellie and Nanny shift uncomfortably behind him, the burning of the Curnow women's eyes on him in scrutiny as they waited for his response.

The bloke was a bloody detective, George thought. But he confidently replied, 'I can appreciate your concerns, Mr Williams. But the key safe was simply installed for easy access between me and Jack. Ellie too, if she needs it for garden maintenance. As for the visitors with clipboards - just the estate agents getting things ready.'

'So, you won't be turning the cottage into a holiday home?' Mr Williams asked more directly. George did everything in his power not to sigh outwardly in exasperation. Talk about exposing him right in front of the people who mattered. He would make a great journalist. But there was no way that George would be admitting his plans for the cottage now. Not with Ellie and Gloria as his audience. So, though it pained him to do so, George slapped on a confident smile and replied, 'not as far as I am aware.'

The guilt was immediate, and George felt wretched all the way back to Ellie and Gloria's blue gate, silently seething at Mr Williams for backing him into a corner like that. This evening, he had been over the moon with getting involved in the community life attached to his estate, feeling more like his grandfather and being one with the people, so-to-speak. Now, he started to wonder whether there had been good reason to keep an arm's length from the people who would criticise his every move - his every decision.

'Would you like to come in for a drink?' Ellie asked from over her shoulder, as she helped her Nanny with the final step over the threshold.

'There's lemon cake left over,' Nanny added, speaking to the floor as she nudged off her 'going-out' shoes and replaced them with a pair of baby-blue slippers. Ellie was now bending down behind her grandmother, scooping a finger into the back, and ensuring her heels were safely inside each slipper whilst George watched in wonder at Ellie's level of care. His mind wandered to the unlikely idea of Tressa or even Wenna being as attentive to their grandmother, but he quickly decided he was being unfair to his sisters.

'As much as I would love to take you up on that offer, I'd best be getting back. Got a bit of work to do tonight before I get to bed.'

'Fair enough,' Ellie said, though George noted a hint of disappointment cross her pretty features. Nanny bid them both goodnight and Ellie waited patiently for her to shuffle further into the cottage and out of ear shot. 'Don't mind Mr Williams. He means well. He's just a bit of a worrywart when it comes to the character of the hamlet.'

George's muscles tightened in his face as he replied, 'perfectly understandable. He seemed a nice enough bloke.'

Ellie smiled. 'He is. They all are. It's a good community here. You'll see it at the open day. They were all buzzing about it this evening, so I reckon you may have won them all over.'

'That's good,' George said, smiling warmly despite his gut twisting and his jaw locking. 'Well, goodnight, Ellie.'

'Good night.'

Despite himself, George memorised the look on Ellie's face as she closed the front door, the way her eyes softened and drew him in. The thought of those eyes turning to disappointment, when it finally occurred to her what he would have no choice but to do, near enough killed him. But it was business at the end of the day and George just had to hope that the community - and more importantly, Ellie - would eventually see that.

# Chapter Twenty-Four

The day before the big Penhaligon Estate Open Day was finally upon them, and with-it torrential rain which drove in sideways along with a vicious wind strong enough to whip you off your feet in unpredictable bursts. Ellie could be found securing everything and anything she could to protect and preserve her gardens, her hair clinging in wet strands to her face and her raincoat acting as a menacing parachute every time the wind took hold. She and Dave made feeble attempts to shelter some of the trained fruit trees against the Kitchen Garden wall with sheets of fleece - something they would usually be applying ready for the winter, not a freak storm in June. Dave shouted something indistinct in her direction, his eyes squinting against the rain and his arms flaying around madly. With much more gesticulation, Ellie eventually decoded that Dave had meant for them to take shelter back in the servant's yard before tackling more of the garden.

'Joseph has made it home okay,' Ellie remarked, reading a message from Joseph, confirming his safe arrival home after she had sent him off early. It had made sense to send Joseph off first. He was a new, and slightly nervous driver living further away from the estate than Ellie or Dave. They practically fell into the staff room, their trench coats dripping all over the slabbed floor. Even with the door open to the elements, the little room was at least sheltered from the harsh winds.

'Dave, I think you should get home now.,' Ellie advised. 'According to my phone, it's gone to a red weather warning, and you'll need to get your animals in.'

Dave, though reluctant to abandon his post in the middle of all this, nodded gravely, his thoughts instantly to his poor horses, sheep, and goats, who all lived in exposed little paddocks on his small holding. 'Don't you go out there on your own. Wait until George has got back.'

'I will. Don't worry. Give me a text when you get home safely.' Dave nodded once and, with a sheltering arm over his head, ran across the yard towards his car. At that very moment, Ellie's phone buzzed in her pocket.

It was Jack.

'Are you okay? I've just passed yours and your van isn't outside. Don't tell me you're still up at the estate.'

'Yeah,' Ellie said, sighing in exasperation. 'It's just taken me and Dave all morning to secure everything. The marquee is getting absolutely butchered out there, but we've taken the sides off and put some extra weights down to hopefully keep it in place.'

'Crikey. What bad timing. I bet Tressa is gutted.'

'I haven't seen her this morning,' Ellie confirmed, a hint of sympathy in her voice but mostly annoyance over her hiding away when things get rough. 'Wenna has put her little coffee van inside one of the barns.'

'Good. Get yourself inside now. The weather report is looking nasty. Where's George?'

'He went to Griggs to pick up some materials for tomorrow in case the weather sorts itself out. Stuff to redirect the public and keep them off the lawn that I had just reseeded.' She blew out a harsh, sharp sigh through her nose, trying to stay calm about the hours of work that was being destroyed at this very moment.

'It's going to be all right, El,' Jack soothed down the phone.

'Get yourself home now. I'm sure Nan is having a fit right now about you being in this. Do you want me to pop back and check her?'

Ellie heard her van pulling into the yard and was relieved to see George returning. She returned her attention to Jack on the phone. 'No, it's okay. I shouldn't be long now. George just got home.'

They rang off and Ellie ran back out into the elements up to her van, which George was clambering out of.

'Leave it!' George shouted over the ever-growing storm, as Ellie went to extract the materials from the back of the van. George grasped her upper arm and steered her back towards the house, following close behind her as a clap of thunder filled the darkening sky.

'Shit! That's getting really bad,' Ellie gasped as they practically fell through the back door into Trixie's kitchen. They stood in the walkway, shaking off as much of the excess water from their coats as possible. 'I need to get back to Nanny!'

'You are not going back out there,' George declared, waving an arm fiercely in the direction of the outdoors. 'I could barely keep your van on the road. It was getting thrown around like a tin can!'

Ellie's mouth gaped open and shut like a goldfish as panic set in. 'I've got to get home! I can't leave Nanny alone in this. She'll be worried sick about me... and... and I need to make sure she's taken her meds...'

George placed steadying hands on her shoulders and guided her deeper into the kitchen, towards the breakfast stools, and flicked the kettle on to make a warming cup of something. 'Can you call her? I'm sure she'll be absolutely fine, Ellie. But you cannot - and will not - be going out in that. It's not safe.'

Ellie bit her lip, looking fruitlessly out of the kitchen window which was running opaque with sheets of water. She dialled their land line on her mobile and tried calling, but the phone just beeped uselessly at her, disconnecting any attempts of a call.

'It's not... it's not connecting!' Ellie cried out, slamming the phone onto the counter. George placed a steaming hot coffee into her hands and, with a warm palm pressed firmly on the small of her back, guided her upstairs into the warmth of the main house. They found Lavinia, Wenna and Beryan gathered in the drawing room, where a roaring fire now filled the room with a warming glow.

'Safe to say this is the first time we've ever lit the fire in June,' Wenna announced, looking as suitably downtrodden and fed up as the next Penhaligon.

'Goodness, Eleanor - you're still here?' Lavinia remarked, appraising Ellie not unkindly from her position on the sofa beside the fireplace. Beryan turned in her chair adjacent, giving Ellie a matching sort of expression. 'I thought you would have gone home with the rest of your team before it got too treacherous.'

'That was the plan,' Ellie said, breathless from concern. 'But I wanted to make sure everything was secure. I left it a bit late.' She glanced at George as if trying to seek permission to sneak out and go home after all, but he looked up at his mother with determination.

'Ellie won't be travelling home in this. She'll need to stay the night if needs be.'

'Ooh, yay! Sleepover!' Wenna sang, bouncing to life at the thought. 'You can borrow some pyjamas if you like. And -oh! - we can do face masks and stuff. Pretend we're teenagers again!'

Ellie chuckled, despite the panic rising like bile in her throat. 'Let me just try Nanny again.'

She started dialling, just as Lavinia asked George a question from across the room. 'How did the meeting go with the lettings agency, George?'

Ellie must have whipped around with interest a little too quickly because a muscle tightened in his jaw and he made a vague attempt to shake off the question, gesturing 'later' to his mum. But it was too late. Ellie was already intrigued.

'I've got friends from Oxford who have already shown interest in staying in August. I told them you would send over the details once you are live.'

George looked noticeably uncomfortable all of a sudden, and Ellie's concern to get home was temporarily side-lined as she approached him. 'What's this? As in, a holiday letting?'

The room went uncomfortably silent then.

'It's not all finalised yet. The agency hasn't even been to help me price it up,' George said, defensively. Ellie must have looked somewhat perplexed, though she had a foreboding feeling that she knew exactly where he was talking about.

'Mrs Pascoe's cottage?' Ellie asked, seeking confirmation of her worrying suspicions. 'I thought we were getting it ready for new tenants?'

George, seemingly unwilling to have this conversation with an audience, nodded in the direction of the library in the next room, encouraging Ellie to discuss this more privately.

'I was planning on telling you. Much more tactfully than that, I can assure you,' George jumped in, as soon as the door was closed, and they were alone.

'You *told* us that we were doing Mrs Pascoe's cottage up for new tenants!'

'No, I didn't,' George replied, firmly. 'I said nothing of the sort. Look, holiday lettings bring in a lot more instant money than long-term rentals do. That's just a well-known fact, and good business.'

Ellie found her jaw dropping involuntarily as she gaped at George. 'So, what about us existing tenants down on the creek? Have you even thought to consult us?'

'About what? What do I have to consult you with?' George demanded, annoyed and defensive.

Ellie threw her arms and shoulders up in an exasperated shrug. 'I don't know, exactly! But a holiday let? In the middle of our tiny little hamlet? Don't you think this will upset the neighbours? Mr Williams? You lied straight to his face the other day after Bingo.'

'Probably. But I've got to do what is right for the estate. That cottage will earn four to five times more a year as a holiday let. And we're the perfect location for tourists.'

She was no hermit. Ellie understood the status of tourism in Cornwall, and she could see the logic behind George's thinking. But she couldn't stop picturing the stag group from last month who had been down on holiday nearby and taken great entertainment in destroying her little boat. What if the holiday let attracted the wrong kind of people?

'I just wish you had been transparent with Jack and I from the start.'

'Would you have reconsidered the job?'

Ellie thought about it for a brief moment. 'Yes, I think I might have. Mrs Pascoe was a very close friend of our community. I hate the thought of her home being filled with groups of people coming down to treat our county like bloody Ibiza.'

Despite the tension building between them, a twitch of a smile pulled in the corner of George's mouth as he sunk his hands deep into his trouser pockets, towering over Ellie in amused appraisal.

'What are you bloody smirking at?'

'Is this about your boat? You know we can put a clause on banning group parties, right?'

That was a reasonable adjustment, Ellie thought. But she was still reeling.

'It's been a long, stressful day with the storm, and you must be exhausted. Why don't you head upstairs with Wenna, and she'll show you where the bathrooms are? Have a shower. A bath. Whatever you fancy. I'll make a start on something warming for dinner.'

She couldn't deny that all of that sounded pretty wonderful

after fighting against the wind and rain all day. She realised suddenly that she was shivering and chilled to the bone, and she was ravaged.

'I am sorry for not being honest with you. I just didn't want to disappoint you,' George added, his voice soft and intimate. 'But I also have this entire estate to save.'

Despite her conflicting feelings, Ellie nodded her understanding. George called Wenna from the other room, who happily whisked Ellie away up the staircase to show the way to one of the bathrooms.

'I'll grab you a towel and some spare pyjamas,' Wenna said, cheerfully. 'I don't think any of the spare rooms have beds anymore so are you happy to share with me?'

It surprised Ellie that such a big stately house as this, with the labyrinth of rooms available, couldn't accommodate one unexpected guest. It seemed that this was the reality of Penhaligon House at the moment. Ellie suddenly had thoughts of Lavinia and Beryan selling furniture in a frenzy to make ends meet, without touching some of the more valuable, antique assets. She wondered what actually went on behind closed doors and that perhaps the thriving gardens under her care were more of a distraction from the fact that Penhaligon Estate was financially in jeopardy.

When Wenna had disappeared off in pursuit of a spare towel and nightwear, Ellie had found herself roaming inquisitively down the stretch of corridor she found herself on. It was surprisingly well-lit but tired and weary from neglect - perhaps even more tired and worn than the downstairs accommodation. There was a notable damp odour coming from the walls and carpet - a faded and busy pattern recognisable as something from the mid to late 1800s. Most of the doors on the corridor were closed off and Ellie wondered what she would find on the other side. Empty rooms covered in dust? That was sadly what came to mind. She was starting to see why George outwardly cringed every time he thought of the idea on needing to make a start with the house. It was going to be a very expensive ordeal.

Coming to the end of that corridor and glancing out of the window to what would be a perfect view of the Kitchen Gardens, had it not been masked by sheets of rain and gusting winds, Ellie turned on her heel and headed back towards the other end where the bathroom was. As she passed a door, which was slightly ajar, her ears pricked at the sound of audible sniffling. She came to a quiet halt and edged towards the door. Someone was sobbing inside. With Lavinia and Beryan downstairs by the fire, and Wenna on a mission to find spare gear, it had to be Tressa.

Ellie took a deep breath and, despite her better judgment, knocked timidly on the door. When the sniffles came to a sudden halt, Ellie committed to her invasion and stepped into the room.

Tressa's room was a disparity from the rest of the house. A light oak floor was visible under a pale Persian rug, whilst everything in the room gravitated around a magnificent mahogany framed queen-sized bed, a scatter of plush cushions and thick cashmere blankets draped over the frame for such an occasion as simply looking bodacious. The carved roll-top headboard backed up against a gentle millennial pink wall which bathed that side of the room with a hint of pastel colour, whilst the rest of the room was humbled in a soft beige. A magnificent circular mirror hung proudly above the bed and the rest of the furniture - the chest of drawers, the bedside table, the occasion chair in the corner - all sat proudly and as solid as the bed. Ellie felt as if she had stumbled across a show room fit for an interior designer.

Ellie had been gaping so unexpectedly at the room, she had almost not noticed Tressa positioned at the vanity table immediately on her left, her usually composed posture bent over in shuddering sobs as she raised her blotchy face in Ellie's direction.

'Are you okay?' Ellie asked lamely, scolding herself for asking such a pointless question. She clearly was far from okay.

'Not really,' Tressa said, her voice thick and scratchy. Ellie waited patiently for Tressa to continue but nothing else came, so Ellie took a couple more steps into the room.

'Everything's as secure as possible outside. It might still clear up by tomorrow,' Ellie said in an attempt to reassure.

Tressa scoffed, throwing her ball of snotty tissue into a little bin, and ripping out a fresh one from her tissue box. 'I doubt it. Nothing I organise, or have anything to do with for that matter, goes to plan. Why do you think they never let me get involved in things? I've spent over a thousand pounds of George's money on this event and now we won't even be able to recoup any of the spendings. I look like a bloody fool.'

'No, you don't. No one expected this storm when you started the preparations. It's June for goodness' sake.'

Ellie watched Tressa dab her eyes, feeling achingly sorry for her. This was the real Tressa behind that supercilious facade - a vulnerable side to a woman who craved opportunities and purpose.

'Nobody blames you,' Ellie said, putting a consoling hand on her bony shoulder and looking firmly into her reflection in the vanity mirror. 'We're only disappointed for you... for us... for the estate. But nobody blames you.'

It seemed for a moment like Ellie might break through the hard exterior of Tressa's demeanour, as something shifted in those narrow dark eyes of hers. But when Tressa cleared her throat, sniffing loudly in indignation, the moment was gone, and she stood up in clear dismissal.

'Yes, well. I shan't be held accountable for the financial loss, and I shan't be doing something like this again. The estate can shove it.' With that, she yanked the bedroom door open and stood back, signalling clearly that she wanted Ellie to leave her be. Possibly deciding she was being unnecessarily rude towards Ellie, she added more softly: 'Thank you. For checking in.'

'No problem,' Ellie muttered, sadly. She stepped back out into the corridor, leaving the perfectly decorated haven of Tressa's bedroom and back out to the tired and stained walls of neglect. Deciding against a shower or bath at this given time, Ellie went to seek out George; he needed to know about Tressa. He needed to speak to her and console her as any caring brother should, putting the estate's matters to one side. When she got downstairs to George's study, she heard murmuring voices within and edged her ears up against the open crack of the doorway. This was becoming a theme for the evening, her snooping in doorways.

'But that's exactly why you cannot pursue this ridiculous notion!' Lavinia's voice rang out clearly, despite her whispering.

'Ridiculous notion? Mother, what century do you think this is?!'

George's voice hissed, low and furious. Ellie had never heard him so scathing. Frustrated, perhaps - maybe even exasperated. But never angry like this. She dared to press her ear closer to the wooden frame, her heart racing and pounding in her chest.

'You cannot be seen to be courting an employee. A gardener for that matter! It's outrageous, and it's embarrassing. The Lord of Penhaligon Estate and a girl who cuts grass for a living. Whatever next?'

Oh, so it was about Ellie. Suddenly, she wished more than anything that she had gone for that shower and that she had not heard those words spoken against her. Tears smarted in her eyes and the floor beneath her began to move and swim. She did everything in her power to keep her unsteady breath from giving away her position.

'Don't you dare!' George growled from inside the room. 'Don't you bloody dare! I've known you to be a snob, Mother.

But I've never thought you to be so damn prejudice and vindictive as that.'

'You have a duty of care for the reputation of this estate, George Thomas Penhaligon. And if you cannot see that this new infatuation of yours will ruin the integrity of your position, then perhaps you were not ready for this after all!'

It was like history was repeating itself, and Ellie thought immediately of Nanny and what she had gone through with Charles.

'You've never given that poor girl a chance! You've never shown any effort to like her.'

'I don't like her, George. I don't like her one bit. Or that damn grandmother of hers. Do you realise the agony this causes Granny on a daily basis? Seeing you lower your standards to such...'

Ellie had heard enough. Her heart and stomach twisted in agony as she ripped herself away from the study door, her blood bubbling and boiling in her veins as she marched down the hallway and wrenched the front door open. The ferocity of the wind matched her temper as she ignored all warnings of the danger, she would now rather subject herself to than being in that God-forsaken house. She pulled the door shut behind her with audible vexation and, realising that George still had the keys to her van, set out on foot to tackle the little track back to the safety of her cottage.

# Chapter Twenty-Five

'No way of contacting you! No way to know if you're dead or alive! I've been bloody sick with worry, I have!' Nanny cried, her rant now at an impressive nine minutes and thirty-three seconds. It was a welcome lecture, despite the frightening tone in which Nanny shouted, because Ellie knew it came from a place of love.

It had been a terrifying hike along the dark track back to the sanctuary of her cottage, and it was fair to say that Ellie resembled a drowned rat by the time she'd finally fallen into the safety of the storm porch on the side of their home. Nanny had wrenched the door open within minutes and, despite her age and fragility, had wrenched a sopping wet Ellie into the warmth and dry. Now, Nanny had finally run out of wind and Ellie dived forward, wrapping her arms around the old lady's shoulders, sobbing inconsolably into her pudgy shoulder.

'I'm so sorry, Nan. I tried to get back but... oh! - Nan, you were right. Those women - they're horrible! They're evil!'

'What did they say to you?' Nanny demanded, grabbing Ellie's face with her cold, gnarled hands and wiping the tears away with a thumb. 'What's happened, my dear girl?'

'It's not what they said *to* me. It's what I... Oh! God!' By this point, Ellie's breathing was so rapid, so suffocating that she didn't know what to do. In a way, she felt like heading back into the storm and being one with the ferocity of nature. But Nanny was insistent and demanded that she give her a breakdown. Ellie took a deep breath and recited everything that had happened, from George insisting that she stay, all the way to the total destruction and breakdown of Ellie's character, courtesy of Lavinia Penhaligon.

'What a bitch!' Nanny growled, her voice low and murderous. 'If I was ten years younger... Lord knows I would punch a tooth out from that precious jaw of hers. I bleddy would!'

'I believe you,' Ellie said, chortling despite herself and blowing her nose loudly into a piece of kitchen roll. The sobs were finally subsiding, and a wave of exhaustion was beginning to come over her from the ordeal of the afternoon. From the day in fact, if she were to include the wrestling of garden items and plants that needed securing and protecting against the elements. Her thoughts momentarily went to the poor garden, distracting her from the pain she was feeling, and she prayed that the gardens would be intact when she returned tomorrow.

Could she even do that? Would she be able to return to that place, knowing now how deeply loathed she was by the Lady of the House. And no doubt Beryan's hatred matched her daughter's. She'd made that very clear from the start. Perhaps Ellie shouldn't even be surprised. The warning signs had been there from the beginning after all.

'Are you ready to eat something?' Nanny asked, her softness and maternal demeanour returning as she squeezed Ellie's hand. 'I've got some nice beef stew on the Rayburn.'

'And dumplings?' Ellie asked, her voice quiet and juvenile.

'Yes, and dumplings!' Nanny said, eyes rolling as she gave her granddaughter an affectionate pat on the knee before shuffling over to the Rayburn to dish out something warm and comforting.

Later, when they were huddled around the little breakfast table, watching the storm continue its war path from the alcove in which it was built in, they tucked into their warming dinner and Ellie began to feel much better, though a festering anger threatened to surface in replacement. Ellie knew from experience that once the tears had subsided and anger had shoved its way to the forefront, it would do her no good to be given the opportunity to give someone a piece of her mind. A text from Jack checking that she had made it home okay tamed her rising temper somewhat and she smiled at his thoughtfulness. At least their friendship was back on track.

A hammering on the door jolted the two women and Nanny muttered furiously about the whole afternoon and evening being a torture on her poor nerves. Ellie rushed to the door, hoping none of her neighbours had ventured out in this horrible weather. When she had wrenched the door open, George's large build filled the entire doorway, his hands braced against either side of the frame. Even in the poor light of the storm, George's face was more thunderous than its competitor in the menacing grey sky.

'Do you... have any idea... how worried... I have been?' George's voice was low and raspy, and he struggled to catch his breath despite usually being in good shape. His large chest heaved, and his shirt clung to his dark skin. Ellie realised then that he stood drenched to the bone, with no sign of a coat or protective gear. She stepped back immediately to invite him into the warmth and safety of the cottage, all current disputations temporarily side-lined.

'Wenna said she was looking for towels for you,' George ranted, as Ellie led him to the kitchen where she could make him a hot drink and get him warm by the Rayburn. 'But next thing I hear is the front door slamming shut. Your van is still in the yard but absolutely no sign of you! I had every dark thought and possibility running through my mind when I realised, you'd only bloody well gone home on foot! You know there's a storm out there, right?'

'I know. I'm sorry.'

'Why the bleddy hell are you the one apologising?' Nanny barked from her position in the bay window, her chest puffed out in vexation. She narrowed her eyes at George and glowered. 'It should be you, my dear boy, who should be apologising. And that wretched mother of yours!'

'Nan!' Ellie protested, feeling her cheeks blazing. George was alarmed by Nanny's outburst and shot questioning glances in Ellie's direction. Her shoulders rose in a shy shrug, and she sighed in defeat. 'I heard you and Lavinia talking. About me.'

There was a noticeable shift in the room and George looked both horrified and furious as he brought his head down and released a heavy sigh through tight lips.

'I knew your mother wasn't fond of me, but I didn't realise just how passionate she was of that feeling,' Ellie remarked, falling flat on her attempt to inject humour into this awkward moment. 'And I'd hoped by now she saw me as more than just some girl who cuts grass for a living.' Her shoulders hunched in defeat, and she shrank within herself, feeling small and inferior.

George swore under his breath and rubbed at his face, as if trying to erase all the bad feelings from his skin. 'I'm so sorry you had to hear that, Ellie. She was being vile. I don't know what came over her.'

Ellie pressed her lips together, not committing to any form of a response. She didn't know what to say. All the tears and fight had left her for today and now she just felt tired and defeated, full and sleepy from Nanny's deliciously warming dinner. She also realised she couldn't be mad at George himself. A sort of pleading apology filled his face as he glanced between her and Nanny, who sat unmoving in her angry demeanour.

'Here was me raring to give you a piece of my mind for putting yourself in danger like you did earlier when it's me who is getting full admonishment right now. With complete justification of course.' He sighed heavily again, and a pregnant silence filled the room, Ellie now beginning to feel quite sorry for him. But her feet stayed firmly rooted to the flagstone floor and she simply mirrored his anguished expressions with her own. 'I'll leave you both in peace tonight. You don't need another Penhaligon ruining your evening.'

He turned towards the door and suddenly Ellie's feet came unstuck from her spot.

'No, wait!' Ellie cried. 'Don't go back out in that, for God's sake. There's some stew leftover and I'm about to pop the kettle on. Stay. You're very welcome. Isn't he, Nan?' Her question, thrown in the direction of the bay window, was very much loaded, and the mumbling from her stubborn Nanny was the only response she could hope to get.

George seemed to be assessing his options, a nervous side-glance at Nanny as her scours continued, before nodding and accepting the offer. He gingerly took a seat at the table, directly opposite the seething old woman, drenched to the bone. Ellie wracked her brain at an attempt to think of a solution for the poor man. He could hardly sit there all evening in his sopping wet clothes, but it was safe to say that no person who took residents in this little cottage came close to the same size in clothes as him.

'Jack!'

Both George and Nanny looked up at Ellie in alarm, and George in particular gave her a bewildering look as he eyed the front door, perhaps half expecting the man himself to come traipsing in.

'Come again?' George asked.

'You and Jack are similar build. I think there's a fleece jacket or something he left behind ages ago.'

Ellie disappeared from the kitchen for a few minutes before returning victorious with a plain black fleece jumper draped over her forearm.

'That should keep hypothermia at bay while you eat your

stew.'

He was visibly uncomfortable at the idea of wearing Jack's clothes, perhaps even more uncomfortable that Ellie just happened to have items of Jack's clothing just casually lying about, but he accepted it all the same and excused himself from the room to change out of his shirt. When Ellie just happened to look in Nanny's direction, she found the old woman scowling.

'What, Nan?'

Nanny shrugged indignantly and muttered under her breath, clearly in disagreement. Ellie chose to ignore her Nanny's disputations and busied herself with prepping George's meal. Despite her feelings being bruised and battered this afternoon, it wasn't of George's doing - she needed to remember that. But it also didn't help that not much before that unfortunate moment, she had also been finding out George's true plans for Mrs Pascoe's cottage. Of course, she hadn't shared this part with Nanny yet for fear of totally riling and upsetting her. The whole community was already sad to see the house looking so empty. To see it subjected to being redundant once again during the seasons where it wasn't possibly invaded by visitor-after-visitor-after-visitor would be the final straw.

'The storm is dying down,' Nanny said, to no one in particular as she peered out of the bay window. She then turned to Ellie and said, 'once he's eaten, send him back home.'

'Nan!' Ellie exclaimed through a whisper. 'I can't just...'

She was cut off as George returned, now donning the borrowed fleece, and looking suitably awkward. As he returned to his seat, Nanny pulled herself up. Ellie had to almost suppress a giggle as George shot back up again in an act of chivalry.

'I'm going for a bath,' Nanny announced, not waiting for a response from either of her companions.

'She hates me, doesn't she?' George asked, once she had left the room.

'She doesn't hate you,' Ellie said in earnest. 'But she's not particularly happy right now either. She's just being a typically protective grandmother.'

George smiled, though it didn't quite reach his chestnut eyes. 'I don't blame her. And what about you? How are you feeling?'

He poised his forearms against the rim of the table, his hands clasped together nervously as he assessed Ellie's expression. She crossed the kitchen with his bowl of stew and a cup of coffee, which he thanked her for. Grabbing her own coffee from the kitchen counter, she took Nanny's vacated seat opposite him, contemplating her response.

'Honestly? I'm devastated.'

George's head hung sadly as he tried to reach for her hand across the table. When she didn't respond to his invitation, he withdrew it and tentatively pushed his spoon through the stew.

'I'm not angry with you,' Ellie clarified. George snorted in disbelief, tucking into the stew hungrily. 'I'm not. I don't blame you at all. I'm just a bit... bruised this evening. You know me. I'll be over it tomorrow, I'm sure.' That last part certainly wasn't true of Ellie's character. On the contrary, she would fester over this for quite some time, perhaps even torture herself with the memory of it in little glimpses for years to come, but she would never let him - or them - know that. As far as the Penhaligons would be concerned tomorrow, she would be well and truly over it and getting on with business as usual. On the subject of tomorrow, Ellie's thoughts suddenly flitted to Tressa. 'Oh! When you get home later, please will you check on Tressa. She was really upset earlier.'

'I know,' George said, through mouthfuls of food. 'I had meant to check on her and coax her out with food at dinner time but... you know... circumstances changed. I'll make sure she's alright later.'

'You didn't need to come after me this evening, you know.'

'Yes, I did!' George scoffed through his stew, giving her a

stern look.

'Why? I'm a big girl! It's not the first bloody storm I've encountered!'

George placed his spoon down with an impatient clatter and crossed his arms, finishing his current mouthful. 'Because - Eleanor Curnow -'

Despite herself, Ellie burst out in giggles. 'Don't call me that! Fuck sake, why does your mother insist on calling me Eleanor?'

'I have no idea!' George said, laughing too. 'Was it on your CV?'

'No!' Ellie cried, her mirth increasing. 'Literally never been called Eleanor in my life! Anyway! Sorry, you were saying.'

She leaned forward, her crossed arms presented on the table. George mirrored her, some of his tension and embarrassment subsided as he picked up where he had been interrupted. 'Because - *Ellie* Curnow - whether you like it or not, I care very much about you. I care very much if a storm threatens to wash you away! And... much to my mother's clear disapproval, as we have brutally discovered this evening... I'm completely besotted by you. Tell me you don't feel the same way.'

The storm powered on unnoticed in the background. In fact, the whole world kept on spinning, kept on being, as Ellie found herself utterly lost in the moment. She allowed herself to be locked into those deep brown eyes of his, his perfectly chiselled jaw, his muscular neck, the play of a smile on those lips.

'I don't think I can,' she finally answered.

# Chapter Twenty-Six

It was to everyone's surprise the next morning that the storm had not only passed but left minimal evidence behind of its existence. Ellie and Dave had clearly done a fantastic job of securing the formal gardens, the Kitchen Gardens and Beryan's favourite little courtyard and pond. Tressa would hopefully be in much better spirits once she discovered the survival of the hired marquee and, though a murkiness still lingered in the skies with no promise of sunny spells for the day, it was dry and with only a little breeze. The open day would continue.

George, though still a little heavy hearted from the dealings of last night, took a quality-check stroll around the gardens first thing, a gentle mist sitting low upon the ground like a plaster healing its wounds from its battle with the storm. It was going to be soggy under foot but perhaps they could redirect the public and avoid grass areas, sticking to the gritted pathways. He chuckled to himself then, spotting Ellie hammer some metal barrier stakes into the ground around the Eastern lawn, just beneath their champion Rhododendrons. On her last stake, she began to tie some blue rope to the first stake, feeding it along to the next. George picked up his pace to a light jog and grabbed the reel of rope, smiling as Ellie looked up to acknowledge him.

'You're up bright and early,' George noted. 'It's not even 6am yet.'

'So are you,' Ellie pointed out, grateful for the extra hands as she now secured the rope to each stake much quicker with the help of George feeding out the rope. 'We need to keep people off the grass today, else it's going to be a mud slide. It'll keep them away from the ha-ha too.'

'Good idea. Do you want a coffee? Wenna is about to fire up her coffee van.'

'Sounds great,' Ellie said, smiling politely. Formalities. All the affection, the joking, and the laughing from last night that had eventually replaced the tension between them had now been substituted for stiffness and politeness. But it was barely 6am, George reminded himself. He would persevere, and he would be keeping his mother well out of it.

'How's Tressa this morning?' Ellie asked, now picking up a new stake to begin the other side of the lawn.

'I spoke to her when I got home last night and consoled her as much as anyone is able to console Tressa Penhaligon.' George blew out a long and exasperated sigh through his lips, making Ellie nod and smile in understanding. 'She seems okay this morning, but as you can see from her current absence, she isn't a morning person. We might be lucky to see her in another hour.'

Ellie laughed softly, continuing with her work. Her walkie-talkie then made a crackling noise, followed by Dave's indistinct mumbling through the speaker. 'That'll be Dave arriving.' Ellie reached around for the device in her back pocket and spoke into the receiver, her hands clasped around the button. 'Morning Dave. We're on the Eastern Lawn - over!'

'Another early bird,' George remarked.

'What can I say? I have a very dedicated team,' Ellie replied, smirking smugly.

In just a couple of hours, they were back on track and almost ready to welcome the public into the gardens for the first time in over thirty years. A sort of excited buzz rippled across the estate as George and Trixie invited all involved to meet together inside the marquee for a complimentary breakfast. Trixie bustled amongst the volunteers, serving out extra sausages and pieces of bacon, whilst George walked around offering refills on hot drinks and engaging in conversations. Grinning ear-to-ear, he found himself enjoying every moment, having an opportunity to talk to the people who were making all this possible. Then there was Ellie. He watched in admiration as she flitted from table to table, a clipboard in hand as she checked in on her team of volunteers and the jobs she had delegated them. He watched as she smiled and laughed amongst them, clearly leading from the front, and earning their attention and respect. Thank goodness he had ignored his mother and grandmother's wishes and hired her. She had been the glue recently and perhaps he didn't let her know that enough.

He shook himself back into reality, pouring the last of the coffees and declaring to Trixie that he was going to return the hot drinks tray to the kitchen to check on his sisters.

'Everything in order, Wenna?' George asked as he first checked in on his youngest sister. She seemed perfectly content, kneeling on the gravel to write a public message on her A-frame blackboard. 'Please cue here!' written in beautiful cursive letters. George paused, assessing the message. 'Q-U-E-U-E.'

'Eh?' Wenna turned to look up at her brother, who was smiling apologetically.

'Q-U-E-U-E. Not C-U-E.'

'Crap. Didn't think it looked right. Would you like a coffee, dear brother?'

'Sounds great! I'm just going to check Tressa is okay at the bottom of the drive, directing the traders. I'll come and grab it from you in ten minutes.'

He left Wenna with correcting the spelling on her sign, her good nature shining through as always, to locate the slightly pricklier of his two sisters. It didn't take long to spot her, shining bright orange in a HI-VIS waistcoat - looking mightily important with her clipboard and a headpiece. As he got closer, he could hear her barking orders at poor Joseph down her little mouthpiece, telling him to get into position in the stable yard to direct the food traders. George could just about hear the stuttering response of Joseph as Tressa cut him off from the line.

'Need a hand?' George asked her when he finally closed the gap.

'Nope.'

George pressed his lips together in mild humour, rocking on his heels. 'Right.'

'Actually, yes. Can you kick everyone out of the marquee now please? Some of the table traders have arrived now and would like to set up.'

'I don't think people have quite finished, Tressa,' George pointed out, keeping exasperation at bay.

'Well, tough! I need the space!'

Deciding it was far too early to start a row with his sister this time of morning, George made a quick return to his more amiable sibling who was now inside the van noisily preparing her first batch of coffees. Hearing footsteps behind him as he crossed the driveway, he turned to see Jack on the same beeline as him to Wenna's van. Jack's expression mirrored George's perfectly as the two men exchanged strained pleasantries.

'Alright?' Jack asked, once they had come level with each other outside the coffee van. He sunk his hands into his trouser pockets and bounced awkwardly on his heels. George nodded his response, a polite but fleeting smile crossing his face. 'Wenna about?'

'I'm in here!' Wenna's tinkering voice could be heard from inside the van.

'You helping out?' George asked conversationally, hoping that Wenna would hurry up with that coffee. It wasn't that he disliked Jack. He was begrudged to admit that he found him to be a pretty decent bloke in fact. But Jack made it abundantly clear of his dislike towards George - and perhaps George couldn't blame him. There had clearly been something between Jack and Ellie. And had George possibly bulldozed right through whatever it had been? In fact, he still wasn't sure what the deal was between them both, but considering Jack seemed to be where-ever Wenna was at the moment, George had to assume his interests had changed. As older brother to Wenna, he wasn't sure how he felt about that either.

'Yeah,' Jack answered vaguely. 'Happy to help where it's needed. Was going to help Wenna with the coffees, but if you need any heavy lifting or something...'

George nodded and smiled, hoping his face didn't crack at the attempt. 'Very decent of you. Thank you very much.'

Wenna's arm suddenly appeared from the back door of the van, the hand clasping a freshly made latte in a takeaway cup. She waved it in front of her brother's face impatiently and George took it.

'George!' It was Ellie and she was racing up the garden path. Spotting him, she waved him over frantically. 'We need you!' And with that, she turned on the spot and raced back in the direction of the marquee by the front lawn.

'It needs to be moved,' Ellie declared breathlessly, as they assessed the muddy mess before them. With the torrential wet weather from yesterday, and despite the shelter of the marquee and the quick installation of field mats, the entire patch under the canopy was now a mud slide. 'It must have been from all the footfall during breakfast. Everyone started dispersing and I started moving the tables because your bloody sister was barking at me to get things cleared for the traders - and you don't have a bloody radio...'

'Wow - okay!' George chuckled, despite his own concerns for this situation. He grasped her shoulder and squeezed it gently in way of reassurance. 'Let's breathe, shall we? Where do you suggest we move the marquee?'

Ellie blew out a sharp puff of breath and made a quick glance at George's large hand, which suddenly felt hot to the touch. Her voice was softer and less frantic as she spoke. 'You're the Lord - it's your decision. Tell me where you want it, and we'll get it moved quickly. But this -' She gesticulated madly at the muddy patch. 'This is going to look shit now to all the visitors! We should have moved the marquee before the storm hit.'

'Right - let's move it around the corner to that open space between the sundial garden and the kitchen garden.'

Ellie looked in the direction of where George was referring. 'How are we going to get it past the beech hedging?'

'Lift it over?'

'You realise this marquee is going to take about twenty of us to move it?' Ellie asked, deadpan. Her walkie-talkie suddenly burst into life, with Tressa's clip voice exploding through the speaker.

'Is everything ready in the marquee - over?!'

Ellie flung her arms up in the air in exaggeration at the sound of Tressa's demanding voice.

'It's barely 8:30am and I'm going to bloody kill her already,' Ellie declared.

A burst of laughter erupted from George and even Ellie gave in to a small smile of amusement. 'OK, so we're on to three 'bloodies' and I can see you're close to tears.'

Ellie was now fanning her face, looking up into the sky. 'I cry when I'm angry or stressed. It's an annoying trait!' She breathed in deeply through her nose and cleared her throat. 'Right, um... I think we might be able to lift it over that wall into the drive where Wenna's van is. It's only waist height whereas not even you and Jack can see over that beech hedge into the sundial garden. Did I see that Jack was here? He can help with the lifting. Can you go and get him?'

George agreed and jogged back towards the drive, leaving

Ellie shouting down her walkie-talkie. 'Can I have all capable bodies to the Italian Gardens please?'

A few moments later, they had gathered up enough people to situate on each pole with a few spares to help with the guiding and gathering of the guy ropes.

'On the count of three, we're going to lift to waist height and slowly make our way towards the drive where the coffee van is!' Ellie instructed. 'It's going to be heavy so please be careful and say if you're losing grip. Slow and steady. Ready?' All nineteen heads nodded their response. 'Right - count of three! One! Two! Thr-'

'What is going on here?' Tressa demanded, in her best Lavinia impersonation. She was marching up the garden path, a face like thunder. 'Why are you moving the marquee? I specifically asked for the company to erect it here!' She was talking mainly at George, who was on the pole to the left of Ellie. Before he had a chance to respond, Ellie jumped forward.

'And I told you that I didn't want it on the grass in the first place,' Ellie rebutted. 'Now we've had a storm, and the ground is sodden.'

'Tressa,' George said, 'we need to move it off the grass and the driveway is the closest open space.'

'Fine! But it's going to totally cock up the whole Feng Shui!'

Ellie didn't seem to be hanging around, and Tressa was forced to step out of the way as Ellie announced the count of three one more time and all twenty poles were hoisted into the air. It was heavy, back-straining work as the group shuffled the large canopy slowly to the right towards the Cornish wall separating the Italian gardens from the grand driveway at the main entrance of the house.

'Everybody OK?' George shouted around his pole, perspiration now forming on his brow and under his arms. He was satisfied to see that Jack was also struggling at equal measures but was astounded to see the strength Ellie presented at lifting the same weight whilst also shouting directions and demands from her position.

'Ellie, dear - Madge and I need to swap!' Kelly, one of the volunteers, puffed from her pole which she was sharing with another lady, both in their fifties and struggling with the weight.

'Tressa. Get onto a pole please!' George ordered.

'Wenna! Get your twenty-six-year-old ass out here and share a pole with your sister!'

There was an eruption of hysterical laughter which rippled around the precariously balanced tent as Wenna came running from her little coffee van.

'That sounded totally inappropriate!' Wenna said, giggling as she and a bad-tempered Tressa took the volunteers' place.

By now, Lavinia, Beryan and Trixie were watching from the French doors of the drawing room, and Joseph had come running from his place at the yard.

'Two blokes from the hog roast company are coming to help and Tom Trengrouse from the cider stall,' Joseph announced.

With another three strong men positioned on the main corners of the marquee, the group were ready to tackle the dry wall.

'OK - everyone to the right of me. Waist height on the count of three,' Ellie began again. 'Joseph, can you get yourself on the other side of the wall with Dave and be ready to guide the men on the nearest side over the wall?'

With a series of grunts, cusses, communication and guidance from Joseph and Dave, they had successfully lifted the first half over the wall, the marquee now straddling it like a giant horse.

'Jesus Christ!' Ellie gasped, as they all paused to catch their breath. George, now safely on the other side of the dry wall, with Jack and Tom Trengrouse, was trying not to laugh at poor Ellie's position on top of the wall, her arms clinging to the marquee's middle pole for dear life.

'I think perhaps we should swap with the back row now that this side is safely over,' Tom suggested. He was a large, rugby-built bloke who made even George and Jack feel a little inadequate, but the three of them were certainly the more powerful of the lot.

'Good idea,' George agreed, gesturing for Joseph and Dave to keep hold of their side whilst they ducked underneath and through the gap between the house and the wall. Once everyone was settled into their new positions, George shouted, 'ready when you are!'

'One - two - three! Lift!' Ellie shouted, and with one more heaving effort from everyone, some shuffling and teamwork, the marquee was finally over the wall and positioned safely on the gravelled driveway.

There was a burst of victorious applause and cheering from everyone; George worked his way through all the volunteers, and the men who stepped in last minute, grasping their hands in thanks and patting them gratefully on the shoulder. Ellie had been doing the same, giving her thanks to her team, and they met in the middle, both laughing a little from hysteria.

'You are a machine!' George said, laughing and wrapping his arm around her shoulders, wedging her into his side. His stomach fluttered madly as her skinny but powerful arms wrapped around his middle in a victorious hug and without thinking, getting carried away with the moment, he kissed the top of her head, his head momentarily spinning from her sweet, floral scent.

They were still entwined in this embrace when Lavinia came marching over, clapping and smiling. George felt Ellie stiffen in his grasp and he gave her a reassuring squeeze.

'Bravo, everyone!' Lavinia sang. 'Wonderful teamwork from you all. Well done, Eleanor. You certainly -'

'Joseph and Dave - shall we go and clear up the mess on the lawn!' Ellie projected across the driveway, ripping herself out of

George's arms and marching past his mother, whose face was that of someone who had been slapped.

'Rude child,' Lavinia grumbled.

'How do you expect her to be after last night?' George hissed under his breath so that only Lavinia could hear. 'She heard every word and you're calling her rude!'

'George,' Lavinia said.

'I don't have time for this right now, Mother,' George said, his cheeriness from the moment before completely dissipated as he walked away to find something useful to do.

# Chapter Twenty-Seven

At 10am, members of the public began to spill through the open gates of Penhaligon Estate, and so the Open Day began.

Despite the grey skies and low temperatures, there was a smile on every face Ellie passed. A delicious scent of wood-fired pizzas, BBQ food and fresh coffee filled the air and the delighted squeals of young children as they ran up and down garden paths. Ellie narrowly averted being ploughed down by two young boys, who were chasing one another with sticks, their faces painted like jungle animals and their hair sticking up wildly from the damp air.

'Sorry!' One of the young boys shouted, and Ellie waved them off, chuckling at their merriness. She located her wheelbarrow on the Broad Walk, her newest project now that she had finally gutted the long borders from their tangle of weeds and overgrowth. She had visions of these beds being filled with drifts of herbaceous perennials, perfectly backdropped by the luscious greens of the yew hedge separating the Broad Walk and the Italian Gardens.

'Ellie, don't suppose you're available to do a little tour around the gardens - over,' George's voice sounded through the radio just as she had sunken down to her knees with a trowel to plant a section of hardy geraniums. Even over the crackling of the radio speaker, his voice managed to be as silky as chocolate.

'Yeah, no problem. Get the group to congregate next to

Wenna's coffee van - over,' Ellie responded, smiling. She held her thumb down on the button again. 'Wenna - can I have a flat white to take around with me? If you have time - over.'

There was a pause before the radio in her hand burst into life again, this time with Wenna's sweet little voice. 'Who the bloody hell do you think you are, Ellie! The Head Gardener!'

Ellie chuckled to herself, staring at the radio, and waiting patiently for Wenna to say more.

'Yeah, no problem, Bird! Jack's telling me off because I forgot to say 'over' - over!'

'Hello, everyone!' Trixie's voice joined in through the radio. 'We have some scones set aside to keep you all going. Come and grab them when you can because they're selling fast. Oh...umm...over.'

'Have you got any cheese scones left?' Someone else asked. The radio was shaking in Ellie's hands as mirth took over her body.

'Hello! No, just sweet ones. I need the cheese ones for the soup. Over.'

The radio didn't stop for a couple more minutes as a proverbial debate erupted over scones and the correct way to layer the jam and cream.

'Can we please stop monopolising the line?' Tressa's clip voice cut through the banter.

'No scones for you then, Tressa!' George's amused voice sang. Ellie snorted in humour, and when the radio finally went silent, she clipped it back onto her trousers and took herself off towards Wenna's van to start a tour.

The day trickled by with what seemed like hundreds upon hundreds of people traipsing happily through the gardens, in the marquee full of craft stalls, and carrying around a variety of different treats to eat and drink. In between gardening and giving tours, Ellie had a look around the artisan craft stalls on offer, buying homemade soap, a tea towel with lino-printed designs of the River Fal for Nanny and even treating herself to a willow hare sculpture from a lovely lady who grew the willow, cut them, and sculpted all from her back garden. Before she knew it, she was making purchases from almost every stall.

'What on earth is that?' George gasped, laughing as Ellie struggled down the path from the drive, the hare tucked under her arm and her hands ladled with bags of goodies. 'Are you getting your Christmas shopping in six months early or something?' Huffing and puffing from the awkward load she was carrying, Ellie gestured for George to relieve her of a bag or two. 'I didn't take you for a shopping type of girl.'

'I'm not! Not usually anyway,' Ellie cried, elated from her purchases. 'But once I'd bought from one stall, I felt the need to support them all! There are so many lovely things on sale and it's all local. We should start a gift shop, you know. Fill it with local produce and crafts like this.' She gestured towards the mixed shape and sizes of brown paper bags happily.

'That's not a bad shout. But seriously, the hare?'

'Lush, isn't he?' Ellie gasped, not even bothering to look up to see whether George agreed. 'I'm going to put him in amongst my cornflowers on our little patio. Then Nanny can see him every morning through the patio doors as she comes into the kitchen.'

George smiled fondly at Ellie, then looked down at the willow hare sitting on the path between their feet. 'So, it's a 'he', is it? You've already decided that.'

'Of course! His name is Harold.'

'Harold the Hare!' George stated his hands on his hips in a matter-of-fact way. 'Of course it is.' The grin which spread over George's face made his eyes twinkle and Ellie felt that warmth rise inside her again, that feeling of desperately wanting to close the gap between them. It was clear that George was about to say something, his chest rising as he took a breath, when a frantic woman approached them, breaking the spell.

'Excuse me - do you work here?'

Ellie answered 'yes' at the same time as George said, 'I'm Lord Penhaligon - how can I help?'

'It's our son! He's wandered off and we can't find him anywhere,' the mother gasped, her eyes brimming with tears. 'He's only four and it's such a big place - and so busy!'

George and Ellie exchanged alarmed looks and sprang into action. George stepped forward to press the mother and father for more details as Ellie grabbed her radio from her back pocket.

'This is a code red, everyone. Can we be on the lookout for a four-year-old boy who has wandered off from his parents.' Ellie released the button on the radio and turned to the parents. 'What does he look like? What's he wearing?'

The father stepped forward now, his face bleak with fear and his hands braced on his wife's trembling shoulders. 'He has...um... sort of blonde, floppy hair. Down to his chin. And he's wearing...umm... he's wearing a yellow t-shirt with a red tractor on it and...'

'Red shorts,' the mum added, sniffling. 'He's wearing bright red shorts. You can't miss them.'

'OK, good. That'll stand out in the gardens.' Ellie returned to her radio and reiterated the description to everyone around the estate. 'OK, we have all eyes around the estate looking out for him. What's his name? I'll start from the bottom of the garden nearest to the river and work my way up.'

'His name's Noah.'

'We'll find him,' George assured them. 'Why don't one of you stay right here in case he comes looking for you.'

'I will,' the mum offered, collapsing into a nearby bench just as Wenna came running from the direction of her van.

'Can I help at all?' She shouted from the other end of the path.

'Wenna, can you make Mum here a strong coffee or something?' Ellie asked. 'Then check the drive area and the avenue.' Wenna nodded and ran back.

'You make your way to the bottom end and I'll start in the stable yard,' George said to Ellie. 'Dad, can you go to all the stall holders and give your description of Noah so that we have as many eyes on him as possible.'

'Thank you so much!' The anxious parents said, and everyone flew off to their retrospective spots.

It didn't take long for Ellie to jog through the gardens, down the jungle and through the stumpery, the increasing collection of tree ferns telling her she was nearing the creek. Once she could hear the gentle lapping of the water beyond the boundary edge of the estate, she slowed her pace right down to scour under every shrub and peek behind every tree, making her way back towards the house. Trying not to heed the secret garden too much notice in her passing, its wooden door still agonizingly shut tight, Ellie called the boy's name through the thick vegetation.

'All clear in the melon yard,' Joseph's voice spoke first through the radio.

'Nothin' down in the stable yard,' Dave mumbled next.

As minutes passed, a small niggle of panic began to fester in the pit of her stomach. It was a vast, dangerous estate for a four-year-old. She hadn't had time to check every inch of the estate for damage from the storm, only the parts she knew would be on show to the public. She quickened her pace at the thought of anything happening to the little boy, her calls out to him more urgent in tone.

When she had eventually searched all areas of the wilder sections of the garden, Ellie and George's paths collided and they exchanged equally panicked expressions.

'No sign,' George confirmed.

'Nothing,' Ellie replied, bleakly. She swore under her breath, thinking hard as she paced a patch of ground. 'If you were four years old, where would you go? Come on - you grew up here!

Where did you like to hide when you were a kid?'

George's face went vacant as he tried to think like his four-year-old self. Then his eyes lit up in realisation. 'Oh, my god!' And with that, he disappeared up the path, in the direction of the walled flower garden.

It was a struggle for Ellie to keep up and she thought for a moment she had lost track of him entirely. The walled flower garden was a magical little spot which Ellie and her team had not been able to dedicate enough time yet to do it justice - and yet, nature had taken over in its very best way, with splashes of colour in every corner of the four red-bricked walls. At the back of it was a raised pergola area, the stone wall and sweeping steps in deep slumber beneath moss and a mass of daisy-like flowers Ellie knew to be Erigeron. The woodwork of the pergola was precariously balanced like the stones of an ancient temple, only held together due to the strong vine-like qualities of the wisteria which surrounded it.

Ellie smiled politely at visitors roaming between the apple trees as she waited at the bottom of the stone steps, hoping George would appear any moment now with the child. Her prayers were quickly answered as George stepped into view through a blistered old door disguised under the vegetation of the unruly clematis at the back. Following closely behind, and barely standing past George's waistline, was a small boy who seemed none of the wiser of the anguish he had created.

'You must be Noah!' Ellie said brightly, beaming up at the boy.

'This,' George said, matching Ellie's friendly manner, 'is Ellie. And she's the Head Gardener here.' The boy's big, blue eyes set on Ellie, and she smiled warmly. A mixture of shyness and delight shone from Noah's face, and Ellie noticed he had a giant Jenga piece in his hand.

'So, your mummy and daddy have been quite worried about you because they didn't know where you are,' Ellie explained.

'Shall we head back together and let them know you're OK?'

The boy nodded, still twisting the long wooden block in his tiny hand.

'What have you got there?' Ellie asked.

'Noah here found my old lawn games,' George said fondly. He crouched down to Noah's level. 'Did you know that I grew up here and this little building was my hideout? My secret den. Only special members are allowed in here.'

A flash of worry crossed the boy's face and he began to chew on his thumb.

'But luckily...!' George continued, snapping a piece of die-back from the wisteria and bending it into a shape. 'Luckily, I'm always looking for new members. And because you discovered it through the special members entrance, I would like to welcome you to the Secret Cool Kids Association.'

Ellie's face beamed in fondness and amusement, and her heart swelled as she watched the boy take the little wicker star shape made of old wisteria vines, his face glowing with pride.

'Now Ellie here is unfortunately not a member, but we will allow her just this once to head through the secret entrance because it's the quickest way back to your parents. Shall we let her?' George looked up at Ellie and winked, a charming smile playing on his lips. Noah nodded enthusiastically and held his hand out to Ellie. Taking his warm, tiny hands into hers, Ellie gave George an expression which said she was bursting with endearment for the cute gesture. George and Noah led Ellie up the concrete steps, through the blistered door which led into the run-down little building with original lead-lined windows and thatched roofing, the floor now littered with Jenga blocks, skittles, and rope hoops. On the other side of the hut was another door, and when George opened it, Ellie could immediately see how the boy had so easily found himself inside it. They descended the narrow little stepping stones and straight onto the driveway where the marquee lay. Noah's parents spotted them immediately and rush over to plant a million frantic kisses upon the little child.

'He's absolutely fine,' George assured the parents as they thanked him and Ellie over and over.

When the parents and little Noah finally said their goodbyes and headed home, Ellie stood side-by-side with George, smiling.

'You are really good with children,' Ellie remarked.

'Am I?' George asked, seeming genuinely surprised by this compliment. 'I do like children. I would love my own one day.' He looked down at her at that moment, his eyes searching. Ellie, who had never really had much experience with children growing up or in recent years, was indifferent to the idea of children. At least for the moment. But she nodded in understanding and smiled warmly.

'He was bored, wasn't he?' Ellie said, looking around at the open day still in full swing before them. 'Noah, I mean. There's not a lot to do for children.'

George turned his attention to the marquee full of delicate crafts and adult beverage samples and handmade soaps, Wenna's coffee van - Ellie was right. It was very adult orientated.

'There's been lots of families today though,' George pointed out.

'Yeah, but how worn out have the parents looked trying to keep their children entertained, besides the face painter - and my lawn,' Ellie scoffed, rolling her eyes as she noticed that her blue rope barricading people from stepping on the lawn had been trampled down at some point during the day, with a patch of the grass now churned up and muddy from the traffic of little feet. 'Do you know what? I'm going to have to fell a lot more trees in the woods and parkland, and we certainly won't need to store all of it for firewood. I reckon Dave, Jack and I could probably make a playground out of it all.'

'A playground?' George said, looking sceptical.

'Very discreet. All made of natural materials. But it means

when we have more of these public events, there's somewhere for the little ones to go and for the parents to relax a little. Maybe over there in that copse of trees so they have shade.' Ellie pointed at the cluster of tall sycamore trees just beyond the Ha-Ha at the bottom of the Italian Gardens.

George nodded, deep in thought. 'What about that little wasted paddock between the Broad-Walk and the Flower Garden? It's easily accessible to the stables where we could later put a visitor centre.'

Ellie lit up, her enthusiasm for their growing idea escalating. 'We could sell plants and Wenna could sell coffee out of her little van.'

'We could even have a proper cafe in one of the stables, with seating!'

'God, we're good!' Ellie breathed, and the two high-fived in earnest, laughing madly.

'You're good!' George retorted. 'Fantastic, in fact! God - I literally could kiss you sometimes!' Ellie's face flushed as she bit down on her bottom lip, a mix of emotions churning away beneath. She was just considering how wonderful it would be to kiss those soft lips, her eyes glazing over in a dreamy state when he added, 'Relax, Ellie. I'm not going to. Though I want to. Come on, we need to tell the others and start planning for this immediately!'

And with that, he grabbed her hand and had them practically skipping across the gardens towards the kitchen entrance to the house, both laughing and giggling like two school children in pursuit of something sweet.

# Chapter Twenty-Eight

'A children's playground? Whatever for?'

Beryan's voice was shrill and bordering on hysteria as George finished telling his family all about the plans for the estate, he and Ellie had conjured together that afternoon. The open day was a complete triumph and, much to everyone's relief, had come to a finish in the late afternoon, with visitors heading home happy and satisfied with their day out. It was now evening, and they had just finished eating together around the dinner table, celebrating the day's success. The mention of a possible playground had suddenly altered the tone around the table.

'Well, Ellie and I agree that having a playground here would provide a facility for families who attend future events, and perhaps we can start looking at having the place open for public more often.'

'But this is just it,' Beryan continued. 'If we have a ghastly playground put in, we're just encouraging these families - with their loud, brash offspring - to take over every time they visit here.'

'Don't we want to encourage families though, Granny?' Tressa spoke up, much to George's relief. 'After all, they tend to bring in the most money in places like this. They're often the ones who will keep returning.'

'I wish they wouldn't,' Beryan grumbled.

'Well, thank goodness you're not in charge of the business side of things here then,' Tressa retorted, sitting back in her chair with a scowl on her face. 'Honestly, it's no wonder we're in the shit that we're in, is it?'

'Tressa Ann-Marie!' Lavinia cried out.

'Well, I'm sorry!' Tressa said, not sounding the least bit sorry. 'But which generation allowed this place to go stale? Which generation closed the gates because they're antisocial and are too posh to mix with the commoners? Never mind making sure the estate can actually afford to run itself - we'll just close the gates and sit on our rotting assets.'

'The child is hysterical!' Beryan exclaimed, turning to Lavinia.

'I think you'd best go to bed,' Lavinia ordered across the table to Tressa.

George opened his mouth to say something just as Tressa burst out laughing. 'I'm thirty-nine years old! I just organised an entire open day - the first open day Penhaligon Estate has had in over thirty years. And all you can do is grumble about the changes George and I are trying to put in place to save the estate and - and send me to bed! Like a scolded child!' Her laugh turned bitter, and George's heart pulled for his poor sister as he began to see all the reasons for her demeanour over the years. He placed his large hand over hers and immediately felt her natural cold reaction. But as she looked up at him, she saw only kindness and support from her brother, and her entire body relaxed in the knowing she had an ally. Perhaps for the first time in a long while.

'You did an excellent job with today, Tressa,' George said, firmly. 'And Wenna, your coffee van was a knockout...'

Wenna, who had remained quiet through the whole thing, straightened in her seat proudly. 'I ran out of milk I made that many coffees! And sold all of Trixie's tray bake bites.'

George threw his arms up in triumph. 'Then let's start

planning the next event. And there will be no more discussions on the playground idea because it's happening!'

George knew he had been ruthless, and he knew that both his mother and grandmother would be sour with him for the next week at the very least. It was these sorts of squabbles and disagreements over the estate that had driven him away in the first place. But - and this was a very rare but - he couldn't allow poor Tressa to be belittled today of all days, not after all she had put together for the open day. He hoped that perhaps this moment of alliance between them would make up for years of rivalry and jealousy - at least on Tressa's part.

After dinner he, Tressa and Wenna began clearing up in Trixie's kitchen, having sent poor Trixie home by the late afternoon after she had been on her feet all day serving cream teas. Covering the last plate of leftovers with some foil and placing it in one of the fridges, George glanced at his sisters. Wenna was her usual animated self, occasionally breaking the silence in the room to give her own perspective on the day from her little van. Though Wenna was often never in short supply of enthusiasm, this evening her excitement was marked with passion and George felt a wave of relief to know that Wenna had found something she had put her mark on and really enjoyed. In the background, silent and sombre, Tressa kept her head down and her gloved arms deep in the depths of the soapy dishwater. George was used to Tressa's silence, her lack of involvement in conversations - but this was different. She looked deeply sad.

'Right, that's enough boring stuff!' George suddenly found himself declaring to the room. Both sisters stopped what they were doing and glanced at their brother in confusion over his outburst. 'Let's go get a celebratory drink down at the pub. Come on - both of you! Grab your jackets, your shoes, hang bags - whatever!'

Wenna squeaked in glee and started peeling her own

marigold gloves from her hands just as Tressa showed as much enthusiasm as a sloth.

'No, thank you. There are a few things I would like to do to round up the day.'

'Like what?' George said, amused and encouraging. 'The marquee isn't being collected until Monday. Everything else is away and secure thanks to our brilliant gardening team. Trixie is going to make a lovely Sunday spread tomorrow for the team as thanks, with all the leftovers.'

'I'd like to count up the takings for the day and make sure all bills are settled,' Tressa continued, not looking up. 'But you two carry on.'

Wenna and George exchanged looks as she shrugged in defeat, quite used to her older sister refusing any opportunity to socialise with the siblings.

'Come on, Tressa!' George persevered. 'This was your big day. It was a huge success! Let me buy you a drink or two.'

'Yeah, come with us,' Wenna said, not sounding quite as convincing.

Tressa paused. It was long enough for George to sense that she did really want to come, but her usual stubborn ways were preventing her from backtracking from her original refusal. George decided, for once, to give his sister the nudge she needed.

'Okay, I'm taking you out for a drink whether you like it or not. You might be the eldest, but I'm the biggest and strongest, and will carry you down to the pub if I must.' George smiled in victory as he caught Tressa's lip twitch upwards. That was enough of an answer for him.

'Right, meet you both out by my car in ten minutes.'

Once George had had a chance to freshen himself up, changing into a casual black polo shirt and chino shorts for the evening, which held a humid warmth typical after the storm they had just had, George then moved his car around from its

Lamorna Ireland

temporary spot in the stable yard up to the driveway to collect his sisters. He quickly punched in a text message to Ellie, inviting her to join them at the pub. He received her reply just as Tressa and Wenna clambered into the back seat together.

*Jack and I are already down here. We'll save you a seat! :) x*

George frowned at his phone screen, trying to bat down any feelings of jealousy. It really did no good to indulge in those feelings. After all, him and Ellie weren't together. She could take herself off to the pub for a drink with another man if she wanted to. Who was he to get funny over it?

'Are we going?' Wenna asked impatiently through the gap between the two front seats.

'Yeah, sorry,' George said, giving himself a mental shake and stuffing his phone into his pocket. 'I've just messaged Ellie to meet us at the pub. But it seems she's already there.' He decided not to mention that she was with Jack, so as not to pass his negative feelings over to his little sister.

'Yeah, I know!' Wenna said, busying herself with her seatbelt. 'She's with Jack!'

*Never mind, then,* thought George, wryly. Then through the rear-view mirror to Wenna, 'Does that not bother you?'

Wenna scoffed. 'No - why should it? They're really close friends. Have been for a long time. I'm not about to get in the way of that.'

George had a sudden newfound respect for his sister and wished he could be so cool and rational.

'You don't have to worry about Jack and Ellie, George,' Wenna continued sympathetically, as George began the slow crawl up the long driveway to the gatehouse on the main road. 'Jack did have feelings for Ellie, but he soon realised it was a platonic friendship. Ellie was never interested that way.'

Tressa sat silently and blissfully unaware of the conversation in the back seat next to Wenna, her face lit up by her phone screen as George regarded Wenna through the rear-view mirror again.

'And you know all of this how?'

'He told me,' Wenna said, shrugging as if this was the most obvious response.

'He *told* you he had feelings for Ellie,' George parroted, incredulous.

'Transparency, brother!' Wenna said, whimsically. George rolled his eyes to the car ceiling; he would have to work a little harder to reach Wenna's level of coolness it seemed.

When they arrived at the pub, it didn't take long for them to find Ellie and Jack, who immediately waved them over to a high table with six stools around it. The pub itself was busy but not packed and had a nice friendly atmosphere to it this evening.

'This is a lovely surprise!' Ellie exclaimed, giving both Wenna and Tressa a one-armed hug around the shoulders. George shook Jack's hand before rounding the table to kiss Ellie respectfully on the cheek, though his hand found hers which rewarded him with one of his favourite smiles.

'What can I get everyone?' Jack called around the table as everyone took to their stools.

'Absolutely not,' George protested. 'I promised my sisters I would buy them a drink, so allow me. What are you drinking, Jack?'

'Tribute. Cheers, mate!'

'Ellie?' George asked, as Jack happily took his place at the table next to Wenna.

'J20, please.'

'Ooh, can I have one of those tequila drink things in the bottle!' Wenna called out, doing unnecessary gestures with her hands to articulate what she meant. 'The one with the lime slice shoved in the top.'

'She means Desperados,' Jack explained, chuckling.

George smiled and turned to his other sister. 'Tressa?'

'Malbec, please.' Tressa had slid elegantly into her stool, straight backed and with her hands poised delicately in her lap. She could not have looked more uncomfortable and out of place if she had tried and George hoped that a few drinks down her long neck would help to relax her.

'Mr Penhaligon?' A voice made George turn as he approached the bar. A couple of older gentlemen smiled up at him from their table, all raising their pints in a friendly gesture. 'Just wanted to say that my wife and I thoroughly enjoyed today. Thank you very much to you and your family for opening the gates once again.'

'Thank you for coming along and supporting us,' George said, smiling down at the gentlemen.

'I don't quite remember the gardens being so vast,' one of the other gentlemen commented. 'We went along in the afternoon with our two grandsons. It's certainly given my wife some ideas for our garden.' He chuckled and added, 'I'll be sending you the bill for all the extra money my wife is going to spend now as a result of being so inspired.'

George laughed with good-nature and shook each man's hand respectfully before bidding them a good evening and returning to the bar. He was accosted a couple more times between ordering the drinks and finally bringing them over to the table, all positive feedback from the day. When he finally got the chance to take his stool next to Ellie with his pint of coke, he felt elated.

'People are raving about today!' George whispered enthusiastically to the table. He then held his glass up. 'Cheers, everyone!'

'To Tressa and her terrifyingly fantastic delegation skills!' Ellie added, earning a hearty ripple of laughter around the table. Even Tressa broke out a small smile of appreciation. They clinked glasses and drank silently for a few seconds, the low rumble of voices continuing around them.

'So, what's the next big event?' Jack asked, resuming normal conversation.

'You'd better ask the Events Coordinator here,' George said, gesturing towards Tressa.

Tressa rolled her eyes and sipped at her wine. 'I know what you're doing.' George shrugged and feigned ignorance. 'We're going to host a classic cars rally next month.'

'No way,' Jack gasped, genuinely looking excited by that news. 'Do you need any helpers?'

'I could do with someone in charge of parking and traffic in and out of the estate,' Tressa offered. 'Joseph needed a bit of guidance today and I could do with being available to oversee everything.'

'Of course!' Jack said, clapping his hands in triumph and swinging his arm over Wenna's head and around her shoulders. George noticed Tressa's mouth purse over that movement, her sharp grey eyes narrowing at the newest couple in front of her.

'How did you convince Tressa to come out, then?' Ellie whispered behind her glass to George.

'I can be very persuasive,' George whispered back, smiling down at Ellie, and wishing he could mirror Jack's smooth actions and wrap his arms around her. She looked extra pretty this evening, out of her gardening clothes and in a simple peach coloured vest top and black denim shorts. Her auburn hair was French braided, with strands of wavy hair framing her face. 'How's Nanny feeling?'

Ellie shrugged, pulling a face. 'Okay. She managed a walk around the hamlet today with a couple of the neighbours, so that's progress. She was pretty pooped when I got home though, so made her a quick poached egg supper and sent her to bed.' She rolled her eyes, though a look of deep worry shadowed the expression. 'Honestly, talk about role reversal.'

George and Ellie's private conversation got disrupted as Jack and Wenna burst out in laughter over something, Tressa even chancing a small chuckle as she tucked into her wine.

'I think it's good you've got her out,' Ellie said, resuming their whispered exchange. 'I think she's a little shy and this will do her the world of good.'

Months ago, George would have laughed in her face at the suggestion that Tressa Penhaligon was shy but as he looked at his sister - at the way she held her arms crossed over her lap; the way she mostly listened and darted her eyes nervously around the room. He'd always taken these traits as something unfriendly and closed off about her. And yes, there were moments when Tressa was just plain cruel and unnecessary with her words, in the heat of the moment. But at this given moment, George had to admit that Ellie had his sister far more figured out than he ever had. This time, he couldn't help himself. As he snaked his arm around Ellie's shoulders, he gazed down at those sapphire blue eyes of hers in wonder.

'You're an intuitive so-and-so, aren't you?'

Ellie shrugged humbly. 'It's a gift.'

'Alright, you two!' Wenna called across the table, breaking the moment. *When would they finally have their moment*, George thought with frustration. 'Enough of your secret little chit chat over there. I'm heading to the bar for more drinks. Who wants what?'

# Chapter Twenty-Nine

Things went blissfully quiet for the next few weeks which gave Ellie the time and head space to plan the next stages for the gardens. She had been head gardener for almost five months now and finally felt she had the established parts of the garden in a satisfactory state, in parts thriving and looking spectacular yet again. Now, Ellie itched to put her own stamp on the estate. She'd already made a start on her stumpery. There was still so much more to do. Starting with the playground.

After ample persuasion and reassurance that a playground would not spoil the gardens or invade the house with noise, Ellie had finally gotten the go ahead and was now standing in front of an open space just under the canopy of some trees with a clipboard, string, and a pile of wooden stakes. She had a design in mind. She just wasn't sure where to start.

Thankfully, before panic and self-doubt could set in Jack turned up with his bags of tools, a pencil behind his ear and a piece of paper flapping in his mouth. He set both toolkits down onto the ground and spat out the paper.

'Alright?' Jack asked.

'Yeah,' Ellie replied slowly, still staring at the open space in front of her, a perplexed look on her face. Jack took a stance next to her, looking at the same spot.

'What you thinkin'?'

'I'm thinking I may have bitten off more than I can chew,'

Ellie admitted.

Jack scoffed and nudged Ellie with his shoulder. 'Says the one who took on a head gardener position for an entire estate. What's the problem?'

'Starting.'

'Okay, well I was thinking something along the lines of this,' Jack began, swiping the pencil from his ear and adding to the sketch he had already planned on his bit of paper. Ellie watched over his shoulder, glancing up at the space every now and again to imagine how it would look.

'I was thinking about putting one of those tube slides here,' Ellie explained, pointing at Jack's sketch, and then pointing at the real spot in front of them. 'I promised the Penhaligons it would be wood only, but the slide I've found online can come in natural green or brown colours.'

'You need a slide, else it'll be a rubbish playground,' Jack said.

'Exactly! There will be no point doing this at all if it ends up being lame.'

'You wait - Beryan Penhaligon will be secretly sneaking off to play in this when no one's looking,' Jack teased. Ellie snickered behind her clipboard. 'She'll be the first one throwing herself down the slide and Lavinia will be on the zip wire.'

It was all too much to imagine, and Ellie and Jack burst into a heap of laughter, nudging and pushing each other in mirth.

'Aww, I miss this!' Ellie sighed, wrapping her arms around Jack's middle, and giving him a squeeze.

'Oof! Not so tight!' Jack teased, draping an arm around Ellie's shoulder, and planting a kiss on her head. 'Me too. Though, we had best stop hugging or a certain Lord is going to be after me.'

Ellie screwed her face up in annoyance and pulled herself out of their friendly embrace. 'I thought we were past all this.'

'I'm not saying it like that,' Jack said, holding his hands up in defence. 'But genuinely - George is keeping a close eye on me. Doesn't help that Wenna told him that I had tried to kiss you.'

'How does *Wenna* know this?' Ellie gasped.

'I told her. She's so cool, Ellie. I told her everything when I was conflicted about you, and she was... just so cool.'

Ellie smiled fondly, bursting with happiness for her friend, who looked doughy eyed at the thought of Wenna. 'I'm so happy for you both.'

'Thanks,' Jack grinned. 'I really like her. She's just so...'

'Cool?' Ellie teased, smiling and winking.

'Alright,' Jack said, now feeling embarrassed and wanting to move on, Ellie chuckling away to herself. 'Let's design a playground, shall we?'

It took an hour of what felt more like faffing than working productively. But by mid-morning, the open space was peppered with wooden stakes sticking out of the ground, and string hung in between to mark off sections of what would eventually be a children's playground.

'What's this bit again?' Ellie asked, pointing at a large square section.

'That is...' Jack began, checking their plan, '...the nest swing.'

'And here?' Ellie asked again, pacing to the next section which was more of a zig zag shape.

'The balance bar and monkey bar bit. If you need to clear any of these older trees, you could use the stumps as step-overs.'

'That's cute. Though, I'm not sure cutting some trees down will help my popularity with L and B.' She whispered the initials of the two older Penhaligon women as if they were taboo words.

'No, you're probably right. Shall we grab a coffee before we start digging?'

'Yes!'

They strolled in companionable silence for a bit, taking the route through the walled gardens and along the Broad Walk,

Ellie deadheading some plants as she went. The Dahlias were looking spectacular, and she made a mental note to pick some of them later for the house and the staffroom, so as to encourage the plants to flourish more over the season. She was enjoying Jack's company again, feeling the strain that had been between them for some time finally melting away. As grateful as Ellie was for this new venture in life - her job at the estate, the new friends she'd made on the way - she had regretted how these changes had affected their relationship. Jack and Ellie had always been thick as thieves, and Ellie had seen that as completely platonic. She had realised soon enough that a lot of that chemistry had been far from simply platonic for Jack and had wondered if they could ever return to how they were before. Now, seeing Jack swelling with happiness and pride over his blooming connection with Wenna made her giddy with happiness and relief - because now her and Jack could continue to be friends, just as they were before.

'I hope you're getting paid for this,' Ellie commented, as they entered the servant's yard. 'You seem to be a permanent fixture here at the moment. I hope you're not doing this just to impress.' She said the last bit in a teasing manner but quietly hoped he wasn't allowing himself to be taken advantage of.

'Of course I'm getting paid! What kind of mug do you take me for?' Jack laughed.

'I did wonder,' Ellie said, winking. 'You should ask for a job here. I'll take you on as an apprentice.'

'Bloody cheek!' Jack laughed, hooking Ellie into a playful headlock just as the door of the kitchen swung open, George's large figure filling the doorway and his face that of utter bewilderment. Ellie's laughter died in her throat, and she wriggled out of Jack's hold to smooth down her hair.

'We're just grabbing a coffee. Want one?' Ellie asked, though her voice came out breathless and squeaky.

'No, thanks,' George replied, his voice clip. Ellie's heart sank.

He was angry. A heavy pause fell between them as George sized Jack up, still blocking the doorway. 'I hope you don't make a habit of man-handling all women like that.'

Jack's eyebrows leapt upwards whilst Ellie's mouth practically fell open.

'George!'

'I just need to know, seeing as Jack here has a particular interest in my little sister.'

Jack scoffed and went to circulate the yard, seemingly composing himself. 'What are you suggesting, mate?'

'You tell me,' George growled.

'Enough, both of you!'

'And there's me thinking we'd come to some sort of truce recently. My mistake!'

'For God's sake! I'm sick of this!' Ellie cried, turning around, and storming off in the opposite direction, ignoring both George and Jack's calls from across the yard. Her blood boiled and those pesky tears of anger smarted in her eyes as she exited the servant's yard and headed straight into the depths and safety of her gardens. She didn't really know where she was headed - only knew she wanted to get as far away from those bloody men as possible. She was tired of tiptoeing between loyalty to Jack as an old friend and this new loyalty she felt - and didn't fully understand - towards George. Whatever it was that was developing between her and George, no matter how unnerving, if it came between her and Jack... then, she didn't want it. No matter how much her body told her otherwise.

So caught up in her thoughts and frustrations, she hadn't realised, until she found herself standing right before the wooden gate just visible through the curtain of climbers and overgrowth, where she had subconsciously taken herself. Her chest still heaved as she scanned the door for any clues to how to get in. She'd tried a couple more times since the first day she had discovered it, to no prevail. So simply standing and glowering at it certainly would not encourage a grand reveal.

In a desire to distract herself, she launched forward and began patting all the stonework around the archway, the old, cobbled path underneath the fallen leaves and even delve deep into the foliage. Nothing. What did she expect to find? A giant golden key or a second entrance?

What she certainly hadn't expected was for the heavy stomps of George to appear and for him to find her so quickly.

'There you are,' George said through heavy breaths.

'Usually, when someone walks off,' Ellie said, her back still to George as she continued her fruitless hunt for a way into the secret garden, 'they want to be alone.'

'It's just... I didn't like it when...' George stumbled over his words and Ellie discovered this was not a common issue usually for George Penhaligon. He heaved a big sigh of defeat and Ellie heard his arms slap down against his thighs. 'I'm sorry. Ellie, please stop trying to climb a wall and look at me.'

Reluctantly, Ellie did so and scoured at him, though she softened a little as she saw his expression. He really was so handsome and at this very moment his usual tall, confident stature was replaced with one of... what was that - vulnerability?

'To be perfectly honest, Ellie. I'm being horribly jealous.'

Though he stood at the very end of that little cobbled path leading to the gate - though he stood a good five metres away - Ellie felt that pull between them.

'Why?'

'You know why,' George said, almost pleadingly. One foot lifted off the ground and he began to step forward down the path. 'You and Jack... I know you're good friends but...'

'We've been friends for years, George. Best friends in fact. And he's happy with Wenna.' Ellie's voice rose the more frustrated she got. 'Why am I having to explain this? Why do you care about me and Jack?'

'I care very much,' George said softly, walking slowly down

the path and closing the gap between them. Ellie realised she was being backed into the closed gateway, like a frightened animal poising to take flight. 'I care very much about you, Ellie. I think, surely, it's been quite obvious. And I've been driving myself mad about it.'

He was merely an arm's length away now, blocking the light from flooding into the dark shadows of the hanging canopy of climbers which framed the old gateway. There was no running from here, thought Ellie - unless she was to physically push through him. But that was only relevant if she wanted to get away. Perhaps she didn't. Her heart raced and her stomach did nauseating somersaults as she fought for something to say.

'You owe Jack an apology.'

'I do. And I will. I promise.' George stopped in his tracks, not daring to move any closer as he assessed Ellie's expression. 'But... he did kiss you. You can't blame me for being driven a little mad.'

'Your sister seems to be handling it just fine,' Ellie quipped.

'My sister,' George said, 'is much, much cooler than I am.' He chanced a smile at Ellie and was awarded with the slightest hint of a lift in the corner of her mouth. 'I like you, Ellie. Very much. And I know I asked you out once, and you said no. And I will respect that. Just... bear with me if I show a little jealousy towards those who can make you smile and laugh the way Jack can.'

Ellie's brows creased with worry and her heart ached and yearned.

'He did get to kiss you, after all,' George added in a repetitive attempt to lighten the mood. The spell was momentarily broken, and Ellie rolled her eyes.

'I don't think you can call ramming his tongue down my throat when he was stinking drunk a kiss to envy,' Ellie said, deadpan. 'Despite that little moment of madness, he's like a brother to me.'

George nodded, his hands finding his pockets. 'So, there's never been anything romantic?'

'No!' Ellie cried, groaning in frustration. 'Look, if you think I'm going to hold back the way me and Jack are or tiptoe every time we're all together, you've got another thing co-'

Suddenly, George had closed the gap, and his mouth was upon hers, his large form crushing her against the wooden gate - his strong hands clasped firmly on her hips. This was nothing like when Jack had kissed her, she thought as her body suddenly awoke in hunger. Her fingers were suddenly entwined in his hair, her mouth bruised against his as they simultaneously forgot to breathe. For a moment they pulled away, Ellie breathing into George's heaving chest as the sounds of chippering birds returned to their ears. George pinched Ellie's chin gently and raised her face to his, tracing the line of her jaw with his thumb.

'You don't know how long I have wanted to do that,' George whispered huskily. 'How much I have wanted you.'

'Now would be a really bad time for your mother or grandmother to rock up,' Ellie whispered back, and they both tittered quietly. Her body practically screamed for more of him, but she became acutely aware of something pressing hard between the blades of her shoulders and something catching on the strap of her dungarees. She wriggled and writhed uncomfortably then, her frontal pressing against George as she did so.

Mistaking Ellie's writhing, George growled longingly and began to help Ellie with the undoing of her strap. 'Ellie, I-'

'Oh my god, George - I'm not suggesting *that* right here, am I? My dungarees are caught on something.'

George reached over her shoulder to investigate just as something clunked on the big wooden gate, causing it to creak open. Ellie let out a little squeal as she lost her footing, falling into the newly opened archway and pulling George down with her, sending them both hurtling down a small set of stone steps into a heap of limbs on the mossy floor of the secret garden.

'Ow, my back!' George groaned, as he and Ellie untangled themselves from one another. 'As far as romantic gestures go, I wasn't banking on that happening.'

As he lay there on the mossy, cobbled floor, Ellie shot up onto her hands and knees, realisation bringing in a wave of excitement.

'The door!' Ellie gasped. 'It's open! How...?'

Ellie was up in a flash, running to investigate the mystery door as George coughed and spluttered slowly to his knees.

'I think you landed on my kidney,' George complained, heaving himself up into a standing position.

'I'm sorry!' Ellie said, pulling a face of sympathy before gesturing him over. 'Look at this!'

He joined her at the gate, which now revealed a whole new surprise.

'Look at the handle,' Ellie observed, twisting the iron ring in way of explanation. 'It's a trick. It doesn't even do anything, and it's on the hinges side. How have I not noticed this before?'

'Probably because you didn't expect our gate to be something out of an Indiana Jones movie,' George quipped, getting in for a closer inspection. 'This is where your clothes got caught. It's a secret latch.' He demonstrated by lifting the section of wood acting as a piece of the support bar, a rusty nail sticking out with threads of Ellie's black denim dungarees as evidence. 'I've never seen anything like this before. Have you?'

'Never.' Ellie and George experimented with the door for a few moments, both speechless with wonder at the clever but medieval-like mechanism. They then turned their attention to the slumbering walled garden before them, blanketed under brambles and ivy. Traces of a once formal garden was just visible under a mountainous jungle of Rhododendrons, roses and Camellias, a dilapidated lean-to greenhouse just visible along the back wall. From where they stood, Ellie noted countless broken panes of glass and the rotting of the white wooden frame which made up the classic Victorian design. It was a time capsule, and nature was claiming it for its own.

'I wonder how long it's been like this,' Ellie whispered, as she tried to part a particularly heavy overhang of unruly foliage. George came up close behind her, his arms snaking around her middle and his chin resting gently on one shoulder.

'Why are you whispering?' George whispered back. Ellie giggled softly and turned to face him, her arms reaching up around his neck.

'Because,' Ellie began, her voice still soft, 'it feels sacred somehow. Like we're trespassing or something.'

'You know I own all of this, right?' George said, grinning arrogantly. He sighed, fondling a curl of Ellie's hair between his fingers before hooking it gently around her ear. 'Please say that you'll allow me to take you on that date now?'

Ellie's face broke out in a smile, and she allowed herself now to sink into the warmth and depths of his dark brown eyes. Her hands braced on the barrel of his chest, and she savoured the feeling of his arms tight around her. As George bent his head down towards her, their second kiss was disrupted by the alarming sounds of Jack's voice belting through Ellie's radio.

'Ellie! Pick up the radio. This is an emergency - over!'

Ignoring George's mutterings against Jack and his timely manner, Ellie freed herself from George's embrace to reach around for her radio from her back pocket, her heart suddenly pounding from the urgency of Jack's voice.

'What is it, Jack?'

'Ellie, we need to go. It's Nanny.'

# Chapter Thirty

In a moment of complete ecstasy, life can have a cruel way of hurtling you back down to the cold, hard ground of Earth in a matter of seconds, and with just two single words.

'It's Nanny.'

It was all Jack needed to say for Ellie's feet to take flight and for her to sprint her way back through the gardens and to her van, where Jack waited with the engine running. They were back at the cottage within five minutes, by which time an ambulance and a small crowd of concerned neighbours gathered. She wasn't given a moment to process anything before Ellie found herself crammed in the back of the ambulance with Nanny, who looked so small and still and frail beneath the white blanket the paramedic had draped over her to keep warm.

'I'm here, Nan,' Ellie had said when she'd positioned herself on the seat beside her, grasping her cold hand for comfort - whether that was for Ellie's comfort or Nanny's, she wasn't sure - as the community of friends and neighbours parted to make way for the ambulance to crawl back through and out of the hamlet.

By late evening, Ellie pacing the tiled floor of a clinical waiting room in Treliske Hospital, a doctor had finally approached her with some updates.

'It's her pneumonia. It's so much worse than we thought,' Ellie explained to Jack moments after the doctor had left. Jack

277

had been out on a hunt for something for them both to eat, given they had been in the same windowless room for over nine hours now. Nanny had been wheeled away almost instantly on their arrival at the hospital, with Ellie being escorted to the little room they now sat in, with only the occasional update on how the patient was doing. Jack was now emptying the contents of a *Subway* bag onto the coffee table and encouraging Ellie to take a seat and eat something. 'They now reckon she has septicaemia, Jack. Septicaemia. At her age.'

Ellie's loud sniffs echoed and bounced against the white walls, and Jack waited a respectable moment before ordering her to sit again.

'You need to eat something, El. We could be here all night.'

'*I'll* be here all night. You're going home to get some sleep before work tomorrow,' Ellie ordered back. She sat down and picked up a 6inch sub sandwich which was oozing at the sides with cheese and Teriyaki chicken. She slopped it back down again onto its grease-proof paper and jumped back up. 'I'm sorry, Jack - I can't eat. I'm too agitated.'

'At least sip the Pepsi and keep your sugars up,' Jack advised, his voice kind and gentle.

Ellie's phone buzzed in her pocket, and she was saved the hassle of politely declining Jack's offer of food and drink to check who the caller was.

'It's George,' Ellie said, looking at the screen.

'Take it outside,' Jack said, pointing at a 'No Mobiles' sign on the wall.

'There's nobody else in here!' Ellie snapped, before clicking the green button. 'Hello.'

'How is she?' George's deep voice sounded through the device, instantly soothing a small part of Ellie.

Ellie took in a lungful of air through her nose, in an attempt to keep another looming sob away, as she answered, 'her pneumonia has gone septic. I haven't been able to see her yet.

It's been hours.'

The phone was deadly silent for a moment before George's smooth voice breathed through again. 'I'm so sorry, Ellie. Is there anything I can do? Are you sure you don't want me to come up and keep you company?'

'Jack's here,' Ellie said, in way of an answer. She added, 'not a word from you please.'

'Ellie. I might have my jealous moments, but I'm pretty good at gauging when it's not the time for it. I'm glad Jack is still with you. Can I speak to him for a moment?'

Ellie creased her eyebrows in suspicion as she silently passed her phone to a bewildered Jack.

'Alright?' Jack said warily down the phone. Ellie could just make out the low rumblings of George's voice in the receiver from where she stood and watched Jack's reactions. 'Yeah. Yeah, of course. No, we're alright for the moment. Yeah. I will, mate. Okay, thanks. We'll keep you posted. Cheers.' Jack hung up and passed Ellie her phone back. 'George said if I need to head back home any time this evening, to let him know and he'll come up and keep you company. Said to promise him I wouldn't leave you here on your own.' Jack snorted. 'Obviously.'

'I hope he wasn't rude,' Ellie sighed, all nervous agitation in her body dissipating and leaving behind an exhausted weariness as she slumped down in the speckled chair next to Jack.

'Not at all,' Jack assured her. 'It's just clear how much he cares about you. He's a good bloke, actually. You could do worse.'

It was Ellie's turn to snort now, despite her worries and concerns for poor Nanny. 'I know.'

'So, what happened between you two earlier?' Jack asked, digging into the second half of his foot-long sandwich.

Ellie shook her head from side to side, leaning back in her chair, her arms crossed, and her eyes closed in anguish. 'Not right now.' Jack nodded in understanding and Ellie forced herself to tuck into a small part of her sandwich, knowing well enough that she would need all the energy she could muster for the long night ahead.

In the small hours of the morning, Ellie woke with a sore neck from where she had fallen asleep scrunched into one of the waiting room chairs. Beside her, a large warm hand encasing hers and his long legs spread out to the middle of the floor, sat George, his eyes closed and his chest moving calmly in a light sleep. He must have swapped with Jack while Ellie was dosing. Without moving, she gazed at him for a bit. His tanned skin; his dark eyelashes shadowing against his stubbled cheek; the way his hair curled in the nape of his neck. Something about his presence brought Ellie a different kind of comfort and she soon settled back into an uncomfortable but necessary light sleep.

'Miss Curnow?' The voice of a young nurse penetrated Ellie's poor slumber and it was all Ellie could do not to yelp out in discomfort as she uncurled from the chair. She could hear George grunting and stretching beside her as they both came to, giving the nurse their full attention. 'Sorry to wake you, love. I'll take you through now to see Gloria.'

Something about the nurse's demeanour flooded Ellie with apprehension. She gripped George's hand as she jumped to her feet.

'Can I bring George here in with me?'

The nurse smiled kindly. 'I think that might be a good idea, love.'

The water on the estuary was as still as a millpond, and a bevy of swans glided idly across the way towards the muddy embankment on the other side. The gentle day-to-day of the hamlet had carried on as usual whilst the stagnant time zone of a hospital had discombobulated Ellie's entire body clock. Her bone-deep exhaustion suggested it was the middle of the night when she returned to their quiet little cottage. But, as a matter of fact, it was mid-afternoon - the distant sounds of strimmers and lawn mowers echoeing from bank to bank and birds twittering gracefully in the trees. Ellie stood on the water's edge, at the base of their long garden, drinking in the view she knew so well - trying to fathom the idea of a life on the river without Nanny.

Gloria Curnow passed away peacefully in the early hours of this morning when the sun had begun to peak over the horizon for a warm day ahead. Ellie had held her hand the entire way through, grateful that she could at least comfort her in the last moments of her extraordinary life.

Her chest ached and her eyes, hooded from the tears she had been shedding since she and George had left the hospital, stung as she drew in deep, shaky breaths through trembling lips.

How would she live her life now, without Nanny?

She was acutely aware of a small gathering by the back door: George, Jack and Wenna, their sympathies and concerns suffocating Ellie even from the other side of the twenty-meter-long garden in which they stood. She did not dare turn around. Just one glance at their pitying expressions was sure to finish her off and she wasn't one for public shows of sorrow. If only she still had her little boat to row away in.

After some time had passed, she eventually surrendered to the fact that she couldn't avoid the people who waited patiently for her out of love forever. When she finally turned around, she was quietly relieved to find that Jack and Wenna had at least gone inside, their movement just visible through the glaring sunlight across the patio doors into the kitchen. George had taken a seat on the patio bench and now his eyes trained on hers all the way back through garden.

He was silent as she stood before him, his face solemn but, thankfully, not that of pity.

'I'm tired,' Ellie said, her voice barely a whisper. She then added, as Jack and Wenna stepped out onto the patio: 'Thanks for coming.'

It was very final and had the desired effect, though Ellie was semi-aware how rude and rejective she was being. Wenna reached across and squeezed Ellie in a tight embrace.

'I'm only a text message away,' Wenna said, kissing her on the cheek.

Jack was more hesitant and seemed hurt by Ellie's dismissal, but she didn't have the emotional capacity to reassure him right now. She just wanted to be alone.

'I'll call in tomorrow morning to check on you,' Jack said, exchanging a strange look with George, both nodding in some mutual understanding they had both concluded to when Ellie hadn't been paying attention. When Jack, after much more hesitation and a solemn glance around Nanny's kitchen, had finally left with Wenna, it left Ellie and George together in a heavy and loaded silence.

'Go to bed,' George ordered. Though his voice was gentle and kind, his body language was distant, his hands tucked deep into his pockets as he stood a considerable distance. 'You need to rest. I'll be here.'

'Won't you go?' Ellie asked quietly. It was half a plea and half a part of her checking she wouldn't indeed be alone, no matter how much she thought she wanted it right now.

George shook his head, then - pulling one hand out from his pocket and stroking her cheek - said, 'get some sleep. I'll be here.'

A week trickled by slowly, with the realities of everything settling in like a heavy cloud. Ellie practically disappeared into the depths of the large estate, putting her focus and energy into the garden, a desperate attempt to busy her mind and keep the inevitable grief at bay. She'd taken a small dose of comfort in the flower garden of all places - it's high, bricked walls acting as a barrier to the world whilst the drowsy hum of bees soothed Ellie like a lullaby, the sea of Dahlia heads nodding in the light breeze as she idly pruned the dead heads.

She had sent half of today's volunteers over to the main driveway, to tidy up the hydrangea bushes which lined the grass verge all the way up, whilst Dave and Joseph led the other half in the Italian Gardens to deweed the beds and give the grass a close cut. Tressa's next event - The Classic Cars Rally - was coming up close and the weather was at least on their side this time. There would be lots of photos being taken of the cars in front of the house, so everything needed to look pristine. Being Head Gardener, Ellie probably should have been leading the groups herself, situating herself in the thick of it all, but she hadn't wanted to be around people all week. Dave and Joseph, though showing their concerns and checking on her in their subtle ways, had respected her need for space, only appearing every now and again to top up her coffee mug.

The one working the closest in proximity was Jack, who was just on the other side of the walled garden, making headway with the natural playground. Though he too respected Ellie's solitary time to grieve, he was lacking subtlety when finding excuses to pass through the Flower Garden about a hundred-times a day, seeking out tools he probably already had or supposedly leaving a vital piece of material in the van. Despite herself, Ellie was grateful for his silent presence.

It was George's companionship in the evening which Ellie held dearest. He'd been away from the estate during the day for most of the week, overloaded with external meetings which Ellie didn't always quite understand. Perhaps if her mind hadn't been so fogged with recent events, she may even question what all these meetings were for. But instead, she was grateful that as soon as she returned home to the emptiness of her and Nanny's cottage, George was there to fill the deafening silence. At first, they barely talked. George simply just allowed Ellie to adjust in her new ordinary whilst he cooked warming meals and slept on the sofa just so Ellie didn't have to be alone in the cottage at night for the first time in her life - not until she was ready.

One morning, groggy from broken sleep and with Nanny's funeral only a couple of days away, Ellie followed the scent of cooking bacon. Even after a couple of weeks, the sight of George cooking in the very place where she would have seen Nanny cooking every single morning caused a jolt of both pain and a confused sense of desire for the man who chose to care for her from a distance - at least for now. Ever since her and George's moment outside the secret garden, through one thing or another there had been no more moments since. Ellie was of course mostly grateful for this. She didn't feel it appropriate to be pursuing whatever this was forming between her and George. But it didn't stop her losing her nerve every now and again and feeling that pang of desire towards him, that longing. And what George was doing for her in the meantime, the way he showed he cared just by being there, meant the world to her.

'Morning,' George said, giving Ellie a gentle smile as he attended to the eggs slowly frying in the pan. 'HP with your bacon and egg sarnie?'

'I swear you're trying to make me fat with all of this,' Ellie mused, sliding into a seat at the breakfast table. The patio doors had been swung open and the sweet, dewy scent of the garden in its morning glory wafted in with a light breeze.

'The number of calories you must burn in a day from all the gardening, I'm determined to keep your body fuelled. Coffee?'

'Please.' She must have looked particularly forlorn, gazing out of the window to watch a robin hop about on the grass. Eventually feeling George's eyes on her, she turned in his direction, her eyes heavy from sleep and sadness. He crossed the room, a mug of steaming hot coffee in his hand which he placed gently on the table in front of her. Then, pulling her up by the elbow into a standing position, he enveloped her in the tightest of hugs, one that could almost glue all her broken pieces back together. She eventually relaxed, moulding into his body and wrapping her arms around his middle, feeling the tightness of the muscles in his back and breathing in his citrus scent. What felt like minutes trickled by, and Ellie buried her face deeper into his chest, feeling a fresh new barrel of sobs overcome her like a tsunami. George only tightened his grip, silent and solid as her body became ragged with heaving tears, juddering breaths catching in her throat. Hours could have passed for all Ellie knew - she felt so succumbed all of a sudden with loss and grief and utter sadness.

And though she felt safe and cared for in the arms of George, his soothing voice a gentle reminder that she would not be alone in this, a feeling of panic consumed her and only one thing echoed in her mind.

How would she ever get through this?

# Chapter Thirty-One

The first early signs of Autumn soon arrived, enveloping Penhaligon Estate in warm hues as trees scattered fiery red and orange leaves to a damp, mossy ground. The hot, sprightly nature of Summer had come to a close for the year and the garden was preparing itself for its inevitable winter slumber.

George was yet to experience a full season of cold and damp weather in the big house, and quietly admitted to being nervous at the prospect. At least over the summer months, the scorching Cornish sun had kept any withdrawals from his Mediterranean life at bay. But now, the promise of colder days was on the horizon, and George felt that pang of desire to feel the Italian sun on his tanned skin once again. The perfect opportunity had arisen. He just had a bit of convincing to do.

Since the passing of Gloria, Ellie had maintained a distance from everyone around her, quietly existing amongst the golden Rudbeckia and vegetable beds swelling with a promising harvest. Her quietening demeanour unnerved George and, despite his silent promises to keep a respectable distance, he was now beginning to think that what Ellie needed was a change of scenery.

'You want me to go with you to Italy?' Ellie reiterated that afternoon, after George had stopped beating around the bush and simply put his idea forward to her. 'To learn about vineyards?'

'I want you to have some time away to clear your head,' George said, pointing out his main priorities. 'But yes. There might be a vineyard or two.' A wide grin spread across his face and he waited patiently for Ellie to consider this offer for a moment, desperately hoping suddenly that she would say yes. He watched as Ellie's chest swelled in a heaving sigh, her eyes trailing in the general direction of the river, as if something over there would give her the answer.

George sighed. Not out of impatience, but with concern. Everything that made Ellie so sprightly and full of life had been sapped away recently and it killed him to see it.

'When my father died,' George began, surprising himself as well as Ellie, who suddenly fixed her sapphire blue eyes on him, 'I honestly thought I would never be able to be happy ever again. That feeling - what you're feeling right now - it consumed me, and it was like a big black cloud hovering over me and... and numbing me. It was strange. I knew I was sad. But the sadness manifested into this general numbness. It lasted for months. And people kept telling me I needed to get on with life. Your father wouldn't want you moping like this, they would say. It's one of the reasons I left and went to Italy. I couldn't stick it, having people dictating how I should feel and when I should stop feeling the loss I felt. And on top of that, being pushed to suddenly step into his shoes and run the estate.'

'That must have been so hard,' Ellie whispered.

'It was. But what I'm trying to say is that I'm not dictating when you should stop grieving. The truth is you never stop grieving. The grief never goes away. It never gets smaller. But time passes and the space around that ball of grief gets bigger. It does become easier to carry that grief and live with it.'

Ellie nodded, understanding his meaning, and drawing in a deep breath through her nose, as if the knowledge from this analogy allowed her to breath just a little easier. 'You're right. At least I don't burst into tears every two seconds now at work.

Though, I think Dave is avoiding me now. He doesn't deal with tears very well.'

George smiled, then stroked her cheek. 'That's progress. But you're not yourself. Let me take you to Italy. Get a change of scenery. We'll take our balls of grief with us, and we'll manage them somewhere sunny and Mediterranean. What do you say?'

\*\*\*

'I can't believe you lived here!' Ellie gasped, tilting herself precariously over the iron balcony to the busy road below. A fortnight had passed between Ellie agreeing and George arranging the flights over to Italy for their excursion. They had landed in Milan Malpenso Airport only a couple of hours ago and now George was giving her the grand, but very short tour of his two-bedroom apartment in the centre of the Italian Metropolitan. 'It's so much more modern than I had pictured in my head.'

'This is Milan, don't forget,' George pointed out, standing in the centre of the main living area, and enjoying every moment of Ellie's animated reactions to the place he called home for ten years. 'It's had a real face lift over the last few years. The city and the apartment, that is. I'll take you to see some of the more historical sights before we head back home.'

Not wanting to intrude on Ellie's exploration any longer, he busied himself with checking through a pile of letters that had been collected for him in his absence. Occasionally he would look up, a strange pull in his chest at the sight of seeing Ellie here in his apartment. Nothing had changed about it. The same white walls gleamed brightly at him; the same oak-finish flooring echoed under foot. The new glass-fronted skyscraper across the road from their building had been freed from its scaffolding and traffic below seemed as busy and hectic as ever. He loaded a coffee capsule to the machine and pressed the button on his De

Longhi ESAM3300 Magnifica. A gift from one of their clients many years ago, the espresso machine was George's favourite feature of the kitchen.

'There's so much space!' Ellie cried, her voice carrying through from one end of the apartment to the other. She appeared through a set of double doors, her eyes bright and sparkling. 'There's so much light.'

George was silent but smiled his appreciation to Ellie, handing her a tiny white porcelain cup of espresso and inviting her back out to the balcony, which veered slightly from the modern views of the city and directly faced an older building, the gap in between no more than around 8ft. The windows of the building had old, sage green shutters with prominent decorative cornices and corbels; scarlet red geraniums were a burst of colour against the ivory-coloured stone. He was automatic in his usual stance and rested his forearms on the iron railings, his espresso poised delicately in his large, tanned hands. Ellie came to stand by him, drinking in every bit of detail.

'Glad you came?' George asked.

'Yes,' Ellie said, nodding in confidence. 'I am.'

They were suddenly interrupted by the clunky sounds of the lock mechanism in the front door.

'Oh, here we go,' George huffed, though his face gave away his delight. 'Whatever happens. Whatever you see or think, remember that I am the handsome one!'

Utterly confused, Ellie chuckled away all the same as the front door burst open, a dark-haired, dark-skinned man stepping into the open space, his shining white teeth gleaming in a welcoming smile.

'Ciao, Bella! You are Ellie, no? George here, he tell me all about you!' Antonio's vivification radiated and filled the room. Dumping his briefcase by the door, he crossed the space between them in no more than five large strides and enveloped Ellie in one of his signature hugs. 'Mi dispiace tantissimo,

Signorina. Your nonna must have been beautiful woman.'

'Thank you. You must be Antonio,' Ellie said, beaming at his energy. George had told her all about his zestful Italian friend and business partner on the flight over.

'So, my mamma tells me!' He turns to George and embraces him, the men patting each other on the back with rigour. 'George, my friend - what you been eating while you are gone? You have got - what do we say - podgy, no?'

'Cheeky shit!' George exclaimed, the laughter rippling through the three of them. 'This is what happens when I don't have a gym to use.' He proceeded to pat his stomach, rock hard and flat, smiling as he caught Ellie looking with a blush in her cheeks. The look that happened between them didn't go unnoticed, and Antonio grinned from ear-to-ear at the sight of them.

'You two are a picture. I take you out for dinner. We celebrate. George, we must show Ellie a night out in Corso Como, no?' He clapped his hands together in triumph, walking backwards in the direction of one of the bedrooms. 'It is decided! We get ready to go in one hour.'

George glanced at Ellie's face and though she was politely smiling, he could see the exhaustion in her features. 'How about tomorrow night, Antonio?' His friend made a noise of protest to which George responded more firmly in Italian, reminding him that he and Ellie had just arrived after a long journey and that he wanted Ellie to relax tonight. 'Calmati, amico.'

'Okay,' Antonio relented. 'Tonight we stay in, we eat good food and drink good wine. I go have shower and then I make my mamma's best Tonnarelli Cacio e Pepe! George! You choose the wine!'

Ellie chuckled to herself as Antonio closed the door to his bedroom at the end of the corridor, bringing back that silence they had had before. George blew a loud breath through his lips and necked his espresso in one. 'He won't be quite so animated in a few hours. He does settle - sort of. But he gets excited meeting new people. You get used to him.'

'You sound like you're apologising for him.' Ellie laughed. 'I think he's great!'

'You might not be saying that later after he's had a few drinks. Come on, I'll show you where you're sleeping and then let you freshen up.'

# Chapter Thirty-Two

Ellie seated herself on the crisp white sheets of George's bed - the bedding cleaned and arranged in a way only a professional cleaner could do - and contemplated the brash decisions that had gotten her here. She could hear the movements of both George and Antonio around the apartment, their feet heavy against the oak flooring and their rumbling voices echoing through the open spaces in fluent Italian.

The initial buzz of going abroad with George had stayed with her out of loyalty for the best part of the journey and for the first hour at least of arriving at George and Antonio's Milan apartment. But now, the early evening drawing in, that excitement had dissipated, being replaced by a hint of homesickness and exhaustion. Despite Ellie's forthcomings, her perfectly placed 'oohs' and 'ahhs' towards George's apartment, which he was clearly proud of, it was a far cry from her pretty little cottage along a Cornish creek. As if to punctuate that point, a proceeding of loud honking sounds from cars below followed by obnoxious vrooming of their throaty engines made Ellie's face scrunch up in anguish. The city life was not for her.

She rose early the next morning, having barely slept at all, in hopes of catching the metropolis in a much calmer time of day. As expected, the roads below were barren and hushed, like the calm after a storm. A dry warmth was setting in already, promising to be another scorching day.

Ellie's bare feet padded against the wooden floor as she tip-toed down the long corridor towards the kitchen and living area. She almost jumped out of her skin as she was met by the soles of George's feet, protruding through a thin blanket, and giving away George's position on the sofa. She bit her lip in guilt. She'd been so tired last night, she hadn't even considered the possibility she would be taking George's only sleeping space. She'd insist he had his own bed tonight and she would take the sofa. It wasn't like she was sleeping much these days, after all.

The coffee machine was merciful and quiet as Ellie pushed a couple of buttons in the vague order in which she had watched George do it yesterday. Smooth, golden liquid pulled through from the machine and into the speckled cup she had placed underneath, the nutty fragrance awakening her senses.

With George undisturbed, Ellie took her espresso out onto the balcony for some fresh air, the hot breeze hitting her instantly. The outside space of the apartment was shed in morning light, the cappuccino-coloured building opposite glowing against the dreary grey concrete of the building she was in now, and she hoped quietly that wherever they were adventuring to later today would have buildings more like the former, with the typically Italian green shutters and bursts of pink from the Bougainvillea clinging to the sides of the old stonework. In fact, less buildings in general would be nice, Ellie thought. Nevertheless, she revelled at the peacefulness of the moment right now, hoisting herself up onto one of the concrete platforms breaking up the wrought-iron railings. She noted that this balcony was in need of some flowers, to break up the greyness of the concrete floor and walls. From her vantage point, Ellie could see the cityscape sprawled out before her - a mosaic of contemporary architecture and historical landmarks.

She closed her eyes for a moment, transporting herself back to their little blue gate - the nodding heads of the Rudbeckia and

Cosmos now blooming in their peak. At the bottom of their garden, the estuary water flowed lazily whilst tall reeds swayed along the embankment - a heron perched majestically on a nearby rock. The smell of short-crust pastry baking in the oven lured her through those double doors into the kitchen where Nanny's hands were adorned with flour, and the saucepans behind her steamed and bubbled away on their hobs.

The warm trickle of tears tracing down her cheek brought Ellie back to the present, the city now waking up around her as she clutched at her coffee. She looked up sharply at the sound of the patio doors clunking open as a dishevelled George stepped onto the warm slabs bare foot, his dark hair curling wildly from sleep. Ellie's chest clenched at the sight of George's bare torso, a scattering of dark chest hair across powerful pecs and a trailing of hair leading down past his Adonis belt. Her eyes rested lazily on the muscles of his powerful chest and shoulders, and though her body reacted, her mind was still dominated by that lingering sadness she carried at the moment.

'You okay?' George asked, rubbing the back of his neck and giving in to a long yawn. 'How long have you been up?'

'Not long,' Ellie mumbled, her eyes darting back down to her coffee. 'I hope I didn't wake you.'

'Not at all,' George replied, then chuckled to himself. 'It is really strange having you here. It is just occurring to me, in my sleepy state.' Ellie smiled, though it didn't quite meet her eyes. George tilted his head in concern and closed the gap between them, taking a seat in front of her and running a thumb gently across her cheek. 'You've been crying.'

Ellie wrinkled her nose. 'Only a bit. I'm fine. Please don't be nice to me or I'll make a tit of myself in front of your friend - who, by the way, snores.'

'Oh yeah - I should have warned you about that. He is also a terrible morning person. Come on. Get changed and I'll take you out for breakfast.'

'Ah, this is something I'm more accustomed to,' Ellie said, feeling herself relaxing at the sight of water. A twenty-minute walk from their apartment block, George had led the way to Naviglio Grande where clutches of cafes and restaurants lined the long canal, the early-morning sun reflecting in the calm waters.

'You should see this place in the evening. It's spectacular.' George's arm snaked around Ellie's waist, and he pulled her into him just in time for a cyclist to come hurtling past.

'I can't imagine how busy it must get in the evening,' Ellie said breathlessly, as she checked her surroundings for more hazards. 'If this is 8am.'

'Hmm, you're right. The nightlife here might not be for you. You're a proper country girl, aren't you?' It wasn't a criticism, and in fact Ellie felt this fondness radiate from George's eyes which caused her to blush ferociously.

'I am,' Ellie admitted. 'Sorry - I hate the city!'

George laughed and, in response, lacing his fingers in hers and grasping her hand tightly, guiding her over the tram line and along the cobblestoned path which ran between the water and the colourful buildings which looked over the canal. The smell of coffee and sweet pastries had Ellie's stomach rumbling as they passed a shock of pink oleander trees, lining the pathway like lollipops. They settled at a cafe with cream parasols, its lemon-yellow building shining golden in the Mediterranean sun. A waiter came to greet them the instant they sat down, greeting them *Buongiorno,* to which George engaged in conversation with the gentleman in fluent Italian. Ellie watched with fascination as George navigated the language with ease, as if it were his first language - both men gesticulating passionately about whatever it was they were discussing.

'Coffee and a brioche?' George asked Ellie.

'Yes please.'

Whilst George placed their order with the waiter, Ellie took a good look around from where she was sitting. The architecture; the people; the smells and sounds of a city waking up for the day. Then she looked back across the table again, to George who fitted like a piece of the puzzle here in Milan, and for the first-time doubt seeped into her chest and a shyness settled in, leaving her vulnerable. In an automatic reaction, she crossed her arms and wished she'd worn something smarter than black denim shorts and a loose t-shirt next to George's pressed white shirt and olive-green chino shorts. An obscured reflection of herself mirrored back from his Ray-Bans, and even from the distance of the small bistro table between them she could see that she looked tired and hollow-faced.

'So, how far is the vineyard from here?' Ellie asked, smiling up at the waiter who now brought out their coffees and pastries. The brioche was enormous and coated in a thick layer of dusted sugar.

'About an hour. Just outside of Lake Como. Antonio will drive us.'

'I've always wanted to visit Lake Como itself. Is it far from there?'

'About twenty minutes. We can visit Lake Como afterwards, if you like,' George said, smiling widely so it crinkled around his dark brown eyes. 'I'll even buy you a gelato.'

'Mmm, now you're talking,' Ellie said, picking up her espresso cup and pulling a face. 'My coffee addiction is definitely going to be significantly worse after this trip with all these espressos. Is there an option for milk?'

George shrugged, his large hands cradling his own espresso. 'You can order it with milk, if you want to be an amateur tourist.'

'Is this the Italian equivalent of putting cream on your scones first.'

George released a burst of laughter. 'Definitely! Consider yourself an Italian emit if you start having milk with your coffee.

But if you do, make sure you don't just ask for a latte, or you'll just get hot milk.'

'Bold of you to assume I'm not going to just leave you to do all the ordering. Your Italian is incredible.'

'Grazie, bella signora.'

Ellie's face blushed for the hundredth time that morning. 'How long did it take you to become so fluent?'

'Trust me, my Italian is still not perfect. Antonio likes to point out all the time that my pronunciation is off, or I'm too formal. But I started taking lessons when I first moved over here ten years ago. It becomes easier once you start using it day-to-day. Especially when you rely on it for sealing business deals.'

'I'd love to learn another language. I was useless at French in school.'

'I'll teach you some basics while we're here,' George said, winking encouragingly. 'Try this one. *Questo...*'

'*Questo...*' Ellie repeated, shyly.

'*...è il mio...*'

'*...è il mio...*'

'*...ragazzo*, George.'

Ellie paused and looked at him suspiciously from across the table but humoured him all the same. '*...ragazzo*, George.'

'Really?' George said, his eyebrows dancing in delight.

'What did you make me say?'

'This is my boyfriend, George. Thought it might come in handy if you need to introduce me.'

Ellie suppressed a smile, her cheeks hurting in effort. She looked around to the empty sets of tables and chairs around them. 'To who? That pigeon over there?'

'Got to start somewhere,' George replied, shrugging. 'Although, in time, I'd like to be more than just a casual *ragazzo*. Someone you are merely dating. One day, if I can finally convince you, I'd like to be your *fidanzato*. Maybe even your *marito*.'

She couldn't be certain, but she was pretty sure she knew

what those words meant, and they made her heart race and her stomach clench with longing.

'You are smooth, George Penhaligon. And also, very presumptuous.'

'Like I said... got to start somewhere.'

After their coffee and pastry breakfast, they walked and talked alongside the black iron railings lining the side of the canal. Despite her dislike towards the busy city life, in the calmness of the morning Ellie could appreciate the beauty of the place - the history. The rows of old buildings looking down on the water are a mosaic of colours, each fronted with quaint little balconies and shuttered windows. Digital billboards flash obnoxiously from both sides, a crude reminder of their urbanised surroundings.

When George leads them up some concrete steps, they cross the water halfway along a black iron bridge where his phone buzzes loudly in his pocket.

'Excuse me,' George mumbles, extracting his phone whilst Ellie looked into the waters below. She looked up in time to catch his face pinching into a frown, a flash of annoyance distorting his face for a split second.

'Everything okay?' Ellie asked, leaning back against the iron railings.

'Hmm?' George's head snapped up as he hurried to stuff his phone into his back pocket. 'Fine. Absolutely fine. Just... Tressa, pestering me about estate stuff.'

Ellie wasn't entirely convinced by that answer but allowed herself the luxury to think of home, not for the first time since they had arrived. She wondered how the gardens were doing in her absence; how Joseph was getting on with the new pumpkin patch in the kitchen gardens; and what the river was now looking like as the luscious green foliage on the embankment evolves into a symphony of fiery reds, burnt oranges and golden yellows. She's soon ripped back to present day as a swarm of

Vespas roar past on a nearby street.

'I think it's time to take you back out into the countryside,' George remarked.

# Chapter Thirty-Three

When it had occurred to George what the email that had pinged through on his mobile had implied, George's chest had clenched, his stomach dropping to painful lows. It wasn't that he didn't trust Lavinia to be a part of the estate's business affairs, but when an email written by his mother, regarding 'Stone's Throw Cottage - Ellie's cottage, is forwarded by one of the officers at Cornwall Council, George couldn't help but feel dread seep in through the edges. Only one question cropped up.

What was his mother up to now?

A picturesque Italian vineyard stretches out before them, with rows upon rows of luscious, green grapevines basking in the Mediterranean sunlight. The air is filled with the sweet scent of grapes and the earthy aroma of the surrounding countryside. Of all the vineyards George and Antonio visited in their line of business, this was always his favourite by far.

A portly man with greying, receding hair steps out of the stone-fronted farmhouse, his arms wide in a friendly welcome, as their car pulls onto the dusty driveway.

'That's Stefano - the owner,' George explained to Ellie as Stefano crossed the yard towards their car. 'His family have been in business here for three generations. Very knowledgeable in his field.'

They stepped out of the car and George and Antonio

greeted Stefano like an old friend, tightly embracing and slapping one another loudly on the back. An exchange of elevated words was had in fast Italian, the topaz sun beating down on them in merry welcome.

'Stefano, this is Ellie,' George said, stepping to one side to reveal Ellie standing quietly behind him. She smiled and stepped forward; a hand outstretched to Stefano in greeting.

'Ciao, *Signora*,' Stefano said, smiling widely and shaking her hand. 'Welcome to Montioni Frantoio e Cantina!'

The sun casted a golden glow over the scene as Stefano led the way, exuding an infectious enthusiasm and genuine love for his craft. He and Antonio moved gracefully between the rows, inspecting the grape clusters, feeling their ripeness between their fingers, whilst George and Ellie held back, relishing in some time to simply walk side-by-side and enjoy the scenery. George lost count how many times he almost gave in to the urge to hold Ellie's hand or gather her in close to his side. Having her here with him, in Italy where he had built a life to be proud of - one he had created himself, and not just inherited - had him thinking about possibilities with Ellie that went beyond physical attraction. He just wished she could see how much she meant to him now.

'Antonio says Ellie here a giardiniera? Uhh...gardener?' Stefano asked, as George and Ellie finally caught up with them at the end of a long row of vines.

'She certainly is,' George said proudly. 'Head Gardener for that matter, at Penhaligon Estate. Our home back in Cornwall.'

'*Molto bene*! Have you ever maintained a vineyard, *Signora*?'

'No, I haven't,' Ellie replied from George's side. She glanced up at him before continuing. 'Actually, George and I considered the idea of starting a small vineyard on our estate. In a walled garden we recently rediscovered. But I wasn't sure whether it's warm enough or the best location for one. Like I said, I'm a complete novice in all of this.'

'People think we here in Italy grow all the wine because of hot, Mediterranean sun. That is important, yes. But adequate sun - long warm summers - and enough cold and rain in the dormant months, that is what makes vines thrive. And good soil! Come! Let me talk you through the varieties we have here.'

George and Antonio held back whilst Ellie listened intently to Stefano's expert advice and tips, his hands and arms gesticulating passionately.

'Call me an old romantic,' Antonio said suddenly, bursting a hole in George's trail of thought. 'But you and Ellie - you are perfect couple!'

George laughed and clapped a hand on his friend's shoulder in thanks. *'Un giorno.* I hope.'

*'Prendilo con calma, amico.* The best things worth waiting for are given time to grow strong roots before they shoot upwards... *Sì? Capito?'*

'Not in the slightest,' George deadpanned. 'But I appreciate your attempt at an analogy all the same.'

*'Signori,'* Stefano announced from where he stood, Ellie examining the soil from underneath. 'It is *mezzogiorno.* My wife Andrea has prepared some delicious food. You will sample our finest wine.'

When they rounded the corner of the old stone farmhouse, they were met by a long, wooden table adorned with crisp white tablecloths and a mountain of different foods, a backdrop of rolling hills and distant vineyards across an expanse of land. It was one of George's favourite views and not the first time he had dined alfresco with the Montioni family, but each time he lay eyes upon the spread of food Andrea brought out, his reaction was every bit as flabbergasted as it had been the first time he had visited here on business. He chuckled as he caught a similar expression on Ellie's face. Her face radiated with enthusiasm and sun as she mouthed a silent but animated 'Oh my god!'

'Please! Sit! I grab the wine!' Stefano cried, kissing his wife on the cheek as she passed him with a platter of capocollo and black olives. Antonio disappeared in the same direction, no doubt to retrieve his favourite red for the table.

George pulled out a chair for Ellie and invited her to take a seat. 'You won't have to drink the wine, Ellie. In the tasting, we'll be spitting it out anyway.'

'It's fine,' Ellie said, simply. 'I won't want to be rude.'

George was about to reassure her that she wouldn't be rude when Stefano and Antonio returned, both with a bottle of wine in each of their hands. Andrea followed close behind with a tray of wine glasses, the sun reflecting brightly from them.

'We start with our dry whites,' Stefano said. 'People in the UK - all you think is Pinot Grigio for white. But - the most widely planted white grapes are Sicilia's Catarratto and Trebbiano Toscano.'

Having heard it all before, George's eyes swept over to Ellie who listened with intent and genuine interest. He smiled warmly at her polite nods and the way she brought a slender hand up to sweep strands of coppery hair from across her face. A sprinkling of freckles was now more prominent across the bridge of her nose and a twinkle had returned to her eyes after such a long time of absence.

Stefano continued, now pouring small portions of his first wine into the glasses. 'Dry Trebbiano wine, it is easy drinker. Very light flavours of green apple and lemon. It has been fermented and aged for many years down in our cellar.'

George accepted his glass, pinching the stem between strong fingers. He winced as Ellie shyly accepted hers, cupping the bowl of the glass awkwardly between two hands. She glanced sideways at him and shrugged.

'Actually, Stefano,' George found himself saying. *'Scusa. Non beve alcolici.'*

'What are you doing?' Ellie hissed. 'It's fine.'

He waved her concerns away and placed what he thought was a reassuring hand on her knee, whilst Stefano and Antonio looked equally perplexed.

'*Niente alcol*? I'm not understanding. How can you be growing your own vineyard if you are not tasting your own produce?'

There was polite fussing and Ellie's hands waving in front of her in embarrassment.

'You're right, Stefano. George, please stop - it's absolutely fine.'

Antonio passed a metal bucket across the table. 'Here, Ellie. You can spit into this.'

'I gave her the spittoon, and still she...how you say...pissed as skunk back there,' Antonio cried, chuckling away to himself in the driver's seat on their way back to Milan.

George turned in his seat from the front passenger to confirm that Ellie was still in the same slumbering position against the car door as she had been almost the moment, they had piled into the car to leave. She looked so peaceful, like she was finally getting the rest she needed after all this time.

'I don't think it's necessarily the wine. She's been through a lot. I'm glad she's getting some sleep.'

George felt brief glances from Antonio's direction in between focusing on the road. 'I think my friend, you are in love. I have not seen you like this before.'

An involuntary smile crept on George's features as he switched the radio on, choosing not to respond.

'Ahh, he does not deny it!' Antonio cried, thumping a hand on the steering wheel with a giant grin on his face. 'George Penhaligon - finally in love!'

'Feel free to keep your voice down,' George said, checking Ellie's state in his mirror. Still fast asleep.

A heavy silence suddenly fell inside the car, farmhouses and green land turning into rows of buildings and billboards as they returned to the city.

'So, what is the plan, amico?'

'I don't mind. We could take Ellie out for dinner when she's had a sleep, or-'

'No... *non è quello che intendo! Uffa!* I mean with us. With the business!' Antonio's voice was suddenly shrill, fast and with accompanying hand gestures which were always a tell-tale sign for George that Antonio was vexed. 'I support you with whatever makes you happy. But I cannot hold the forte here forever while you playing His Lordship in England with your castle.'

Despite himself, a spurt of laughter erupted from George's chest, causing Ellie to temporarily stir on the backseat. 'I don't live in a bloody castle, but your perception of my life in Cornwall is hilariously inaccurate, my friend.' He filled his lungs slowly, biding time whilst thinking of an answer to Antonio's questions. He'd been questioning it himself for a little while now, what his new future held for him in regard to their merchant's business. He'd naively assumed he could swoop in, sort out any issues with the Estate and get the finances all in order, and swoop back out again, returning to his blissful, controlled life here in Italy.

But, of course, he hadn't accounted for the endless issues that came with a large 18th Century stately home, not to mention the creative ways in which they would need to bring in an income in a modern world. And he hadn't accounted for the possibility of meeting someone who would actually make him want to stay. Everything he had been so certain of, of the life he had built in Italy, of his commitment to his company - it had all gone topsy-turvy now.

'Hello, Lord Penhaligon?' Antonio teased from the front seat. 'What now?'

George released a heavy sigh. 'I'm sorry, *amico*. I don't know.'

# Chapter Thirty-Four

It was the rush of loud voices from the streets down below and the roaring of cars bursting through Ellie's open bedroom window which disturbed her from her deep sleep. She blinked multiple times, bringing the blurriness of the room into focus.

That was the best sleep she had had in a long time.

It was at that moment that the door opened, and George's face appeared in the gap.

'Just in time, sleepy head,' George said. 'Fancy going out for dinner?'

A yawn and a stretch momentarily took over her body before she could answer. 'What time is it?'

'It's six o'clock.'

'You're joking!' George shook his head. 'So much for visiting Lake Como and making the most of our trip. I'm so sorry, I'll get up.'

George rushed in to reassure her, perching on the edge of the bed. 'Why on earth are you sorry? You clearly needed it.'

'I did,' Ellie relented. 'That wine knocked me for six.'

'It'll do that,' George said, smiling. 'How are you feeling?'

'Better for a sleep. But I feel a bit embarrassed for passing out like that. I wasn't drunk! Just exhausted.'

'When was the last time you had a drink?'

Ellie paused, rubbing her eyes, and releasing another yawn. 'Five...six years?'

George's eyes widened. 'Not suggesting that everybody needs to be drinking, but that's-'

'Unusual, I know.'

George's phone pinged in his pocket. Checking the screen, he said, 'Wenna says hi. And hurry home.'

'Oh dear,' Ellie said, her thoughts immediately going to the idea of Lavinia, Tressa and Beryan being up to their usual antics and driving Wenna and Trixie up the wall.

She watched George's thumbs tap away on his phone as he messaged Wenna back. He was wearing a navy t-shirt which stretched over his biceps and desert tan shorts, whilst Ellie felt scruffy and discombobulated in a loose black vest and grey cotton shorts. Whilst George finished sending his message to his sister, Ellie made an attempt to tame her unruly hair. She was pretty sure there was a hair band in there somewhere which had somewhat lost control of her mane.

'You did really well today,' George said, now bringing his attention back on Ellie. 'Antonio reckons Stefano would have offered you a job if you lived here.'

'Really?'

'Believe it or not Ellie, you are excellent at what you do. In a garden or in a vineyard, you are brilliant.' Ellie felt herself glow with something that felt very much like pride. 'And you even managed to get through a whole tasting session, without spitting and without hitting the deck. So, I remain exceedingly impressed with you.' His voice tittered off into a chuckle as they both laughed together, Ellie relishing in that feeling for a moment. Laughter had felt unnatural and misplaced since Nanny had died, but today she felt lighter than she had in a while.

'What made you quit alcohol? Or stop? Swear off it, whatever it was.'

Ellie frowned, wondering why George focused so much on her sobriety. Her body language changed, and she seemed to

307

brace herself, gathering her knees up to her chest and trying hard to think of an answer that didn't make her sound like a complete idiot.

'It's going to sound ridiculous to you,' Ellie complained, her brows creased in worry.

'No, it won't.'

Ellie released a defeating blow of breath. 'It was on Jack's birthday, I think. We went out with some of his other mates to Falmouth for the shanty festival. Lots of drinking. I got embarrassingly drunk. All I remember, before Jack had to take me home, was throwing up all over the payment outside one of the pubs.'

'Classy,' George said, smiling to show he was only teasing.

'I woke up the next morning at Jack's house - splitting headache - only to find out that Nanny had been taken ill during the night and had been rushed to hospital by one of our neighbours. When I checked my phone, it was filled with endless missed calls, messages from people in the hamlet explaining what had happened, where to find her, who was with her. And there was me, drunk, unconscious, and utterly useless to anyone. I was her only next of kin once Pappy passed away, and they couldn't even reach me in her hour of need.' Even now, the memory of it caused a self-loathing she would hold on to forever. Her features contorted in rage against herself as she remembered how vulnerable Nanny had looked in her hospital bed when Ellie had eventually sorted herself out and hitched a ride from a neighbour to see her. The way Nanny had tried to reassure Ellie that is had been alright, despite the undertone of betrayal in her voice. Or perhaps Ellie had imagined that through her riddled guilt - it had been hard to tell.

'It had been a water infection which had given her a funny turn, so nothing too serious. But it could have been, and I wasn't there to safeguard her. So, after that, I swore off alcohol. I realised that Nanny's age would mean it potentially wouldn't be her last hospital visit. That, one day, she would need me to step up as a regular carer. Which turned out to be true.'

'Oh, Ellie...' George's voice was low, and his eyes penetrated her as he leaned in, holding onto her every word.

'It sounds neurotic, I know. But it made me realise that you can never plan when a loved one is going to get poorly. It could happen at any time, and Nanny's health had already been taking a slow decline - so I wanted to make sure that from then on, I was always available - able to drive, et cetera. And actually, as time went on, I realised I actually preferred not drinking. So... yeah...'

Her explanation fizzled out and she braced her hands on her knees, suddenly feeling exposed. George was silent for a while, his expression unreadable.

'I think I'm struggling to switch that part of me off, you know,' Ellie suddenly admitted, surprising herself with this revelation. 'It's like a habit now - being on standby in case she needs me. But she doesn't need me anymore, does she? In fact, I'm completely redundant now. I don't know how it all works without her now. I'm feeling totally lost.'

In a split second, the gap between them was closed and George enveloped his arms around her, his fingers lacing through her hair.

'I think you might just be the most caring person I have ever met, Ellie Curnow,' George declared softly in her ear. She pulled away gently to look up at him, her chest pounding and her skin roaring with desire. She traced the line of his jaw with a fingertip, relishing in the feel of his stubble against her soft skin, then raised her mouth to his, brushing her lips against his. Like an elastic band pulled taut, their restrain finally snapped and suddenly his mouth claimed hers and their hands began their long, anticipated exploration. Their breathing quickened and a groan of longing escaped Ellie's lips. An unidentifiable feeling stirred inside her. Excitement. Desire. Anticipation. Something that had been absent for a long time, and she was almost reassured to learn that she was still capable of feeling it. George brought himself over and pressed her body with his into the mattress, the heat of his hands leaving imprints all over her body where he touched.

Her hands had found the buckle of his belt just as there was a thumping on the bedroom door, causing them to both jump like forbidden teenagers.

'Are you both getting randy in there or are we getting food?' Antonio's muffled voice broke the spell between them, and George nuzzled his face into the crook of Ellie's shoulder in exasperation, their quickened breaths slowing together.

'Should have... stayed in a hotel,' George mumbled through puffs, causing Ellie to snort with laughter, her arms snaking around his middle and her hands fondling beneath his short. Back muscles rippled under her touch, and suddenly she wished Antonio would bugger off.

A barrage of vexatious Italian could be heard in the corridor, Ellie and George suppressing laughter as they peeled themselves off the bed.

'We'd best take him out for some food. He's hangry,' George said, touching his lips against hers one more time before leaving her to get ready in private.

# Chapter Thirty-Five

A crisp autumn breeze welcomed Ellie back to the hamlet as she stepped out of the taxi to face the river. In the few days her and George had been away, what had been left of the greenery that surrounded the water had fully morphed into blazing red and orange hues. Autumn was officially here, and with it a feeling of change.

'Italy is beautiful,' Ellie said, as George rounded the taxi to stand by her side. 'But this is pretty spectacular, isn't it?'

George shrugged and pulled a face. 'It's alright. Ouch!' He laughed as Ellie dug her elbow into his ribs, gathering her into his side with an arm and kissing the top of her head. 'I must say, this is the first time ever that I am glad to be back on Cornish soil. With my Cornish maid.'

Ellie screwed up her face, both with affection and something along the line of a grimace. 'We'll have to work on better pet names. That made you sound like a gropey old man.'

A distant sound of shouting caught their laughter short in that moment. It was then that Ellie realised how deserted the hamlet seemed.

Where was everyone?

Before they had even reached the end of Ellie's long track to the cottage, her questions had been answered, her eyes wide with bewilderment at the scene unfolding in front of them. Ellie was momentarily brought back to that harrowing day when an ambulance had taken Nanny from the cottage, the crowd of concerned neighbours surrounding the property holding only good intentions for the wellbeing of a fellow creek resident. But this time, the gathering which formed around her little thatched cottage buzzed with anger and tension.

Shouts of accusation flew through the air as Ellie abandoned her luggage on the rocky track and fought through the dense crowd, recognising her neighbours from not only the hamlet but further down the river too. Her heart hammered in her chest, George close behind and cursing under his breath. When she turned to look up at him, his face was drained from colour and he suddenly grabbed Ellie's arm, attempting to pull her away from her advance to the front. He was at least half a foot above the tallest member of the crowd - what had he seen that her shorter stature could not?

'Ellie, let me deal with this,' George said, a panic in his voice.

'Deal with what? What is it?'

'Ellie! Oh - oh, thank goodness you're back, my love!' It was Mr Williams, followed by Larry from the pub, Vivian next door and even Harold and Irene from along the river. 'I'm so very sorry you must return from your travels like this. We are here for you, me 'ansome.'

Blood rushed loudly in Ellie's ears as she tried to comprehend the situation, feeling herself being ushered forward by her overwrought neighbours.

'She's here!' Mr Williams called out, with surprising amount of force in his otherwise soft voice. 'Stop everything you are doing, because Ellie is here!'

'Really, Mr Williams - there is no need to create such a scene.' The sound of Lavinia's voice ran Ellie's blood cold and when she finally arrived by the little blue gate of her and Nanny's cottage, her mind raced for ideas as to why she would be here at all. A suited man with a clipboard shuffled nervously beside her, assessing the growing crowd and the escalating situation before him.

'Mother, what are you doing?' George demanded, reaching Ellie's side once again.

It was clear that things had gotten out of hand and that Lavinia was doing her utmost to maintain composure, despite hysteria growing behind those stern, hazel eyes of hers.

'George, I think we may have to call for some reinforcement in a moment. These people are being quite unreasonable,' Lavinia said tartly, her speech quickening and higher than normal.

Ellie was near to speechless, an attack of emotions bubbling away inside as she looked from her cottage to Lavinia, to the man with the clipboard, piecing together the possibility of something she couldn't begin to comprehend. She looked at George for some comfort, some reassurance, but only found his handsome features to be contorted by rage and anguish.

'What is she doing, George?' Ellie asked, but George's silence only added to her fears.

'I'll tell you what they've been doing!' Mr Williams cut in. Ellie had never seen him so wound up, the kindness in his face masked by fury. 'They plan to turf us all out - one by one! First it was our dear Mrs Pascoe's place. Now Gloria's. It isn't right! It isn't proper!'

'Hear, hear!' A ripple of agreement spread through the crowd.

Ellie fixed her eyes on George, his face grim and distant. He wasn't denying any of it. Something shifted in Ellie's chest, and she felt that her knees might give way.

'That's why you took me to Italy, isn't it?' Ellie said, her voice quiet and unsteady.

'What? - No!'

'You needed me out of the way. Away from the cottage.'

'No! Ellie, please listen...!' George pleaded, gathering her hands into his and shooting nervous glances at the crowd.

'George - Mr Callaway here needs to be at another appointment in half an hour,' Lavinia continued. 'We really must get on with it. Perhaps you and Ellie could bring this conversation inside.'

Appointment for what? Get on with what? What was happening that involved Nanny's cottage - Ellie's cottage - in her absence? Ellie was rooted to the spot, unable to move and unable to piece together a single sentence to defend herself. She tried to give George a pleading look, but he was doing everything he could not to look directly at her. Something in her chest plummeted to her stomach, leaving her feeling nauseous and clammy.

'Mr Callaway, I apologise that you're having your time wasted here,' George said, bringing some authority back to his voice. 'But I did not request this meeting.'

'Oh, well I...' poor Mr Callaway began, checking something on his clipboard as Lavinia cut in again.

'I arranged it, George. Because we've put this off long enough. It's been weeks - months even. So, I took it upon myself to set the ball rolling.'

'What ball rolling?' Ellie cried, finding her voice again. 'You can't be suggesting you're claiming my Nanny's cottage? I still live here!'

'Not for much longer, I'm afraid.' Lavinia concluded, though her voice was quiet and hesitant. A single tear trailed down Ellie's face and a numbness descended over her, leaving her unable to breathe. George's eyes were closed, like he couldn't bear to risk seeing the betrayal and heartbreak on her face. He just closed his eyes, his nostrils flared, and his jaw clenched. But he said nothing in her defence and Lavinia continued. 'It was Joseph and Gloria Curnow who were the named tenants. Now they...' Lavinia paused, assessing her words carefully as she eyed up her audience. 'Now they are sadly deceased, we are within our rights to claim back the property and re-purpose it as we see fit for the financial wellbeing of the estate.'

A fresh wave of anger exploded from the crowd of neighbours, shouts of 'This isn't right!' and 'What about the wellbeing of your tenants?' and 'You should be ashamed of yourself!' In a rush of relief Ellie caught sight of Jack running up the track and forcing his way through to her. She resisted the urge to leap into the safety of his arms, like a big brother saving her from a band of bullies, not wanting to appear melodramatic in a situation already escalated beyond belief. She merely grappled at his hands, in search of his keys.

'I can't do this,' Ellie gasped. 'I need your house keys. Please get rid of everyone!'

George reached for Ellie's arm, but she batted him away, her face white with anger. 'Do not touch me!'

'Wenna's keeping away,' Jack explained. 'She's in the car now. She'll take you to mine. I've got this - go.'

She was faintly aware of George's voice calling out to her, of Jack's telling him to leave her be and ordering the neighbours to step down before she disappeared around the corner towards the safety of Jack's van in the distance, Wenna visible from the front passenger window.

Ellie fumbled with her keys in the dark, stabbing at the lock and eventually letting them into the warmth of the cottage. It was as quiet as if nothing had happened, the cottage welcoming Ellie back with open arms, the thermostat coming up in the nick of time to heat the place ready for a chilly autumn evening. Jack and Wenna followed closely behind, Jack placing Ellie's luggage in the hallway as she switched on some lights.

As she walked into the kitchen, Ellie noted no evidence of Lavinia and Mr Callaway's presence. Had they gone through with the appointment after all? Or had Jack ushered them all away - the crowd of well-intentioned neighbours, Lavinia, and the agent? And what of George?

Ellie's chest clenched painfully at the thought of George as she threw her keys down on the kitchen side, bashing a clumsy hand down on the kettle switch. A part of her didn't want to believe it - how could he betray her like that? It had clearly been Lavinia's doing, but he did not deny any of it either. He did not come to her aid or try to correct it. He just stood there - sorry that he had been caught.

'Tea? Coffee?' Ellie mumbled to her guests. Though she was surly, and terrible company right now, she was grateful to Jack and Wenna and held absolutely no grudge against the youngest Penhaligon.

'I can order in pizza or something if you like,' Jack said, checking Ellie's fridge freezer which was, of course, bare due to her absence all week. He shut it with purpose having not found anything worth eating. 'Or Chinese? Indian?'

'You guys get going, if you like,' Ellie said. 'You don't want to waste an evening with me. I plan to just stew over it all, stuff my face with chocolate and get an early night. I'm exhausted.'

Jack and Wenna exchanged concerned expressions. Wenna then pulled out her phone and took a seat at the kitchen island. 'As healthy as that coping mechanism sounds, we'll stay. Make sure you eat at least. Pizza?'

Ellie thought back to less than forty-right hours ago when she and George were eating real Italian pizzas along the Naviglio Grande, excitedly planning ideas for Penhaligon Estate's first vineyard and talking about the future. Their future. Where it had made her heart swell, the whole thing left a sour taste in her mouth now.

'Not pizza,' Ellie replied, firmly. 'Chinese sounds good.'

A couple of hours later, empty Chinese takeaway tubs scattered over the kitchen island and a stack of dirty plates by the sink, the three of them lounged in the breakfast nook, nursing full bellies. Jack heaved himself up to grab one of his beers from the fridge.

'Drink, anyone?'

'Glass of water, please,' Wenna said. 'Chinese always makes me so thirsty.'

'Ellie?'

'How many beers have you got?'

Jack glanced at her over the fridge door. 'Really?' When Ellie shrugged, a look of determination on her face, he said, 'one beer, coming up!'

Wenna's phone pinged for what seemed like the hundredth time over dinner, and Wenna's nervous glance in Ellie's direction made her narrow her eyes.

'Is that George?'

Wenna scrunched her face up, looking bashful. 'He's just checking in. He really had no idea about the whole thing.'

'He did know that I wasn't a named tenant though. And he chose not to inform me.'

'Did you not know? That you weren't a named tenant?'

'No, I didn't,' Ellie said, now looking bashful herself. 'I feel like maybe I should have known that. Perhaps I should have thought about these sorts of things before Nanny had passed away.' She leaned forward, her elbows on the table, and buried her face in her hands. 'It's all such a mess now.'

'George will come up with something. You'll see.' Wenna's attempts to reassure her thawed Ellie's bitterness and for the first time that evening Ellie sent a grateful smile across the table - albeit a frail one.

'You're a good sister. And a good friend.'

Wenna looked slightly crestfallen but smiled all the same, Jack placing a hand on her shoulder and offering Ellie a wink of reassurance.

'I'm really sorry about Mother,' Wenna said, tears prickling in her eyes. 'When she's worried about something - in this case, the estate's finances - she gets a little crazy.'

'Mmm,' Ellie said, trying not to add *I hadn't noticed!* 'But it's not her decisions to make, surely. It's George's.'

'It is,' Wenna replied. 'But I sometimes wonder whether she regrets never being given a chance to run the estate herself. But only males have ever been allowed. So, it went straight from my grandfather Charles to George. My father was obviously not bloodline, and our parents got a divorce when we were young anyway.'

'I didn't know that! George never said.'

'Probably because he took the divorce horribly. He was a teenager at the time. I was super young so can't remember much. But I recall George and Tressa being absolute horrors!'

'What happened?'

'Father cheated,' Wenna said, her face scrunched up for the second time and sadness washing over her pretty features. 'And then he passed away about eight years later from leukaemia. Despite his infidelity and their separation, Mother had been heartbroken. I do feel sorry for Mother a lot of the time. She's gone through a lot over the years. But I know she doesn't help herself sometimes.'

The curious part of Ellie wanted to ask further questions, but the cynical side of her didn't want or need to know more about the family who had wronged her and her Nanny multiple times.

'Anyway, all families come with flaws and quirks,' Wenna said, sliding out from the nook to wash her hands in the sink.

'I guess,' Ellie relented, her own mother coming to mind. She reasoned for a moment that perhaps her own mum-issues were not much better than that of George, Tressa and Wenna's. At least Lavinia remained present in her children's lives. At least she cared, in her own Lavinia way.

Jack lounged in the corner of the nook against the window, swigging his beer. His eyes bored into Ellie's. 'You okay?'

'I will be. Just need some time to figure out what I'm going to do.'

A strangled sob escaped Wenna's throat as she looked up

from what she was doing at the kitchen counter. 'Oh, please don't tell me you're going to quit! You are so absolutely brilliant at your job, Ellie.'

'I don't see how I can carry on working there. I'm sorry, Wenna,' Ellie began, before realising that Wenna was peeking through the contents of the shoe box Ellie should have stored away before she had left for Italy. But in her excitement to get away and the lack of foresight that George's mother would go snooping in her own home, she hadn't thought to. 'Wenna! Do you mind?'

'I'm so sorry!' Wenna pleaded, sniffing loudly. 'I was just entranced by this beautiful handwriting.' She lifted a letter up for closer inspection.

'It was my Nanny's handwriting. Some of them will be...' She looked up at Wenna then, unsure how much she knew.

'Our grandfathers. George filled me in.'

Jack exchanged an expression of sadness with Ellie and a heavy silence filled between them.

'Oh my god,' Wenna gasped, raising a photograph from the box.

'Stop snooping through Nanny's things!' Ellie cried from the table, a small laugh of exasperation erupting from her throat.

'I know, I'm sorry! But... have you seen this?' Wenna brought the photo, browned with age, to the table and placed it down for the three of them to see. 'I never knew that Granny and Gloria were once friends.'

'Eh?' Jack leaned in for a closer look. The photograph was blistered and browned, but three young women of their late teens dominated the sepia picture, arms looped, hair in ringlets around their neck and happy smiles upon their youthful faces. This wasn't new to Ellie; she'd already seen it when Nanny had first presented her with the box of her mysterious history. In the photograph, they were clearly at the beach, dressed in 50s-style swimming costumes with a glimpse of the sea in the background. In the middle, Ellie recognised her late Nanny's twinkling eyes and dimpled smile instantly. She had been beautiful, even in her last days, but as a young woman her looks had been devastating. Flanking either side of her were two women who now, on a second inspection, seemed much more familiar to her now. She recognised Beryan instantly, her distinctively strong bone structure and large eyes, her curve-bridged nose and prominent brow. It was a wonder now that Ellie hadn't noticed her before. But Nanny hadn't been keen to scan through the photos too closely before.

'Who's the other woman?' Wenna asked.

'That's Mrs Pascoe,' Jack said. 'I'd recognise that smile anywhere. Bless her.'

Ellie and Jack gazed at the photograph in wonder whilst Wenna pondered.

'They all look so happy. Like best friends,' Wenna said, sadly. 'I wonder what happened to Granny and Gloria's friendship?'

Ellie knew, and her expression gave her away instantly. Her friends' eyes narrowed at her, and she contemplated her options for a moment.

'I will tell you some of the truth,' Ellie relented. 'But some of it I must protect for Nanny's memory. But I think it's important you know some it, seeing as it's linked directly with your own family.'

They nodded, Wenna's forehead creased with worry and anticipation as she added, 'Of course.'

Ellie took a deep breath, navigating around the best way to tell her Nanny's story.

# Chapter Thirty-Six

'What on earth are you doing, child?' Beryan grumbled in the doorway of her bedroom. 'Do you realise what time it is?'

Wenna was standing in the corridor outside her grandmother's room at the crack of dawn, both seeming nervous and determined in some way, a tatty old shoe box in her arms. Beryan regarded the package for a moment, wondering what on earth her youngest granddaughter could be up to. She realised on closer inspection that she had perhaps mistaken the look on Wenna's face as nerves when it was suddenly very clear how upset she was.

'What's the matter?' Beryan asked, more demand than affection in her voice. She'd never been very good at that and tried her best to soften her voice. 'What's in the box, my darling?'

'I'm sorry to bother you so late, Granny. I've barely been able to sleep. I was going to show you this at breakfast, but this needs to be done more privately. Do you recognise this?'

To Beryan's surprise, Wenna held up a photograph. An old photograph, with three young, determined women with bright futures ahead of them. Beryan was instantly flooded with nostalgia, fleeting joy, and a strong pang of regret. She gripped the doorway with one aged hand, the other gripping her cane as she did her best not to collapse in a heap on the floor. 'What do you mean by showing me this?'

'Can I come inside? So we can talk?' Wenna asked. Usually radiating with positivity and sometimes, for Beryan's old nerves, exhaustingly energetic. This morning, it had seemed like whatever bothered her had aged her young granddaughter overnight, and suddenly Beryan felt a responsibility to listen to her every word. She nodded and they stepped inside, the door closing behind them.

Beryan found herself outside the blue gates of a little thatched cottage she had not set eyes on in many a decade. It was as quaint and understated as she had always remembered it and provided a warmth despite the emotions coursing through her at this moment. She looked back at her granddaughter, who was waiting patiently in the car behind her, and received a smile of encouragement. Dear Wenna.

With a determination borrowed from the youngest of the Penhaligon family, she lifted a shaky arm to the blue door and knocked. It took a few moments, but eventually the door creaked open, and a bewildered Ellie stood before her, appraising the old woman suspiciously. It was only to be expected and she couldn't blame the young girl.

'May I come in?'

'Umm,' Ellie began, fumbling over a million excuses to say no Beryan expected. Again, she couldn't blame her. But it seemed that Ellie's politeness got the better of her and she nodded, stepping to one side to let her through. Even in the many, many years that had passed, Beryan felt recognition towards everything that was Gloria as she passed through the small property into the kitchen. It was starting to rain, the water patting down on the glass which lined the entire back of the kitchen, giving a panoramic view of the river in its autumnal state. Beryan wasn't proud enough to admit that it was a beautiful spot to come to for breakfast every morning.

'You have a lovely home down here, my girl,' Beryan began,

not knowing quite what else to say. Ellie paused with the kettle under the tap.

'Thank you,' Ellie mumbled. 'Obviously not for long.'

'It's partly why I am here, actually. But I shall get to that in a moment.' Silly woman, she thought to herself. She was nervous about this. She hovered in the middle of the flagstone floor, upon a handwoven rug of ghastly colours. Ellie must have sensed her discomfort and mumbled an invitation for her to sit at the breakfast table. Beryan assessed the situation of the seating and relented to the idea that she would have to slide, something she hadn't done for a long time. But slide she did and found herself with the perfect angle of the estuary. She thanked Ellie for the tea which was placed in a simple but delicate teacup and waited for the young girl to take a seat opposite her before she began.

'I am assuming you already knew of my and Gloria's friendship... back in the day.'

'I did.'

'Do you know much more beyond that?'

'I do.'

The girl wasn't giving her much to go by here, but Beryan installed some patience and continued.

'I don't suppose you will know that it was not I who chose to marry Charles. Nor was it his.' This fact seemed new to Ellie and so she pressed on. 'It was an arranged engagement with our families. Quite common back then, you see. Now, I will not deny that the arrangement did please me. He was a lovely man and held great prospect as a loving and secure future.'

The light, airy room soon felt close and stuffy, and Beryan arranged her next words carefully.

'I was very young. And very foolish. And like any eighteen-year-old seeking out a husband, horribly self-absorbed. I put my own happiness and security before Gloria's. I know that. I've known for a very long time, and it keeps me awake at night. And the jealousy I felt towards her, and how she was perceived in the eyes of the man I was to marry, was masked with cruelty. Unkind words.'

'So, why didn't you say all this to Nanny whilst she was still alive?' Ellie said, impatiently. 'You could have said this years ago!'

'You're absolutely right, my girl. I could have. But stubbornness and pride won over morality here I'm afraid. I'm not proud of it. Not one bit.' A deep sigh of regret erupted in Beryan's chest, and her eyes pricked with tears. 'I hadn't laid eyes on the photographs your Nanny kept so dear for quite some time. I was never one for sentimentality you see. But sifting through some of the things Gloria had kept in that little shoe box you so kindly lent to Wenna - well, I was touched. There's not a lot I can do about that now. Nothing I can put right with Gloria now anyway. But I would like to put things right for you, my dear.'

Ellie didn't look convinced. 'What do you mean?'

'I'd like to first apologise for my initial behaviour towards you when we first met. One can get very good at tucking away old emotions and memories as the years roll by, particularly when hidden away without so much as a sighting of those who make you face your crimes.'

'Mmm, I think you'll find Nanny was pretty good at avoiding you lot too,' Ellie admitted, rolling her eyes.

'Yes well... I'm afraid it shook me something dreadful that day - when I realised who you were. The resemblance was uncanny, and I could see Gloria's features on your pretty face straight away. It felt like Judgement Day for me that day, like the past was rearing its ugly head and forcing me to face it square on. You are a spitting image of your grandmother, Ellie dear. And you clearly have her strength and spirit too.'

The young girl rightfully took it for the compliment it had aimed to be, a smile forming on her sad features. Then, to

Beryan's horror, Ellie's face creased as she broke down in tears. She was terrible at this - comforting people in a state of distress. Even when Lavinia had been young and when the grandchildren had been young, if there had been any tears, she'd wanted to quieten them with firm words and nothing more. Charles had been the affectionate parent and grandparent, the one to enclose the children in warming cuddles and kiss bruises and scrapes better. If only he could be here now to put things to right.

'Here,' Beryan finally said. She offered a clean handkerchief from her handbag and Ellie accepted it with a quivering thanks. 'Despite everything, I was very grieved to learn of Gloria's passing. I can only imagine that she was a remarkable woman.'

'She was.'

'Well, then.' It was time to get down to business. Beryan had exhausted her patience with all things emotional for one day. 'Wenna tells me you are handing your notice in.'

Ellie sniffed and blew her nose loudly. She shrugged. 'Well, I... I think I will have to.'

'The gardens are looking wonderful, Ellie. Truly wonderful. I think I can safely speak for all of us that it would be a great loss to the estate if you were to leave.'

'I doubt Lavinia will feel the same way. No offense.'

'My daughter always has her best intentions for the estate. I'm afraid she took after me for forgetting to counter in the emotional aspect to decisions. What she did yesterday was wrong and she's seeing that now. I'm afraid I allowed my own feelings and prejudice to pass down to my daughter when she was growing up. I allowed her to adopt an *us and them* attitude when it came to the house and your community down here on the river. Between us, we allowed the public events to fizzle out and shut ourselves away in the safety of the house and gardens. I'm afraid the spirit of Penhaligon Estate died with my dear Charles.'

Ellie pressed her lips together in a sympathetic smile, her chest heaving in a shuddering sigh. Beryan took the pause as an opportunity to sip on her tea.

'George,' she continued, and she noted immediately the way the young girl's expression changed at the mention of Beryan's only grandson. 'He's very much like his grandfather. Both in looks and personality. He, and his sisters, will do wonderful things with the estate.' Ellie nodded, agreeing with her. 'But I have always said that behind any great man is an even greater woman.'

The old lady smiled coyly at Ellie, and she was relieved to receive one in return.

'None of this is George's doing, my dear. I do hope that after our conversation here this morning, you will give him your time. I know he is driving himself potty back at the house. I'm not completely blind to see that my grandson is utterly smitten with you.'

'But Lavinia-' Ellie began.

'She'll come round,' Beryan said, kindly. 'Now, do we still have a Head Gardener? Because I do believe Head Gardener benefits from their own lodging. One with a gorgeous view of the estuary, I hear.'

Beryan winked mischievously, feeling younger and lighter than she had in years, and realisation washed over Ellie, her pretty face breaking out in an enormous grin.

# Chapter Thirty-Seven

'I did the maths last night. If we convert all of this to begin with, we have the potential to take in the equivalent of six of the small terrace cottages down on the hamlet.' Tressa was on a mission this morning and had dragged a reluctant George to the stable yard with a clipboard and the many pieces of paper she had scribbled on the night before.

George was cynical, his arms crossed, and one eyebrow arched as he looked at the dilapidated stone buildings in front of them. They had been nothing but dusty storage to old machinery for many decades now, their roofs leaking, and the pointing of the stonework crumbling and barely being held together by the stubbornness of wild ivy.

'I get what you're saying. But again, you're forgetting a minor detail here. How do you propose we pay for all of this?'

Tressa's face was deadpan as she glowered at her brother. 'Well, genius! There's such thing as bank loans for investments like this. Grants can sometimes be applied for if it means the project will benefit the preservation of Cornish heritage - which this estate is a part of. Do some research every now again!'

George relented, unfolding his arms and throwing his sister an apologetic look. 'Sorry.'

'It's okay,' Tressa said, her voice softening. 'I know you're going through a lot right now. I'm just trying to help with a bit of damage control.'

'I know you are. Okay!' He rubbed his face, resetting himself. 'Let's hear it all. So, this section here - all holiday lets. This section here?'

'The plant centre and possibly the café. Wenna is adamant she wants to be in charge of this bit, so I've told her she needs to commit and work on her attention span.'

A small laugh escaped George's mouth, despite himself. 'It all sounds great. I can't believe we could fit six holiday lets here. If, like you say, we can get some sort of financial help for the building work, this could pay for itself in a matter of years.'

'But we cannot have holiday homes down in the hamlet,' Tressa said, passionately. 'It's non-negotiable. We need to maintain a good relationship with our tenants, and if holiday lets are going to line the estate's pockets, better that we hold them up here with us than force them upon people who have no say in the matter.'

'Wow,' George said with earnest, looking at his sister with a sense of admiration. 'Perhaps you should have been put in charge. You're much better at this than me.'

'Oh please,' Tressa drooled, rolling her eyes. 'Don't start moping again. We haven't got time for that. And besides, I'm female - which apparently is a huge problem.'

'Yeah, well - I'll be having that changed in whatever rulebook states that,' George scoffed. He scanned the buildings which surrounded the square yard and sighed at the monumentous but exciting task ahead. 'I can't do any of this without you.'

Tressa snorted. 'Obviously. I'll settle with manager of the estate.'

A wide grin spread over George's face. 'Deal.'

In that moment, Tressa's car pulled into the yard, with Wenna in the driving seat.

'You let Wenna drive your car?' George said, surprised.

'It was an emergency,' Tressa shrugged, mysteriously.

With that, Beryan unfolded from the front seat, her cane

making contact with the ground, closely followed by Ellie who stepped out from the back passenger door furthest from George. She gave him a hesitant smile from over the car's roof as Beryan shuffled past him, looking tired but triumphant.

'What have you been up to?' George mumbled, narrowing his eyes at his grandmother.

'I've warmed her up for you. Don't mess it up, my boy.'

She disappeared through the archway and towards the main house, Tressa and Wenna following closely behind, leaving George and Ellie alone in the yard. He assessed her face for a moment, his hands in his pockets as thought of what to say.

'I'm so sorry,' was all he could manage to begin with. 'I'm so, so sorry.'

'It's not your fault.'

'It's not going to happen. I promise you. Not in a million years.'

Ellie walked around the car to face him, her hands laced together in front of her. 'Rumour has it that Stone's Throw Cottage is to be assigned as Head Gardener's Lodge.'

George's body relaxed and he smiled. 'Granny told you then.'

'Granny told me,' Ellie echoed, her too relaxing as they closed the gap between them.

'I was going to tell you. About the whole thing with the tenant's agreement. But I'd only discovered it the night before we were due to leave for Italy and I didn't want to spoil anything. I was never going to act upon it, for God's sake. But then Mother got involved...' he added, rolling his eyes. 'As she does.'

'Mmm,' Ellie added, non-committing.

'She's actually mortified. Now it's dawned on her what she tried to do,' George said, followed by Ellie's scoff of disbelief. 'No, really. It was Tressa who broke through her.'

'Tressa broke your mother?' Ellie joked, wickedly.

'Broke through her!' George corrected, suppressing a smile.

'Tressa is a force to be reckoned with, but I've never seen her reprimand the way she did last night. It was quite something. She really cares for you, you know? Tressa, I mean.'

'Well, I wasn't mistaking you to meaning your mother. Trust me.'

George sighed. 'My mother means well. I'm trying to see that. And one day I might forgive her for what she tried to do to you.' He paused. 'I've just made Tressa manager of the estate. Or - correction - I just got bullied into making her manager of the estate.'

'Good decision,' Ellie said, nodding her approval.

'And these buildings here,' George said, gesturing wide arms towards the old stable buildings. 'You're looking at the new holiday lets.'

'Excellent decision!' Ellie beamed. 'You guys can deal with the emits!'

They both erupted into a fit of laughter and whatever tension had sat between them dissipated immediately.

'No, I'm only joking,' Ellie said. 'Holiday lets do make sense, and tourists will really enjoy exploring the estate on their visit. Perhaps I could do that private tour and evening meal idea now as part of the stay.'

'So, you'll stay?' George asked, in hope.

Ellie nodded, a suppressed smile breaking out into a wide grin as George closed the gap between them and kissed her with earnest, his arms enveloping her and pressing her firmly into him. Her hands rested on his chest as her head tilted up to him in longing, her coppery hair cascading down her back. He pulled away for a second to gaze down at her, a hand resting on her cheek before his fingers laced through her hair. 'Fancy running an estate with me?'

'What a romantic gesture,' Ellie said, lightly. She kissed him gently on his lips and shrugged. 'Sure. Why not?'

# Epilogue

'I wish George would hurry up!' Tressa complained, checking her wristwatch for the hundredth time. 'The crowd is getting restless, and the caterers wanted to dish out the food half an hour ago.'

Gathered in a huddle inside the walls of the newly reclaimed Secret Gardens, Ellie

'He'll be here. He got caught in traffic going through Playing Place,' Ellie said. 'Beryan, why don't you take a seat on that bench for a bit. You too, Ernie.'

'I think that's Ellie's way of telling us *we're old and we need to sit down'*. Beryan grumbled, though she winked in Ellie's direction and did as she was told.

'Fine by me,' Ernie said. 'My hip is killing me. Just an expression! Stop panicking, girl!' The last bit was aimed at Ellie, who's eyes went as wide as dinner plates as she ushered her oldest gardener to the nearby bench. She had been delighted when Ernie had approached her just a couple of months ago with the request to join her team for one day a week. It had been, as he stated, a way to keep the old joints moving. She had accepted gladly and was grateful for his expertise and knowledge of the gardens, his years with the estate proving to be an invaluable asset. 'My hip is hurting the normal amount for a man in his late seventies. Don't fuss!'

'Yeah, well - I told you to take one of the easier tasks from the white board this morning,' Ellie nagged. She was distracted, much to Ernie's relief, by the arrival of George. Even now, six months into their relationship, his dark chestnut hair and tanned skin sent butterflies to her stomach. She smiled longingly at him and allowed herself to be gathered up in his arms, excitement radiating from his every being.

'We did it!' George announced, to Ellie and all his family behind, who stood to attention in quiet anticipation.

'You got the green light?' Wenna cried from her position by the free-standing display boards, the panels adorned with photographs and information about the history of the newly discovered gardens, and details of the project undergone by Ellie and her growing gardening team. 'The council have said yes?'

'Permission has been fully granted!' George confirmed. The family celebrated, along with Ernie, Joseph, and some of the other members of the gardening team who were present. 'We can start the renovation of the holiday homes, the plant centre and Wenna's café straight away!'

'Please don't call it Wenna's cafe, for God's sake!' Tressa said snootily to her younger sister. 'It'll lower the tone.'

'How about Jack's Diner?' Jack joined in, winking at Tressa and laughing at her deadpan expression.

Laughter echoed and bounced against the stone walls as everyone celebrated the good news. Tressa clapped loudly, getting everyone's attention.

'Now his Lordship has graced us with his presence, can we get on with it now?'

Ellie reached for her walkie-talkie. 'Dave, you can lead the crowd back to the secret garden now. George is here. Over.'

'Thank Christ for that,' Dave's voice mumbled through the speaker. 'I woz runnin' out of things to say about the bleddy cock pit.'

'Cock pit?' Ellie asked, looking pointedly at Ernie.

'Down by your new stumpery thing,' Ernie answered from his spot on the bench next to Beryan. To everyone's surprise, she was chuckling away at the whole thing. 'T'was used for cockerel fighting back in the 1800s. Hence the name. Also known as 'the sod'!'

'Really?' Ellie asked, checking that Ernie wasn't pulling her leg like he often did. He nodded with earnest. 'Sorry I asked. Right, Dave's on his way with the public. Trixie's holding the fort with the food back up at the house.'

'Mother's on the way with someone from the newspapers,' Tressa confirmed, checking her phone.

'Fantastic. That just leaves one thing. Joseph?'

Joseph's eyes widened in alarm at the sound of his name, and he skulked forward nervously to stand with Ellie and George.

'Before everyone arrives and things get hectic with the grand opening,' Ellie said, speaking to Joseph loud enough for everyone around them to hear too. 'We all wanted to first congratulate you, Joseph, for completing your apprenticeship. You have been absolutely fantastic and should be really proud of yourself for everything you have achieved.'

'Hear, hear!' Everyone around them cheered, Joseph turning scarlet red in the face, matching his hair spectacularly.

'To thank you for everything you have done for the estate, we wanted to present you with something,' Ellie said, excitement radiating from her face. She turned to Ernie, who heaved himself off the bench and accepted an A4 brown envelope from Tressa. He then stood beside Ellie and faced Joseph.

'Joseph, I remember your first day at Penhaligon Estate and the first thing I thought to myself was 'Oh bleddy hell, who's idea was it to burden me with babysitting duties?''

'Nice one, Ernie,' Ellie deadpanned. Everyone laughed, including Joseph who nodded bashfully, remembering the day himself.

'And even though I was hard on you sometimes. Alright, a lot of the times. I discovered very quickly that I had needed someone like you on the team for a very long time. Someone who's endless energy and creative would help drive us forward,' Ernie paused for a moment, his cheeks reddening at expressing such emotions. 'And I remember Dave turning to me one day and telling me 'Ernie, that kid might be clumsy. He might be a bit scatty at times. But that boy is going to be one hell of a gardener one day!'

His bottom lip caught between his teeth, and tears welling in his eyes, Joseph nodded his thanks to his former Head Gardener. 'Thanks, Ernie. That's really nice to hear.'

'We'd like to offer you a full-time contract, Joseph,' Ellie declared. Suddenly all eyes beamed down at Joseph as Ernie presented him with the brown envelope. 'As Deputy Head Gardener.'

A second cheer rippled through the small gathering and suddenly everyone was shaking the boy's hand or patting him on the back in congratulations. Joseph hugged Ellie and shook George's hand, beaming from ear to ear.

'But what about Dave? He's been here much longer than me!' Joseph cried, always looking out for other people over his own gain.

'I don't bleddy want it,' Dave grumbled as he ducked under the ribbon barrier, the crowd of public congregating on the other side with flutes of champagne in their hands and smiling faces of anticipation. 'I'll be retiring soon. Ellie needs a deputy who doesn't get out of breath an hour into his shift.'

'Then I'd be honoured,' Joseph said. 'Thank you so much, Ellie. Thank you, George.'

'You are welcome, Joseph,' George said.

'If we could now proceed with the ribbon cutting,' Tressa said, ever the timekeeper. 'Mother has just arrived with the photographer from the West Briton.'

There was a hustle and a bustle as everyone took their places. Jack passed George a large pair of scissors and they stood before the audience, the white ribbon acting as a temporary barrier into the walled garden.

'Good afternoon, ladies and gentlemen,' George announced, his voice booming out with confidence. 'We'd like to thank you for joining us in this very special moment, where we will be marking a moment in history for Penhaligon Estate. Ellie and I accidentally rediscovered this walled garden back in May last year, and we've been trying to reveal its history ever since. It comes with quite a story, and though my grandfather Charles Penhaligon never got to set foot in these gardens, he used this little hole in the wall as a way of sending love letters to his first love, over seventy years ago.'

There was a small 'ooh' sound which rippled through the crowd as Beryan cried out from the bench, 'the scoundrel!' Everyone's laughter danced into the trees and Ellie looked back at Beryan knowingly, receiving a wink from the old woman.

'But of course, he then met my wonderful grandmother, Beryan, and they lived a happy life together,' George said, grinning at his Granny and her wicked humour. 'Upon further discovery...'

'...and lots of bonfires to clear all the brambles,' Ellie added.

'It was discovered that this walled garden was once named *Tus an gwlas*. Which roughly translates from old Cornish as '*The people of the land*'. It was community land and old journals from our collections had revealed the intentions of my ancestors. I had had visions of turning this into my own private vineyard...'

This earned a few chuckles amongst the listening crowd.

'But that didn't sit quite right with me. Don't worry, I'm still getting my vineyard. In fact, my closest friend and viticulture expert is in the audience today, all the way from Italy, to advise me and Ellie on the best place for one. Give us a wave, Antonio!'

'*Ciao a tutti!*' Antonio shouted out from the depths of the crowd, waving animatedly from his position.

'So, you'll be pleased to know that this walled garden has been cleared and prepared ready for you, our community. There will be allotments, communal gardens, raised beds for local schools and charities.'

There was an eruption of applause and George paused his speech to take in the positive reception. There wasn't a single face in the crowd or the gathering of family around him without a beaming smile. Well, apart from Tressa who was now gesturing for him to get a move on.

'I'm being told by the manager of the estate to hurry along now. So, all I need now is for my grandmother to come forward and do me the honours.'

Wenna and Jack supported a shocked Beryan out of her seat and led her over to the ribbon, George placing the large scissors in her hands and planting a kiss on her cheek.

After a moment to compose herself, Beryan positioned the scissors and spoke clearly to the audience. 'I declare the newly instated Community Garden now open!'

The Grand Opening had been in full swing for over an hour, with the walled gardens alive with laughter, happy chatter, and the joyful squeals of young children as they explored their surroundings. Food and drink had been enjoyed by all and now guests and family alike exchanged stories, reading about the history of Penhaligon Estate from the displays on show and some even approaching Tressa to claim allotment patches straight away.

Ellie and George found each other in the crowd, having circulated for the last thirty minutes to integrate with the community. They smiled at one another in triumph, Ellie tilting her head and snaking her arms around his neck to bring him in for a kiss. They relished the moment in each other's arms for a moment, in semi-privacy by the glassless frame of the old Victorian greenhouse, which one day would be renovated to its former glory.

'We did it,' Ellie cooed, settling in the warmth of George's arms, and trying her best to resist the temptation of sleep. They had been working solidly for the last month to get the community gardens ready for the big day.

'We did,' George said, smiling down and kissing her on the nose. 'Want to go out and celebrate tonight?'

'Mmm, yes?'

'Want to stay in and collapse in front of the TV tonight with snacks and a movie?' George corrected himself.

Ellie grinned. 'Now you're talking. Let's go out and celebrate when I've slept off the exhaustion.'

'Sorry to interrupt, you two,' Lavinia said, stepping forward and exchanging a meaningful look with her son. 'George? Shall we?'

George nodded, then turned to Ellie. 'Mother and I have a surprise for you.'

Lavinia led the way across the walled garden to the far side where the start of the communal gardens was beginning to take shape. Against the red brick of the back wall, a raised patio area had been created by Jack for members of the community to sit and bask in the sun whilst admiring the fruits of their labour. Jack and Joseph were, at that moment, placing a brand-new teak bench on a newly concreted base, it's curl-shaped back against the wall, centred perfectly for any person who took a seat to gaze upon the entire garden. A golden plaque shimmered in the sunlight, and Lavinia was inviting Ellie to take a closer look.

'In loving memory of friends Gloria Curnow and Lizzie Pascoe. Forever watching over the creek community.' Ellie's voice cracked and a sob threatened to surface as her hand flew to her mouth. 'It's beautiful.'

'And a little something extra,' Lavinia added, smiling proudly at her efforts as she gestured to a newly potted rose, its peony flower golden in colour and tinged with pink, radiating in the spring sunlight. 'It's called a Gloria Dei rose. This was Mother's doing actually. She found the variety in her rose catalogue and had Tressa order it straight away.'

'We thought it seemed appropriate that Gloria and Mrs Pascoe keep an eye on things around here. Keep these lot in check,' George said, winking at Ellie in good humour.

'Nothing new there then,' Ellie quipped, wiping away tears and wrapping her arms around George's middle. 'I love it. Thank you, Lavinia.'

Lavinia smiled, satisfied with her efforts. 'Small steps towards making amends for the future.'

As she walked away, George said, 'That was quite whimsical for Mother.' Ellie snorted with laughter, burying her face in his chest to hide her reaction.

'Now all the emotional stuff has been announced,' Jack said, Wenna appearing from nowhere and almost barrelling him over as she dived into his arms. 'Can we go and try out the new zip wire in the playground now?'

'Last one there has to empty the dog-poo bins!' George shouted, as the four of them raced out of the communal gardens and through the jungle, birds scattering in flight from nearby trees.

Penhaligon House could be seen standing proudly on its hill, its formal gardens peppered with visitors, its grandeur shared by all who stepped through it once again. Cattle grazed in the parkland and boats could be seen in scatters across the widening estuary. The future of the Cornish estate was bright, and the beaming rays of the afternoon sun shone down on its people below.

*The End*

# Acknowledgements

The Thankyous

I cannot begin to express how much I enjoyed writing this book. But like all of my novels, none of these stories could have been written without special people in my life.

For all the words I am able to throw down when creating a fictional world, it's the acknowledgements I dread. Not because I don't want to express my thanks but because I always worry that I will miss someone out or not fully express my gratitude towards people who have made a difference to my writing journey. So, I will do my best, but please know that if I haven't named you, I want you to know that I am still grateful to you.

To my fabulous Mum and Dad, who regularly astound me with their knowledge of plants and all things gardening. Mum – I meant every word of the dedication. You have gifted me with an endless hobby and an expensive spending habit in our favourite garden centres. Without you, this book wouldn't exist.

A huge and heart-felt thank you to my wonderful husband, Martin - who has supported me effortlessly in my dream to be a published writer. Who picks up extra bedtimes for the children, plies me with snacks and never questions me when I ask him obscure questions about something random for my storyline, always having an answer at hand. For never once grumbling at having the children for the day when I have had book signing events or craft fairs. You are honestly my rock – I couldn't squeeze in my writing time in our busy schedule without you.

I am lucky to be surrounded by talented colleagues in my English department at school, and even more lucky to count them as good friends. Thank you to Leah for being my guinea pig and doing a read through in record timing, your keen eye spotting errors from a mile off. To Lana, for your advice and timely GIFs to keep my sanity in check, and for kindly pointing out my grammatical mistakes when things got tough. And of course, to my bestie Chrissi – always a quick message away with a 'you've got this!' and endless literacy knowledge when I needed it!

I have made so many friends and contacts in the last few years since I began my published writing journey. I am constantly humbled by the talent of the writers in Cornwall Writers – a massive thank you to Tracey and all the other writers in our anthology projects for helping me in my constant growth as a writer. Your critique, advice and support is vital and massively appreciated. Thank you to James (JC Berry) for beta-reading one of my drafts and offering such fantastic advice to drive it forward.

To the talented Heather at Heather-Rose Designs for creating such beautiful illustrations for my book cover. You captured the personality of the book perfectly and I am so excited to see it all come together.

A massive thank you to my loyal stockists – the independent businesses around Cornwall who have been selling my books from the beginnings. Duchy Nursery, Hurley's Books, Shrew Books, Ladyvale Bakery, Wheal Martin – you're all incredible!

Finally – a big thank you to my reading community. To you for buying this book and for seeing it through to the end. I hope you enjoyed it and I hope you will stick with me through this writing journey. There are still so many more stories to be written. Your support and kindness mean the absolute world to me.

# About the Author
# Lamorna Ireland

A proper Cornish maid with a rich Cornish heritage, Lamorna Ireland has taken inspiration from the beautiful county from a very young age. Whilst teaching English in a local secondary school and being a dedicated wife and mother, Lamorna has always taken joy from the written word. She has released two novels set in Cornwall: *Unexpected Beginnings* and *Unexpected Truths*, and a Christmas Novella, *A Merry Trengrouse Christmas*. She has also been involved in various short story anthology projects with Cornwall Writers, recently publishing her short story *These Little Moments in Time*.

Lamorna's love for coffee and quality food inspired her to write a blog for some of her favourite tearooms and cafés, whilst taking her debut novel on its own unique book tour. Her blog Lamorna Corner can be found bursting with positive vibes and yummy places to visit, including The Elm Tree tearooms, Ladyvale Bakery and Duchy of Cornwall Nursery.

Lamorna continues to spend her free time adventuring around her beautiful home county, her feet firmly rooted to the place of her ancestors.

You can follow the latest news and updates on Lamorna's work on her website (www.lamornaireland.co.uk), as well as Facebook, Twitter, Instagram and LinkedIn.

Printed in Great Britain
by Amazon